The Tripartite Soul
by
Eve S. Nicholson

Dedicated to my husband Jeffrey, my personal Jovan.

And to my brother John, with a prayer for this book to find you.

Acknowledgements:
Thank you to my mom, Julie Stringham for being my best cheerleader, to Debbie Burns for the incredible patience and care taken while encouraging and educating me, to my husband Jeffrey for telling me the only way to move forward is to write the story, and to Sandi Roberts and Tina who keep me grounded in reality all while fostering fantasies.

Baleful (adj) wretched, miserable

"Come to me, Eviona." His smooth, deep voice caressed each syllable. I cringed. How dare he speak with such a tender tone? How dare he ask me for anything? I closed my eyes against the plea, and turned over in my bed.

"Come to me."

My words may have been muffled by the pillow, but he heard well enough. "I don't want to meet you, Dyre. Stop asking."

Each day as I woke he pleaded the same request. Most of my life he and Zefforah would shut me out, but not since the battle. If I wanted to be alone, I had to build my veil. My dreams and memories each night stole the respite I might have claimed. I simply did not have the strength it took.

He sighed and stretched his legs against the cold floor looking up toward the ceiling of the dark space.

I pulled my legs to my chest fighting the reality of morning under the warmth of my blankets.

"How long must I wait?" He cupped his hands below his head as a makeshift pillow.

"Why couldn't you stop? This could have gone so differently if you had only listened to me!"

"It doesn't matter now," he replied a hushed regret. The reality pierced our hearts all over again.

The emptiness ached. "It didn't have to end this way."

"It's over," he whispered. "I only have one desire left. Please. Come to me. Meet me face to face now."

"You are in no position to have desires. I'm the one with the power now, and I do not want to see your face. Why should I indulge the man who never once willingly indulged me?"

He breathed in audibly, thinking very carefully.

"Would it make a difference if I told you I have a message for you?"

"A message from whom? Zefforah? What would it matter? You've ruined everything!"

"Before he died, Marjeàn asked me to tell you something."

My heart quickened at the mention of his name. My fingers found their way to my temples massaging the thoughts out of my head. He knew all too well how to manipulate me. "If you have a message for me—" I agonized as I begged, "Tell me what it is."

"This is something I have to tell you in person, in the flesh."

I had hoped to be strong, but found myself quickly failing. My desire for news of Marjeàn won over any resolve I had left, just as Dyre knew it would. "Please." He easily heard the defeat in my voice.

"I will tell you, when you come."

"I won't come!" I cried hitting the bed to enforce my insistence.

He whispered a malevolent inquiry. "Why haven't you told Jovan where you are?"

"I want to," I answered reluctantly.

"What you will learn from me will help you heal."

I barked, "Liar! You supply me words only to purchase your wishes. You can't control me anymore. I'm not coming to see you."

"There was a time you hoped to meet me." His casual confidence burned my soul like a spark of fire on exposed flesh.

"That was a very long time ago," I whispered defiantly. "Before I knew... anything."

"I felt your urgency." He paused allowing the memories to flood back into my mind. "You would have done anything to meet me."

"Zefforah," I spoke the name with the reverence she deserved. "I wanted to meet Zefforah."

A solemn silence flowed between us.

He stood and paced back and forth. Ten feet repeatedly from one wall to the other.

I closed my eyes fighting the scenes my memory refused to forget.

"How different things might be now if I had only allowed it," he stated repentantly. Then the man I thought was devoid of feeling closed his veil allowing me to be alone.

Tripartite (adj) made of three parts

The growling of my young, empty stomach bothered Dyre as he tried to sleep. The hollowness sounded clear with far too much volume. Zefforah had to have been awake somewhere because her veil remained unopened to me. I hoped it meant she couldn't feel my hunger, but I suspected otherwise.

My food supplies had been spent days earlier, and I hadn't seen any rodents or insects to catch for a meal in a long time. Unfortunately, I had been in this predicament before. Minuette often left me for extended periods of time. I wouldn't die soon, but as my strength decreased uncertainty accompanied the starvation.

Because Dyre knew exactly how hungry I felt, I could usually depend on him to remind Minuette of my need for a meal. This time, no such prompt could be made. Minuette had not been seen since Dyre last saw her through my eyes.

Dyre's squeezed his eyes shut tighter then opened them and focused on the floral shadows cast by his fire onto his high ceiling.

I asked in a small voice, "Where is Minuette?"

He barked, "Why would I know?"

"Ask Horrish."

"It's the middle of the night."

"You want food in my stomach too," I snidely reminded.

He reluctantly rolled out of bed and pulled a pair of slacks over the hem of his cotton night shirt. Then he grabbed a candle and searched the manor for Horrish.

Not finding him in his bed Dyre went to the front foyer counting on him to come home sooner or later.

He stopped by the kitchen first to grab something to eat, a disappointing attempt to fill the emptiness of my stomach.

When his candle had almost reached its quick Horrish stumbled in, swimming in the stench of alcohol and sweat. Dyre never showed his disgust as he sat reading in a red velvet wingback chair in the entry of their manor, but I felt it.

Horrish lurched until he reached Dyre's chair. Once he steadied himself, he asked as if he were accusing Dyre of a crime, "Don't you have better things to do with your nights?"

Dyre didn't flinch. He merely sat with his eyes focused on the page number of the book.

"I'm talking to you."

Horrish raised his fist, but Dyre caught his strike and squeezed the offending hand, pushing it downward until the large man begged for mercy on his knees.

"Who were you addressing?" Dyre's voice sounded calm, but his body tensed with anger.

Horrish gave in quickly, spouting everything he may have wanted to hear. "You Sire. My Lord. Your Majesty. King Dyre."

Dyre released him, throwing him to the floor as he did. He paced as Horrish knelt and rubbed his sore wrist. He slapped the book into his palm with every step, lording over the man. "Where is Minuette?"

Horrish twisted to his feet with loathing in his eyes, but humility in his shoulders. Then he shrugged at Dyre, an odd response from a man who never tired of his own voice.

"Well?"

"She could be dead for all I know. She's been missing for days." He didn't seem disappointed.

Dyre asked, "Where does she keep the girl?"

"I don't know. She may be my wife, but she keeps her own secrets." He sneered with disgust, "Which is fine with me." A threatening stare from Dyre pushed the man mentally enough to have him repeat the words with a nearly begging tone, "I swear, I don't know!"

"You will go now, and find Minuette. Do not come home until she has fed that child!"

"Of course, King Dyre." Horrish's head bobbed forward, bitterly acknowledging the command.

Dyre tossed his book onto the chair and started toward his room mumbling, "It better be soon."

He halted as Horrish called out to him. "When you are King you will not forget who helped you to the throne."

Dyre turned slightly looking back at the man who had so long ago placed him on his journey. His words did not reflect the revulsion Dyre felt. "Horrish, my good man, how could I... ever... forget you?"

Horrish humbly backed toward the door. The house shook as it slammed behind him.

As Dyre stormed back to his room, his loathing returned to me. "She's gone, Eviona. Find a way out of there!"

"How?"

"You must have figured out something by now. You've been living there your whole life!"

"I can't escape. What if she comes back?" I whispered.

"Minuette is gone. It's been days," he grumbled. "I find it hard to believe you've never thought about escaping before now."

"Minuette would kill me."

"I'd kill her, and she knows it. I need you out of there now. Go find some food!"

"I'm scared."

A raging growl escaped his lungs. "Stupid girl!" He

slammed his bedroom door as his veil went black.

I stoked my fire and prayed for sleep.

I woke the next day to a familiar cry. "Zefforah?" I raised my head off the floor and scratched at the dirt encrusted on my face.

The cry came again, growing louder. It wasn't through her ears I heard, it was through mine.

"Zefforah?" I screamed.

Dyre's laughter resonated through my head. "Ah ha! We found you."

I saw my tiny prison through his eyes; a small, squalid shack, barely noticeable from their vantage point. If it weren't for the thin stream of smoke still rising from my chimney, they would have never found me.

"If you want to see her, Eviona, all you need to do is find a way out of that hole."

I measured my fear of Minuette against my desire to see the ethereal creature who had always been kind to me, Zefforah.

"Come and help me."

"You can do it, Eviona. Try."

It would take me a long time to force the blocked door open, but this time, I wouldn't give up like I had in the past.

This time, I wouldn't allow my fear of Minuette or my fear of the world outside these four walls to control me. This time, I wouldn't stop until I escaped.

The door had been barred from the outside. I still could hear the finality of it going down into the latch. A sound which played over and over in my mind each time Minuette left me. A hideous echo of abandonment my memory would never release.

I knew the crack in the door. Dyre had been right. I'd been examining it for years with the hope of one day mustering the courage to escape my prison. The location could have been better, but I would make it work for me. I took out the small knife I had made and worked at the crack until it was thick enough for me to shove a sturdy stick through. Several broke in my attempts. I gave up and whittled the crack until I could get my hand through enough to lift the bar.

Both Dyre and Zefforah watched my efforts. I occasionally heard Zefforah cry as they flew overhead encouraging me.

Finally, I felt the crack in the door was wide enough to thrust my hand through. I scraped it badly as I did. Both Dyre and Zefforah grunted their discomfort. I didn't have to lift the bar very much, but I found it more difficult than I had hoped. Pain raced through my hand and wrist in the struggle before I felt the bar give way. The door opened quickly with the weight of my slight body. My hand still stuck through the crack dragged me outside.

I blinked into the blinding light of the sun. I closed my eyes and breathed in the fresh and clean air.

"You're free," Dyre sighed.

"Free," I repeated unbelieving. I quickly wrenched my hand from the hold of the door, picked up my makeshift knife and ran in their direction.

Dyre pushed Zefforah forward. I assumed he steered me in a direction away from where Minuette might be. I followed them as fast as I could even though my breathing became difficult and my sides ached.

"Zefforah, Dyre, I'm coming." An unquenchable desire rushed through my staggering body.

I had spent my entire life inside their heads, seeing their sights, hearing their words, feeling their experiences. Finally, I would be with them. Happiness filled me as I imagined the scene.

Zefforah's emotions matched mine, but Dyre felt opposite. His customary loathing toward me returned, and he maneuvered them to fly over a town.

I knew I was a monster. No one had ever seen me except for Minuette, and she reminded me often of my ugliness. I shouldn't have run into the town, but I wasn't thinking about how people would react to me. I only thought about Zefforah and Dyre.

"Let's go!" Dyre commanded Zefforah and kicked her side a little too harshly. My body tensed, repelling the sting his kick triggered in my ribs.

Zefforah paused confused. She wanted to see me as much as I wanted to see her. Dyre said we could meet if I escaped.

"*Go! Now!*" His voice threatened. "We only needed to help her escape. She can't help us gain the throne!"

Zefforah felt conflicted. Hesitant.

Dyre leaned down to speak into her ear. "She's in a town now. Do you really want to be close to people?"

Fear gripped at Zefforah. Reluctantly she rose higher into the sky.

"Zefforah!" I screamed. "Zefforah!"

I physically ached at having them so close, and yet my heart broke at their retreat. I trailed their course as best as I could, straining to see them both more clearly. Dyre shoved his hand in my direction as if he could push me away.

Zefforah's eyes looked back as she continued her flight away. Her heart twisted as she watched me become nothing but a tiny speck.

I stopped running, grief-stricken and beaten.

"Close your veil!" He ordered, and she obeyed.

"NO!" I bawled falling to my knees. "Let me meet her. Can't I come with you?"

He closed his veil as well and left me in the isolated worthlessness of my own mind. I pulled at my hair, trying to rip it from its roots to hurt him, but stopped thinking of her. "Zefforah, come back."

A door creaked open. It was the first time I realized I hadn't seen any people in the town.

I hid the repugnance of my face behind my hands and peeked through my fingers as a set of faded black boots approached.

"What kind of monster are you?" A deep voice echoed the words Minuette used to ask.

He must have already seen my face. I frowned at the man glowering over me.

An angry woman with a long crooked nose called to him from a nearby doorway, "Ask him why he called to the beast."

He grabbed my arm to pull me up. "I think it might be a girl." I knew his tone. Minuette used to speak to me like that, just before her anger erupted. I purposely fell pushing my weight to the ground. His grip loosened and I kicked him in the leg. He lost his balance and his hold on me.

I ran, forcing my way past a few bewildered people coming from their hiding places to see the scene. I needed to escape. I ran hard and fast and two rows of houses over I tripped and fell. My hands caught the brunt, but my face and knees felt the agony of the fall. The doors in the town remained closed even as I cried. Not one person came into the street to help me. After all, who would help something as horrific as I was?

Dyre's veil dropped. "Are you trying to hurt her? Because you are."

I sobbed, pushing small stones and dirt from the flesh of my hands. "Why can't I meet her? She's the only one who has ever been good to me."

"We only wanted you to escape. She didn't really want to meet you," he snarled.

"That's not true!" As I yelled, Zefforah screeched. She too opposed his statement.

Our frustrated heartbeats raced in unison.

"Why does a monster like you even exist?" Dyre mumbled.

Zefforah shifted hard to the side until Dyre lost his hold on her. I was grateful to have her retaliate a bit on my behalf, although, she allowed him to fall for a long time. We all felt his panic and knew death would come to us all if he hit the ground. Zefforah dove to catch him just in time.

"That was too close," he grunted as he caught his breath, straightening himself on her back. "This whole thing would be so much easier without her."

Zefforah snorted.

"We are one mind," I stated.

His loud guffaw hurt my ears. "Differences like ours could never occupy one mind."

"We have one heart."

"Ignorant girl. To be one heart, suggests a commonality of feeling. We may feel each other's emotions, but mine are mine, and yours are yours."

I pushed, "We are one essence."

"No, we are not! The three of us are separate, individual entities. I make choices for me, she makes choices for her, and you make your own stupid choices."

"We are one," I said in a small, yet forceful voice.

His head bowed downward, and his eyes glared over his left shoulder in a well-known movement. We both knew he wouldn't see what he looked for. Me. He didn't want me there, constantly in his head.

I continued. "I see through your eyes. I hear through your ears."

Dyre glanced down at his hands and the wounds my actions had created. As Zefforah's legs stretched forward, blood flowed into the air as they flew. I glanced at my own hands displaying my injuries in the same place. "See, we even bleed together. You experience everything I go through, just as I do with you."

He growled, bitter about my existence as well as the truth I had stated.

"Do you know how this happened?" I asked.

His lips turned to a snarl. "I didn't ask for it!"

"If we are not one, what are we?"

He spat the words, "I am to be the greatest ruler Sylvaria has ever seen. Zefforah is beautiful, and powerful; magnificence personified. And you? You are a miscreation!" His veil closed.

I rose to my feet and raced again in the direction I'd last seen them. I must have stood too fast, my eyes went dim, and I couldn't feel where my feet planted themselves.

I shook my hands praying for my sight to return. When it did my speed had taken over, and my direction pointed straight into a wall. Sudden pain burst in my nose and forehead. The world went black.

Sodality (n) an association

I was chasing Horrish, but I wasn't me, I was Zefforah. I felt the crunch of the brushwood under my hooves and could feel my wings crashing against the branches of the forest as I knocked down trees to allow myself closer access to him. Horrish wasn't screaming the way I wanted him to, he ran silent, horrified in front of me. It wasn't hard to catch him, and no one was around to call me to stop. When I reached him, I slapped him to the ground with my tail. As I stood over him, he pleaded with me, making promises I knew he would break. The last expression I saw on his face was dread. I apathetically crushed him under my hooves. A slight whimper followed, and I stomped again and again until no sound could be heard. He would never hurt me or my friends again.

I woke slowly. Zefforah had killed Horrish. I knew it. I couldn't help but wonder if Minuette had come to a similar fate. It took me a minute to shake the awfulness of the dream away. I pulled at something which brushed against my neck and realized I had been covered by a blanket. A woman's voice sang softly, and two other voices whispered low. My face hurt, my stomach cramped, and my head felt like it would explode. I moaned.

"Mother, she is waking up."

"She looks really horrible." A woman's voice confirmed Minuette's words. I felt a hand on my head and turned away covering my face in panic.

I tried to open my eyes. The light of the room made my head hurt even worse. I slammed them shut.

The girl's voice said, "Maybe some water will make you feel better."

I attempted to roll away from their voices but fell

onto the floor where I hastily covered my face again.

"You poor thing." I watched through my fingers as a young girl approached. I couldn't help but stare at her. She had light olive skin the color of a newborn deer, with dark brown doe eyes to match and a mane of deep brown hair down to her waist. Beautiful. She asked, "What happened to you?"

I wasn't sure if she was asking why I was feeble, or why I was a monster. "I don't know."

A man took me from the floor, placed me back on the bed and sat next to me. He appeared normal enough in his leather apron and nicely trimmed beard. Confusion choked my mind. Why would he help me? Why weren't these people running away from me?

His eyebrows rose to expose deep sympathetic eyes. "May I examine your face?"

I shook my head emphatically it made my head feel like it would burst, but I knew once I took my hands away they would all run, just as Minuette had always told me. Run from the freak, the horror, the savage that I was.

"Now, now. I don't think it's all that bad. Let me look." He pulled at my fingers gently, and I turned my head as I allowed him to move them, I flinched knowing what their reactions would be.

"Hmmmm." His eyes continued with their kindness as they studied my face. "You look quite bad."

I had expected a much worse reaction. Only looking quite bad sounded quite good to me.

"Sanura, will you bring me some juice and rags?"

"Not the juice," the woman protested. "I don't have enough to last until next season. Water will be fine."

The girl looked to the man who seemed displeased but nodded her on. She then moved quickly. My eyes, nose, and face were being blotted moments later. I wondered how wet rags could make me less of a monster. I didn't mind though, his soft touch felt nice.

"Hand me a cup of water."

The beautiful young girl approached and placed a cup in his hand.

The woman worked at a table nearby. She was just as beautiful as the girl. However, she had a much more appropriate reaction to the demon which had invaded her home. Darts of distain shot at me from her eyes. I couldn't blame her.

The man encouraged me to drink. I gulped it down quickly. After I had drained the cup two more times, he lay me back down on the bed and left me to myself for a while.

The room wasn't large, but it looked like it facilitated all of the needs of a family. There were two doors. One obviously to go outside, I couldn't determine where the other might lead. Perhaps a closet.

"If you have things here I need to get into the shop." The man said.

"Yes, you go ahead. Sanura and I will keep an eye on the urchin," answered the woman.

"She is a girl, Aurel." He reprimanded her with a smile as he kissed her sweetly then left through the curious door. I had never seen a kiss like that before, genuine, without want or condition.

The girl came and sat on the bed next to me. "I'm Sanura. What's your name?"

"Eviona."

"What a pretty name. Would you like some breakfast, Eviona?"

My eyes grew wide. "Really?"

She giggled at my response and asked, "Would you like to eat in bed, or do you want to come to the table?"

I loved being on a bed, having never had one before. But I hadn't ever sat in a chair either. "I think the table."

"Come on then." She motioned for me to come with her, offering her hand to help me up.

I couldn't believe she would be willing to touch me. Surely she should fear me, but she showed no apprehension.

I stood up with her help and swayed a little as the blood rushed to my head. She put her arm around me to help me walk. I appreciated her gentle touch. I hadn't ever been handled in kindness before. It felt foreign and yet pleasant.

A small plate of food was placed in front of me. I grabbed it eagerly with my hands and started eating with delight. A grunt of repulsion and a giggle stopped me. I glanced from the disgusted face of the woman and then to her daughter.

Sanura shook her head at me with a smile and held up a fork. I shook the food from my fingers and swallowed hoping to try to start again and do it right this time. I picked up the fork in front of me, and both women nodded.

I thought using a fork would be easy. Dyre made it look simple, but it took me a while to get the food onto it. And once I did, it didn't always stay there until I moved it to my mouth. I felt clumsy and stupid. It would be so much easier if I could simply eat with my hands, but I didn't dare.

After the meal, Sanura asked, "Would you like to get cleaned up? I have a dress you could wear and we could wash your clothes."

"No." I looked at her and her mother in horror as I grabbed the collar of my coat and wrapped it tight around my neck.

"It's alright." She tried to still me by rubbing my back.

I arched pulling away from her fingers certain she would feel my dreadfulness through the clothing.

"I promise we won't do anything to hurt you." She took my hand and pulled me gently. Her tender eyes entreated me to get up until I reluctantly gave in to her beckons.

We moved to the door in the middle of the house. On the other side was a shoe shop. The man smiled from his workbench. Sanura continued pulling me until we reached another door.

She opened it to a room just about the size of my prison. In the middle rested a tub of water. I'd seen one before. Although, Dyre never left his veil opened when he bathed I understood it to be where he scrubbed himself clean. I wondered what it would feel like to be completely immersed in the water.

Sanura handed me a large sheet. "I'll be back with something for you to wear."

I didn't dare undress myself so I simply stood there until she returned.

She giggled when she came back and asked, "Why aren't you washing?"

"I don't want you to see me."

"We're both girls." She giggled again. "I promise you will be left alone until you are clothed." She put the clothes down next to the tub and scooted out of the room. She had called me a girl. I felt elated.

I bathed as quickly as I could and attempted to dress. It took a while to figure out how to put on the clothes and in what order.

There was a white under-dress, a grey dress over that and a bibbed white apron. The clean and crisp layers of fabric covered most of me, yet they did not cover my face and hands therefore still exposing me as the vile creature I was.

I stepped from the little room. Smiling, albeit awkwardly, at the pleasant man and the brooding woman as I found the door of the living quarters.

Sanura greeted me as I came in. "I'm going to brush your hair."

My smile transformed into panic as I remembered the way Minuette would grab and pull while cutting my hair clean to my scalp. It had been several months, but the memory was fresh enough. Sanura touched my shoulder gingerly and sat me in a chair. She tugged at my hair repeatedly with her brush, but tried to be gentle. Not like Minuette.

"Your hair is a very interesting color."

I only flinched at a jerk of her brush.

"It isn't cut very well. I'll bet if you let it grow out a little it could be really pretty."

A half smile could never express my inward euphoria. She said something about me could be pretty.

I spent the day watching the two females in wonder. They tried to include me as they worked but I felt much more comfortable when they didn't acknowledge me. As time went on, they seemed to understand and only looked to me occasionally with a smile or a nod. They spent the morning in lessons of math and reading.

In the afternoon they cleaned the house, washed clothes, sewed buttons on shirts, made butter, and bread, and laughed and talked the whole while. I had never seen interactions like this. I enjoyed it.

Toward evening the woman asked, "It's time to make some dinner. Sanura it's your turn to cook. Perhaps your new friend could help."

Excitedly I offered, "I can make crackers."

Minuette started to leave me for several days at a time even when I was very young. She would stock me with a few supplies each time she came. She had shown me how to mix flour with water and bake it in the oven which she instructed me to always keep lit, both for warmth and also to cook with.

When she felt I could fare well enough by myself, she left me for weeks at a time and would only come back when Dyre screamed at her for how hungry we felt. One summer night I accidentally forgot to restock the fire when I fell asleep. I burned myself terribly the next day as I attempted to light it. Of course, Dyre yelled at me for hurting him, but it moved him to teach me, although his lessons were never pleasant.

"Are you blind? Don't you see that stick right there in front of you?"

"There are quite a few. Which one?"

"Oh, you are such an idiot! Just grab that little one there."

I picked one up, "This one?"

"No! Imbecile! Do you see the smallest one?"

"This one?"

"Finally! How am I supposed to live my life connected to such ignorance?"

Even though he hated and yelled at me, at least he talked me through it so I would do it right without burning myself.

My crackers weren't pretty. Globs of paste baked into globs of dry, tasteless sustenance. Sometimes I rolled them into long strings. They didn't taste any better, but I could imagine them to be snakes or worms and enjoyed the meal more because of it. As time passed, I made them into other things patterned after the insects and mice which scurried about my prison with me.

I wouldn't consider my first attempts very successful.
I fashioned tools out of the rubble of the house. A
broken piece of glass wrapped at the end with a cloth
formed a perfectly useful knife. I'd shape my little
crackers and carve them with hair, ears, and a long
skinny tail. Over the course of time, I continually
worked to perfect them.

Dyre watched me in curiosity one day as I placed my
supper in the oven.

"What do you think?" I asked.

"You aren't seriously going to eat that, it's
disgusting!"

"They're easier to eat than the real ones." Excited I
asked, "Did you think they were real?"

"I hate to admit it, but yes. I did." Then he laughed
aloud and said, "You should eat one in front of
Minuette. She'll be sick for a week thinking you ate a
mouse hair and all." We both delighted at the thought.

The next time she came, I made sure to have one
ready. As she entered, I held it by the tail above my head
and lowered it into my mouth. Sure enough, she left
immediately and vomited repeatedly outside the door. I
laughed internally. Dyre laughed out loud.

My little stunt had very good effects. From then on
she left me more food and even started to vary it a little
bringing me things like nuts.

Of course, I had tasted other foods, really
exceptional foods through Dyre. He had always been
spoiled with meats and sauces, cheeses, and sautéed
vegetables, fruits of all kinds, such wonderful tastes and
textures. I rejoiced each and every time he ate while
opened to me. However, I simply enjoyed having nuts
for myself. They served a great purpose as well. I could

fashion them into perfect little cockroaches.

I loved watching Minuette react to the things she saw me eat. Eventually, she brought me potatoes, or an occasional piece of fruit. I treasured those treats, and I would always make them into something wonderful, simply for my own enjoyment. I never let her know of my talents and used them against her often.

Sanura and I prepared supper for the family while the man and woman worked in the shop. Dyre's veil opened. He had gone to the theater, and though his eyes looked at a stage, I could feel him watching me. I could understand why he opened his veil. He was bored mindless by the poor production. My new surroundings suddenly felt a bit odd, not being able to talk to him whenever I felt the urge. I wondered if he ever felt that same kind of peculiarity. Probably not. I'm sure he never really had the desire to talk to me.

Sanura showed me how to make food which actually tasted good, and I showed her how to make mice shaped crackers. I loved the way her voice went up and down as she laughed when she saw my finished project.

"Last week was my birthday. I turned 12 years old. How old are you? Sanura asked.

"I don't know. I've never had a birthday."

"Silly girl, everyone has a birthday. Why don't you ask your mother when you go home?"

"I don't have a mother."

"What about your father then? You could ask him."

I shrugged, "No family."

"Who takes care of you? You can't be alone in the world."

Dyre interrupted my thoughts with a whisper.

"Eviona, tell her your parents died, and you are alone. As far as we know it's the truth." I heard the hope in his voice and couldn't help but understand how much he wanted me to stay here. Food, clothes, baths, it seemed a dream.

I very hesitantly told her what he suggested, hoping along with him. Her eyes grew wide with my words, and she went to the door which led to the shop.

"Mother, Father. I think I need to talk to you."

She went into the shop and closed the door. "Dyre, do you know when my birthday is?"

He shook his head while clearing his throat and rolling his eyes.

Voices from the next room came through the door. The woman yelled, "She can't stay here! We hardly have food to feed ourselves."

My hopes fell with my heart until I heard the man. "She has nowhere else to go. I refuse to send her out into the cold."

Their tones softened again. I didn't know what to think. I looked at the bread on the table and my coat still drying by the fireplace. I could quickly grab them both and leave.

Dyre cupped his hand over his mouth to lower his whisper, "Go listen at the door."

I tiptoed and pressed my ear to the door.

"Mother, I could share with her."

"You barely have enough as it is."

Dyre sneered. "Selfish."

"My darling we aren't used to having much. We have a roof over our heads; we have clothing, and food. What more do we need?"

"If you could see all we *could* have. All we could give to Sanura."

"I have never known the life you knew before, but I have known hunger. I can't turn away this girl when we still have enough."

During a long pause a lump formed in my chest. Hope.

"Have you looked at her?" My heart sank. My ugliness would have me cast out for certain. "She can't look like that because of nothing. What if she's a –"

"She's a girl. The same as our Sanura. Please, Aurel."

Silence.

The woman then sighed heavily, "Roan, how can I deny you anything?"

Sanura squealed, "Let's go tell her."

Dyre let out a breath he must have been holding in anticipation.

I felt the same desire for release but couldn't yet. I heard them approaching, ran back to the table and attempted to look busy by putting the plates and forks in their places. I now wished I had paid a little closer attention to Dyre's place settings each day.

They approached me, and the man bent down in front of me to look into my eyes. "Eviona? Do you have a place to go?"

"I've been staying in the forest. I could go back there." I bowed my head and looked toward the woman who rolled her eyes and looked away.

Sanura came and took my hand. "We are poor people, you will have to work as we do, but you can stay here with us."

I nodded earnestly. "I will work hard. I promise."

Sanura squealed with joy and put her arms around me. I shied, and she hugged me tighter not allowing me to pull away. "I've always wanted a sister!"

Augury (n) omen, token, or indication

"I want you girls to go out to the fields and find some obiberries." Aurel handed us each a basket.

I did my best to say and do everything Aurel asked of me, but her hatred toward me still hadn't changed even after months. As we wandered to our destination, I asked Sanura, "What are obiberries?"

She laughed, "You are so funny. Sometimes I wonder if you fell out of the sky. Do you really not know what obiberries are?"

I did my best to search my memory, but I never recalled hearing about them from Dyre. I finally said, "I think I may have had some once."

"Of course you have," she replied. "Everybody has. Their juice is medicine. Mother has me drink obiberry juice when I have headaches, and it helps to clean cuts and things. I know you've had some."

We came to a field of silver and gold which glistened in the sun.

"Those are the berries," she said.

"The sparkles are obiberries?"

She grabbed my hand and ran. "You'll see when we're closer."

The bushes were unlike any other I'd seen, with three beautiful, silvery-green leaves at the end of every branch which nestled three berries, perfect balls of glistening gold.

"Aren't they lovely?"

"They are," I agreed.

"I'll begin over there. You start here, and we will meet in the middle. By then our baskets should be full enough to head home."

I nodded, and she left me alone to work. I picked a berry. It felt warm as if it had just been taken off a hot stove.

I quickly dropped it into my basket and wondered how long my fingers would hold out with heat like that.

I looked over to Sanura already happily picking on the other side of the field. Their temperature didn't seem to bother her. I would not allow it to bother me either. I picked more.

With only a few berries in my basket, I couldn't bear the pain of the heat any longer. Sanura said the juice could be used as medicine, I thought perhaps I'd squeeze the juice from the next one I picked to ease the pain of my fingers.

The moment the juice touched my skin it bubbled. I'd only touched a drop, but my finger felt like flames. I wiped it frantically on my dress and then put it in my mouth to calm the burn. Pain seared my tongue and lips. I spit, and rubbed my mouth against the sleeve of my dress while wiping my thumb ferociously. Nothing seemed to help, I couldn't stop the burn.

Dyre yelled at me. "Are you eating fire?" Zefforah dropped her veil as well.

As I spat, I gave them one word. "Berries."

"Let me see them," he demanded.

I glanced to the bushes to allow them to see.

"Those aren't just any berries. Don't touch them!"

"I found that out," I barked.

"What's going on?" Sanura ran to me. "What happened?"

Still panicking I showed her my thumb, red and blistered.

"Oh my! We should put some juice on that."

"No! The juice caused it! I need water."

"Oh." She pointed down the lane. "There is a stream over there."

I ran, and the cooling water calmed the fire of my

finger. I immersed my mouth for a very long time as well.

Dyre took a deep breath feeling the relief of the cold water washing over the burns. "I don't know anyone who has a reaction to them like we do, Eviona. Be careful, or obiberries will be the death of us all."

Roan darted into the house gasping and white as the powder he used to clean grease spots off the shoes in his cobbler shop. "Bar the doors. Lock every window."

Aurel and Sanura rushed to obey. Confused by the alarm, I didn't question, I simply followed their lead.

Aurel asked, "What happened?"

Breathlessly Roan answered, "The beast is back. I saw it myself heading toward the next village."

I didn't understand. I'd never heard of a beast other than myself.

As I boarded the shop window, other shops did the same. The whole town shut down in a matter of minutes. I didn't know why to be afraid, but attempted to seem fearful simply because it seemed correct. Dyre warned me to act like everyone else, so I did.

I grabbed Sanura's shaking hand. "What's the beast?" I asked in a whisper, not wanting Aurel to be angry with me. She hated my ignorance almost as much as my ugliness.

Sanura's umber eyes widened. "You don't know what the beast is?"

Aurel glared at me, just as I knew she would. "Who's never heard of the beast? Honestly, are you stupid?"

Roan glared at her then approached me tenderly. "Eviona, you must know about the beast. It's ruined villages all over Sylvaria. They say it's capable of destroying the whole kingdom."

"How?"

He knelt down on one knee to look into my eyes. "It's huge, and can fly."

A rush of hope washed over me. It sounded like Zefforah. "Is she a horse?"

"Yes, only much bigger."

"White and brilliant like the sun?"

"White like a ghost," was his concerned reply.

Shallow breath and the size of my smile couldn't force the words from my lips fast enough. "With wings like a dove, and the tail of a lizard?"

"There," he sighed. "You have heard of it. I believe we are safe for now. It passed over our village."

"Where did she go? Where is she?"

"I saw it flying toward Gockin."

My heart raced. How would it be to go and see her? "Can't we go to her? She sounds so beautiful!"

"It's not beautiful! It's terrible!" Aurel chided.

They'd never understand. I snuck to the window as they continued to defend against my friend. I wished with all my heart to see her again, even if only for a moment.

To my surprise later that night Zefforah opened her veil with panic racing through her veins.

We had all settled in bed and were just on the cusp of sleep. I gingerly slid from beside Sanura. Roan stirred. I froze for a long time praying not to be noticed. I didn't move until the soft sound of steady breaths resonated from sleeping bodies. I delicately lifted my coat from the hook near the door, wrapped it around my shoulders and tip-toed to Roan's shop.

I breathed in and out deeply and whispered to Zefforah. "What's wrong?"

Zefforah whined. I had the distinct impression something happened with Dyre.

"Is he open to you?"

She nodded.

"Tell him to connect to me so I can find out what is going on."

She grunted. Which I took to mean either she wouldn't ask him, or he had already refused.

I had no idea how to help. "Did you know you were close to me tonight? When you flew to Gockin, you flew over my town."

Her eyes widened. She reared, and stomped her feet. A very affirmative yes.

I mumbled fruitless ideas of what she could be anxious about. All of which she shot down with grunts and growls until I asked, "Is Dyre in Gockin?" She stopped moving and neighed. I'd guessed it. I couldn't bear the ache to run and see her, so close again. Only one town over.

"Tell him to open his veil! I can't help if I can't tell what's going on.

There were a few moments of silence. I wish I knew how they communicated. He could understand her somehow. I could only feel her.

His veil opened to me, and I could see his surroundings, a small empty room, a door, nothing else. His hands pushed together behind his back. A rope scratched against his wrists and wadded fabric pressed against his tongue with another piece tied around his mouth.

"Dyre, you're in trouble."

His head nodded slowly, deliberately, as if telling me I was stupid for stating the obvious. Ropes tied each of his ankles to a leg of the chair he sat on.

Zefforah circled the town searching for any indication of where Dyre might be.

"Zefforah's already over Gockin," I reassured Dyre. "And I'm coming." I moved to the outside door, unlocked it and readied myself to run.

He struggled in his chair, shaking his head and moaned muffled screams. He didn't want my help. He forbade it.

Defiantly, I pushed the door open and buttoned the coat around me to the top. I may have been young and ugly, but I could still help.

His hands fisted, and he grunted a hard growl.

A man's hand clapped on Dyre's shoulder making all three of us jump. A hushed voice whispered, "Comfy, Dyre?"

He inhaled and adrenaline raced through his body as a knife appeared in front of his face. I gasped in fear as the tip of the blade in front of Dyre pressed slightly against his chin. Zefforah landed, urgent to find Dyre and help. She watched for humans and any clue of Dyre's location.

Keeping the blade steady the man appeared in front of Dyre. He wore a black hat and a mask over his eyes so only his mouth could be seen.

"Here is the question," the man spoke low and clear, "Do I allow you to live until I receive the order to kill you? Or should I simply do it my way?"

Zefforah huffed, and I felt her control sifting from very slight to even less. Dyre attempted to free his bound hands.

The man laughed watching him struggle. Then he placed the blade of the knife against Dyre's neck. The cold blade pressed into his throat too tightly. I swallowed to relieve the pressure. It didn't help.

Zefforah's stress raced in my veins. "Zefforah, you have to do something," I whispered.

A noise in the next room distracted Dyre's captor,

and he tapped Dyre on the cheek with his knife before exiting the room.

Zefforah's fear took control. When she saw a flicker of light in a home she whipped her tail through the door. Slicing through it like an ax through a stick. Screams rose, but her fear for Dyre seemed to override her own. She entered the place desperately searching for him. After searching, she emerged once again on the street. Screams surrounded her from nearby windows and doors.

Not to be thwarted from her quest Zefforah moved to the next structure. A bell in the village tower sent a warning through the town. Chaos ensued in a matter of moments. People ran and screamed as Zefforah's hunt continued.

When she emerged from another unsuccessful hunt of a shack, rocks and torches came at her. The townspeople had taken a defensive position. She took to the sky and landed quickly in a different part of the town where she continued her search.

She searched everywhere. Another exploration failed, and the mob of angry villagers attacked her again.

When she landed on yet another deserted avenue ready to search, I stopped her. "Zefforah, stop and listen!" She hesitated and listened only for a moment before returning to her work. "Zefforah! Listen through Dyre!"

We both listened from his ears. Quiet. He didn't hear the screams. Only the sounds of Dyre struggling from his ropes could be heard through his ears.

"Dyre isn't in Gockin."

Zefforah witnessed with new eyes the destruction she'd caused.

The torches people had launched at her had created

raging fires through the panicked town. And then there were the homes she'd ruined looking for Dyre.

Dyre finally freed a hand and ripped the gag from his mouth. "I'm in Hammill Cove."

Zefforah dashed into the sky, looking back with brutal guilt to the devastation of Gockin.

I barked at Dyre, "What are you doing there? Who captured you?"

"I'm not sure, but if he comes back soon, we're all dead."

He squirmed from the lashes around his other wrist and then from his ankles. He stood, and I felt the tip of a knife blade once again. This time pressed squarely in the center of his back. Dyre straightened, and his captor pushed the blade to meet his movement. "Let's go, Dyre."

Dyre held his hands up as his captor prompted him forward with his knife. They moved into a lit hall ornamented with statues and art. The man pressed Dyre forward with his knife. Zefforah reached her destination. The homes of Hammill Cove weren't shops and shacks like Gockin. Its buildings were manors with two and three stories as well as large yards.

Zefforah shuttered in fear but crashed through the roof of one with several lights on. She whipped through the home and though terrified each time she saw a person, even though most of them looked to be more frightened of her. She continued her search crashing through rooms and breaking out through windows. Three manors later screaming could be heard through Dyre's ears. She'd found the right house.

At the commotion, the masked man pushed Dyre into a stairwell. Dyre whipped around knocking him with his elbow. He turned to face the man and hit him in the face just as we received a kick to the ribs. Dyre grabbed for the knife and a struggle ensued. The blade moved from a position too close to the man's face to that of nearly piercing Dyre's chest and then back toward the other man's throat.

Dyre's hand twisted under the strength of the other man until the blade dropped. When he moved to pick it up a hand came down hard between Dyre's collar bone and his neck. He fell to the ground. I fell landing hard on my back. Zefforah struggled to steady her own legs.

Dyre attempted to open his eyes, but by the time he managed to focus, the man had disappeared.

Dyre called for Zefforah until she centered herself enough to continue her search. She ripped through only two or three more doors before she found him and lifted him onto her back. They raced into the night. Relief.

She looked back at the ravaged homes. Her self-loathing consumed every muscle in her body.

"No Zefforah, this is not your fault. You did the right thing. You found me. You saved me, saved us."

She didn't feel like a savior. She despised what she had done, and I felt she knew the people she feared had every right to fear her as well.

Teratoid (adj) resembling a monster

I snuck back to bed. Soon the sound of the town bell peeling woke Aurel and Roan. A murmured conversation between them gave my heart a moment to calm down. I pretended to sleep until Roan shook me.

"Sanura, Eviona, wake up."

I moaned and faked waking. I put on my coat quickly and reached for my bonnet which tied beneath my chin and hid my cheeks, and if I bowed my head, most of my face as well.

Aurel grabbed my wrist, "Come, girls, we have much work to do."

"My bonnet," I pleaded.

She pulled me toward the door. "There is no sun shining into your eyes, you don't need it."

"Mother," Sanura's voice begged in my behalf.

"No! We have more important things to worry about." Aurel pushed us from the shop without the protection I depended upon. My hands covered my face. I did my best to bow my head and hide in the shadows, but fear ate at me every second. Like Zefforah, people would see me and fear me.

Minuette's words haunted me. *"You are terrifying to look upon! You must always hide. Hide everything. Hide your face. Hide your hair, and most importantly never, never allow anyone to see your back. No one should be subjected to the horror of your freakish looks. I can't stand to look at you!"*

I stayed glued to Sanura's side as we went to work helping the people gathered in our town square. Some of them had lost their homes, some were simply too frightened of the beast to return to Gockin. Roan and Aurel loaded our arms with blankets, and firewood to distribute.

Our home barely had enough room for the four of us,

but Roan offered his small shop for a sleeping place. Four or five people could sleep well enough on the floor if we pushed his work bench and tables to the wall.

Provisions were brought to some who would stay in the square; others found homes or shops in which to stay. Things finally calmed, until a piercing scream split the night.

No one spoke, all eyes moved to the source of the scream and the woman with the crooked nose standing with her finger pointed at me.

Then their eyes moved to me.

I pulled my coat up over my face and burrowed into Sanura's side.

A gruff voice asked, "What's wrong?" I knew the voice, the man who grabbed me when I'd first come here.

"It's her... the girl, the beast... there," the woman muttered.

The rough voice rose and barked at me. "Show your face girl! I wouldn't forget a face like that. You brought this destruction on us! Show your face!"

I whimpered as his heavy footsteps approached me.

"She's only a girl." Roan's voice stopped the steps.

"She's a monster in cahoots with the beast. She called for it, cried after it. When it came tonight, it must have been looking for *her*!"

Whispers buzzed through the crowd.

Steady and calm, Roan's voice demanded attention. "This girl had nothing to do with what happened in Gockin tonight. She slept not two feet from me. Leave her alone."

It seemed a lifetime before anyone breathed.

The heavy footsteps moved away, and the murmurs started again.

Roan whispered to Sanura, "Take her home. Go to bed."

I stayed buried into her side until we arrived safely in the small room we lived in. She gently pushed my arms from around her. "It's alright, Eviona. You are safe."

I nodded, but I never wanted to be around other people again.

We went to bed. Soon Sanura's breathing became steady and calm.

I couldn't sleep. In a way, that man had been right. I did help to bring the destruction. I hadn't discouraged Zefforah from destroying those homes.

How selfish I'd been. My thoughts were focused on how we might die if she didn't find Dyre. Guilt weighed my heart. Zefforah and I were too innocent to be connected to someone like Dyre. I hated our connection as much as he did.

The door opened, and Aurel and Roan entered whispering a conversation.

"She can't stay here. I said it from the beginning. I said this would happen. I knew that girl meant trouble."

Roan answered, "I won't send her away. She's a child. She doesn't have anyone else."

"I can't live like this. She speaks to herself when she thinks she's alone. She insists on absolute privacy even though she and Sanura are both girls. She eats like she's never seen food in her life. When I ask her to help in the kitchen, she makes the food into creatures causing me to constantly lose my appetite."

Her volume didn't increase, but her anger did.

"She will surely drive me to insanity. And now to think she is connected to the beast! Don't you remember her face last night? She really did want it to come here!"

"You're imagining that."

"No, I'm not! The worst part is that you don't seem

to see everything you give to that girl is something you take away from our daughter!"

"Is that what this is about? Then there is a solution I think we might agree on."

"You would agree to send Eviona away?" Aurel whispered hopefully.

"There is one place I would send her. However, you know she will only be accepted if I send Sanura with her. We've talked about it so many times. I can't give Sanura everything, but everything is available to her. I'd bet she'd go with Eviona."

"I'm not giving her to my sister," Aurel cried softly.

"Your sister has asked to have Sanura as her ward for years. Think of the fine young men she would meet there. It won't be long before she marries."

"Don't say such things. She's still so young."

"She's getting older every day. Haven't you noticed how she flirts with the boys in the town?"

Aurel sighed deeply, "Yes I have."

"Would you like her to marry a boy from my social class?"

Her tone changed, "I found the man of my dreams there."

"Look what you gave up by marrying him."

She sighed, "But she would be without her mother and her mother without her."

Roan replied, "Her mother could go with her, at least for a while."

"Must I only have my daughter or my husband? Why can't I have both?"

"I am not welcome at your sister's house."

"It would tear me in two to be separated from you."

"Then you will occasionally have to come back to check on your poor husband." I could practically hear the smile on Roan's face.

Aurel lashed out in angry whispers, "This isn't about Sanura. It's about Eviona."

"Your daughter sees Eviona as a sister and has from the moment she stumbled into our lives."

Soft sniffles could be heard as Aurel cried, "I don't want to give up my daughter, but Eviona must go."

"I will not have that girl go back to where she came from; back to being beaten, starved, and scared."

Aurel didn't speak for several moments. "We should warn my sister about her."

"We will do no such thing!" Roan whispered harsh and low. "Eviona deserves a fresh start."

"What if she goes running after the beast like that man said?"

"She won't."

I felt a twinge of guilt.

A thoughtful hush filled the cold air, and their conversation quieted. The door opened and closed. Then the quiet rustling of cupboards and drawers were all I could hear.

I promised myself to run away before morning. I'd wait until they were sleeping then I'd go back to the forest. Perhaps I could find a cave for shelter, and I could finally meet Zefforah. The forest was a safe place for both of us. I simply needed to wait until they slept.

The rustling continued. I forced my eyes to stay open, praying they would return to bed soon. I blinked slowly. My tired eyes burned. I pushed them closed with the thought of holding them tight only until the flames stopped. I needed to leave. Once Aurel and Roan slept I'd sneak out. I'd miss Sanura and Roan, but I would be safe. They would be safe.

Exordium (n) the beginning

Dyre rode in a coach seated next to his best friend. Toe-headed Laroke with his brilliant eyes, strong chin, and easy laugh. At the time they were probably about my age, eleven or twelve. I was only a toddler then.

The boys played a game, clapping their hands together and onto their legs in different rhythms. Trying to repeat the pattern the other had created. They attempted to foil each other with complexity or speed. Dyre managed much better than Laroke following his cadences easily with concentrated focus. Laroke played off his losses with smiles and sniggers and his wins with whoops and chortles. Dyre, on the other hand, played each round with seriousness. Composure and inward evaluation were the extent of his emotions whether he won or lost.

Across from them sat Horrish. A large man, very well dressed with a boyish face and long unkempt charcoal hair. One might guess him to be rich but would never know he was one of the wealthiest men in the kingdom. He didn't carry himself quite right, a little too irreverent, and a bit too crass.

They journeyed to the side of town which reeked of poverty and seemed shadowed in darkness even in the full light of day. Their carriage stopped in a low alley in front of an uninviting pub. Dyre gazed out the window as his companions stepped onto the cobblestone street. His nose crinkled with the disgust he made no attempt to hide as he evaluated two other boys running up the road. They were filthy and rude as they stepped over a fallen drunkard. Dyre followed them with his eyes until a woman scolded them and beat them as she pulled them into a door down the way. The drunk attempted to rise repeatedly, only to forfeit the futile task and scoot to the nearest building to curl up against its outer wall.

Dyre slowly stepped down as he spotted three men talking in whispers, hunkering over some secret exchange between their hands. Then he stepped back up into the coach when a woman scuttled past with wide coveting eyes.

"Come on boy!" Horrish demanded.

Dyre closed his eyes but could only think of the filthy hands of every person he had inspected. Unclean things sickened him. Having to step into the heart of such a foul place brought the bile from his stomach to his throat. "Why do we have to meet him here?"

"He lives here and refuses to leave his room," Horrish answered with impatience. "Come on."

Dyre swallowed hard and exited the coach to join Horrish and Laroke.

"You may pay the old man's rent, but you can't bring those boys in here." A large black man dressed in what might have once been a proper pair of slacks and a vest folded his arms and moved to block the door while Horrish endeavored to push Dyre and Laroke forward.

Horrish stepped back and evaluated the innkeeper. He pulled a small bag of coins from his pocket and tossed it to him, then pressed the boys through the door.

The innkeeper glowered with thick eyebrows and a hard lined mouth and called after them, "Keep them in the back. I'll let him know you've come."

As he entered, Dyre coughed and choked on the sickening air of the smoke filled room. The rancid smell of stale liquor filled his nostrils which flared their disapproval.

The people outside seemed a tad more welcoming compared to the untrusting scowls and bitter features of the sully patrons.

A roughly clad woman approached Dyre and Laroke

and stroked their faces with her leather hands. "What sweet little ones we have here." Horrish pulled the boys by their collars away from her. The woman's greedy eyes considered the gold buttons on Horrish's coat as her fingertips played with them. "How about you honey?" He pushed her aside, obviously disgusted.

She strolled away, but as they sat at the back table, Dyre noticed her watching them. He grimaced at her, and she winked at him in return. A cold shiver ran down his spine.

Horrish hit him hard on his back as he let out a loud laugh. "She's messing with you boy."

The innkeeper came and escorted the three of them up a rickety staircase and opened a door. "Have a seat at the table."

They sat, and the door slammed rattling through the decayed walls.

Then a skittish old man with wide eyes entered. Horrish motioned an impatient greeting. Dyre watched the awkward figure with curiosity as he scampered and tripped toward the table. As the old man settled into the seat, his wild eyes surveyed the boys in front of him.

Horrish carefully inspected every corner of the room from where he sat next to the old man. When he deemed the area free of threat, he barked quietly at the newcomer. "Grandfather, this is the boy. Tell him about your vision."

The old man's body convulsed as he coughed repeatedly. When his chest cleared itself of phlegm, he raised a boney finger to point at Dyre. Shaky and gasping for each breath of air his voice finally spoke the words, "You belong to that...that... animal?"

"You mean Zefforah, a big flying horse with a lizard like tail?"

A slow nod of the old man's head followed by another coughing fit confirmed the question.

Dyre chuckled. "I guess you could say I belong to her."

"She is part of it. The perfect ruler of Sylvaria."

Dyre's posture became straight and haughty, even his voice changed to drip with the self-importance of a superior being. "Me and Zefforah?"

"There's more," the old man stammered.

"Let's concentrate on the essentials." Horrish interrupted.

"He must understand all of what I saw."

Horrish grabbed his arm digging his fingers into the thin, wrinkled flesh. He spoke through his teeth with an unmoving jaw. "Where's the map you made? It is the important part."

The old man pried the heavy fingers from his arm with spiteful eyes and retrieved a very large piece of dark parchment. He unrolled it on the table. Dyre marveled over the tiny dots covering the page.

"Do you know what this is?" He asked Dyre.

"It's the stars of the heavens."

"This is the all important map?" Horrish sank back into his chair and pushed away from the table with a glare of contempt at the old man. "Rubbish."

Dyre defiantly stared at Horrish then he pointed to several spots on the page. "See this constellation, and this one, and this one? This is a map of the stars. He has it perfectly done."

He stopped and concentrated on the page. "...other than these seven. I have never seen this configuration in the night sky."

All four figures huddled together over the diminutive dots to analyze them further. The eyes of Dyre remained steady as he labored over the page. His three companions sporadically peered from the page to him, watching him in his employ. The silent examination interrupted only by occasional coughing fits from the old man, a sniffle or two from Laroke, and the movement of Horrish's head monitoring the room.

Then Dyre noticed a particular pattern. With one finger he traced an unseen line from one point to another and then to another and another. The seven stars he had pointed out earlier. "It must be a date," he said. "A time when the stars will be in these exact positions, probably only visible like this from one location."

Horrish looked around nervously and whispered, "Then that is where and when you will gain the kingdom!"

Dyre smiled and looked over to Laroke who nodded with excited eyes.

Horrish's mouth turned up in an evil grin. "So now we plan."

His grandfather grabbed him. Shaking fingers pressed fervently into Horrish's hand. "No!" He choked out several heavy coughs, and his eyes once again became wild and feverish. "It is the boy's destiny it will come to pass without help."

Horrish shook off the weak grasp of his grandfather. "Quiet old man, I need to think."

Cull (n) to select, pick, or choose (v) picked out and put aside as inferior

I woke to Sanura's voice whispering, "Eviona, wake up."

My eyes flew open. Morning sun shone through the small window. I cursed myself for falling asleep I didn't need to see that dream again. The night Dyre learned he was to rule Sylvaria had been dreamed too many times. I had other, more important things to worry about.

"My Aunt Delsa is here. We are going to live with her."

I didn't bother to appear ignorant. I simply moved slowly and spoke little as I gathered my things to take in the closet where I changed my clothes. I didn't put on the dress the family had given me when I first arrived. I slipped on the old trousers and shirts I wore when I lived in Minuette's prison. They still fit me, they'd always been large. I pulled Minuette's coat on and buttoned it to the top to hide my rags. I would find a moment to slip away and live in the forest; away from villages, constant judgment for my looks, and people who would keep me from ever meeting Zefforah.

Now we both knew where she could find me. I wouldn't give up that opportunity. Zefforah and I were destined to be friends. I'd known it from my earliest memories of flying with her. She soared above the clouds and turned circles in the air to hear me laugh. She'd been the only kindness I'd known until I met Sanura and Roan. I loved her far before the first time I saw her through Dyre's eyes. I wanted nothing more than to meet her. I closed my eyes to imagine the scene. It would be soon.

As I emerged from the closet, I tripped and fell, awakening Dyre.

He groaned and pulled the pillow over his head as if layers of feathers could drown me out. "Close your veil, Eviona!"

"You close yours," I whispered. It took conscious effort to close the veil, sleeping with it up proved impossible although all of us had tried to do it, several times.

He growled at me but didn't close his veil. He simply closed his eyes.

Sanura rushed to me pulling me toward her father and whispered, "Come, say goodbye to Father."

Dyre's head lifted from the bed. "Where are you going?"

I looked into Roan's eyes. I'd miss his deep sense of compassion. Roan had been the first man I ever met in person. I expected all men to be like Dyre and Horrish. Roan showed me some men were good. Happy with the simple miracles hard work and love can bring. My heart broke to leave him.

He embraced me. I leaned into him, but my arms stayed low knowing no one really ever wanted to be this close to me. Roan never seemed disgusted by my looks though, he embodied kindness. "Be a good girl."

I nodded wanting to tell him of my gratitude, but when I opened my mouth tears streamed down my face, and nothing came out.

Dyre scoffed, "They are finally casting you out." He pulled the pillow back over his head and rolled over. "We knew it would happen sooner or later. Don't be so juvenile."

His words only brought more tears.

"You don't need to say anything," Roan assured me, "I think I know what you're feeling. You should know I am as grateful to you as you might be for finding us.

You have given my little girl something I have always wanted to give her, and I shall always love you for it."

Dyre and I were both confused by his words. I searched his face for his meaning. Surely, I had nothing to give Sanura. He smiled and wiped the tears from my cheeks.

I noticed one falling down his cheek as well, but he didn't cry for me. I turned away from him. Reminding myself each step moved me closer to Zefforah.

As I reached the cottage door I turned to observe Roan and Sanura in their final goodbye, their mouths moved, but I could not hear.

Aurel and Roan followed Sanura only footsteps behind me. As they stepped from the house, Roan turned to his wife. He held his arms out to her inviting her for a last embrace. She held a bag. Her eyes were puffy and red. Then Roan did the oddest thing. He laughed. I stared at him with curiosity.

"Oh, Eviona!" Sanura dashed to me and squeezed my hands. "Mother has refused to leave my father, even for a short while to help us settle in. Isn't it sweet? They are so in love."

I glanced at the couple, a laughing wife being smothered in kisses by her husband. As much as she hated me, I understood her. If I had someone like that to love me, I would never leave him behind.

Sanura took my hand and began to pull me toward the coach. My feet did not move. "What's the matter?" she asked.

I looked at Sanura, but I didn't see her. I only thought of the forest behind me, the chance of meeting Zefforah and the freedom from people who would judge me by my hideousness.

Sanura stepped toward me, "Are you concerned about what's to come?"

I nodded.

She took my hands in hers. "I am too," she whispered. "Isn't it wonderful how we have each other? I wouldn't have agreed to go without you."

Did Sanura need me?

"When Father told me he had been to see Aunt Delsa last night I knew why. She's been asking me to come for years, and father has begged me to go live there. I didn't want to go. Not alone, but now I have you."

My heart wrenched in my chest. Didn't I want to meet Zefforah?

Sanura tugged on my hands. "Are you ready?"

With Sanura's beauty, she didn't need to be scared. Roan said I'd be giving her something, would she really not go if I didn't? Would her future be decided by my choice?

I looked back toward the woods, Zefforah and the simple goodness of familiarity and dreams coming true.

I looked forward toward Sanura and the terrifying world which would shun me and condemn my dreams.

Then a woman who looked like Aurel stepped from the coach. She wore the finest dress I'd ever seen, except through Dyre's eyes. Her hair, which had been combed into a lovely waving chignon, matched the chestnut brown of Aurel and Sanura's, and her umber eyes equaled theirs as well. However, the fractious look on her face made all of her beauty dissipate.

Dyre snarled, "What's *she* doing there?"

She approached me before I could pull my bonnet over my head. My hands rushed to cover my face.

"Put your hands down, girl!"

Minuette like tones forced my obedience, but I pushed my chin to my chest hiding as much as I could.

She placed her hand under my jaw lifting it to

examine me. She recoiled. Her eyes opened with obvious shock, but her face never lost their severity. "I don't like the look of her."

"Aunt Delsa!" Sanura pulled me away and pushed my face into her shoulder protecting me from the woman. "Please speak to her kindly. Can't you see how difficult this is for her?"

Dyre said, "I hate that woman."

Was he trying to comfort me? Then I remembered her face. Dyre did know her. She and Minuette were once friends, which meant she must live close to where Dyre spent his youth. I would be in a place Zefforah knew well. I could meet her, and be with Sanura too. I felt the liberation of hope.

I took Sanura's hand in mine. "I'm ready," I announced.

"You'll never be accepted. Don't forget what you are!" Dyre snapped. I smiled and closed my veil.

Dulcify (v) to make more agreeable, appease

I sat next to Sanura in the coach as Lady Delsa examined us through a monocle's lens. She offered a slight nod of the head to Sanura and eyed me only momentarily, her face stony and severe.

"Thank you for taking us in on such short notice," Sanura said.

"I've always felt you should be brought up properly. What type of future can you expect when you only associate with people in such a..." she hesitated as if choosing her words very carefully, "...humble town?" She glared toward me.

Who could blame her? I was a creature, not a companion for any real girl, rich or poor.

We passed a large house I knew well. It was the house Dyre grew up in, although from the road it looked like it had been neglected for quite some time. "Who lives there?" I asked quietly.

"Oh," Lady Delsa took a handkerchief from her sleeve and patted her eyes as if there might have been tears, though I saw none. "Do not ask me to say. In my loss I cannot speak of it." Her show of grief had been lost on me, but Sanura patted her hand to comfort her.

Not far down the road we turned into the large drive of a very intimidating looking manor.

Lady Delsa's home left me feeling uncomfortable in a way I'd never felt before. I'd only lived in small places before; a prison, and then Roan and Aurel's home. This manor held distress too much space would always hold for me. Wide eyes and new faces stared at me from me around every corner. I kept my head down with my bonnet as protection but every time I'd look up another new person would react to seeing me.

Sanura held my hand tightly. Her warmth comforted

me and urged my feet to continue forward.

I tugged on the brim of my bonnet pulling it as far over my face as I could without completely cutting off my sight.

As we were escorted through a foyer, one wall had been completely covered in glass. As we passed, I saw my shoes in it. A mirror. I cowered from it. I already knew I looked horrible. I had no desire to investigate my reflection.

We came to a stop. Delsa gave orders, and footsteps retreated. I could only hear one or two other people in the room with us. I lifted my head.

A meadow unlike any I'd ever seen appeared before me. Blue roses blossomed over a lattice gate. Tall green grass swayed to the music of sweet birds. The whole scene pulled me in until I realized it couldn't be real. My eyes focused. It had been made with threads and hung on the wall. Intricate and amazing. I stepped towards it with outstretched fingers.

"STOP!" I halted at the sound of Aunt Delsa's cold voice. I dropped my hand and stood unmoving. She lowered her volume, but her tone sounded harsh. "One must not touch the tapestries." She cleared her throat softly, as if a cough were beneath her. "Now," she motioned toward a couple of girls not much older than Sanura and me, dressed in brown frocks and white aprons. "Sanura, you will be taken to your room upstairs." Sanura began to follow the girl Lady Delsa motioned to. I followed along. "You," she motioned to me, "will be taken down to the servant's quarters."

"No!" Sanura glued herself to my side.

"It's alright," I whispered to her. "I don't mind."

Lady Delsa stood stunned, clearly appalled at Sanura's audacity in questioning her commands.

"You do not make the rules in my house young

lady."

"I will not sleep upstairs if I know Eviona is in a lower place." She made her tone as firm as her aunts.

"She is not your sister. She is nothing. She has nothing. We only arranged for me to bring you both here. I never had the intention of treating her as your equal."

"She will either stay with me, or I will stay with her. I will not be separated from her." Sanura held my arm as if we were conjoined.

"You are as foolish as your mother," she warned Sanura.

"Like my mother, I will take the lower place rather than be separated from those I love." Sanura hugged my arm so tightly I thought it would fall off. I didn't mind though.

Lady Delsa lectured, "I want you to be a lady. A goal you will never achieve it if you continue to cling to the lower class."

Sanura did not falter.

"Foolish, foolish girl."

Sanura didn't speak. Her chin steady, her stance strong.

"You will have all the less because of it."

"I do not need much," Sanura replied.

With disgust in her step Delsa left our care to a servant. Sanura slightly curtsied as she walked away and then she breathed.

She had been scared, but she fought for me. I wondered if she would regret bringing me along. When she reached around me and squeezed, I knew she didn't yet.

"I couldn't be without you," she cried.

I didn't understand Sanura's goodness toward me,

but I loved her for it.

We were escorted to our room and left alone. We squealed and hugged. Then I noticed a freestanding mirror waiting in the corner. I bowed my head and looked elsewhere. Sanura raced to it. "I've never had a mirror before." She touched her face and twirled watching her reflection. "Would you like to see?"

"No." My voice trembled on the short word.

Sanura nodded her head and thought silently for a moment. She then turned the mirror to face the wall. "I think I like it better that way." She moved a small chest three or four inches as well. "There, now the room is perfect."

It was perfect. High walls textured with intricate velvet patterns, pictures of people who must have been relatives, chests, and credenzas and a beautiful stonework fireplace. The bed in the center of the room seemed gigantic compared with the one we had shared back at Sanura's home. It had a high canopy over it, and curtains pulled back on each side. We eyed each other with eager faces and climbed onto it laughing and jumping until we couldn't breathe.

Sanura rested her head on my stomach, an odd and uncomfortable position for me. I wriggled off the bed and opened a wardrobe. A high pitch scream startled me, but soon Sanura bounced on her toes next to me giggling with delight.

"Look at all of these beautiful dresses." She appraised them, pulling them out and holding them in front of her. I watched her with a smile until she pushed a dress against me.

"Only you shall wear this one. It is the same color blue as your eyes."

I never knew my eyes were blue. If they were indeed the same bright blue of the dress, they might have even been pretty.

"I'm going to put one on." She began to undress.

I would have loved to try on the dress in my arms, but I couldn't remove my clothes with her there. The reactions from the few people which had seen my face were bad enough. I knew better than to allow anyone to see my body. Even Sanura.

Minuette stomped and strutted, pacing in raging footsteps while yelling at me. "I found you in the garbage. Garbage! That is exactly what you are. You are repulsive! You are disgusting! Exactly like this place you live; foul, contaminated, and sickening!"

She approached me with her claws at the ready, and I curled myself into a ball. She ripped the back of my shirt allowing the cold air to shroud my skin. "There!" She shrieked. "There is the most grotesque thing I have ever seen in my life! Your revolting back!" She stormed, pacing in semi-circles. "You are heinous. Every part of you." She spat. The cold slime crawled down my ribs and dripped to the floor.

I did not move as she walked away, but when she opened the door, I looked up to see her leave. Her breathing once again pushed from her lungs in regular patterns instead of the seething heavy huffs I always seemed to invoke in her. She spoke to me tenderly although her words defied her tone. "My sickening little urchin."

She stirred toward me. Her hand moved in a way to make me think she would cup my chin and perhaps show kindness to me, but she stopped before touching me.

She whispered, "Ugly, dreadful creature. People will see you as a monster. If you do ever allow anyone see you, they will run from you in terror. You're lucky I took

you in and let you live. You are hideous and unlovable."
She reached into her bag and pulled a large rather ragged coat from it.

"Hide yourself. You must never allow yourself to be seen. Not by anyone! Ever!"

After dressing Sanura examined herself in the mirror then peeked out from behind it to see me. Her smile quickly faded. She thoughtfully looked at my petrified stance. She motioned toward the other side of the room. "Will this be enough? Or should I leave while you change?"

She had indicated a free standing partition in the opposite corner of the room. I stared at it, still reliving the memories of Minuette's words.

"I'll leave."

I nodded and waited with gratitude until the door closed behind her. Thinking of undressing, I didn't like the space of the room. I opened a chest with several drawers like those I'd seen Dyre use many times for underclothing and other odds and ends. In it, I found the proper undergarments I'd been taught to wear at Sanura's house. I pulled out an underdress and took it to dress behind the partition.

I felt eyes everywhere. The cold air on my skin reminded me of a million prickly stares. I quickly took off Minuette's coat and the rags it hid and slipped the underdress over my frame. I added the blue frock on top of it and felt almost like a real girl.

The rags I once wore burned with a low hiss in the fireplace. I would never truly be free of Minuette, but I enjoyed destroying evidence of her existence.

Aperture (n) an opening

Soon Lady Delsa began our education. She hired a tutor, and we spent most of our time with her. Elina, though not fine-looking, had spirit and made learning fun. I liked her. I enjoyed learning and discussing the world with her. Aurel had taught Sanura to read and write so her lessons were different than mine. I had only the knowledge I'd learned from Dyre.

"Having you around is like having my own private hell!"

Dyre barked the words at me. I felt the same way about him, but I wouldn't back down this time. Our connection held my only portal to anything outside my prison, and I intended to use it to my advantage. Anytime his veil dropped I begged.

"Please, Dyre. All you have to do is go gambling and let me watch."

"No!" He closed me off.

I huffed and waited. He could shut me off during the day, but as soon as his veil closed when he fell to sleep, I'd start again.

"Dyre. Dyre, wake up."

He pulled his pillow over his head and snarled.

I hoped the pillow would make my voice echo in his head. "It's not like anyone will see me."

"Aaaaarrrgghh. You've been doing this for weeks! You must stop!"

I purposely made my voice as innocent as possible. "All you have to do is take me with you."

"Fine! Tomorrow."

Shocked into silence, I didn't respond. I couldn't form a thought to say as he turned over in bed and closed his veil again.

Once I gained my wits, I squealed and clapped my hands. I waited for an eternity to pass until he would let me watch him play cards the next day.

As he stepped out of the manor, my questions started. "How is it they let you gamble? Isn't seventeen a little young?"

"Horrish is with me most of the time, but sometimes he has other things to do. I think they're accustomed to seeing my face. I always have plenty of money to play with as well. They're not going to turn that away."

As he walked in, excitement filled us both.

As he walked out frustrated would more aptly describe the mood.

"You are such an idiot," he grumbled as he walked home.

"I didn't make you lose."

"I can't play with a stupid child asking me questions through the whole game!"

"I simply wanted to know what you were doing."

"I couldn't very well tell you right in the middle of it!"

"I want to learn Dyre. Teach me." I did want to be taught. Anything.

Once again I used our connection to my advantage, and I wouldn't let it go. I wanted to learn, and he was the only one who could teach me. Our little ritual continued month after month, me begging to be taught and him simply wanting me to disappear.

He finally crumbled. "If I teach you a game will you let me have some peace?"

"I will give you a month of silence, I swear."

"I want the silence first!"

"Done!"

I didn't trust him. I knew he would probably never teach me, but I wanted to try. We settled the dates.

Dyre told Minuette not to speak to me or make me speak. I don't know if he told her why, but she did it. It was the most pleasant time I ever spent with her. She would drop things off and leave me quickly. I preferred it to her usual criticisms.

After three weeks Dyre forgot about me. He even left himself open most of the time, which I enjoyed very much until one evening when he and Horrish visited a new place. I didn't like how he felt when he looked at the women there. No emotion, only want. Several women eyed Horrish and Dyre as they entered. One approached Horrish. Low whispers were exchanged as Dyre's eyes moved from woman to woman. Occasionally his focus rested on things I didn't care for, an extra low neckline, or a hemline pulled up exposing a thigh.

Horrish pointed out two women to the woman he had been conversing with. One approached him and the other circled Dyre. "Hello, honey." She ran her fingers across the back of his shoulders as she passed. Dyre liked it, but it felt creepy to me.

"Hello." He grabbed her wrist to prevent her from moving away.

Dyre could block me, but I didn't know how to do the same to him, and I didn't dare ask him to do it. I didn't even clear my throat. If I alerted him to my presence now he would be mad, our whole deal would be broken, and I wouldn't ever learn anything. I kept my mouth closed and my body still as I sat in the darkness of my prison; watching, without a chance of evasion.

The woman's coarse fingers touched his cheek and moved down toward his chin. "You're younger than my usuals."

Her lips closed in toward Dyre as she spoke. Her

breath smelled disgusting, like Horrish's breath sometimes smelled when he came home late at night walking and talking funny.

"He's man enough." I heard Horrish say.

Her eyes shifted from Dyre's only momentarily to size up Horrish. Then she took Dyre by the hand. His heart raced with excitement. Mine joined it with a different emotion.

"Would you like me to talk to you through our time? Or would you rather just keep things quiet?" She asked Dyre as she led him to a small room in the back.

"Talking is good." His voice cracked on the last word. She smirked as his face flushed hot with embarrassment.

I crouched myself into the corner of my prison. As she started to speak, I opened my mouth and flattened my tongue to allow the bad taste of her words to fall out. They may have been exciting to him, but they sounded sickening to me.

I closed my eyes and concentrated on the songs of the crickets outside, hoping they could somehow drown out her oily voice. As I paid closer attention to the shrill creaks and chirrs they made, a thin green whisper of color appeared in my mind. Although much thinner and lighter, it reminded me of his veil. An idea took shape inside my head. I concentrated on smaller, less obvious sounds hoping to increase the weight of the color between me and Dyre.

I focused on the faint scratches of the mice scraping through my food supplies, and the click of the cockroaches as they scrambled when I wiggled my toes. The more attention I paid to the noise surrounding me the fainter the echo of his setting grew until the first layer of my veil had formed.

I almost gasped with excitement. I focused on it,

mentally picturing myself grabbing it with my hands and yanking it between me and the sounds he heard. Released from her words, I wanted to cheer.

But then her hands moved to unlace her bodice, and Dyre's focus rested there. My own hands instinctively flew over my already closed eyes trying to block her out. It didn't help. So I focused on the crickets again, and the mice and the cockroaches. It didn't work this time. I cringed against the sight of her skin. I opened my eyes wide and looked at anything that could distract me from the woman. I couldn't see much of anything in my little prison after the sun set, only some shadows and a small ray of moonlight coming through a slight crack in the door. I gave it my full attention. Could I see the bits of dust in it? I moved to the light and stirred my hand on the floor. Dust danced in the air. As I became engrossed in the sea of tiny shapes, a deep blue layer of fabric appeared in front of the green. I mentally pulled it down between us, grateful to not be watching her anymore.

Then it clicked. Sound for sound. Sight for sight. I only had to overwhelm each sense with my surroundings to block his out.

I inhaled only to have the familiar reek of waste and urine fill my nose. Too commonplace to me to be a nuisance, but he inhaled at the same time; smells nastier than my surroundings.

I felt him pressing his nose against her skin breathing in something like smoky musk with too much sweat. I didn't like it. Fortunately, the scents around me were stronger and as I concentrated on breathing them in, a yellow sheet formed in my head. I pulled it into place blocking off his sense of smell. I rubbed at my nose, the potency of her odor lingered not in my nose, but too pungent in my memory.

I debated which sense to block next. Did it matter? They were all too strong. Before I could decide the taste of something stale and rancid filled my mouth as I felt his mouth exploring hers. When I started to gag on the flavor, I knew I really had no choice. I didn't have much around me I could think to taste. Only one thing came to mind, but it would be terrible. Another wave of her tang filled my mouth so I did the only thing I could, I brought a finger to my lips and licked it. It almost seemed worse than tasting her tongue. I cringed as I placed it in my mouth, sucking off all the nastiness and grime, and swallowed. A red layer of the veil came into view, and I placed it as quickly as I could between us.

I felt exhausted. My head hurt, and I wanted to be finished. I looked at the veil between me and Dyre, deep enough in color to allow me to not be experiencing his night. I lay backward on the ground and felt Dyre make the same movement. I panicked when I felt the unbuttoning of his shirt. Her leather hands moved down his torso and I bolted upright and wrapped my arms around myself pulling my knees into my chest for protection.

"No," I whined frustrated with how much work it took to close my veil. Dyre made it seem so easy.

I placed my hands on the ground moving them from side to side, allowing them to experience my world. The green moss I had watched growing over the last few weeks felt slimy and cold under my left hand. Dark black gravel pressed its ragged edges into the palm of my right.

A slight haze of purple revealed itself, much too thin to help. Her body pressed against his. I forced my back against the wall and pressed myself into it feeling the bumps and grooves. The haze grew deeper in color but not enough. I pushed my fingernails into the skin of my ankles. Dyre shook his foot but at this point, I didn't care if he felt me or not. One way or another I needed to be away from him. The deeper I dug my nails, the stronger my purple shroud became.

Then finally I couldn't feel him. I couldn't see him. No sounds, smells, or tastes invaded me from his side.

"Whoo!" I yelled. Then I yelled again louder. I jumped up and reached my arms up as high as I could. "YES! I did it!" I screamed. I danced and jumped, delighted with myself until I fell down with fatigue.

I slept. Then in the morning I built my veil first thing. Then I removed it and placed it again and again and again. Practicing constantly until it became as natural to me as opening and closing my eyes.

A week later at the end of my month, I woke early and yelled, "Dyre!" Then I placed my veil. A few minutes later I repeated the actions.

After five or six times he screamed at me. "Stop it, you little creep!"

"Stop what?" I giggled and placed the veil while he yelled at me again. When I pulled back my veil still laughing I felt delighted by his frustration.

"When did you learn to do that?" he asked.

"When you forgot about me! You swine!"

I felt him pause, "Forgot about you?"

"When you and Horrish went to that place with those women and..." I couldn't finish. I shuttered as the memory crept down my back.

"Oh, that." Did I hear sorrow in his voice?

"Yes, that!"

"Well, it's about time you learned how to block me off. I shouldn't have to be the one to do it all of the time."

"It's also time for you to teach me cards."

"I'll think about it," he said as he placed his own veil.

Surprisingly, he kept his part of the bargain. For the next several weeks if he found himself alone or bored he would take out his cards and teach me.

He started my education with numbers and early math skills. They made sense and learning came easily. He still called me stupid, but I think he could tell I loved learning.

He then taught me all of the games he knew and strategies to play them. He enjoyed being crafty and cheated sometimes. I think he might have been testing me because he seemed pleased when I caught him.

He also taught me a trick. One magic card always ended up on top of the deck at the end. I loved that trick. Someday if I ever played cards, I would do it.

Once I mastered the card games, he let me watch him play when he went out to gamble. At first, I only watched and tried not to ask questions or make comments.

I loved watching for the numbers as they were played and eventually I learned to count the cards. I helped Dyre by knowing what cards had already been played and the chances of the others. Of course, he enjoyed winning and together we won quite a bit. I think I even gained a little respect in his eyes. Maybe I wasn't a stupid little girl after all. But if he ever thought that, he never said it.

Echelon (n) a level of worthiness, achievement or reputation

Even though I loved learning with Elina, and Sanura made my life happy, I wanted some time to myself. It had been three years since we'd come here and Zefforah still didn't even know where I lived. I needed time alone so I could talk to her. I hadn't thought through those kinds of details when I came here. The occasional moments Zefforah's veil opened to me I'd be with Sanura and couldn't speak. It drove me mad wondering if I would ever meet her. If I hadn't come here, I wouldn't have been made to wait. Sometimes, I regretted that decision.

One day Elina knocked on our door. Sanura greeted her, "Elina, are we late for our lessons?"

"No, but there has been a change of plans." Her eyes seemed happy yet cautious.

Sanura and I exchanged curious glances. "Is something wrong?" Sanura asked.

Elina shook her head and smiled at Sanura and then shot a worried look to me. "Lady Aurel has come to visit. She's waiting for you downstairs."

Sanura jumped up and down hugging our tutor and then ran to hug me too. "That's wonderful!"

Elina cleared her throat. "She only wants to see you, Sanura."

Sanura's face dropped. "No, she's coming to see both of us."

"She and your aunt wish to have your company for a few days. Only yours."

Visibly the fight built inside Sanura. She wouldn't let them cut me out, but I only thought of the opportunity this would create for me to spend some time alone.

I quickly interjected, "I don't mind. I know you miss

her."

She didn't give in easily but finally hugged me in gratitude. "I do miss her. I'm sorry she—"

I interrupted, "I'm not sorry. Go. Enjoy your mother."

Obviously torn she finished putting on her boots and reluctantly left with Elina. If only she knew how happy this little change in plans made me, she would have been more willing to go.

I quickly dressed and with the finishing touch of a large bonnet to sufficiently cover my face I headed out to explore. I had the goal of finding the house Dyre lived in with Minuette and Horrish. Zefforah would certainly know its location. I recognized the house quickly.

Of course, Zefforah had her veil closed. I trudged toward the house a bit deflated wishing she would see where I was.

The overgrown yard told me it had been deserted since Dyre left. I couldn't imagine why no one would agree to buy it from him. It had once been quite a grand manor. I found a back door, lifted it ever so slightly and pushed to the left the way I remembered Dyre doing. It creaked and fought against my body and then groaned as it recognized the familiar pull and opened.

The kitchen, the servant's quarters and offices I explored were unfamiliar, but I found myself soon enough in the main entryway.

I took a deep breath as I saw the ghosts of the furnishings which used to occupy the space. I stood where Dyre's favorite wing backed chair use to stand.

I looked at the room the way he used to, like a throne room. Huge double doors opposite his chair were the front doors of the house. Sometimes Dyre would sit here until someone came simply to intimidate them as they walked in.

I wanted to show him where I stood. I wanted to gloat the way he used to with me, strutting around this grand place as I suffered. I first found the only room Dyre never entered. Minuette's room. I couldn't think why I would want to go there. I had no hope to see her. Perhaps I only wanted verification of her absence.

I inspected the door thoroughly before turning its handle. I pushed it open slowly wondering what terrors or marvels I might find on the other side. Nothing greeted me. No screams from Minuette's ghost, nor angels rejoicing her nonexistence. I moved to the windows and pulled back the curtains to allow light into the room.

Two figures scampered about the overgrown weeds of the yard. I quickly jumped out of the light. After a moment I peeked around the curtain, the figures had disappeared. I breathed. They hadn't seen me.

Then voices rang through the house. "Hello? Hello. Where are you?"

I hid, crouched in the large dark fireplace in the corner of the room hoping the shadows would hide me if they searched there. The door opened. "I'm pretty certain this is the room," a voice said.

"You go ahead. I'll search down the hall," said another.

A young man came into the light and went to the curtains I'd opened earlier. "I know you're in here."

I didn't move. He couldn't know.

"Come out. I won't tell anyone."

I remained still, barely breathing.

He slowly moved around the room. "Hmmmm, maybe I *should* tell someone we saw you. It would only be right to report a trespasser."

"You aren't supposed to be here either," I panicked.

"Ah ha! I knew you were here!"

I stayed in my corner and trembled as he approached. "Please don't come any closer," I cried.

He took one more cautious step. "I didn't mean to frighten you."

"I don't want to frighten you either. Please stay where you are."

He stopped.

Relieved thanks fell from my lips.

"Are you," he paused, "frightening?"

To avoid answering I asked, "What is your name?"

He thought for a moment before responding. "I'll tell you my name as soon as we meet properly."

"I'll never know then," I responded.

"Maybe you simply need to know me better before we actually meet. Ask me what you will, I'll gladly answer."

As I thought, footsteps came down the hall. "Hey! Did you find anything?" boomed the boy running to the room.

He shook his head, "It's getting late. We should head home." He pulled the door closed behind them and added in a loud voice, "I think I might come back tomorrow to do a more thorough search."

Did he say it as a cue for me to meet him here again? I giggled at the thought of a boy with an actual desire to spend time with me. I'd hide again in the darkness of course, but I certainly wanted to be there when he came back.

I easily convinced Elina to allow me more time to myself. After all, she'd been hired as Sanura's teacher. Lady Delsa wouldn't object to her taking the time for herself.

Sanura didn't come to our room that night. I suppose

she chose to stay with her mother. It made it easy to steal away to the kitchen while everyone slept. I had a plan. I wanted to take my new friend a gift.

Delitescent (adj) concealed, hidden

"Hello?"

"I'm here," I called from the fireplace.

"I knew you would be. Are we to meet today?"

"No, but I do have questions for you."

"I welcome them." He paced the room slowly and from my crouched position I could occasionally make out his facial expressions in the dim light.

"What is your name?" I asked.

He grinned and put up a finger swaying it back and forth. "Tsk, tsk. Not until a proper meeting."

He'd caught me. I laughed. "How old are you?"

"I'm seventeen," he responded. "How about you?"

"My friend tells me I'm sixteen."

"Your friend? Don't you have parents?"

"No, but I'm about the same size as my friend, so when she has a birthday I assume I'm a year older too."

"That's interesting. Have you actually met this other friend?"

I giggled, "Of course I have."

"You never know about people who lurk in shadows," he stood in the light allowing me to see his face clearly. His features were strong, yet youthful. His face glowed in the dim ray of sun. "What other questions do you have for me?"

"I was wondering…"

"Yes?"

"Would you be willing to eat a mouse?"

"Is there a reason I would need to?"

I smirked, "I made you some. Mice are my specialty."

Disbelief spread with a grin over his face.

I instructed, "They're on the window seat."

He pulled back the curtains exposing the three little white mice I'd made. "My cat does this for me, you know."

I giggled.

He picked one up. "The weight is wrong. Cooking it shouldn't make it this much lighter."

"Try it," I encouraged.

Hesitantly he put the rodent to his nose and breathed in. His eyebrows shot up. "Surprisingly tempting."

"My friend taught me how to make them taste good."

He took a bite and chewed with a smirk on his face. "It's a pastry!"

Happy with his reaction I confessed, "I wanted to test your bravery."

"I like that," he announced. After finishing the tidbit he added, "I like you. I like the way you think. Find another challenge for me."

"Tell me what you are good at and I'll do my best to try you."

"I'll pass any test you present me. I assure you."

"I wonder what the best test of pride would be," I chuckled.

He smiled, "My father tells me it's one of my weaknesses and assures me it will find me trouble."

"Oh a weakness," I feigned surprise. "And here I thought you perfect."

"I have others as well," he protested.

"Really? What is another?"

"You'll have to find them for yourself."

"Another ploy to have me show myself, I suppose?"

He laughed. "Perhaps."

"Next question," I moved on. "What do you think you will be like when you are old?"

"Wait. I'd like to know a thing or two about you."

"Like what?"

"I don't know... What do you want out of life? Are

you one of those girls who simply wishes to meet a man, become his wife and have some children?"

"I could never hope for anything so grand."

"Grand? What do you see yourself doing in the future?"

"Well, I never thought about it. I wonder if I'd be allowed to work in a kitchen."

He laughed, "Your goals are much too modest."

"And yours?" I retaliated.

"I am going to be a captain. It's the highest rank one can achieve in the king's army."

"That's lofty."

"And I am going to find the lost princess. Well, I'm not truly interested in finding her, but if I did perhaps I could marry her and become King. That would indeed interest me."

I chuckled, "I believe your goals may not be quite modest enough. Who is the lost princess?"

His head jerked toward the fireplace. "Have you been living in there your whole life?"

"No," I answered timidly. "And who will rule if the lost princess isn't found?" I asked thinking of Dyre.

"The king and queen have young twin daughters now. I think the eldest is Princess Rika."

"Why don't you court Princess Rika and become king that way?"

He hooted a chortle. "Perhaps because she is five years old."

"I didn't know. Don't laugh at me," I muttered.

His laugh stopped short. "It was never my intention to offend you. I'm sorry."

I didn't know how to respond to such sincerity.

"Tell me about the lost princess."

He paced the floor slowly. "Here is what I know of her. At only two or three years old, she vanished."

"How is that possible?"

"That is the question. People were with her every moment of every day. Her bedroom had been set up on one of the top floors of the castle. Two nurses even slept in the same room with her and guards were awake just outside. But one night – poof, she disappeared."

"How?"

"If they knew how they would probably be able to find her. The king and queen still believe she is alive. There are many stories though."

"Like what?"

"I've heard people say she crawled into her fireplace during the night and burned to death. Fireplaces aren't exactly safe, you know."

I snickered at his intimation.

"Some people speculate whether or not she ever existed at all."

"Really?"

"There are those who say the walls of the castle itself swallowed her, and you can still hear her cries late at night.

"That's terrifying," I over-exaggerated the fear in my voice.

He snuck a snarky glance in my direction. "Do you want to hear something truly terrifying?"

I answered hesitantly, "I don't know…"

"Do you want to know why this house is deserted?"

I did want to know, but I wondered if any of his ghost stories could truly tell me the answers. "Yes."

"This is where the beast used to live."

"Oh?" I hoped to sound surprised.

"If you go out to the stables you'll see where walls were torn out to house something huge. There are also chains still there. The ones they used to hold it captive.

A few years ago the owners disappeared. My father tells me both of their bodies were found months later trampled to death. The beast took its revenge."

Zefforah hated Minuette for her cruelty, as much as I did. I wish I didn't know how true his allegations were.

"I know it was here. I've seen it myself three times." His voice insinuated I should be impressed. "It hasn't come in years though. I think it fears this place, if it's possible for that thing to feel fear."

My heart sank knowing now I'd never meet Zefforah. I should have stayed in the forest.

"You're so quiet. Did I scare you?"

"It will take more than stories to upset me," I faked a positive tone.

He looked pleased with my comment. Then glanced outside and said, "It's late. I should probably go."

Urgently I asked, "Tomorrow?"

"No," he replied sadly.

Disappointed I said, "I understand. I'm sorry we won't be able to talk more."

"Oh, this isn't the end. I plan on meeting you properly."

Butterflies beat their wings against my stomach walls. "It won't be often, but when I can, I'll come here."

He bowed toward the fireplace and smiled before he exited.

I waited quite a while before coming out of my hiding place for fear he might have lingered. Then I found the stable. I knelt down beside the huge metal cuffs which once held Zefforah captive. I could still feel the way they rubbed against my ankles.

"Zefforah? Will we ever meet?"

Machinate (v) to plot with evil purpose

A knock jolted me awake. My heart pounded with
the start. The knock came again. A woman's voice
moaned, and a hand nudged my hip. "You answer it." It
was Dyre feeling it, not me. I closed my eyes but felt too
tired to build my veil.

Dyre grunted and sat up, pushing his hands through
his hair. Lighting a candle, he dressed sloppily and
opened the door only a crack. "What do you want?"

A very handsome, well-dressed man with golden
blond hair greeted Dyre with a smirk on his face. "I
want an audience with the future king of Sylvaria."

Dyre cheered as he acknowledged his old friend. "Ah
Ha!" He threw the door open and offered his arms to the
man. "Laroke! It has been too long. I didn't even
recognize you."

Laroke's laughter joined Dyre's as they embraced.

The woman's voice behind Dyre interrupted their
reunion. "Shhhhh. You two are going to wake the whole
town."

Dyre pulled Laroke into the house and closed the
door. "Laroke this is Listy."

Listy nodded to him once through squinting eyes.
"Charmed. Now see if you two can hold it down so the
world can sleep."

Dyre hummed at her as she sauntered back to the
bedroom, shaking her head.

I joined her in her sentiment. "Dyre I can't keep my
veil closed while I sleep. Close yours."

He grunted and closed me off.

Not much later I awoke again with a pinch on my
arm. Dyre purposely woke me.

"Ouch!" I cried.

He looked over his shoulder and raised his eyebrows

like he expected me to be there whenever he wanted me, and he changed the subject of the conversation. "I've thought we could do a bit of gambling tomorrow. Are you up for it?" Dyre spoke to Laroke, but I understood he wanted me to answer his question as well.

I hadn't been gambling with Dyre for quite a while.

"I'd like that," I told him, grateful to be able to have some fun since Sanura would still be with her mother.

"I'm not much of a card player," Laroke admitted.

"Come on, be a man." Dyre urged him.

"Can't we simply go find some women?"

"Women are too easily had. I hoped to do something a little more lucrative. Besides, I have Listy right now."

Laroke laughed, "You believe in fidelity now?"

Dyre laughed. "You know me too well for that. I'm only staying another week or two here. Remember that one red head I —"

"Ugh," I interjected rolling my eyes. "Are we going or not?"

Dyre returned to the original question, "Never mind about women. What about gambling?"

"I don't have the money."

"I'll give you some."

Laroke shrugged, "Then how can I refuse?"

"Good! We'll go tomorrow."

When the conversation turned back to women, I closed my veil.

The next day I anxiously waited for Dyre to open his veil to me. Half way through the afternoon his senses rushed to join mine.

"Took you long enough," I pouted.

He grunted and looked around.

Other than Laroke all of the players at the table with him were men we had played with before. Laroke sat to

Dyre's left and on his other side sat a fat middle-aged man with a scar on his left cheek who went by the name of Killer. It seemed silly for a man like that to have ever had the physique or skills to be called Killer. He did make for a fair opponent though.

A young good looking man named Toril sat across from Dyre. A beautiful woman at his side fondled his hair and whispered periodically into his ear making him smile. He had a different woman on his arm every time he played. I didn't like Toril. He cheated. I had suspected him of it since the first time we played against him.

To his left sat an old man named Gup. White hair flew from his head as if he had just come in from a wind storm. He hadn't, his hair always looked like that. I didn't enjoy playing with him. He was hard faced and difficult to read.

They had already been playing for a while and from the look of things Dyre hadn't been as successful as usual. I gloated a bit in my head and even though he didn't hear me he pinched his arm as if he had read my thoughts.

"Ouch!" I hissed. "Do you want my help or not!"

He sighed heavily and massaged the soreness as a peace offering.

Within an hour Dyre had made a comeback and had a good amount of the winnings. Toril fumed visibly. He ignored his companion and constantly raised the stakes in each game.

Gup left early with a few dollars still left in his pocket, and Laroke proved he truly couldn't play. At the end of the night only Killer, Toril, and Dyre still played.

I focused on the cards in Dyre's hand. "Don't smirk," I reminded him when I felt the corner of his mouth turn up as he picked up the two cards on the table. He relaxed his face and looked at Toril.

Dyre's cards were a pretty sight. Only one other hand could beat it and I'd already seen the top card Toril would need for him to win.

Toril pushed everything in front of him to the center of the table. Killer threw down his cards and pushed himself away from them in frustration.

"There is no way he can win," I encouraged Dyre.

He eyed Toril and hesitated. I read his mind when he paused silently asking of my certainty.

"I'm positive. He can't beat you."

Dyre peered at the money in front of him. A small fortune. He pushed it all into the center of the table trusting me.

Toril turned his cards over one at a time. I sneered as he turned over his last card to reveal the exact card I had assured Dyre couldn't be in his hand. I yelled. "Cheater! Count the tens. I know he cheated!"

With grinding teeth, Dyre picked up the cards. Toril quickly cleaned his money off the table and bolted out the door.

Dyre shot an uncertain look toward him as he made his exit. He then went through the deck throwing the tens down as he found them. "One. Two. Three. Four." He kept searching… "Five." Two cards with the same face stared up from the table.

Dyre raced outside just in time to pull Toril from his coach. The woman inside screamed as Dyre threw a punch at Toril's face. Toril fell to the ground. Dyre waited for him to rise with his fists up.

Several sets of footsteps behind Dyre told me Laroke and others had followed him out.

As he moved to stand Toril pulled a small knife from his boot. Then he lunged forward and crammed it into

Dyre's right leg.

Agonist (n) A chemical capable of activating a physiological reaction

I screamed! Then I silenced myself so as to not draw the attention of the entire house. Zefforah's veil dropped, and she wailed. Dyre grabbed the knife and pulled it out. His spiteful eyes went to Toril who hit the horse attached to the carriage and then ran with it until he jumped into the coach. He stood on the door ledge and waved with an evil grin at Dyre and the other men. Some ran after him but couldn't keep up for long.

One of the men promised, "He'll never play in this town again." He helped Dyre to stand.

Laroke put himself under Dyre's arm. "Let me help." Zefforah's screams hurt my ears.

I exposed my bleeding leg and whimpered watching the red substance stream to the floor.

Dyre instructed. "Put pressure on the wound."

"I'm not an idiot." Laroke came back defensively.

"Take care of it!" Dyre barked at me over his shoulder.

"All right! Don't yell at me." Laroke shouted.

I watched closely and pressed my leg the same as Dyre did. Laroke took a kerchief from his pocket and wrapped it tightly around the wound. I followed his lead with a kerchief I found in my dressing table.

Zefforah's cries were still horrendous. I asked, "What about Zefforah?"

Dyre gritted his teeth, "I can't take care of her right now."

Laroke sneered at Dyre. "Weren't you going to leave her soon anyway?" Laroke looked clearly disgusted at how Listy seemed to be Dyre's current concern. He picked Dyre up and supported his left side as the two men hobbled home.

Zefforah ran wildly, then dropped agonizing in the

pain. Dyre and I felt the impact and jerked.

Laroke encouraged, "We're almost there."

Listy must have seen the men coming. She ran out to Dyre as they approached. "What happened?"

"A creep stole my money."

"So you took it out on your leg?" She moved to Dyre's other side to help Laroke move him into the house.

They seated him. Listy ripped off the temporary binding and tore the leg of Dyre's pants to examine the gash more closely. She instructed Laroke. "Go find the doctor. He lives in the town square. There's a sign above his door." Laroke ran out.

She looked at Dyre a bit sideways, her eyebrows up. "I'm going to use the juice."

"No!" Dyre grabbed her shoulders forcing her to look into his eyes. "I've told you before obiberry juice is poison to me."

"I've used it a million times. Trust me."

"You need to trust *me*. I can't have it!" He shouted and pushed her back slightly as he released her.

She left the room and returned with a pitcher and went to pour its contents on his leg. He seized her hand to stop her.

"It's only water. I need to clean the cut with something." She bit at him.

He let go of her hand in consent. As the liquid poured onto his leg, a wave of fire seared mine.

"Aaaaahhhh!" Zefforah and Dyre screamed together. I buried my face in a pillow hoping to muffle the sound.

The skin on Dyre's leg bubbled and burned and we all writhed in agony. I released the grip on my leg certain my flesh would be missing from the bone. Instead, the cut which had been there moments earlier seemed to dissolve together into a simple, pink line while the flesh around it gurgled and merged.

Splashing water cooled Dyre's leg and the flame of the poison, but only momentarily.

"More water!" Dyre hollered.

Listy obeyed quickly and ran from the room for more water. After several douses, the pain moved from a flame to a smolder.

Dyre raised angry eyes to Listy's face.

"I'm sorry," she whispered turning to bring more water.

Dyre growled at her. "You should have listened."

"I'm sorry," she repeated as she continually tried to cool his leg.

Laroke came in with the doctor. "When did the flood happen?" he asked as he stepped through the pool of water on the floor.

"It's a long story." Dyre stared harshly at Listy.

The doctor sat down in front of Dyre and looked at Laroke in confusion. "I thought you said he had a knife wound."

"He did." I felt Laroke look over Dyre's shoulder.

The doctor immediately pulled several items from his bag and started to work on Dyre's leg. "This is a burn if ever I saw one."

After he soothed the burn, he applied ointment and dressed it. The doctor told Dyre how to care for it and packed up his bag. "You'll have a bad scar I'm afraid, but I'm sure your leg will function as well as it always has."

Listy walked with him, stopping him at the door to ask more questions.

"You won't let this stop you," Laroke said with a questioning tone.

Dyre returned with a scalding hot expression. "Of

course not."

"I've never seen you panic like that before, it's unlike you."

Dyre agreed with a nod and motioned for his friend to help him move.

Laroke settled him comfortably in a chair in the bedroom. As he left he said, "I'll go help Listy clean up the lake in the other room."

Zefforah settled down and found her way to a large pond where she immersed herself in cooling water.

I still stared at my newly mended skin. "Dyre, what happened?"

He whispered in frustration. "Did you miss it? Listy poured obiberry juice on my leg."

"I know that. I mean with the knife wound. I thought obiberry juice only eased pain. I didn't think it could heal anything."

"Heal? Does my leg look healed?"

"Mine is. Zefforah stopped screaming. Your knife wound has completely disappeared." I touched the faint pink line on my leg.

He growled, "It didn't burn you?"

"Are you talking to me?" Listy interrupted our conversation.

"No. I'm talking to myself again," he muttered.

"Are you ever going to forgive me?" She stood in front of him, her eyes pleading with soft remorse.

Dyre put his hands around her waist pulling her toward him and onto his good leg. "Now maybe you will admit I am always right." If it had been me, he would have never been so kind.

Pleased with his forgiving tone she rubbed his nose with hers and kissed him.

"Hey! You two are not alone here," I called at the

same time Laroke cleared his throat to interrupt. I placed my veil.

Late into the night I felt a chill and woke to the voices of Laroke and Dyre. I kept my eyes closed not intentionally eavesdropping, but doing so nonetheless.

"Do you always travel at night?" Dyre asked.

"I find it best."

"Very good, my friend. I appreciate your news and everything you are doing. Do you still feel good about your contact?"

"Yes."

"Is he high in rank? Will we be able to use him?"

"I should think so," replied Laroke. "I will be exactly where I want to be when the time is right."

"Good!" Dyre slapped Laroke's back as they parted. "Until we meet again."

Oeillade (n) an amorous glance

Aurel made it a practice to come every month and stay a few days with her daughter and sister. Elina took those days to herself, and I looked forward to each time I could go back to the house and hopefully see my new friend.

"Hello?" I called.

Footsteps rushed in my direction. I ran upstairs to beat them. Giggling, I found another new hiding place.

He hurried in panting, "Are you in here?"

My giggling gave me away.

"I almost had you today. I caught a glimpse of your dress this time. You're wearing yellow."

"Yes. I am," I relented from behind the window curtain.

"One of these days I am going to catch you out in the open," he said.

He'd stated my worst fear. I enjoyed our friendship and knew if he ever saw me he wouldn't come running to see me anymore.

He paced the room and inquired, "What tests do you have for me today? Questions about current events? Perhaps you'd enjoy learning the proper course of action when meeting a notable dignitary."

"I found some new words," I announced.

He rubbed his hands together eagerly, "Vocabulary! My favorite. Do your worst."

"Litigious."

"Too easy," he laughed. "A litigious person is argumentative."

"Ensconce."

"It is what you are doing. You are ensconced, or hidden, in the drapery."

"Atrabilious," I stumbled over the pronunciation.

"Ah." He repeated the word enunciating each syllable so I could hear it correctly. "It is exactly how I feel each time I come here and cannot find you. I leave in quite a bad temper."

"I come as often as I can," I assured him.

"As do I," he agreed. "Do you have more words?"

"Oeillade."

"That's cheating, it's French. Although I do know it," he grinned. "I believe it is what you are currently doing to me."

I blushed. Of course he was correct.

Quietly he asked, "Hasn't this gone on long enough? Are we never to meet?"

"I don't think that's a good idea."

"Why?"

I didn't know how to respond.

He turned my direction and quietly spoke. "I assume you've been hiding from me because of your appearance. Am I right?"

I acknowledged him with a hum.

"Do you think I won't want to be your friend after seeing you?"

"Yes," I answered sheepishly.

"You think me that petty?"

"No!" I quickly exclaimed.

He sighed heavily, "It's been months since we met. I like spending time with you. I'd like to spend time with you outside of these walls. Like riding horses or having picnics."

"The winter will be here soon," I objected.

He huffed, "Well then, hay rides and fireside readings until it snows." Then he softly added, "What if I promise never to look at you?"

I chuckled, but his seriousness remained.

"I'm going," he announced.

I fell silent. I knew I wouldn't keep his friendship forever, but I hoped to hold onto it longer than merely half a year.

He stepped to the door then waited with his fingers on the handle. He'd be waiting a long time if he hoped I would come out to stop him. "Goodbye." He whispered as he exited.

Heartbroken at the sound of the door clicking shut I turned to my only solace. I opened my veil. I couldn't connect with Zefforah, but Dyre surprisingly didn't close me off. When he saw through my eyes, he scowled, "Aren't those the curtains of my old room?"

I peeked out. As a child I loved this room. Dyre had a warm bed with soft blankets, sofas to sit on and clean water to wash with. Even now with all of the furnishings removed its high ceilings and textured walls made it beautiful. "I used to love this room."

"I hate that place."

I pulled the curtain back over me and asked, "What was it like to live here?"

"Zefforah and I were happy before we were taken there. We lived in the wild. She would only leave me alone for an hour or two at most and only when I needed something." He smiled as he remembered younger days. "We never walked anywhere. We always flew. I think I had the best childhood of any boy who ever lived. Even the winters when we lived in caves were wonderful."

It felt good to sense him remembering something so fondly. Until the anger set in. "Then Horrish and Minuette followed her. In one moment our lives changed. They grabbed me before she could reach us." He shook his head and closed his fists, as the anger increased. "If they allowed me out, she would be chained. When she went, someone guarded me. We had no choice but to stay with them from then on. We were captives like you. Our prison didn't look like yours, but it was a prison nonetheless." His hands relaxed as he sucked in a deep breath. "I could have left easily after a few years, but by then I'd been told my future. I couldn't imagine going back even though Zefforah often begged me. I guess she made her own way out."

"I'm grateful to her," I muttered.

"For some reason she loves you." He spoke with a soft voice, gentle even.

I whispered, "You could tell her where I am. So I could meet her."

He glanced over his shoulder and smirked, "Not a chance."

"Why?" I pouted.

"Because you're you. Besides, she doesn't like people. They scare her."

"I wouldn't scare her."

"You live with people now, in a wealthy part of the kingdom. Those are the ones she fears the most. She won't be coming to visit any time soon."

"That's not fair!" I yelled.

The door opened, footsteps echoed in the room. "It's unfair for me to wait?"

He came back. Wrapping the curtain to protect me I answered, "What are you doing?"

"You never came out."

It felt wonderful knowing he'd waited for me.

He moved toward the window. Not too close but standing in the light allowing me to see his profile. "You were supposed to come after me."

I whispered, "You must have known I wouldn't."

"But then you never came out to leave either. How long do you wait after I've gone?"

Smiling, I admitted, "Each time we've met I've

waited longer."

He chuckled, "I've waited longer as well."

Dyre growled, "Who is that?"

Then my friend said, "When shall we meet again?"

"I thought you were finished with me," I replied.

"I hoped it would encourage you to come out. Obviously, my plan didn't work. So things will have to continue as they are."

Dyre felt the size of my grin.

"As soon as we can I guess."

"I look forward to it." He bowed again and left pulling the door closed behind him.

Dyre scoffed, "Explain."

"A friend," I continued to grin as I closed my veil.

Politesse (n) formal courtesy

"But you must come with me! It's my chance to meet some boys," Sanura had been begging me for two hours.

"I can't go to a gala."

"I know you don't like the way people look at you. But honestly, it's not that bad."

Sanura had never mentioned my appearance before. Of course she noticed how people looked at me. Almost everyone reacted the same way. Some looked and looked again, huge disbelieving stares, and some even literally backed away from me. At least Minuette's promises of people running in terror weren't true.

"Please, Eviona! Aunt Delsa is convinced I need to be accompanied everywhere. If you won't go, I'll have to go with her or Elina. Please. I need you."

I didn't know whether to be excited or fearful as we exited the coach. We held hands which shook together as we approached the door of the magnificent home. I squared my shoulders and reminded myself to ignore the stares.

Music filled the front foyer and urged us to move into the party. I turned in panic to Sanura when we saw the ballroom. "I've never danced."

"Father used to dance with me, although it has been quite some time. I remember it being easy." With her beauty she could afford to be brave that way.

As we moved forward the reactions came just as they always do; wide-eyed stares and people moving away from me. Sanura didn't allow it to bother her. I did my best to imitate her.

Sanura searched through the faces finding several young men. She would point to one and giggle at his hair. Or to another and comment on his very beautiful eyes. This would be a fun night. Our entertainment was short-lived, however, as a young man approached. I turned my face before he could see me.

"Good evening ladies," he said with a bow.

Sanura giggled and curtsied, grabbing my arm to pull me down with her.

"Would you like to dance?" He offered his hand.

"Oh yes!" Sanura placed her hand in his, and he escorted her toward the ballroom. She seized my upper arm dragging me along.

I pried her fingers away. "I don't think he can dance with both of us at once."

"Oh no!" She stopped and looked at me with a bit of panic, "I can't abandon you."

I pushed her gently toward him. "Go."

She grinned and hurried along.

I wandered the halls, hiding as much as possible. Still, I took pleasure in the chatter of conversations, the music as it drifted from the ballroom and the tinkle of glasses and dishes as people enjoyed refreshments.

On the second floor, one particular room appeared to be filled. I hurried past its doorway until I heard a familiar voice. I peeked in surprised to find my young friend addressing the group. I tucked myself in a back corner to observe.

The crowd asked him question after question, like I usually did. Of course, he had answers to almost everything. I snickered when sometimes people thought he knew the answers simply because of how he worded telling them he didn't.

I also liked how his responses never made anyone feel ignorant. Even when people asked absurd questions about what he thinks might happen in the future as if he were clairvoyant, or questions even I could have answered with my limited experience. He addressed every one with kindness and an eagerness to enlighten.

Then, in the middle of a sentence, he saw me. His eyes shot open, his head jerked back, and the attention of the room turned to me. I bowed my head in panic but couldn't escape. I'd put myself too far into the mass to exit quickly. When he saw his audience reacting to me, he reeled them back in with a clever end to his answer and an immediate move to the next question.

Grateful for his quick thinking I wondered if somehow he knew it was me. I decided to stay.

As the night progressed, ballroom music called, and the aroma of fine foods pulled people from the room. Eventually, we were left alone.

He looked at me seriously as the last few people stepped out of the room. I stood as he approached me quickly with curious eyes.

"You are absolutely the most pulchritudinous creature I have ever beheld."

I hoped he didn't know it was me. Obviously my appearance appalled him.

Then he touched my face like it was a model to be studied. He moved my chin examining me from different angles, scrutinizing every part of my face. "Isn't it amazing," he mused, "how we can have the same features, and yet yours are organized in such a manner as to completely alter the rules of presentation."

Hurt I pushed his hands away. "I am not an object for you to handle."

His eyes shot open. "Ah ha," he sang. Then he threw his arms around me, lifted me up and twirled me around. All the while repeating, "It's you!"

I choked with surprise.

He set me down and again put his hands on my face. "Oh, it is wonderful to meet you! Wonderful!"

"Well," I coughed, "we haven't met properly yet."

He stood straight and offered me his hand. I took it and he bowed pulling my fingers to his lips in the sweet gesture of a kiss which surprised me in every way possible. "I am Jovan. And you are?"

"I'm Eviona."

He grinned widely. I couldn't help but smile back. I couldn't have dreamed a reaction like this. Then his eyebrows buckled, and his eyes moved once more from my eyes to my nose, lips, chin and ears, studying me again. "Pulchritudinous," he whispered softly with a smirk.

My heart sank. I had momentarily forgotten my ugliness. I pulled my gaze to the floor and pushed all of the humiliation I felt into a forced smile and said, "Well, you are not the first to call me such things."

"Undoubtedly." His confident tone turned the dagger even more into my chest. He grabbed my hands and asked, "What tests have you for me tonight, my friend?"

A weight lifted. Despite my appearance he called me friend. "I hadn't planned one."

"Think of one quickly. You must!"

As the music wafted in the air and I had a thought. "Will you teach me to dance?"

He chuckled, "Why do you suppose I hide up here away from the ballroom? I have knowledge of many things. Dancing, however, is not one of them."

"You promised me you would be able to pass any test I placed before you," I complained.

He bowed, "Then I shall. Though, this one will take me some time to prepare."

Just then Sanura strolled by on the arm of a boy and spotted me. She pulled him into the room. "I must introduce you. Eviona, this is Trew."

"Trew," Jovan grabbed him, "guess who this is?" He

didn't wait for an answer. "It's her! This is her!"

Trew smiled at me and bowed graciously. His eyes remained on me as he spoke to his friend. "She is clever, just as you said. I think her wise to hide from you. You wouldn't have given her half a thought if you'd seen her first."

I glanced with hurt eyes at Jovan humbly hanging his head. He squeezed my hand still holding his. At least he still wanted to be friends, which thrilled me.

Sanura immediately berated me, "You've been keeping secrets from me."

I sheepishly told Jovan, "I've never mentioned you."

"Oh," he seemed hurt. Then he snapped his fingers, "This is your friend. The one you've actually met."

I introduced them, and the four of us went for refreshments.

"How do you know each other?" Sanura asked the boys.

"We're cousins. What about you two."

"We're sisters." She winked at me.

As we talked I'd catch Jovan recurrently studying my features. He frequently took opportunity to touch me. Whether brushing a crumb from my chin, explaining to me way the muscles in my arms work, or moving a stray hair from my cheek. Perhaps he imagined how awkward I felt in a crowd and determined to be overly attentive to make up for other's reactions.

At the end of the night he and Trew escorted us to our carriage. Jovan again kissed my hand as he helped me into the coach. My heart raced and I fell even more infatuated with the brilliant boy who had seen me for what I am, and still flirted with me. I couldn't wait to see him again.

Veracious (adj) characterized by truthfulness

Sanura insisted I take her to the place I'd met Jovan. "He's not always there when I am," I told her.

"But he may go looking for you more now that you've met. Besides, he may bring Trew with him."

Of course my wishes weren't the real reason behind her desire, but I didn't mind. I wanted to go as badly as she did.

As we entered the front foyer, we bumped into Trew, "Well hello." His face grew into a grand smile as he called for Jovan. "I found them."

"Hello Trew," Sanura gleefully bounced as she offered up her hand.

He graciously took her away. Obviously he had hoped to find her here as much as she had hoped to find him.

I swallowed and smiled as Jovan approached. He took my hand and said, "Hello, my friend. It's nice to see you." He overemphasized the word 'see'.

"Will you teach me to dance today?" I asked.

"It's only been a few days," he exclaimed. "Trew and I have come here every day hoping to catch you. I haven't had much time for study."

Praying for the embarrassment to wane in my face I quipped, "I guess I'll never know the joy of dancing."

"Now, now," he objected. "I made a promise, I intend to keep it."

"What shall we do today?" I asked.

"I don't care what they do. I plan on taking a walk with you. Outside." He offered me his arm. We left by way of the front door.

I asked, "Why would someone as intelligent as you are, choose to be a soldier?"

He smiled and bowed his head. "I should caution you

on how you compliment me. Remember? My pride?"

"Well, you are quite smart."

"And that, young lady, is why I shall ever adore you. Feed my ego, more please."

I chuckled. "There are so many things you could do with your intelligence. Why have you chosen service, rather than something more notable?"

"Several years ago after a heated disagreement with my father I ran away from home."

He glanced at me, visibly hoping for a reaction. I opened my eyes widely to express shock.

Then he asked, "Didn't you ever run away as a child?"

I wondered if I'd ever share the story of how I escaped from my prison. "I did."

"I think everyone should at least once." He winked. "I decided to go so far away my father would never be able to find me. I wanted him to search in vain. I concealed myself close to the road until a coach passed by with the intention to quietly jump on for an easy ride." He laughed as he remembered. "It didn't happen that way. I leapt, hit the coach, and collapsed to the ground."

I tried not to laugh, but his animation encouraged it.

"Of course the coach halted right away. As fortune would have it, the owner of the coach was none other than his majesty the king traveling incognito with none of his usual fair. He personally came to my assistance and nursed my bruises."

Jovan looked down visibly moved by the memories. "My father came to explain on my behalf. I'll never forget the countenance of the king as he heard my father's story. He showed genuine concern. Then he told my father to return home. I thought fortune had smiled on me. I would now have a new home. The castle." His face showed the excitement he must have felt as a child.

"What happened then?"

"I accepted the king's invitation into his coach and sat across from a young man a few years older than I. As we began to travel the king told me of his lifelong desire for a son. I assumed his wish had come true and acknowledged the young man with us. However, the boy informed me he did not hold the title of prince. The king interrupted him declaring his devotion to the young man despite their lack of blood relations. Then he talked of how the young man and I were different. Unlike me, he had no family. When the king met him a few years earlier, he had no father to disagree with, or to run away from."

I teased, "Did you feel guilty?"

"Yes, but it would become even greater guilt when the king talked of his own father and how they had not always seen eye to eye." He stopped walking, his eyes glazed and thoughtful.

"Did something happen?" I asked.

"Something happened to the king. He cried. I had never seen a man cry before. As he told me how much he missed his father, tears streamed from his eyes. He talked much of his father and how he missed him, even to bicker with him once more would be welcome."

"That evidently left quite an impression."

Jovan began to walk again. "It did. Our discussion lasted half an afternoon and at the end he asked if I would like to go home. When I answered affirmatively, he beckoned to the driver. The coach stopped. The door opened only yards from my front door." He snickered. "We must have been driving in circles the entire time."

We chuckled together.

"That's a really sweet story, but it doesn't tell me

why you want to be a soldier."

"I learned several lessons that day. Including how grateful I am to have such a man as our king. I am determined to be an asset to him. I've considered my options and feel the best way for me to do so is to become a component of his military. I hope to benefit him as much as he did me and my relationship with my father."

I hadn't met anyone who had actually had interaction with the king. Suddenly Dyre's plans for his future hit me with a bit of reality. I wondered for the first time if his ambitions were wrong.

Immersed in my thoughts, I jumped a bit when Jovan asked, "Is something wrong?"

I realized my face had been scowling. "You are the first person who has made the king real for me. I wish you could talk to a friend of mine."

"I'd be pleased to," he offered cheerfully. "Next time we are both in the same place you will have to make the introductions."

I laughed, "I doubt that will happen."

"Well, perhaps you could tell your friend my story. You have my permission if you wish."

"Thank you," I said wondering how I might broach the subject with Dyre.

"I don't think I've ever been this far out into these woods," Jovan said.

Looking around we were far enough into the forest I couldn't see where we'd come from. When I realized what we might find if we continued. I stopped.

"Shall we turn around," Jovan suggested.

I glanced toward the direction from which we'd come and then turned the opposite way. How many more paces would it take until we found my prison? It couldn't have been too far away from their house.

Minuette brought me supplies even during winter. We were close. I could feel it.

"Can we walk a while longer?" I asked.

"Of course."

Jovan didn't say much. He seemed to sense I had a purpose in moving on. Then I saw it and struggled forward.

Pure filth stood black and squalid, with marks of age etched deep into its character. I closed my eyes, trapped again in the prison where I once lived.

"You slimy little worm, how dare you touch me!" I dropped the hand wanting to clench the hair on my head as she pulled it. I hoped to decrease the pain by doing so but had accidently brushed her hand as I reached up. The dull scissors cut right against my scalp and occasionally pulled the hair out in clumps rather than cutting it.

"Ouch!" I flinched, which only pulled out more hair.

"That's what you get for moving! Hold still!"

I watched the small bits of hair fall to the ground and wondered if the floor may have once had some kind of covering. Now I only saw dirt, a bit of moss here and there, or the rubble of something that may have once resembled a household item and my tiny pieces of hair.

Would I ever know my hair color? I had tried before to examine the pieces she cut off after she left but the thick walls allowed little light in from the outside through their mortared grooves. I'd hold it up to one of the small windows which permitted a few rays of sun into the space. Unfortunately, they were too high for me to see out of or use in my research.

"There! You awful monster. Now perhaps the bugs will not try to live in your hair."

I looked up expressionless.

"Aren't you going to thank me?" Her tiny mouth spit the words, and I turned away.

"I didn't feel any bugs," I whispered.

She screeched, and I cowered.

She dropped a bag on the floor and precious flour spilled. I scooped it up with my hands salvaging as much as I could.

I felt her eyes watch me from the doorway and wished she would leave me alone. My wish came true and the bar falling into the latch on the outside of the door reminded me of how alone I'd be.

My heart raced as I advanced toward the horrible place which once held me prisoner. Large hands of dread clenched at my throat trying to suffocate me. I forced my way forward to its entrance.

The door rested only a bit ajar. I pulled it slightly and immediately gagged as my stomach wrenched. I couldn't believe I had once been forced to live here. It was worse than I had remembered.

"This place is terrible," Jovan said as he examined how the door was barred on the outside.

Pure hatred filled my heart as I choked on a sea of horrid memories.

I turned to walk away. I had only taken three or four steps when my contempt bested me. I would not allow any trace of Minuette to remain.

I turned to Jovan, "There is something I must do."

"Can I help?"

I instructed him to gather some dry wood. Meanwhile, I lit a fire not far from the opened door. I placed the tips of several logs Jovan had gathered in the center of the fire. When they held full flames, one by one, I threw them inside. Each one left my hands with the violence I'd wished I could have fought with as a child. The flames spread easily. When the wood had all been used, I grabbed rocks and threw them spinning the ash in the air. Eventually, nothing remained of my prison but some charred stone. I hefted a large rock and pounded against them trying to break them down to nothing.

Jovan grabbed the stone from my hands and pulled me into his chest. I sobbed. He allowed me to weep in his arms until my cries slowed. He wiped my tears and put his arm around my shoulder moving me back toward where we had come from.

I felt liberated, yet incredibly vulnerable. Though I would never again be in that hole with Minuette or allow myself to be so helpless, her voice still rang in my ears. How would I ever explain my actions to Jovan?

We walked back to the house in silence. When we met Sanura and Trew, Jovan never insinuated anything amiss.

"What have you been doing? Your coat and dress are a mess." Sanura ran to me.

Jovan spoke before I could, "We went for a walk. Eviona fell." He gazed at me intently. "I think she's better now."

Looking into his eyes I nodded, grateful for his concealment of my secret.

"Are you in pain?" Sanura examined me.

I pushed her hands gently. "I'm well." I looked to Jovan. "Thank you."

In his eyes I read questions I didn't want to answer. He then gently placed his lips on my forehead. I almost collapsed with shock, especially after what he'd witnessed.

Sanura giggled and pulled me away. As we walked home she said, "It looks like you had a good afternoon."

I touched my forehead where I could still feel the

pressure of Jovan's lips. "It wasn't like that," I insisted, but she didn't believe me. I needed to redirect the conversation and did so with one question. I asked about Trew. It worked.

Inutile (adj) of no use

Sanura squealed and jumped up and down, obviously ecstatic about a letter she'd received. She ran to me, "You and I have been invited to Sylvaria's most prestigious winter gala."

"Is that what it says?" I pulled the paper from her hands.

"Well, no, but it's given by Trew's father every year. I'm sure it is wonderful."

I laughed at her and felt the butterflies in my own stomach. Though we'd tried several times, I hadn't seen Jovan since that day and wondered if perhaps he didn't want to see me again.

We entered the gala and had given our coats to the doorman when Trew found us. He bowed and made the expected small talk until I shooed them away.

Sanura beamed at me, waving as she disappeared into the throng of people.

Then I remembered my face as stares from the other guests ensued.

I didn't know if I'd call it the most prestigious gathering, but I'd certainly consider it the most crowded. I wormed my way through the horde attempting to find a comfortable spot to hide for the night.

"Here you are," a familiar voice accompanied a hand touching mine. "I've been waiting for you."

I turned as Jovan's lips touched my hand. Excited butterflies fluttered in my stomach. I blurted, "I've missed you."

His eyebrows arched with surprise, "Here I thought you were avoiding me." He smiled pleasantly and offered me his arm.

As we pressed our way through the crowd, I asked, "Where are we going?"

"I believe I made you a promise. Tonight I shall teach you to dance."

I stopped and looked at the mass of people. My desire to dance disappeared.

He must have read my mind. "Perhaps a more secluded setting?"

He clearly could see the relief in my face. He offered his arm yet again. We didn't speak as we struggled through the gathering. We moved up the winding staircase to the second floor. Behind a wall of thick curtains, he opened a door leading to an outside balcony. As we slipped out into the chill, the silence seemed just as deafening as the mob of people.

"Did you really learn to dance?" I asked.

He nodded.

"But you already knew how." I stated it as a fact.

"I most certainly did not," he remarked, offended. Then he reassured, "It's a skill I never felt the need to learn, before you."

The blood rushed to my face which I attempted to hide by focusing on the air bitterly snipping at my arms. I rubbed them with my hands and Jovan moved to open the door we had just exited.

Dyre showed up in my head. "Eviona, go inside. You are freezing me to death."

"Where are you going?" I asked Jovan.

"It's too cold out here. It may be crowded inside, but I think we'd be better off."

"Now there is a smart man. Listen to him," Dyre said.

"No," I countered. "You promised to teach me to dance."

Jovan smiled so affectionately I thought it might

warm me simply to look at his face.

Dyre grunted.

Jovan made a show of closing the door and returned to my side. He took my hands and placed one on his shoulder and held the other gently in his. He then placed his other hand at my waist. I wished I could pull myself further into his warmth. His eyes looked down as if he were reading an invisible book. The hand on my waist pulled me tenderly toward him. I did feel much warmer, but the source may not have been Jovan. I blushed.

He talked me through what I should do with my feet. Logistically he knew it all very well, and I felt confident enough to try. When we began to move, we constantly stepped on each other's toes and jerked in awkward patterns. We laughed as we tripped and stumbled, and eventually fell together to the ground.

"An utter failure," he chuckled.

I laughed even harder as his laughs increased.

"Oh, this is pathetic." Dyre demanded, "Go inside!"

I barked, "Why don't you leave?"

The shock I felt from Dyre as well as Jovan's confused expression made me regret my words immediately. I pulled the veil between me and Dyre.

Jovan's eyebrows buckled. "I'm sorry?"

Humiliated I whispered, "I'm so embarrassed about how clumsy I am. I was talking to myself."

He stood with a concerned expression and offered his hand. "The fault was mine. Please forgive me."

I took his hand and rose. "You are too kind, Jovan."

"And too gauche for dancing tonight. Shall I give you a tour of Trew's house instead?"

"Can I hold you to your promise of a dance on a later date?"

His kind eyes filled with what looked like gratitude.

"I would be disappointed if you didn't."

We moved inside to the warmth and multitude of people. We found almost every room as crowded as the previous one, but Jovan finally spied a vacant chair close to a fireplace. He motioned for me to take the place then sat next to me on the hearth.

"It is rare for this gathering to be so congested," he said.

"I assume you come every year."

"Yes, but this year with the early flash storm last week, people are urgent to fill what's left of their time before winter. Everyone came tonight because this is probably the last gala until spring. How are your fingers?" He grabbed my hands massaging life into them.

I paused and spoke slowly. "I'm certain you've been busy but are there other reasons I haven't seen you lately?"

His eyebrows buckled, "Yes."

I asked reluctantly, "Do any of them have to do with…?"

He moved to say something then stopped and put his head down to think. His fingers moved slowly in their work, and his tone softened intently. "First, you must know I tried as often as I could to see you. Each time ended in concern because of this very question. Second, if you want to tell me, I will gladly hear. If you don't want me to know, I can pretend I never saw anything."

"Why would you do that?"

He grinned slightly and his fingers regained their speed. "We are friends. Are we not?"

"Why are you my friend?" I asked.

He smirked, "Look at our interactions." His eyebrows rose challenging me to recollect our friendship.

"You are the most intriguing being in all of Sylvaria, I am sure of it. Wouldn't you want to be your friend?"

I laughed and took my hand from his. "I have some challenges for you." I pulled out a list I had worked hard to create.

He cleared his throat. "So now, what is your first inquiry?"

I asked him my questions and took pleasure in his answers as much as he seemed to enjoy being challenged.

Time passed too quickly, and a tall man with silver grey hair approached Jovan.

"Jovan, we need to go. A storm is approaching."

Jovan rose and gestured to me. "Father, this is Eviona."

I stood and offered the gentleman my hand despite the wide eyes he greeted me with. He glanced at Jovan as he said, "My son told me about you. He certainly knows how to pick his company."

Jovan grinned at me as I eyed him with curiosity.

We left along with the rest of the crowd, everyone rushing to avoid the storm. Jovan held my hand as we struggled our way back to the entry of the manor where I found Sanura panicked.

"The storm is almost here. We need to be home before it hits or I'll never be allowed out again."

We donned our coats and moved quickly to our coach. As we drove away my eyes found Jovan who beamed a smile which melted my heart.

We beat the storm home and giggling dressed for bed telling each other our adventures until Sanura's eyes drifted into dreams while her mouth continued to babble. I chuckled at her attempts to stay awake. Soon, I too neared sleep and let my veil fall open.

Dyre's eyes were closed. I thought he must have been sleeping as well until I felt his position. He stood upright and his forearm rested above his head against something velvety. The scent of floral perfume filled his nose. And his lips moved against another's.

I forced myself awake and started to place my veil. "Eviona?"

"Dyre?" I answered in shock.

I winced as a hand whipped against his face, and his eyes opened to the very upset face of a girl. "My name is *not* Eviona!" He watched with a slight grin as she stormed away from him.

I whispered, "I'm sorry, I didn't mean to interrupt."

He rubbed his cheek. "How were your dance lessons?"

"Disastrous. Too many people to dance inside, too cold outside, we decided to try again later."

"Later." He whispered the word with a snicker.

"A while ago I learned something."

"Good for you."

I laughed at his mocking tone. Then I asked him a question I thought I might regret. "Have you ever met the king?"

"Hey, I have news." Laroke's voice approached him from behind. Dyre put his head down and looked over his shoulder the way he did when he didn't want me there. His veil closed and I easily drifted into dreams.

That night, and many nights after, I dreamed of Jovan. He made me laugh and in my dreams I was beautiful. He often kissed me, and I'd wake wondering if Dyre had seen. To my relief he never talked about it. After all, he had embarrassing dreams sometimes too.

Pulchritudinous (adj) physically beautiful

Sanura woke me early. "I have a surprise for you. We must hurry so we don't miss the chance." I rubbed my eyes as Sanura picked out dresses for us. She changed quickly and threw a dress at me.

I yawned, "What's going on?"

"Dressed," she said as she stepped out of the room giving me time to change.

Dyre growled, "Close your veil."

"It's morning. Wake up," I said with cheer, purposely annoying him.

He closed his veil, but it soon fell as he slept again.

I quickly donned the dress and opened the door for Sanura to come back in. Then she sat me down and took a brush to fix my hair. "I have a surprise for you today." She told me as she brushed.

Dyre groaned and sat up feeling defeated.

"What is this surprise?" I asked.

"You are going to be introduced to one of the most beautiful girls in Sylvaria."

"Why would I want to meet her? I have you to torment me with your beauty."

Dyre's ears perked and he rubbed his face to wake himself. He wanted to see this beauty too.

"I think you will enjoy meeting her," Sanura said. She sang playfully as she braided my hair. One long braid down my back. She walked to the front of me and moved aside some wisps of hair which had fallen on my forehead. She smiled with her head cocked to one side. "Yes, I think that will do."

"Where is this lovely girl?" I asked.

Sanura's eyes opened wide like saucers, and her voice sang with excitement. "Oh, she is here in the house today."

"How could she come in the middle of winter?"

"It doesn't matter. She's here."

"Don't you think Lady Delsa will be angry? She doesn't like for me to bother her visitors."

Sanura's eyes became mischievous as she whispered to me. "Aunt Delsa doesn't even care to speak with her."

"Humph," Dyre muttered. "I'm not surprised."

"What?" I couldn't believe it.

She continued with her whispering, "Yes, I think she is intimidated by her beauty." She had a look of pure pleasure and smiled at me with her huge brown eyes.

I laughed. I loved how animated Sanura could be. "When will she be here?"

"She's here already. We need to hurry and meet her before Elina calls us for lessons."

"Well, hurry up then." I tried to take the brush from her and accidentally knocked her over on to the bed. We laughed excitedly as we readied.

Sanura's enthusiasm rubbed onto me easily. I found myself anxiously anticipating meeting this lovely girl. Dyre felt the same.

Sanura took a long scarf from the dresser. "I need to blindfold you." She held it up to my eyes.

I pushed it away. "Why?"

She pursed her lips. "You will simply have to trust me."

"I trust you." I squinted into her eyes. "I think you are ridiculous, but I trust you."

"Good!" She squealed and quickly placed the blindfold over my eyes.

Then she led me through the house. We went up stairs, then down stairs. We wandered in what felt like circles for a very long time.

"Can you not find her?" I finally asked.

"No, I know where she is. Does that mean you are ready to be introduced?"

I slapped her hand to reprimand her.

"Ouch! Now I shall never take you to her," Sanura teased.

"Lead the way, silly girl!" The desires of both Dyre and I had begun to gnaw at me.

"All right."

We walked a few minutes more. I had no idea where in the house we finally came to a stop. Sanura placed me and ordered, "Stay right there. Don't move."

I heard footsteps and then from the far end of the room Sanura's voice said, "Take off your blindfold."

I pulled the cloth from my eyes and looked in complete amazement at the girl in front of me. Her beauty was shocking. I felt so overwhelmed by it I took a step away from her. She reacted to my ugliness the same way. We both caught ourselves and curtsied our apologies. I raised my hand to greet her, and she motioned at the same time. We giggled together, too synchronized to be real.

Then realizing I stood in the room which held the great mirror on one wall, I looked back to the girl across from me finally understanding. Dyre grasped it moments before I did.

"Eviona," he whispered in disbelief. "That's you."

"That's me?"

I heard Sanura's voice and watched in the mirror as she approached. "I've never known why you have hidden from yourself, but I thought you should know the truth. I hope you approve of my method." She held my hand when she reached my side.

Truly my opposite with her striking dark eyes and hair Sanura smiled at me with me with my light skin and features. I knew her intense beauty well, but couldn't believe what I was learning about myself. My eyes were large blue pools, my hair sunshine, and my lips deep red cherries against pale, peach skin. I'd seen others with similar features but never imagined my reflection would hold such unbelievable beauty.

"I can't be beautiful. This is a trick."

Sanura smiled at me and gently pushed me closer to the mirror.

I touched it and then my face. My soft feminine features were not that of a monster. I smiled at myself in the mirror. The corners of my eyes smiled as well as my mouth. I then placed my hands on my face and watched them move with astonishment.

"Wow," Dyre whispered. He couldn't believe it almost as much as me. All these years we had been wrong. "You're beautiful," Dyre spoke softly. I wondered if I heard regret in his voice.

"Thank you," I whispered.

"You're welcome," Sanura whispered back to me.

Minuette's screams hurt my ears. I screamed with her.

"What!" Horrish rushed to investigate the tumult.

Minuette's voice shook as she yelled over my volume, "Her back! Look at her back!"

He didn't touch me, but after a moment he shouted, "You have to kill it! Do you know what that is?"

"I can't kill a baby!"

"It's not that small," he sneered. "Besides, you don't care about it."

"That's because it...she shouldn't be here."

"Well, it's here! We have to deal with it somehow! If anyone sees that back—"

Minuette interrupted, "I know! I know! Could

anything be worse?"

"I don't care what you do. Kill it or not it's up to you, but I want it out of my house! Now!"

Minuette screamed again but this time out of frustration instead of fear. My own cries continued.

"Eviona, wake up." Dyre's voice pulled me from my dream. "Wake up. It's a dream."

"Is it?" I wiped the moisture from my forehead and cheeks. "Did it happen? Do you remember?"

"I don't know. When you were a baby, I closed you off most of the time. I knew they feared something about you. What is on your back?"

"I don't know."

"If it's enough to scare Horrish it must be terrifying."

"I promise, I won't show anyone."

"Good!"

"Goodnight, Dyre."

He exhaled heavily and closed his eyes. "Dream sweetly, Eviona."

Facile (adj) easily done, performed, used, etc.

The winter dragged on with its flash storms and seclusion. Every year the whole of Sylvaria halts for at least two months, while the kingdom is covered with a thick white blanket of snow and ice.

We were confined to the house with Elina who refused to listen to any more about boys. Plans had been made for her to take a summer holiday to see her family, so she used our isolation to cram information into our heads. Though I loved learning, I did feel she worked us extra hard.

Spring arrived, at last, bringing with it an anxiousness to see the boys. When the snow melted and the grounds dry enough for us to go walking, Elina finally gave in and allowed us a day. The air still bit, even through our coats, but we were determined to go to the house where Jovan and Trew might meet us. We made a basket for lunch, just in case, complete with some of my treasures.

We chatted and giggled until we arrived and snuck in. The house seemed too dark and quiet, and very cold. Though we searched thoroughly, the boys were not there.

Sanura broke down into tears. I did my best to comfort her to no avail. I convinced her to walk with me a bit outside where it felt warmer. Tears continued as we walked through what had been left of the paths of the garden. We came to a small overgrown circular patio. A cracked and broken fountain stood in the middle with a small seat off to one side. We sat, and she cried.

I rubbed her back attempting to comfort her. "I know they will try to see us. It won't be too much longer."

"It could be weeks, or months," she complained.

We waited for a very long hour, and the sun began to warm the garden. Then the best sound vibrated towards us. Laughter. "That's his laugh." Sanura darted. "Trew! Trew, we're over here." She ran in the direction of the sound and I took a deep breath deciding to wait. Hoping my composure would impress Jovan.

I occupied myself in the study of the flowers, surprised any were evident after the winter and the weed infestation. Dead yellow and vibrant green climbing vines combined covering a trellis archway, and purple and red buds had begun blooming. My favorite buds were on a row of rose bushes. Blue roses. I remembered them vividly from Dyre's youth. The most magnificent flowers I had ever seen. I couldn't wait to see them in bloom through my own eyes this year.

"Would you like to dance?" His voice came from behind me.

I turned smiling and nodded my head in approval.

He took my hands and placed one at his shoulder and held the other in his. Then he started to move. He hummed a tune as we turned and flowed for several minutes around the small circle. I laughed and allowed him to move me to his will. Then the music in his head must have ended because he stopped, looked into my eyes and smiled.

"How did you do that? Last time we failed so miserably."

"Practice," he grinned. "I learned if I knew exactly what to do it would not be necessary for you to know. You simply needed to trust me."

"Ah, that may be the crux right there. What if I didn't trust you?"

"But you do," his eyebrows rose. "So we shall always be perfect dance partners."

I snickered while a bit of embarrassment evidenced on my cheeks.

Our conversation hadn't changed our stance. My hand still rested on his shoulder and his on my waist. Our eye contact became more intense as silent seconds past.

I broke the tension. "That word you called me on the day we met. Say it for me again."

"Pulchritudinous," he answered placing his warm hand against my cheek.

"What does it mean?"

He stared at me curiously, "It means physically beautiful. I thought you knew."

The blush in my face deepened. I took his hand and moved toward Sanura and Trew setting out our meal.

"What did Trew mean when he said you wouldn't have felt the same about me if you'd seen me first?"

He dropped his head and shot a scrutinizing glare toward Trew before he answered, "I've never given much credit to girls in general, especially pretty ones. You absolutely ruined my theory."

"What if I had been ugly?"

"In my head I pictured you scarred, or deformed in some way. Yet, the more I talked to you, the less it mattered to me. I think I would have adored you even if you had come out of your hiding place looking like the beast."

"Well, she's beautiful, quite honestly."

"You've seen her?"

"I have," I grinned thinking of the times I've stolen glimpses through Dyre's eyes.

Jovan mused, "Terrifying and beautiful."

Trew approached, "You must be talking about Sanura."

I laughed, but Jovan hit him on the shoulder. Sanura beckoned us, and we sat on a blanket for our picnic.

"What is this we are supposed to eat?" Trew studied

the food presented.

I began to explain but Jovan interrupted me, "Let me see. The birds look like they might be fruit, the cockroaches in the salad are nuts, and the rabbits will be the most delicious breads you'll ever eat." He looked to me for an affirmation.

"I hope so," I confirmed with a grin.

Trew studied everything with deep scrutiny, watching us enjoy the meal before joining in.

Our conversation twisted and turned, focusing on everything from town gossip to the weather. I enjoyed the conversation immensely until we talked about the snow months.

Trew announced, "Next winter Jovan will be snowed in with 100 men."

"What do you mean?" I asked.

Jovan answered, "In the fall I will be nineteen, finally old enough to study with the military. I'll leave just before winter begins."

My heart sank.

He nudged me and added, "I'll be back for visits."

I felt a bit better.

Trew broke in, "He'll have to brainwash them into thinking he's brilliant and a good fighter so he can make captain."

"I'll fight you and win." Jovan hit Trew's shoulder.

Trew winced and rubbed the spot. "That's true, but then again Sanura could probably fight me and win."

She giggled.

I asked, "What all do you have to do to become a captain?"

"There are several tests. Strength, knowledge, strategy, character—"

"Don't forget social standing," Trew interrupted.

"What kind of social standing?"

"I'm from the kind of family they want. Only the wealthiest and most high-bred families in the kingdom are eligible."

Sanura declared, "That cuts the pool down quite a bit, doesn't it?"

"Oh yes," Trew answered. "Not only that, but if his father ever convinces him to wed, he must marry a woman of high standing as well."

I met eyes with Jovan. I'm sure the disappointment showed on my face, he looked away after an awkward momentary glance.

Soon Sanura and Trew went for a walk, and I began to clean up.

Jovan helped me put things into the basket and fold the blanket. He touched my shoulder as I put it away. "You're so quiet."

I gathered all the strength I could into a smile. Fake or not I would have to appear fine. "Oh, today has been exhausting. The winter weakened me, I guess."

"This summer both Trew and I will have a lot of time. Can we plan more things like this?"

"Of course." Could he see the tears I fought to keep hidden?

He wrapped his hands around my face and placed his forehead on mine. "You know; you break all my rules."

"What do you mean?"

"Never before has a girl been important to me. My only essentials were training, studying, and preparing for the future. I still need to do those things, but I really want to spend time with you too."

I pulled away from him. His sweet words sang through my head. Yet, knowing I'd never be eligible to be anything more than simply friends weighed on my heart. Determined not to be a deterrent and still desperate to spend time with him I said, "I will make sure you prepare then. You'll study all summer." He bowed humbly, agreeing with my words. "When you're not studying alone, you'll study with me."

He smirked. "Another reason to adore you. I look forward to these months more than ever now."

He called to Trew, and we said our goodbyes.

Obviously, Trew would be a while longer so Jovan began to walk alone. I watched him go. I couldn't ever allow him to know how much I'd fallen in love with him. I'd control myself for his sake. When he showed interest in me, I'd find a way to redirect him. He had his dreams. I wouldn't be the reason he didn't achieve them.

When Sanura finally came back from saying her goodbyes, I found myself mindlessly pulling the buds off the vines.

Aleatory (adj) pertaining to accidental causes

That summer we spent a lot of time with Jovan and Trew. Their homes were not far from Lady Delsa's, and we took turns spending time in different places.

When we weren't together, I spent hours researching so I might help Jovan with his studies. When I'd try to challenge him, he seemed to know everything about everything, even more, if it had to do with the military. He knew all of the wars and battles which had ever been fought. Where they were fought, why they were fought, who fought in them, who won and why. He knew how a soldier should act and behave and all of the protocol which went along with it. I had no doubt he knew everything about being a soldier and how to be a good one. I would ask one little question, and he could go on for hours to answer it.

He also loved to talk about politics. He liked our king and the way he ran the kingdom. But had many ideas on how things could be improved, or at least modernized. I often wondered what the conversation might be like if I could ever introduce Dyre and Jovan.

When it came our turn to host Sanura and I decided to eat a small lunch on the patio. I made the food while Sanura made us beautiful. It must have been amusing to watch her do my hair while chasing me around the kitchen as I worked.

The boys arrived, and after we finished the carefully sculpted treasures I'd made, Trew took Sanura by the hand. They wandered off to explore the surrounding fields.

Jovan stood to put things away. I helped him place things into a basket we had brought with us.

Nodding over to our retreating friends, I asked, "How young is too young to marry?"

"I'm certain he will ask her as soon as she turns

eighteen."

"Her birthday is in the winter."

"Then next spring I guess. The wait will kill him," he chuckled.

I chuckled with him, knowing the wait would kill her as well. I only inquired because Sanura asked me to find out if Trew had said anything to Jovan.

"So, did you learn anything?" Sanura asked as we climbed into bed that night.

"Yes."

"And?" Her eyes couldn't grow any wider.

"Jovan is pretty certain he will ask you."

She squealed and rolled back and forth. "I knew it! When? How? What should I wear for a dress? Oh, there's so much to plan."

"Jovan said it probably wouldn't be until after you turn eighteen."

"That's months away," she moaned. She turned over and huffed out a sigh.

Wanting to raise her spirits I asked, "Has he kissed you?"

She squealed again and turned to face me again. "No, but he almost did during our walk today. I'm sure he will soon. What about you and Jovan?"

"No. And he won't."

Her eyebrows pulled low into a frown, "Why?"

With a smile, I reminded her of the conversations we'd had a few weeks earlier. "Jovan needs to marry a woman of social high standing."

"But we're from high rank. Just because Father isn't doesn't mean..." She stopped when she saw how my face dropped. "I feel like we're sisters."

I smiled at her sadly, "Me too."

"I forgot. You were pretty beaten when you came to us. How did you end up at my house that night?"

I only shook my head. I'd never tell her the story.

Horrish, Dyre, and Laroke sat around the grand table of Horrish and Minuette's dining room planning. Dyre and Laroke still wore their school uniforms, they only recently arrived home. Horrish glowed, obviously pleased with how things were going. Apparently, Dyre disagreed.

"I think there might be a better way to do this," Dyre complained.

Horrish responded, "You are too young and naïve right now. Someday you will see I am right and come back to thank me."

"I don't like doing this with Zefforah. She's peaceful and good, she loves people. She will never be happy if everyone is scared of her."

"She is only an animal. You think of her as an intelligent being."

"She is an intelligent being!"

"She is also a great part of our plan. If you will only trust me, once you have the throne you can let everyone see her for what she really is."

"I don't like it!"

Horrish ignored Dyre's anger and turned to Laroke. "You know what you are supposed to do. Are you up for it?"

"Absolutely." Laroke's eyes seemed to shine with excitement.

"Good," Horrish grumbled to himself as he studied the map of the stars his grandfather had given to Dyre.

"My Grandfather may not have been the brightest man in the world, but he had his purpose. Between his dream which led me to my fortune and the other which

123

led me to you, he certainly knew where to find treasure."

Ignoring his ramblings Dyre yelled again. "I don't want to do it this way!"

Horrish stood up grabbing Dyre by his shoulders. Dyre's rage ran through his body as his hands wrapped into fists.

"We have already begun! This is the only way it can work." Horrish spat. "This is the way it started. It must be the way it ends!" Then darkness fell as Horrish's words echoed.

I woke shaking with anger. We all woke.

I whispered, "Horrish has been gone for a long time. It's over now. You were dreaming."

As we began to relax, he repeated the words, "This is the way it started. It must be the way it ends."

Imbibe (v) to receive into the mind, such as knowledge or ideas

Before the next time we met the boys I asked one of the male servants in our house if I could borrow some clothing. Sanura laughed at my plans but went along with me anyway. The pants were much too large, and she helped me fit a scarf around my waist to keep them up.

We were to meet at Jovan's house that day. The man who greeted us at the door looked over my outfit several times before showing us into the front foyer, but he kept his opinions to himself.

Jovan's father was a different story. He came to welcome us and outright laughed when he saw me. "My girl. What on earth are you wearing?"

"I'm determined to help Jovan in his preparations for this winter. Today I will be his dueling partner."

He continued to giggle but was obviously pleased. He excused himself returning shortly to present me with a gift. He held it up by its handle and blade. "May I introduce you to the first sword I ever fought with? I would be honored if you would use it while you serve my son."

I bowed gratefully and moved to take it.

He gently pushed my hand away. "I'll carry it until we find the boys. I think they are out in the yard. Follow me."

Trew rushed to meet us as we came into view. "Sanura, how wonderful to see you." He acted surprised as if he hadn't seen her almost every day for the past month.

"Hello, Trew." She lowered her head to appear shy.

I rolled my eyes and looked for Jovan. I'd chosen the right activity. He swung and moved with his sword in a graceful and delightfully dangerous dance.

"Jovan," his father called. "You have a guest."

Jovan grabbed a towel to mop his face then ran to us, squinting at me as he came.

"Hello, Jovan."

"Eviona." He nodded to me with a smirk.

His father presented him with the sword and said, "It seems you shall have a training partner today."

He took the sword from his father who left us alone. Then he did nothing but beam at me.

"Will you teach me to use a sword?"

"Really?"

"Is something wrong with that?"

"Well, girls don't usually do those kinds of things."

"I break all the rules."

"Yes, you do," he grinned. "Come on then." He motioned for me to follow him.

He took me to where he'd been training, and he handed me his father's sword. The tip of it fell to the ground with a thud. Jovan laughed.

"It's heavy. You made it look easy," I complained.

"It is easy, but I have been doing it since my childhood." He looked thoughtful. "Let's begin with a weapon of a more appropriate weight."

He put the blades aside and disappeared into the house. He returned shortly with two wooden swords. He handed one to me and stood opposite.

"No, no, no. Your hold is incorrect. Place your right hand just under..." He screwed up his face and put his sword down. Then he took my hands manipulating my fingers to the position he wanted. "Like that."

I nodded.

He took his sword and instead of standing opposite me, stood next to me. "Follow me. Everything I do, I want you to do."

I did my best to imitate his moves, but every once in a while he'd stop and move my hand or reposition my feet or hips. He showed me several things before he decided to stand opposite me again asking, "Would you like to try?"

I nodded and as we moved felt surprised at how naturally my body mimicked the actions he'd shown me. We maneuvered rather slowly, Jovan didn't actually move much at all. After a few minutes, I tried to touch his stomach with the tip of my sword. When he play acted death instead of parrying, I complained, "You aren't even trying."

"It's your first day," he grinned.

"Well then, you better start teaching me." I swung at him.

"Alright then!" He protested playfully. "Let's learn." He swung around me quickly and hit my rump with his sword.

I jumped in shock. By the sting of the blow, I would have quite a nice welt. I whimpered playfully and then buckled down and spent the rest of the afternoon doing my best to challenge him.

I loved the feel of the movement and Jovan obviously enjoyed his role as a teacher. He possessed great patience and continually pushed me to do better. By the end of the day, I tried holding the real sword again and did it with a bit more grace this time. Although, not much. My arms weren't strong enough.

Sleep didn't come easily that night, and once it did I woke to Dyre moaning, "Whoa, Eviona, what did you do to your arms, and what about this welt on my backside?"

"Oooh, I'm so sore." I grabbed my arms and tried to squeeze the ache out of them. "I learned how to use a sword. I had no idea it would hurt so much."

"Why do I have to suffer for your stupidity? At least think of Zefforah before you make decisions which will cause us all pain."

"Only if you will as well," I agreed.

I didn't know it would be so agonizing. I could barely hold up a finger let alone a sword for the next three days.

When we saw the boys, Jovan laughed at me and rubbed my arms to make them feel better. I loved it when he touched me, but pushed him away when I realized he enjoyed it as much. He showed me stretches I could do before and after our lessons so I wouldn't feel the smart of developing muscles.

Jovan and I dueled often and eventually I felt I might be able to one day beat him, or at least be good opposition for him. As we'd duel I'd pepper him with questions I thought might be useful for his winter training. He loved how I made him concentrate on two things at once.

Some nights my dreams of Jovan weren't as pleasant as they first were and I wondered if they were actually my dreams.

Dyre and Jovan would stand opposite each other on either side of a table where Dyre's map lay open for examination. He'd changed it little by little over time. The seven stars he originally pointed out had been marked and clearly stood out from the rest. As if they were going to be brighter on the night they would be in their places.

Lines connected them making three triangles connected to the brightest star in the center. Similar to a mark I knew Zefforah had on her back.

Jovan would tell him his plans were futile, and his

strategies weak. He proclaimed him a fool and a failure.

Dyre argued and fought each time; debating and yelling, and Jovan would simply shake his head and define Dyre's ideas as reckless and ignorant.

Other times Dyre pounded the table with his fists and then attempted to fight Jovan physically, or sometimes with a knife or sword. I hated watching them fight and always begged them to stop.

As each dream ended Jovan would kiss me and apologize for my discomfort before parting.

Dyre would angrily roll up the map and leave me standing alone.

Those mornings I woke and immediately closed my veil. I didn't want to be yelled at for dreams which I could not control. I couldn't determine whether the things Jovan told Dyre were part of my thoughts or Dyre's. Either way, I didn't want to be in trouble for it.

Solicitude (n) cause of anxiety

"Is she asleep yet?" Dyre asked me late one night.

"Sanura...Sanura?" I whispered. "It looks like it. Why do you ask?"

He shrugged, "I wanted to talk to you. You haven't been alone for two seconds lately. I wondered... how you are."

"Dyre?" He had never asked about my welfare before.

He didn't say anything for a long time and then swore under his breath. Then he was gone.

He surprised me when he chose to remain open the next morning. I didn't speak to him but saw no harm in having him along for the day. He might even be willing to help me.

"Hello, ladies." Trew bowed and took each of our hands as we exited the coach.

"Hello." Sanura beamed at him.

Jovan came to take his place at my side. He offered me his arm. I gladly walked with him. We had decided to go for a horseback ride. Actually, they decided, and I fought the idea from its conception. I'd flown with Zefforah but only in my mind. This would be a physically present horse. I'd also felt how it should be through Dyre. He loved to ride, not only with Zefforah but regular horses, but riding a horse myself terrified me.

Jovan patted my hand as we walked to the stables. "How are you this morning, Eviona?"

I tried to hide my fright. "Well. Thank you, Jovan. And you?"

Dyre chimed in mockingly, "How are you, Eviona?"

Jovan, obviously pleased with me for squashing my fear, answered optimistically, "Looking forward to a beautiful ride today."

I gave him a sulking look so he knew I didn't feel any better. "I promise your fears are for nothing. Do try to enjoy yourself."

I sighed and pushed him to go tend to the horses with Trew.

As they readied the horses, I sat with Sanura outside the stable.

"Don't worry," Sanura said. "You are going to do fine."

"Or maybe the opposite of fine," I said.

Dyre laughed.

"Well, at least you're among friends," Sanura smiled.

I teased, "Oh, is that what you consider Trew? A friend?"

She blushed. "He told me he has already started to build his wedding room."

I didn't know what that meant, but I congratulated her. "That's wonderful."

"Do you think my parents will ever allow me to marry so young?"

"I'm sure Roan will love him as much as you do, and Aurel will forever hate him for taking you away."

Sanura smiled knowing my teasing tone. "What about you? Are you sure Jovan hasn't changed his mind about being captain? You two have been spending a lot of time together."

"That is because you and Trew always leave us." I accused her.

"He is sweet though." She motioned with her head toward Jovan. "You can't deny the way he watches you."

"Humph!" Dyre disapproved.

Belligerently I answered Sanura though I spoke to Dyre. "We're friends. I like him very much."

"I can't understand why." Dyre's terse reply grated on my already overtaxed nerves.

"He is knowledgeable. *He* likes to teach me things. I never have to beg him. He does it naturally and willingly. He's good-hearted, and always thinking of others." I hoped to dig under Dyre's skin.

"You don't have to convince me," Sanura said in defense of my sharp words.

Dyre snarled in my head.

I felt a little pleasure at causing his frustration. I wanted to confront him. "I am going to take a little walk. Do you mind?" I asked Sanura.

"Go ahead. We won't go anywhere without you."

I hurried down the lane, and when I reached a safe distance I demanded, "Why are you so angry?"

"I don't like him," He told me dryly. "I don't like the way you feel about him."

"Since when do I need your approval? You aren't exactly spending time with my choice of people."

"He's such a sapient."

I scoffed, "I don't even know what that means."

"He would know. He thinks he knows everything."

"That's what you have against him? He's too smart, too good? You are such a hypocrite." His emotions were raising, and mine weren't helping. I decided to shut him off for the day. "Goodbye."

"No, wait!" He tried to calm down by inhaling deeply. "I love horseback riding. You know I do. I've been too busy. I simply wanted to come with you today."

"I wanted you to come, so you could help me," I admitted. "You know I've never been on a horse."

"It's not hard. I am sure your sapient will teach you everything you need to know." He said it with sarcasm, but I knew he thought it to be true.

"Will you be able to be civil toward him?"

"You know I can't promise that."

"Ugh, Dyre, I am trying to be nice to you. Can't you give a little in return?"

"Alright, alright. I'll refrain from commenting about your charming scholar."

"Thank you." I walked back to where Sanura waited.

"I think everything's ready. Are you going to be alright?" She stood and looped my arm with hers.

I slowly nodded, and we went to meet the horses.

Jovan talked me through how to approach and handle my horse. Since his father owned them, he knew the mildest of the small herd and introduced us. The good-natured animal ate some oats from my hand. It felt funny, but I enjoyed it.

Jovan talked me through mounting, and Dyre interjected instructions as well. He told me exactly what I needed to do and where I should put my weight in order to mount with a bit of grace. Between Dyre and Jovan I almost felt confident.

Jovan held the reigns of my horse until he left me to mount his own. I could feel Dyre wanting to comment on his assistance, but he stayed good to his word and didn't say anything.

Sanura and Trew enjoyed themselves from the beginning. They chased each other over the hills until I couldn't see them anymore, then they would race back to Jovan and me. Jovan attended me much more closely, keenly aware of my desire to go slow. He took his horse to a gallop only for a few moments at a time and then made a loop to come back and check on my progress.

We only rode for a little while when Zefforah's veil opened. She felt happy as she flew.

Dyre playfully said, "Don't do anything too crazy,

Zefforah. It's her first ride."

Zefforah whinnied and dashed upward.

Already worried about falling I couldn't take the time or mental effort to place my veil to her. I knew she only wanted to have some fun with me, but she made things harder. She occasionally flew low enough to brush her wings against tree tops or skim them across the water. It didn't hurt, but I could barely concentrate on the path in front of me. I felt sure I'd fall at any moment. I held the reigns of my horse so tightly my fingernails embedded themselves into my palms.

Jovan encouraged, "You are sitting quite well. I think you should try to go a bit faster." He rode ahead, probably to motivate me, and momentarily disappeared around some trees.

I couldn't concentrate on my own horse or surroundings, too worried about the mountain top Zefforah would soon collide with.

Dyre yelled, "No Zefforah, you're scaring her!"

She dashed upward just before she hit the hard surface. My reflexes had already kicked in. I'd lunged hard to the side.

No one saw as I fell off of my horse. My foot remained in the stirrup which caused my body to drag along the ground. I couldn't scream, I couldn't think.

"Zefforah!" Dyre flustered. Zefforah's eyes closed trying to help rectify what she'd done.

"Help!" I finally managed to force a word out of my mouth.

Before I could call again, Jovan had stopped my horse. He dismounted and helped my foot out of the stirrup. "Eviona, are you injured?"

"My arm." The sleeve of my dress had been ripped from my shoulder to my wrist. Jovan tore it revealing a long, deep scratch.

I panicked. My head felt heavy and little black spots formed in front of my eyes. Larger spots followed and then the whole world turned black.

Fire raged down my arm. I screamed lifting my weighty head off the ground and opened my eyes.

"Shhhhh," Jovan whispered.

"That's obiberry juice, don't let it touch me!" The pain was incredible.

"I've never seen it do this before."

Didn't he realize how badly he was scorching me? "Jovan, stop!"

Dyre tried to calm me, "Let him be, Eviona."

"It's healing you, but it's burning me!"

"Shhhhh," Jovan reassuringly repeated.

"I don't know what he's doing," Dyre said. "But it's different than before, I don't even have a scar. Can you watch?"

Even Zefforah seemed curious about what was happening.

Jovan quickly took off his belt, "Bite down on this to help with the pain. I need you to not move as much as possible. If it touches raw skin, it's bad."

I did as he directed.

"This is incredible. When I apply it to the wounded area, it completely heals. Watch how it mends." Jovan had a small vile and carefully administered a drop onto my forearm.

I sucked in hard but kept my eyes open to watch as Dyre requested.

The blood bubbled, and the once torn skin pulled together underneath it. Then Jovan quickly wiped away the blood and juice with a rag. Though the heat lingered, not only had the wound disappeared but the skin held no scar.

"I'm sorry about your shoulder," Jovan cowered for a moment before bringing his eyes to meet mine.

I pulled my eyebrows down in question.

He explained, "I used too much and didn't wipe it off fast enough... obiberry juice doesn't usually burn like that. I tried to act quickly, but I'm afraid you might have a scar there."

"Ugh." Dyre sounded disgusted. "I'm pretty sure he sucked it off. You missed a lot after you fainted."

I allowed Jovan to continue and watched with Dyre and Zefforah as the wound disappeared under drops of the poisonous juice.

"It can heal us," Dyre stated in amazement. "But it will damage anything which isn't hurt. I say we still stay away from it."

Zefforah and I agreed nodding our heads.

Just before Jovan finished Trew came with a carriage. "Sorry it took me so long, Eviona. Jovan wouldn't allow anyone to put you back on a horse."

Jovan finished cleaning the last of the juice from my arm. "Look at that, Trew." He took the belt out of my mouth. "Is the pain better?"

I nodded wanting to make him feel like I was okay.

"You're as good as new."

He helped me stand, but I still felt faint and quickly grabbed Jovan to steady myself.

With both arms supporting me he relented, "Well, maybe not yet."

Trew said, "Sanura went for the doctor, I'm sure they'll be at Lady Delsa's by the time we arrive."

Jovan sat next to me in the carriage, "Is it still painful?" One of his arms rested behind my head and with the other, his fingers traced down my skin where the cut no longer existed.

"It still feels hot, but tolerable now."

Dyre closed me off after grunting, "Doesn't he ever stop touching you?"

Jovan's fingers then graced my shoulder making a little circle around the red scar there. "I'm sorry about this."

If he knew the way my insides fluttered with pleasure, he might have been a little less sorry. My thrill only increased when he kissed it.

I grabbed his hand and sternly ordered, "Stop, Jovan."

Sorrow graced his expression, and guilt grew inside me, but I couldn't have him thinking I enjoyed his touch. He couldn't feel that way about me, even though I loved him with all my heart.

"I'm glad you were here," I offered.

He shook his head. "I never thought anything would go wrong."

"I don't blame you."

"You were so nervous. I shouldn't have insisted."

"Jovan, what does sapient mean?"

He looked at me puzzled, but he answered my question. "It means full of wisdom, or well learned. Why do you ask?"

I smiled, "Someone called you a sapient."

He grinned. "Well, I am pretty smart to always carry a panacea with me." After watching my face scowl with question he added with a pleased chuckle, "Obiberry juice is a panacea. It means universal cure."

We arrived at Lady Delsa's, and Jovan's strong arms carried me in. He refused to leave me until the doctor insisted everyone leave the room. Even then I could still hear his footsteps as he paced up and down the hall stopping only occasionally and for short periods of time.

The doctor looked me over and declared me sufficiently healthy. He packed his bag and suggested I rest. When he left the room Jovan shot questions at him. I couldn't make out the words, but I heard their voices. Sanura came in a few minutes later. "I'll be downstairs if you need me. He said you should rest until you feel better."

"I feel fine," I protested.

"Just rest," she commanded.

She left, and I sat up in bed. When my head swayed a bit, I lay back down. Maybe it would be good to relax.

A little while later Dyre said, "She only wanted to have some fun."

"I know." My voice held more severity than I wanted.

"She wanted to be your first ride."

I replied callously, "If you would let us meet..." I closed my eyes and grit my teeth. "Leave me alone."

As I closed my veil he said, "I'm glad Jovan was there to help you." I felt like he actually was.

Abnegate (v) to refuse or deny oneself

"Where is she?"

I jumped out of bed when I heard Roan's voice. He'd only just entered my room when I reached him in an embrace. We hugged enthusiastically and laughed together. "Should you be out of bed? Sanura said you'd been hurt."

"I'm better now, especially seeing you. What are you doing here?"

Our embrace ended but he held me up, worried I might still be weak. "Well, that's one reason I wanted to see you."

He motioned toward the bed, and I climbed back in. Roan sat on the foot as I pulled the blankets over me.

"Do you like Trew?" he asked.

I smiled knowing the real reason for Roan's visit. "Does it matter?"

"Your opinion matters to me."

"She is so in love with him. I think she'll be happy."

He sighed deeply. "He wants to ask her while Aurel and I are here."

"That's sooner than I expected."

He bowed his head in a moment of thought. "You can't stay here once she's married. Will you come home with me?"

I thought about going back to the little house with Roan and smiled momentarily. His goodness filled me with gratitude. "What would Aurel say?" I asked.

He shook his head humbly. We both knew she wouldn't approve.

I reached for him, and he scooted closer to take my hand. "I'll find a place to go."

He didn't say anything but stood and squeezed my hand.

My life would change now whether I wanted it or

not. I'd been given so much over the last few years. Somehow I'd find a good life.

Before he left Roan said, "Oh, there's a young man downstairs. They say he's come every day. If you're strong enough, I'll walk you down."

Jovan, of course. "I'll be dressed in a few minutes."

Roan assisted me to a sitting room where Jovan stood waiting for me. He rushed to my side. "Here, allow me." He took my arm from Roan's and helped me find a comfortable place to sit.

Roan quickly excused himself and smiled at me as he pulled the doors closed behind him.

"I've been very concerned about you, Eviona. Are you feeling much better?"

Sincere and wonderful, I loved him more than ever. I then realized his hands were shaking. "Jovan, is something the matter?"

He looked at me apprehensively and moved to sit closer to me. He closed his eyes as if gathering his thoughts. "I don't...." He took my hand in his and turned it over gently, obviously avoiding eye contact. "I couldn't...." He stood up and walked to the window.

I wanted to comfort him and stood. Too quickly. I swayed as my head rushed with blood. I put my hand down to steady myself on the arm of the couch. He must have noticed because I quickly found myself being held up by him. I smiled but pushed his hands away.

Once he made sure I could stand on my own he looked into my eyes, "I want to marry you."

"Jovan?"

"I know. It's rather sudden, but I've been thinking. Trew is asking Sanura today, he wants to marry her before the summer is over. I think we should be married too."

"You don't want to be married," I reminded him.

He touched my cheek, "You break all my rules."

My heart leapt for joy as my head reminded me of what I must do. I lowered my eyes, "Not that one. Not with me."

"Father said you could come live in the manor with him until my training is complete. It won't be long. I know you aren't in love with me, but I promise I would make you happy."

I reminded myself of the pledge I made not to be the fall of his dreams. Grateful he didn't know how much I loved him I said, "I don't think that can happen."

"You don't think I could make you happy?"

"Nothing could ever happen between us." My heart broke as I spoke. "You saw where I came from. Remember?"

"You never said... I'm still joining the king's army."

"But there would be no chance for you to be a captain."

He knew I was right. He cradled my cheek in his hand, inhaled deeply, and placed his forehead on mine. "What's one more broken rule?"

I fought my feelings to say what I needed instead of what I wanted. "I won't marry you."

He lifted his forehead from mine to look into my eyes. "Where will you go? You can't stay here. I know how Sanura's mother feels about you. You can't go there either. Where else do you have to go?"

"That's not your concern." I patted his hand indifferently.

He gazed at the movement with a protruded chin, feeling the coldness I meant for it to have. "I'll see you at the wedding then." He moved toward the door with the same lack of feeling I'd given him but paused before leaving. He rushed back to me, drawing me into a long embrace and whispered softly in my ear, "Change your mind."

After he'd gone, I jumped at the sound of a slamming door, but it wasn't from Jovan. Dyre's eyes whipped open at the interruption, and he stood to greet Laroke as his veil closed. I realized he had seen the whole thing.

That night I dreamed about me. I dreamed everything I'd experienced that afternoon with one change. I told Jovan I would marry him. As my dream ended, we kissed. Through it all, I felt simply miserable.

Segregate (v) to practice, require or force separation

I made a request for an audience with Lady Delsa. She hesitantly invited me into her sitting room.

"I understand you wish to speak to me." Her aloof eyes did not meet mine.

I curtsied before I spoke and stood straight giving her the respect I knew she wanted. "I appreciate your taking the time to see me."

"What is it you desire?" She sounded as if she knew I would ask to stay.

"I am hoping you can help me. As a child, my mother served in a kitchen." A lie I hoped she wouldn't care to ask further about. "I think it would be best if I followed her example."

The look on her face was pricelessly shocked. "It is very wise of you to ask. I will find somewhere for you to go and be of good use."

She asked to see me a few days later. "I found a home for you to be a teacher. I wouldn't want to waste the education my good money paid for. You will leave the day after the wedding."

I had a place to go, and Sanura had her groom. All seemed well in the world.

On the day of the wedding I could hardly contain my excitement. Jovan came to find me as things began.

Just outside Lady Delsa's home, a large crowd of people had begun to gather. The air seemed saturated with happiness, celebratory even before any sign of the bride or groom. "Why aren't the guests coming into the house?" I asked.

"Do you really not know?"

"I've never seen a wedding before."

Jovan beamed, happy to be able to teach me more. He explained, "The festivities happen outside. You'll soon see Trew's wedding room. A choice groom always builds his own room on wheels. Trew's will be pulled by horses. Some of the less wealthy have theirs pulled by family members or friends. One side of it is a whole wall with a door; the other three sides have only half walls. So the room is almost completely open. Inside there is usually a bench or two small chairs because the couple spends the day there as the festivities happen around them."

"Huzzah!" The crowd cheered. We peeked out the window and saw the room coming down the drive. Though small, it held extreme beauty. The wood girders and door frame had been carved and painted with flowers and birds. And an array natural flowers and vines weaved their way around the beams.

As it came closer, some of the people helped push, and others moved out of the way until it found its place in front of the house.

Then silence washed over the crowd.

Sanura peeked around the door. "Did they stop cheering?" Her ocher hair had been fashioned into curly locks framing her doe eyes. The elaborate gown she wore only added to her striking appearance. She smiled freely. Her perfect lips seemed to know no other emotion.

I jumped to hug her. "You are beautiful!"

"Do you think he will like my dress?"

"I think he could care less about the dress. He's only going to see his bride."

Sanura giggled, "I'm a bride."

Jovan motioned to us and said, "Trew's singing."

Sanura jumped to the window to hear.

A soft melody wafted from the wedding room. A shaky voice sang a simple and sweet song.

"I'd better go downstairs." Sanura trembled as she embraced me again and fled the room.

Jovan whispered, "It's a beckon to his bride. If you listen carefully, you'll hear her name followed by a plea to come out and join him. The words give her a choice to remain inside or to be with him forever. Then overtures of love and promises are made."

As the song repeated one voice coupled with Trew, and then another and another. When the whole crowd seemed to have united in song, the front door of the house opened. Trew's father who had been standing next to the wedding room approached the door. In his hands he held a small offering.

Jovan explained, "The gift is the key to the door of the wedding room. It is usually taken by a close friend or family member of the groom. A family member or friend of the bride takes it from him and gives it to her, signifying the families and friends of the couple approve of the marriage. If the bride wants to marry this man she will take the key and go out. When she unlocks the door and walks in to greet her love, they are married."

"That's it?" I asked.

"Well, they usually kiss, and an epithalamion will take place."

"A what?"

He chuckled. "It's a song in honor of the bride and groom. You'll hear it. Then we will celebrate for the rest of the day. They will stay in their room though until it's all over, symbolically saying they will always be together as if in a world to themselves."

We watched together out the window. Sanura would have run to the wedding room door if it hadn't been for all of the people in her way. She made her way through and dropped the key twice while trying to open the door. She laughed and looked around nervously before she finally opened it. Trew waited for her with a smile equaled only by hers. She stepped in and Trew threw his arms around her and picked her up to kiss her.

As the congratulatory song rang through the crowd. I glanced over to Jovan. His eyes already rested on me. I wished I could have read his thoughts. Mine went to places and things I knew could never be. I allowed myself to see this as our wedding day. The song floating in the air being sung to the two of us as my arms wrapped around him and just before my imagination allowed our lips to touch Roan popped his head into the room. "Come on you two, everyone to the party."

I pulled my eyes from Jovan's and back to reality. We joined the crowd and the celebration. I wanted to congratulate Trew and Sanura, but couldn't fight my way through the throng. It didn't matter though. They didn't seem to notice anyone other than each other.

Jovan found me later and asked me to dance and to my joy we spent quite a bit of the celebration dancing. My mind played tricks on me often as it pushed the same wonderful thoughts of this day being for us repeatedly through my mind. I forced myself to remember his ambitions and dismiss my selfishness. His eyes did not meet mine often, which only made it more comfortable for me to stare at him.

"She's been found!"

A cry in the middle of the celebration pushed everything to a halt.

"She's been found! The lost princess is at the castle!"

The crowd went wild with celebration.

Discussions and conversations not only focused on the wedding but on the newly found princess as well.

I took Jovan's hand, "I'm so sorry," I mocked.

"I'm pleased for the king and queen," he said

solemnly. "Can you imagine losing someone you care about that deeply?" His face did not smile as his eyes pled with mine.

"I'm happy for them too," I muttered, flustered by the suggestion in his tone. His head bowed. He squeezed my hands and turned away from me. He walked down the road away from the party. He didn't say goodbye. Perhaps it would be easier this way.

Roan found me and pulled me back into the celebrations by dancing with me. I had never seen him happier. As the evening died down and the guests slowly withdrew, I hugged him. "You took me in when you had so little and treated me as if I had been your own. I will always be grateful to you."

He said nothing, but patted my cheek affectionately and hugged me once again. As we parted, I think we both knew I would never see him again.

The next day Lady Delsa had a coach ready to take me to my new home. She had generously ordered some clothing more appropriate for a teacher and had given me an old bag to place my things in. Sanura would be back in a few days to collect the rest of the beautiful dresses we had shared.

I rubbed the fabric of my favorite gown between my fingers memorizing the way it felt against my skin. I had grown accustomed to beautiful things. I wondered if it wouldn't have been better for me to have spent these last years with the servants as Lady Delsa had originally planned.

When I came downstairs, I found Jovan waiting for me in the foyer. No longer dressed well I felt a bit uncomfortable when I saw him, but I couldn't help but think it would remind him of why I'd made my choice to go.

"I thought you left without saying goodbye."

"I would never forgive myself," he replied.

I placed my bag on the floor and fell into his embrace. Traitorous tears filled my eyes.

"Did you change your mind?"

I pulled away touching his cheek. "You are so wonderful!"

He smiled at me tenderly.

"I wouldn't think about depriving the king of his best captain by taking you away."

His countenance changed, but I knew he would not regret letting me go. Before me, he had only ever wanted to be a soldier. "Where have you arranged to go?"

"I have a place as a teacher. I'm glad to be going to where I'm needed."

"I need you."

I laughed softly, "You don't need anyone. You have everything you need right here." I put my hand on the side of his head and rubbed my thumb across his temple.

He placed his forehead on mine and positioned his hands on my waist. His grey eyes closed and we didn't move for a long time. "Yesterday my closest friend abandoned me to marriage, and today I'm losing you."

I countered, "I could say the same thing."

He chuckled and moved his head to the side and placed his face next to mine. He kissed me sweetly on the cheek and whispered, "I will always be thinking of you."

I wanted to believe him, but I also hoped time would erase the memories we shared. "I know you'll achieve your ambitions."

He stroked my hair. I took his hands and placed them at his sides as I stepped back. He pressed his lips together in a tight smile, bowed, and left me. My heart wanted me to race after him, but my head told my feet to stay still. I breathed in a long breath, gathered my things, and said goodbye to Lady Delsa's house forever.

Guile (n) crafty or artful deception

Dyre watched out the window of the carriage with me as I traveled. He didn't say anything, but I felt comforted to have him there. He and Zefforah were the one constant in my life. Even when Dyre treated me poorly, at least I knew he would always be with me. When the carriage stopped, I looked in confusion at the homes on the street. As the driver helped me out I asked, "Are you certain we have come to the correct address?"

"This is it," he responded coldly. He handed me my bag and drove away before I had knocked on the door of the house.

This section of town held small, impoverished houses. Not even large enough to hold servant's quarters. Certainly, these families would not have enough money to pay for a teacher. I knocked on the door lightly, confident I would be told I had the wrong place.

The door opened, and a finely dressed, middle-aged woman opened the door. "Oh! You're so pretty." Her face glowed in excitement, "Come in. Come in."

Chaos seemed to be the theme of the home, and a slight reminiscent smell of my childhood wafted through the air. I entered the small home and began to introduce myself. "I'm…"

She interrupted me before I could start. "My husband told me you would be here today, although he didn't mention how attractive you'd be. My, my! Now, you must know. We haven't done much for the children with their education to this point, but now that we have this kind of money we will make up for it I am sure. Here is a list of your duties."

She produced a piece of paper for me. "I know you

will have no trouble in preparing the meals. I understand you used to work in the kitchen before you were educated. That will prove quite handy to us. Of course, I am sure you know how to clean and organize. The household chores will certainly be easy for you as you teach the children. The two really do go hand in hand."

I understood the words coming out of her mouth but had a hard time believing them. They had hired me as a teacher but expected me to be a cook and be a housekeeper as well. A team of household servants wouldn't have been able to help this dwelling.

She continued to prattle as she led me through the clutter-filled house. "Follow me this way. My husband is a gambler. Yes, I know, I know, but you mustn't think less of him for it. He is good to us when his winnings are good. Look at all of the wonderful gifts he buys for us."

I couldn't imagine the clutter in the house being considered nice gifts. To me, it all looked like rubbish.

She led me through a small hallway and up a narrow set of stairs, the whole time the woman's voice constantly filling my head. "Now the children are here upstairs. We prefer if they stay in their part of the house. It's better for everyone. Our oldest son takes care of things when we need him to. His name is Kellam, and I am sure he will help you out whenever you need. We also have two younger children. They are all a bit wild. I can't understand why they don't have better control of themselves."

We walked into a large room littered with toys and clothing. The sound of screaming filled my ears as two children jumped and ran around us. They surrounded their mother with arms up. She pushed them off as if they were dogs jumping on her.

I felt Dyre lean back as if their volume pushed him

backward. "Children." He closed his veil and escaped the noise the way I wish I could have.

"As you can see they are a bit unrefined." She raised her voice to be heard. "You will certainly help them over this phase, I'm sure." My eyes grew wide with the impossibility of her expectation. "This is your room." I looked around wondering how it would be possible to sleep in such chaos. A bed in the corner as well as a trunk, both covered in various items, were the only signs of a space one might live. "Chandi will sleep with you here. Kellam and Wilton sleep in the next room. The trunk by the bed has been emptied for your things, and I am sure you won't mind sharing a bed with Chandi. She is such a little thing. So, here you are. I'll be waiting for you in two hours with our dinner. Have the children prepared to eat with us." As she left the children pulled at her skirt. She slithered around the door shooing their hands, almost closing it on their fingers.

I stood in shock as the two children ran and screamed.

Zefforah opened her veil. Dyre must have complained about the children. As strongly as Dyre desired to flee from them, she felt opposite. She listened to their screams and watched with satisfactory delight. I could barely refrain from reaching out to them, her desire to touch them seemed to ache in my own fingers.

The two little ones played a sort of tag with long sticks which looked like they may have once been a broom and a mop. When the boy hit his sister a bit too roughly, she ran to me and took comfort in the hem of my skirt. I bent down I placed my hand against her cheek wiping away the tears, and she burrowed her head into my chest. Zefforah's heart felt like it would burst with pleasure. Soon the little girl ran from my arms back to play, and Zefforah sighed anticipating the joy of my newfound position.

I smiled and looked at the children in a new light. Perhaps if Zefforah spent time with me, I would love this work and even find the joy in the multitude of tasks set before me.

Then I saw a boy sitting quietly against a far wall with his knees pulled to his chest. Perhaps ten or eleven years of age, he had a slight frame and a head of dark hair with matching eyes. He must have felt me staring at him. His head and body didn't move, but his eyes did, toward me. I didn't have the kind of time I needed or wanted, but I had an idea and would need his help.

"You must be Kellam." I walked toward him holding my hand out to shake his.

He looked at my hand without moving until I dropped it.

I knelt down next to him and whispered, "Listen, I have an idea. The first few days I am here I will need your help."

He continued his cold stare.

"Since you are obviously often left in charge of your siblings I need you to continue in that task."

His eyebrows rose lazily. He seemed certain I would be leaving soon anyway and had little care of it one way or another.

"I promise, I won't let it stay like this."

He rested his chin on his knee and closed his eyes.

"I'll be back before dinner."

I left him and the bedlam of the younger children and went downstairs to make a nice dinner. Mice would be our main course.

As I placed the plates in front of the family, the little children looked ecstatic to be eating something as exotic as mice and quickly bit into them. Chewing with their mouths open and jumping up and down occasionally on their chairs. I did nothing to stop them but watched the faces of their parents as the children crunched on their dinners. Neither parent moved to eat a bite. Kellam looked from one adult to the next, shaking his head when he reached me.

I smiled at him and lifted my fork to cut into mine.

My master asked, "Why in the world would you feed us mice?"

"Oh, mice are full of good nutrients. They'll make the children strong."

His wife whispered, "You'd need a strong stomach to eat them."

"Oh not at all, they are quite delicious. Aren't they children?"

The children nodded their heads in agreement and continued to munch their treasures jumping from their chair to the other's and back again.

Kellam picked his up with his fingers and took a bite. He looked over at me in curiosity as he chewed lifting it up and tipping his head.

My master threw his napkin on the table and stormed from the room, followed shortly by his wife.

"What is this really?" Kellam asked after they left.

"Kind of like crackers."

He almost smiled. "What are we having for breakfast tomorrow?"

"I thought maybe some fried roaches." I winked at him.

"Goodie." The children shouted as they headed toward their parent's plates.

Pedagogy (n) the art or science of teaching

"Is there a word for someone who always gets what they want?" Kellam asked.

I studied him. Sometimes he would ask me questions simply to test my responses. "Do you mean someone who is self-indulgent?"

"Is that what you would call yourself?"

"Ouch!" I laughed. "Do I always get what I want?"

"It seems that way to me. The day after you came my parents hired a cook, and after a week of having us help you clean the house we had a housekeeper as well."

"Your younger siblings helped with the housekeeper," I grinned at him.

"Only because you had them clean the fragile things and they broke so many of them." He snickered.

"I think the word you are looking for is manipulator. To manipulate something means to skillfully control something, but it's not a terribly nice thing to call someone."

We were sitting in my room at a small table working on vocabulary. A subject I enjoyed immensely because it filled my mind with thoughts of Jovan.

After the cook and housekeeper were hired, Kellam and Wilton moved into the room with Chandi. The cook and the housekeeper, and I all shared the room across from them. Since winter called for afternoon quite time for the little ones, Kellam and I often came into my room for some one on one study.

"I like you." The eyes which had only held distrust for me a few weeks earlier now looked at me admirably.

"I like you too, Kellam."

"You talk to me, and treat me like a person."

"Of course I do. You are an intelligent and fascinating young man."

"My parents don't like me."

"Kellam. That's ridiculous."

He rolled his eyes. "Have you ever seen my parents talk to me?"

I thought about it for a minute and scowled, disappointed in my memories. "No."

"Two years ago I thought I would try an experiment. I decided not to talk to my parents unless they said something to me first. I haven't spoken to either one of them since."

"Oh." My understanding of his pain ground deep.

"It's better now. I have you," he smiled.

I squeezed his hand.

"I keep thinking my Father might respect me if I could play cards with him. I don't suppose you play cards?"

I grinned at him and raised my eyebrows.

His eyes grew excited. "Would you teach me?" He pulled a deck out of his pocket.

"Where did you find those?"

He smiled and attempted a shuffle.

I took the cards from him and showed him how to do it correctly. "I learned math by watching card games."

"Your teacher must have been a very interesting character."

I laughed at the thought of calling Dyre a teacher. "Well, he is interesting, but he isn't a proper teacher."

"Is it your father?"

"No, I never knew my father."

"Really? That would be wonderful."

I laughed and handed the cards to him for another try. "A friend taught me card games."

"A... friend?" Kellam kept his eyes on me but turned his head to the side to scrutinize the meaning of the word.

"I'm not allowed to have friends?" I asked him wide eyed with a grin. I chuckled at his distrusting stare. "Deal us both five cards. I'll teach you your father's favorite game."

Cognizance (n) awareness, realization, notice or knowledge

"Going out again today?" Cookie asked as she packed a basket for us. Chandi and Wilton ran around the kitchen gathering up any spare morsels of food left from the preparation.

"The children and I have found a wonderful little lake up in the mountains. It's a great place to play, and we have plenty of ways to keep busy with our studies as well." I told her.

Kellam added. "After the long winter, it's nice to be able to be out of here. There is far more room up there for Eviona to teach me how to duel too."

He shot me a grin. Every day since he learned I knew how to fight we had been sparring. I loved it as much as he did. Wilton and Chandi loved the action as well, but with them it would always only be play. Kellam had a very natural talent with the sword and worked at it regularly.

As Wilton chased her around the kitchen, Chandi slipped and fell. She began to cry and came to me with her arms upstretched. Zefforah's heartbeat quickened. She loved it when I picked up the children. Zefforah spent a lot of her days with us. She loved the children and felt especially happy when they would laugh or if I touched them. I loved having her open to me so much. She filled me with happiness.

Once Chandi had been comforted we grabbed our things and were soon hiking up the familiar trail to our sanctuary in the mountains. The younger children ran ahead of me while Kellam preferred to stay at my side.

"Promise me you will never leave us."

I wished I could make that promise to him. "I can't."

He looked away from me, obviously unhappy with

my response.

I nudged him, "I like being with you. I see a lot of myself in you."

"You do?"

"I didn't have the greatest childhood either."

"I'll bet you grew up someplace better than my house."

"No."

"Really?"

"And I didn't start any kind of real education until I became older than you are."

"But you're so smart."

"I still have a lot to learn," I chuckled.

"And a lot to teach!" He grabbed a stick from the ground and swished it around like a sword.

I couldn't have anticipated a better student than Kellam. He noticed everything and learned quickly. Often at the lake, he would bring a book and read as I worked with his younger siblings. At night once they slept he would take advantage of our time alone. We often had impromptu lessons while he should have been sleeping.

Today as I set up I saw Zefforah flying and could feel her desire to be close to us. She flew silently through the air scouring through mountainous places looking for us.

I glanced at the other side of the lake. "You have to stay over there, behind the trees," I whispered.

She impressed her assurance on me.

"Who are you talking to?" Kellam asked.

I ignored his question. "Do you know where the city of Flicktlemit is?"

Kellam responded, "Of course I do, that's where we live."

I smiled at him, and Zefforah changed the direction she had been flying elated to know where we were.

"What direction do you think we are from the city?"

"If you have taught me correctly this lake is about a mile and a half North East of there."

"I think you are exactly right," I grinned and started to shake with excitement. I would see Zefforah. Actually see her with my own eyes. I knew I couldn't meet her the way I wanted to, but even the thought of seeing her again thrilled me.

I had to move or my anticipation would burst out of my body. I suggested a race across the field with the children. They happily obliged me.

It wasn't long before her huge shadow passed over us, and my heart skipped with exhilaration. I watched through her eyes as she spied the children and me.

I felt a craving to be with her, unlike any need I had felt before. Her snowy, silk hair glowed, almost translucent. She stretched her gigantic wings. I thought it impossible but they were even more alluring than her body. Her feathers, the size of my arms, sparkled when the light hit them just right as if they had been made with gemstones. And though her tail was like that of a lizard, instead of scales, the same shining, iridescent, white hair covered it like the rest of her body. She couldn't have been more beautiful.

I needed to distract the children. "Okay everyone, let's go swimming."

The children happily jumped into the water and remained too busy to notice our visitor. She landed so I could see her just on the other side of the lake and hid behind some tall trees enough to watch us but still hopefully remain unseen.

I ached to go to her. If I hadn't had the children with me, I would have swam the lake to be with her. The short distance between us tortured me.

"Hello Zefforah, how wonderful it is to finally meet you in person." I softly greeted her. She looked at me to acknowledge me. I felt her happiness as great as my own. "You are beautiful, even more than I remember."

She and I stared at each other across the lake for several moments. How I longed to be there with her. I felt her longing as well, not only for me but for the children.

She stayed and watched until we needed to go home. As I called the children out of the water, she took to the sky. I relished the experience of flying once again as she flew away from me. I only wish I could have found a way to physically connect with her during the day. But grateful she had been willing to not come close enough for the children to see. Their parents would never understand if one of them talked about her.

After evening meals, I tucked the children into bed and sang to them quietly until Chandi and Wilton were sleeping. After Kellam and I worked on a bit of history and math, I stood to leave.

He grabbed my hand. "How do you know it?"

"History?"

He shook his head. "That thing."

"What thing?" My heartbeat quickened, I knew he was asking about Zefforah but hoped differently.

"That big, white…are you going to tell me?"

I pulled my hand tenderly away from his and as I closed the door. "Goodnight, Kellam."

After what seemed to be only a few moments of sleep Chandi crawled into bed with me. I knew I would probably be joined shortly by Wilton as well.

Dyre groaned. "Oh, not again!"

"It doesn't happen every night," I whispered.

"It happens much too often." He complained.

"At least it's Chandi tonight. Once she is asleep, I

will go and sleep in her bed. I can't do that if only Wilton comes in. He shares a bed with Kellam."

"Someday I hope you have a huge, comfortable bed all to yourself."

I laughed quietly. "Well, it sounds nice, but it won't happen tonight."

After a few minutes, Wilton came in as well. When he kicked me in the ribs, Dyre grunted loudly. I slipped out of the bed and went into the next room to sleep in Chandi's bed.

Once settled I looked over to Kellam and saw him smiling in the soft moonlight of the room. "Wilton has quite a good pair of kicking legs, doesn't he?" he snickered.

I playfully growled at him. "You didn't send him in there did you?"

He opened his eyes wide in an attempt to look innocent.

"Hm, go to sleep, Kellam." I closed my eyes.

A soft whisper broke the silence. "I love you, Eviona."

I felt Dyre smile, and Kellam rolled over.

Relinquish (v) to let go

Once again Zefforah had left her veil open. As we began our hike, Kellam's anticipation rose from him like an odor. He asked me other things instead, but I knew he wanted to know about Zefforah.

Once we arrived, he found his usual position propped up against a tree with a book. I sent Chandi and Wilton to play while I set up class for the day.

Zefforah's shadow covered us as she flew overhead. I glanced toward Kellam who seemed oblivious to it. Zefforah landed on the opposite bank of the lake and moved to watch us from behind the trees.

"Thanks for hiding," I whispered. "Kellam saw you last time."

As I started my math lessons with Wilton and Chandi, a splash startled me. Kellam swam hard and fast. I knew exactly what had happened. He only pretended not to see her and would swim the lake to reach her. I understood his desire. I would have done it myself. The expanse of the lake wasn't large but a young boy of eleven years with only occasional swimming practice would not be able to make it the whole way. I panicked. Zefforah's feelings mirrored my own.

I needed to occupy the other children for a while. "Can you find twenty bugs, Wilton? Chandi, see if you can find twenty stones all about the same size." I hoped it would keep them busy long enough for Kellam to make it to the other side.

Toward the middle of the lake, he slowed. I chewed my fingernails as I paced back and forth. Zefforah watched in terror from the other side of the trees. He stopped. My heart sank and so did Kellam. I counted to five and whispered in panic. "Zefforah."

She instantly glided across the clear water and

plucked him out of it with her tail. She placed him on her back and took off into the sky.

She had reached him before any real danger. I closed my eyes and breathed in relief as Kellam laughed.

She took him for the rest of the day. Soaring with him through the sky, taking him to many of the places she'd shown me during my childhood. She left her veil open allowing me to experience the happiness she felt and keep tabs on Kellam.

Wilton, Chandi and I had our lessons and then I allowed them to swim, grateful they hadn't noticed Kellam's absence.

As I packed up our things at the end of the day, I whispered to her, "Zefforah, it's almost time for us to go home."

Staying out of sight, she brought Kellam to the canyon and left him not far down the trail. Even though he had to climb uphill, he ran the whole way. When he reached me, he threw his arms around me.

I motioned for him not to say anything, but he grinned the whole way home. That night as I left their room he told me, "Today was the best day of my entire life."

"She is wonderful."

"*So wonderful!*" He agreed with me.

The next day her veil didn't open to me. She wouldn't be joining us. Dyre probably had her occupied. She wouldn't tell him about spending time with the children or coming to find me, I'm certain she knew as well as I did he would be cross with us both.

I assigned the other children into gathering some supplies for our classes that day and went to talk to Kellam searching the sky with his eyes behind the cover of his book.

"She's not coming today."

"How do you know?"

"I know. I can't explain it better than that."

"Tell me about her." He insisted.

I looked over to the other children and inhaled deeply. "He's going to hate this," I whispered to myself as I gave in. "Her name is Zefforah."

"She's nice. Like you."

I nodded my head with a smile and sat down next to him.

Contagious excitement filled his eyes. "Have you ever flown with her?"

"In a way."

"What does that mean?" He scowled at me.

I scolded him. "You shouldn't have tried to reach her."

He grimaced and studied my expression. "You're jealous. I can see it in your face."

I sighed, "I am very envious of your time with her."

His eyes softened and grew puzzled. "Why don't you go to her?"

"Who would take care of the children?" I chuckled without any real emotion.

He read me too easily. "Even if they weren't here, you can't. Can you?"

"It's complicated." I shook my head.

"She has an interesting mark on the center of her back. Three triangles connected in the center."

I vaguely remembered seeing it once. It looked a lot like the lines Dyre drew on his map connecting the stars. "Yes, it's an interesting mark."

"What does it mean?"

I pondered momentarily about how much to tell Kellam, against my better judgment I told him. "Well, I'm not sure, but I do know someday the stars will align in a pattern just like that."

"Who put the mark there?"

I didn't know the answer. She'd had the mark for as long as I could remember, but Dyre knew about the stars for longer than that. "I don't know. Does it look like a brand?"

"That's not the place to brand a horse." He objected. "Besides, it doesn't look like a brand. It's more like the hair there is a different color, like she was born with it."

"I wish I could tell you more about it."

"Next time she comes, can I go with her again?"

I shook my head. "I don't know if you are a strong enough swimmer."

"I will be." He grinned and gazed at the water.

I looked over to the lake and back to him. Kellam's face shone with anticipation. "Go on then."

Every day Kellam grew stronger and by the end of the summer he could swim across the whole lake to reach the other side. On the days she joined us they both begged me to allow them to be together. I never held back. I would have joined them if I could.

When the younger children noticed Kellam's long absences I would simply tell them I had sent him exploring, and he would be back by the time we went home, which always happened.

As fall began the chill in the air brought a change I never saw coming. I was called to talk with my master and his wife. As I entered the small sitting room, their faces were solemn, and I feared that someone might have reported seeing Kellam with Zefforah.

"Sit down, Eviona." His features were so like his son Wilton. I studied his face trying to discern what emotions were housed there. Anger? Guilt?

I sat and appraised his wife wiping away evidence of

sadness; a pink nose, sniffles, and red eyes.

"You have been good to our children."

I nodded, waiting for the real purpose of this meeting.

"We have seen remarkable improvement in their behavior, as well as their knowledge. We are grateful to you for being the teacher we had hoped you would be."

I waited. My skill as a teacher could not be the subject on their minds.

"You won't be staying with us any longer," his wife said.

I stared at them, disbelieving their news.

His wife took my hand. I pulled it away.

Her husband did not look at me as he explained, "Last night I found myself with nothing left to wager. I had a good hand. I shouldn't have lost." His obvious irritation overshadowed his attempt to keep his composure. "I am sorry. Go pack your things, then you will be taken to a new home."

"But the children," I protested.

"We will find them a new teacher when we can." His wife cried softly.

I sat motionless, a piece of me dying at the thought of leaving them.

"Come Eviona." He offered his hand to help me stand. "You will need to go and tell the children now."

I didn't try to hide the contempt in my eyes as I left.

I walked into their bedroom and immediately caught the eye of Kellam. A scowl on his face made me wonder if he knew what had happened.

"My plans worked against me," I told him.

He cleared his throat and his arms folded across his chest. "What do you mean?"

"Well, with a cook, and a housekeeper, and me, if one of us had to go which do you think your parents would choose?"

His chin began to quiver. I put my arms around him, and he shoved me away. He stormed down the stairs, and the house shook when the front door slammed.

Wilton and Chandi looked at me with fear in their eyes. I explained, and we sobbed together. They cried for the love and attention they had become accustomed to with my presence, I showered them with it and wept knowing their parents would not do the same when I left.

As I packed the front door slammed again. Kellam broke his silence to his parents and yelled at them until a lightning-like crack. He'd been slapped. The hush of the house after weighed heavily on everyone's ears.

I finished packing and took Wilton and Chandi downstairs with me. Kellam stood like a stone statue facing away from the hallway where I waited.

I called to him. "Kellam?"

He didn't move.

I walked to him, standing in front of him waiting for him to make eye contact with me. When he didn't move, I touched his chin pulling it upward, but he jerked it away. I wrapped my arms around him.

"I love you, Kellam. I promise it won't always be like this." I kissed him on the cheek. He still didn't look at me. I crept away hoping he'd stop me for one last embrace.

Zefforah had seen the events of the morning. Her sadness weighed as greatly as my own. She cried with me as I held Wilton and Chandi and whispered my love for them. I touched each of their faces expressly for Zefforah. Then for me, I kissed them on their cheeks and encouraged them to be good and to keep learning.

After my goodbyes, I stepped into the coach and

watched out the window as the children cried and begged for me to stay. As the coach pulled away, Kellam ran outside after me.

I called to him and reached my hand out the window. "Kellam."

"Eviona!" Tears streamed down his face as he reached toward me. I heard the driver crack the whip for the horses to go faster. Kellam stayed close as he ran. A half mile down the road he fell to his knees. I pulled my hand into the coach but continued to watch him. His face never lifted. Instead, he hit the ground with his fists and remained still until I couldn't see him any longer.

Cicatrice (n) blemish from a previous injury

As I rode Dyre opened his veil. "Zefforah told me something bad happened. Are you alright?"

"No," I replied honestly.

"Where are you going?"

"I don't know. My master placed me as a wager in a card game last night and gambled me away."

Dyre didn't leave me, but he didn't speak to me either. I allowed myself to release the heartache I felt and cried until the carriage started to slow. When we came to a stop the door opened and the driver handed me my bag. I stood, once again, alone on a doorstep. I knocked quietly and waited while an old housekeeper went to call her master.

Dyre growled in my head as soon as he saw the face of the man approaching me. "Toril." He whispered with distain.

I recognized his face as well. My hand instinctively moved to cover the part of my leg which still held a scar from his knife. The cheater. Anger filled me as I remembered the words of the children's father, 'I shouldn't have lost.' He'd probably been right. Toril cheated again. I wanted to confront him on it. My own anger, combined with Dyre's, caused my hand to fist, and I had to remind myself as his servant it wouldn't be wise to hit him.

Dyre snarled. "Tell him he owes me money."

Toril approached me with his eyes raking over every curve of my body. He moved to take my bag. "Oh no." I protested. "I won't be staying here." He chuckled at my stubborn stance, which only made me angrier. "I'm a teacher. What use might you have for me?"

"I am sure I could think of something." He raised his eyebrows and spoke in the smooth, charming way I had seen women fawn over before. He approached me reaching toward me with the charm I had seen him use on serving wenches at the gambling houses.

Dyre's anger grew. His teeth clenched. "If he so much as touches you…" His fist matched my own.

I pulled away from him and made my voice hard and threatening. "I will not be staying. You may either arrange for me to go back to the children or find me another situation."

"I don't think you understand your position. You belong to me." He spoke condescendingly to put me in my place.

"I understand perfectly. Your swindling ways brought you some money. And I happened to be on the table."

His face lost the charm from a moment before, and his lip twitched as he responded to me, "I won you straightforward."

"Straightforward? You won me by fraud, the way you always win."

He tried to appear calm. "Your last master must have been pretty upset to accuse me of cheating."

"He didn't accuse you. I did."

He no longer tried to hide the blaze in his eyes.

"Watch him," Dyre warned.

I pushed him again with my words. "Where do you keep your spare cards, up your sleeve or in your boot with your knife?"

He seized me by the arm and threw me to the ground. I heard a gasp and looked over to see his housekeeper. Her terrified face showed she obviously had never seen this side of him.

He pushed his shoulders back and picked me up while clearing his throat. "Are you alright? You must have tripped."

The small woman helped him lift me to stand and looked at him nervously.

"Why don't you bring her a cup of water?" He told her.

I glared at him as she left the room. "She's your housekeeper, are you trying to protect your reputation with your servants? I'll be happy to fill them in."

His fury and confusion combined into an interesting glower. He grabbed my bag and stormed from the room.

"Are you alright?" Dyre asked. "I never thought I'd see him threaten a woman."

"I'm sure no woman has stood up to him before." I brushed myself off. "He's too accustomed to getting his way with them."

Dyre chuckled, and I smirked as Toril came back into the room. Seeing my smile did not make him any happier. He swiftly pulled on his coat as he moved to the front door. "I have locked your things in a safe place to keep you here. I wouldn't want anything I own to be wandering off." He scowled.

I simply continued to stare at him.

"I wouldn't want to keep a monster like you anyway." The daggers in his eyes as he slammed the door didn't bother me.

Dyre laughed. "Good for you, Eviona."

The housekeeper returned with a cup of water. "He's in an unusual mood today. Don't worry dear, the master is usually quite amiable. Why don't you have a seat and wait patiently for his return? He'll feel better if you are right here waiting for him."

I nodded to her and sat as directed and she left me to go back to her work.

"Do me a favor," Dyre said. "Take a walk."

"You want me to run away?"

"No, I simply want you to take a walk."

I grinned when I realized what Dyre had planned. I did as he requested. As I passed a woman on the street, I stopped her to ask, "Excuse me, what is the name of this town?"

"Why this is Heding Town, Miss."

"Thank you," Dyre said it to me as I spoke the same words to the woman.

I took my time getting back to the home of Toril. I studied the outside of the building for quite a while before entering.

I found Toril fuming. "I thought you had left us for good, robbing me of my property."

I didn't hide my irritation and glared at him.

He called a coach for me and brought my bag. "I have found you a home in which you will be a servant, I didn't think it wise to have children exposed to you as a teacher."

Simply grateful to be leaving so quickly, I snatched my bag from his hand and entered the coach. "A friend of mine will be coming to see you soon. You owe him a great deal of money. I suggest you start putting it together."

Obviously confused, Toril frowned at me as the coach drove away.

"You shouldn't have warned him," Dyre stated.

"You don't want your money?"

"I hoped to beat it out of him."

I laughed, "You may still have your desire. He probably thought it an empty threat."

"I hope." I felt Dyre's teeth grinding, "I hope."

Rejuvenate (v) to restore to a former state

I liked being back in a large home, and once my talents were heard of, I quickly moved to the kitchen. Different households periodically traded or hired me out. I found myself enjoying going to new places and meeting new people, but remained kitchen staff from then on. My skills with food honed and grew as most of my masters found my creations quite amusing. I felt more at home in the kitchen than anywhere else.

I ended up being sought after by one specific master. Because he entertained quite frequently, he encouraged me to freely experiment. In fact, it seemed a whole week never passed without the broadcast of visitors to the house. On one such occasion we had been told we would be having a whole company of soldiers with their spouses coming to visit for three days. We planned and prepared.

A bit of a fluster raced through the staff when we discovered we didn't quite have enough servers for so many people. The head housekeeper decided many of us could play dual roles. We would do our usual work and also act as servers for the meals. Even with the difficulties of such a large amount of people coming, the house felt alive with energy and the whole staff enjoyed the festive mood.

The night our guests arrived we made a simple banquet. I had been given the task of breads. Because Jovan had a sword like those of the king's soldiers I had been able to recreate them in bread form. When our master saw them, he beamed with enchantment.

Several of us changed our clothes and positioned ourselves as servers while they announced the evening meal. As the soldiers came in with their wives and I couldn't help but look at each of their faces, hoping perhaps Jovan would be one of them.

Each new face entering the room pushed my heart to skip in anticipation. I heard his laugh but disbelieved until he walked into the room.

His eyes took in his surroundings, and his face showed his pleasure in being there. I immediately looked at the people closest to him. My heart dropped at the sight of his hand on the shoulder of a woman in front of him until I noticed her holding the arm of another man. I bit my lip trying to conceal the wide smile coming to my mouth. I couldn't speak to him, but I prayed he would notice me. I simply wanted him to see me and acknowledge me with a smile. I loved his smile.

He picked up his sword-shaped bread and studied it for a few moments, then nudged his neighbor to chat about it. He admired my work before he tore a piece off to pop in his mouth. Did he recognize it as my work? I wondered if he thought I might be here and if he might want to search me out. I wanted so badly for him to know I stood only a few feet away, but he never looked around at the servants.

The conversation and banter of the table entertained us all. They talked of their training, and it seemed this group had been together for some time. They frequently would talk of inside jokes and I enjoyed watching Jovan's face as he would laugh. Disappointment entered my heart as the meal came to a close.

As we cleared the plates from the table, the girl next to me accidently dropped one. She and I picked up the shattered pieces. Our good master tried to alleviate the sudden tension by saying, "Thank you, my dear, I have despised that plate for far too long." It did help the mood as everyone laughed. When I turned to look back at Jovan, he was staring straight at me. Smiling.

I smiled back at him, and he winked at me. I began to

shake like a child.

As the company moved to another room, he approach my master. I cleared the table close to where they stood and overheard their conversation.

"My dear sir, you have a lovely home," Jovan started.

"I am grateful to you and glad to have your company."

"I have a small favor to ask of you."

"Please ask. I will see if I can grant it."

"As you can see I am without a companion. All of my fellow soldiers have been married or are otherwise engaged. I am the only single gentleman here."

"So you are."

"I am hoping you will help me rectify the situation for the few days I am to be here with my company."

"I do not have daughters if that is what you are asking. I will not have working girls in my home." He seemed a little put off.

"No, no. I assure you. I only wish for someone to accompany me through the next few days."

"Did you have someone in mind?" My master asked.

"Yes. I see you have several young girls who work as servants in your home." His eyes peeked at me. "Could I perhaps borrow one to use as a companion?"

I smiled as I picked up a dish and put it on my tray.

My master looked around at those of us working. "I don't think any of them would have anything appropriate to wear." He whispered as if his comment might offend us.

"I'll take care of that. No one other than her fellow servants will ever know she is not a lady."

"As you like." My master said as he left the room.

Jovan looked at me. I found my face reflecting the

huge grin he wore. I put down the items in my hands as he raced to me, picked me up and twirled me around. I squealed, and the other servants eyed us curiously. He placed me back on the ground and put his forehead on mine.

"Hello, beautiful Eviona."

"Hello, wonderful Jovan."

"What are you doing here? I thought you were a teacher."

"I actually work in the kitchen now." I giggled. "I told you that was my aspiration."

He chuckled. "I will find you a dress, and you will be my companion."

"I don't know how I will be able to finish my work and be with you at the same time."

He pulled his face away from mine and gave me a grave look. "I will tell your master who I have chosen. He will dismiss you I am sure of it."

"But we are short staffed already, the workers need me."

His face fell. "Don't you want to spend time with me?"

"You know I do."

"Then stop fighting with me."

I smiled and sighed, "I will find a way to spend time with you."

"Good! Finish what you need to tonight and come to my room. I'll arrange everything."

"Come to your room?" My eyes grew wide, questioning him teasingly.

"I believe you rejected me," he laughed. "Am I in danger being alone with you?"

I shook my head.

"I'll give you a dress and tomorrow you'll be my companion."

"I am so happy to see you, Jovan."

He laughed, "I simply want someone to duel with who I'm sure I can beat." He let go of me and walked to the door.

"Then you'd better find me attire for that too. Don't be thinking I won't win." I shook my finger at him.

"You need another welt on your backside?" He teased as he left the room smiling.

I worked as hard and as fast as I could that night. The girls working near me whispered behind my back, but I didn't care what they thought. I simply wished to spend time with Jovan. After the work had been finished, I snuck up to the guest rooms.

Once there, I realized I had no idea which room he occupied. I stood in the hallway for a long time debating about what to do.

An obvious cough clearly trying to gain my attention interrupted my thoughts. Jovan stood in a doorway down the hall with his arms and his ankles crossed as if he had been standing for quite some time watching me struggle.

"How long have you been there?" I whispered.

"A while." His eyes sparkled as if he had been watching me for hours.

I moved to him putting on a sour expression.

He smiled broadly and raised his eyebrows, my cross look didn't last for long.

"Come in. See what I have."

True to his word, he loaned me some of his clothing and a belt. He also had several dresses laid out on his bed. "One of my colleague's spouses packed an extra-large trunk," he said. "Pick out the ones you like the best."

I felt like I had won a prize. He had also borrowed

ribbons for my hair and shoes as well as a few other baubles. I picked two dresses which fit my taste and some of the accessories. Then I gathered everything into my arms.

"These are wonderful. In the morning when you see me I will be a new woman." I turned to leave, and Jovan blocked my path. "What are you doing?" I asked him confused.

"I think you need to pay for the use of those dresses," he smirked.

"Oh really? How much do I owe?"

"Hmmm... perhaps a kiss."

I rolled my eyes at him and snuck under his arm. I turned around and made a face at him as I walked backward down the hall.

He smiled at me and then laughed as I tripped and almost fell.

When I came up the next day, my master introduced me to the party as a companion to Jovan. With a twinkle in his eye he said, "I'm pleased your detainment at your last position did not deprive you from a visit at my house."

The servants knew, but none of them let on. They all treated me as one of the company.

After the morning meal, one of the wives approached me. She whispered, "This is one of my favorites, I am so glad to see it on you. It's never looked more beautiful."

I blushed, thanking her profusely. Then I asked which of the rooms she stayed in so I could return them promptly at the conclusion of my time with Jovan. When I noticed Jovan watching me, I kissed her cheek.

She started a bit with surprise but kissed my cheek in return as old friends do.

Jovan approached us and offered me his arm to escort me to a sitting room where the company was gathering.

"That should have been my payment." He nudged me with his arm.

"They aren't your dresses." I happily reminded him.

Dyre came into my head as I sat enjoying the conversations around me, "You are extremely happy. What's wrong?"

I laughed at him and without speaking let him see whose hand held mine.

"Oh." I felt his smile change to hostility.

I said nothing as I blocked him. Dyre would not ruin this for me.

My time with Jovan felt like heaven. We walked in the gardens and talked of old times. He told me about Trew and Sanura. He didn't see them much but knew they had been blessed with a child; a son, healthy, strong and he looked like his father.

As we walked, we came to a large gazebo. He took my hand and led me inside. He looked at me with excitement in his eyes. "Come here." He said as he pulled me close to him.

I hesitated until he took one of my hands and placed it on his shoulder. He then placed his hand on my waist and hummed a tune.

We turned and swayed to the music in his head, flustered I tried to remember what to do. I stepped on his feet more than once and at one point tripped us both. We giggled as we sat on the floor.

"You are not supposed to lead, Eviona." His contagious laugh tickled me.

I opened my eyes wide to emphasize my embarrassment. "I'm sorry."

He stood and pulled me to him.

"Again?" I asked. "I'll try to follow you this time."

"Then we might actually dance," he teased.

I let him move me the way I knew I should, relishing the moments as they passed.

"Who did you practice dancing with when you realized you needed to actually practice?" I asked.

He laughed and stopped turning, he hesitated and cleared his voice. "Trew."

I laughed at the thought of them dancing, and enjoyed watching him grow a bit uncomfortable.

"He knew how to dance. After our first failure, I asked him to teach me."

I smiled at him placing my hands back in position to show I wanted to dance more. He gathered me into his arms, and we danced again.

At dinner I enjoyed the dialogue around the table. Every once in a while, a question would be asked and in his usual manner Jovan would enlighten anyone willing to listen. I loved listening to him talk. He knew everything. It seemed he knew even more than when I first met him. His wisdom showed in his eyes as well as his conversations.

At the end of the evening, everyone went to their rooms. Jovan purposely kept me in the sitting room so no one would see I didn't sleep in the guest rooms.

"It's been a fine day." He smiled honestly.

"It has." I agreed. "This has almost been as wonderful as our time at Trew and Sanura's wedding."

Jovan's smile faded, and he bowed his head humbly. "I look forward to spending tomorrow with you."

Declension (n) an act or instance of declining

That night I dreamed of life if I had married Jovan. In my dream, we were well enough off. We lived in a large and comfortable home with many beautiful things. We were often invited to parties and social gatherings, but Jovan could not find contentment. Without the status of captain, his life could never be what he wanted. Nothing I did or said could alter his spirit. I felt like a wretch having traded my own happiness for his.

When I awoke the next morning, I knew I had made the right decision when I had turned down Jovan in the first place.

Dyre's voice spoke to me as soon as he realized I had awoken. "Did he ask you to marry him again?"

"No," I whispered so as not to awaken the other servants.

"Is he going to?" He asked almost too loudly to contradict my whispers.

"Why does it matter to you?"

"If you are going to marry him, I had better figure out how to block you more effectively. I can't imagine having to wake to the sight of him each day."

"Stop it. Why are you so awful to him?"

"I'm simply trying to plan for my future, Eviona."

"You don't need to worry. I'm not going to marry Jovan."

"Good."

I blocked his smug voice. Then hurried to help prepare the morning meal and ready myself to meet Jovan before the call for it to be served.

Jovan waited for me in the foyer with a smile. "Hello, beautiful Eviona."

"Hello." Despite what I had said to Dyre I did love Jovan and wished I could marry him. I would struggle to turn him down if he asked me again.

"Is something wrong?" He must have seen the sadness in my eyes.

"Nothing could go wrong today, Jovan. I'm with you."

He smiled, but his eyes questioned me as if he knew I lied to him. He offered me his arm and we walked through the house.

I quietly thought about my dream from the night before.

"Something is wrong," Jovan stated.

Thinking quickly, I came up with a good alternative. "I simply wish we had more time to spend together."

Jovan smiled at me. I found myself smiling at him in return. We joined the others for the morning meal.

As we ate with the other soldiers and their wives I couldn't help but note how very comfortable Jovan seemed. He had been meant for this life, this element. I couldn't take him away from it.

When the meal concluded my master announced there would be a special play put on for the soldiers. He directed us to the front of the house where a stage had been put in place.

Jovan leaned over to whisper in my ear. "I have other plans for us. If it's all right with you."

"What would you like to do?"

"How do you feel about a duel?" His eyes sparkled with anticipation.

"Are you sure you're up for it?" I asked him with faux seriousness.

"Well, I haven't lifted a sword for a whole three days. I'm not positive I am." He winked at me.

Jovan had borrowed a sword from a fellow soldier for me to use. We found a secluded spot on the side of the house to duel.

"Wow, you remember your lessons very well." He commented after a particularly fun round.

"I am a natural."

He chuckled, "And we thought I had pride issues. You can even lift the sword now." He teased. "Come on then, let's see if I can win again." He raised his sword, and I gladly took his invitation.

We had such fun and laughed more than we fought. It felt good to laugh with him again. I did have the feeling my arms would burn from all of the work, but I didn't care. We changed, and I took Jovan's clothes up to his room.

We didn't join the company again until evening. At one point during dinner, I found myself the topic of conversation.

"Where were you raised?" A young wife near me asked. I looked around and noticed the attention of more than a few of the couples.

"Um, close to Jovan," I replied a bit tense.

"What is your family's business?" Her husband joined the conversation.

"My family's business?" I looked to Jovan for help. He simply looked at me with raised eyebrows wondering what I would say.

"My family doesn't have a business," I said humbly.

Suddenly it seemed the whole table looked at me.

One of the wives chimed in. "How would it be to simply come from money like that?" I thought I had freed myself until she looked at me and asked. "So, what hobbies do you have?"

I quickly glanced at my master and said, "I very much enjoy sculpting."

Another soldier down the way asked, "I fancy myself a bit of a sculptor. What is your favorite medium?"

"Well, there are so many to choose from, I use a large variety."

"You must be quite talented."

"Yes, I am." I blushed when I realized how I must have sounded.

Jovan laughed and finally decided to say something. "She is quite gifted. I've never seen anything like the work she does."

I smiled at him gratefully.

The soldier spoke again. "Really? Might I have seen some of your pieces?"

I am sure I looked scarlet red by this point, but I continued on with my charade. "You may have." I knew full well he had the night they arrived. "But I do not sell any of my work."

"Why not?"

I thought about it for a moment and decided I could twist truth a bit. "It is commonly understood most artists are never well known during their own lifetimes. I am waiting to sell mine posthumously."

The roar of laughter around the table pleased me enormously. I felt even more pleased as the conversation turned to other things and people.

I glanced down the table at my master who smiled at me knowingly.

Jovan leaned over to me and whispered. "Nicely done. You obviously have learned from watching me in action as I answered impossible questions."

I tapped his hand playfully and whispered, "Which of us has pride issues?"

He snickered.

At the end of the day, we went for a walk.

"Eviona, it has been delightful to spend time with you again. I can't believe how quickly our time has gone."

"You shall never know how happy you have made me," I told him honestly.

"You know, Eviona," Jovan took my hand and held it as we walked, "I could make you happy all the time."

I felt it coming. Even though I had prepared myself, it wouldn't be easy to say the words. "Jovan," I stopped walking and looked at him in all seriousness. "I would only be like a bad debt to you, and you would end up hating me for all I took you away from."

"I could never hate you." He looked down as if to dismiss the thought.

I moved my hand under his chin and raised his head so I could look into his stormy eyes. "You know it is the truth. One day with your ambitions taken from you and your life no longer new you would come to despise me."

His eyes gazed at me with such intensity. "I want to take you away from this."

I died a little internally as I told him, "I will not have you."

His expression pained.

"If I do, in the end, you will not have me."

His tone escalated a pitch. "It is futile to try to talk to you. You always go back to these same arguments."

I softened my tone in response. "We both know I'm right."

He sighed and pulled me close, rested his forehead on mine, and placed his hands on my face. "Eviona, I don't have to be a soldier. I have other options."

I shook my head, "I know you too well, Jovan. You wanted this life far before you met me."

He sighed, "What can I say? What can I do?"

"Go become Captain Jovan. It is what you were meant to do."

He inhaled deeply and breathed out slowly. He

released me from his arms. We walked back to the house in silence with our hands clasped together. Then he kissed both of my palms, placed them together as if in prayer, and looked deeply into my eyes. "I have given you three chances. I have tried to be convincing each time, and yet you always come back to what you see is best for me."

I hugged him tightly for a long time and turned to leave him. I missed him the second I walked away, but I knew I had done the right thing. I prayed he would forget about me. I went to change into my serving attire and return the lovely dresses. As I held my own clothes, my breath seemed to stop. I cried into the rough cloth.

Tacit (v) unvoiced or unspoken

A long while passed before anything changed after my time with Jovan. Dyre never asked me what had happened. Thankfully, he left me alone with my regret.

He had been organizing something or maybe a few somethings. He dreamt constantly of his map. In those dreams I saw him adding to it, understanding it better and being led toward the time and place in which he needed to be. He'd found the place. A beautiful place. I wondered what would happen there.

In the times I could see he planned, wrote letters, made notes, and paced the floor with hopeful feelings.

I often found new foods to create in the kitchen. With any free time I had, I would take walks in the surrounding country to observe the many plants and creatures. In their shapes, I made cakes, breads, salads, and meats. My master, his many guests, and the other house workers were fascinated by my artwork, and I loved finding new things to create. One of my favorites was a salad made with silver beets. The rainbow colored chard made for a beautiful, coiling serpent. The scales were the hardest part because each scale held importance to me. It took me forever to perfect it and so little time for it to be devoured.

One day the headmistress of the house took me into her planning room.

"You need to prepare yourself to leave. You are being moved to another house."

"Have I done something which displeases the master?" I didn't want to leave. Jovan knew where to find me. For the first time since I left the children, I honestly wanted to stay in one place.

"A man approached our master. He has heard of your talents and wants you in his own kitchen."

"Isn't there some way to say no?"

"Please prepare yourself to leave." Her tone softened as she saw me struggle. She came to me and put her hand on my shoulder. "You have a gift. Many people will want to use your talents. You know our master loves what you do. This man offered to pay quite a high price for you." Tears surfaced in my eyes. She patted my shoulder and gently reminded me, "You had better prepare yourself to go. You leave in the morning."

I begged for her to find a way to keep me. She escorted me out the door and closed it without another word.

My heart sank. Jovan would have no idea where to find me, but I had no choice. I walked slowly down the hall to my room realizing I'd left my veil open. Dyre had seen the conversation. I placed my veil to block him out.

The next morning, I climbed into the carriage reluctantly and took a deep breath. It took several hours to reach the new house, evidently miles beyond anything else. I found it hard to believe anyone would want to live this far away from anybody or anything else. I watched out the window in hopes of spotting some creatures on the way or perhaps some beautiful countryside but felt too miserable. It might as well have all been grey.

Finally, I saw the incredible house. I'd never seen such a large structure and the country surrounding it reeked of wealth.

For the last half mile, the drive held huge statues alternating with gigantic fir trees. The courtyard housed a large fountain surrounded by patterned floral arrays.

The entryway of the house consisted of four great pillars and a porch with gigantic potted plants. I wondered why someone this rich would want to live so far away from any other society.

The coach drove to the rear of the house. Members of the staff greeted me and quickly showed me to my quarters. My room held four single beds, next to the kitchen of course. The sounds and smells of which comforted me. Beside each bed sat a trunk much the same as the last few houses I had been in. I soon found the staff to be quite large, but for an estate this size, there would have to be many people to keep it up. The size of the kitchen staff surprised me after I heard our new master would be a single man and did not plan to have many visitors. Even with all of the servants, I didn't feel we needed quite so many people to prepare the meals. I must admit I liked the idea of having more time to create my art.

I quickly learned not one person had met our new master. He had hired us all in the last few weeks and would be arriving for the first time in two days. I met my three roommates and delighted to see we were all close in age. Even though we had come together quickly, we became fast friends. We shared stories and laughed as we worked together.

Our conversations covered all sorts of subjects, but one subject came up more than I wanted. Dyre and Zefforah. People talked of seeing the beast and how ferocious she was. They talked of Dyre and his opinions of the kingdom and recruitment of men for his ranks. I shied away from the conversations.

The days flew, we had worked hard and when our new master arrived we were prepared. We came to the front of the house and formed a line in front of the pillars to greet him.

As he stepped out into the light of the morning, the surprise among us felt almost tangible. We had expected an older gentleman. Our master looked young. His strong build and square face emanated authority. His jet black hair and ice blue eyes struck me as more than simply handsome. His gaze met mine and he smiled slightly. I felt like he singled me out to stare at as he approached our line and began asking everyone's name. I couldn't help but feel an attraction to him. Easily the most handsome man I had ever seen, but something about him seemed to actually pull me to him.

As certain people introduced themselves, he knew their names and talents. A man named Bren caught his attention right off. He had been hired as a personal assistant and our master talked with him for some time before moving on. He also spoke with one gardener named Godin for several minutes. Evidently he had a great talent for sculpting plants. The master had hired him specifically to beautify a private garden.

As he came closer to me in line, I couldn't believe the incredible craving of my arms to reach out and touch him. I put them behind me and intertwined my fingers to keep myself in check. Servants cannot simply reach out to touch their masters.

When he came to me, he tipped his head as he had to the others. I nodded back to him, "Hello. I'm Eviona."

His dark eyebrows raised and his head tilted up a little with a slight smile. He spoke with a gruff voice and accent I hadn't heard before. It sounded like it hurt to talk, though his face showed no discomfort. "Ah, the food artist."

"I hope to please you with my creations."

"I am sure you will." He raised his hand. I felt like he would reach out to touch my face. The magnetic pull I sensed yearned for it and I found myself leaning forward a bit with anticipation. His hand instead went to his thick wavy hair, and he pushed his fingers through it.

I smiled at him, and he nodded to me. Though I put my head down, I felt his eyes on me.

When he finished hearing our names, he stood in front of us and raised his rough voice, "I am Marjeȧn. I hope you can find it in yourselves to address me as such. I have hired you for an undetermined amount of time. My life is unpredictable and busy. I will be here as often as I can, however, I will travel some as well. I require days of seclusion. On these days I wish no one to interrupt me. However, if you see me, I encourage your interaction and conversation is welcome. I do not tolerate deception or idleness. As I hired each of you, your past masters have vowed to me I will not see these traits in any of you. I hope to find this true, and I hope you will all be happy in your service here."

As he walked into the house, my body again leaned to him as if telling me to follow him. I wanted so badly to be near him. Instead, I squared my shoulders and focused on the work I needed to do.

I found myself reflecting on his speech. Easily the most interesting speech I had ever heard from a master. The other staff members also expressed how different he seemed than anyone they had worked for in the past.

We weren't surprised to hear he did not allow dishonesty or laziness. However, he had invited us all to converse freely with him, call him by name, and hoped we were happy.

Most masters didn't care how their staff felt, as long as his household ran as it should. Free discussion with one's master however, seemed too peculiar. They all felt precautious and weren't sure how to act around him. I, on the other hand, couldn't wait to be near him again.

The next week after picking vegetables in the garden I was hurrying through the hallway counting my carrots to see if I had enough for a particular dish I wanted to create when suddenly I bashed into something. Vegetables flew everywhere. My eyes grew in horror as I realized what I had hit. My master sat a few feet from me on the floor.

"Oh! I am truly sorry. Are you alright?"

He laughed and stood before I could even think. "It seems we were both lost in our own worlds for a minute." He saw my mortified face and his eyes looked into mine with incredible kindness. "But it's a good thing we ran into each other. I have been meaning to talk with you."

I quickly rose to my feet, not sure of my capability for forming complete words. "Me?" I frantically began to gather vegetables.

He helped me to pick up the items. "I have wanted to tell you I have been incredibly pleased every day as I am brought my meals. You fashion something wonderful for each one. It means a lot to me to know you take the pains you do." His speech slowed as he placed the last of the carrots into the basket. His voice turned as soft as I imagined he could manage with its hoarseness. "But I want you to know it isn't necessary to do for every meal, I don't want you to feel it a burden."

"It is never a burden. I immensely enjoy creating my little masterpieces."

He laughed quietly. "Humble, aren't you." He raised his eyebrows.

My eyes grew wide with embarrassment. "Oh," I stumbled backward, "I never meant," I caught myself from falling but still couldn't seem to find words.

"You do indeed create masterpieces. I didn't mean to cause you alarm." Again he raised his hand, and I found myself moving forward into his gravity. I felt such disappointment as his hand pushed his hair out of his face.

I tried simply to breathe. "Thank you for your help. Good day." I bobbed a curtsy.

He walked away from me. I wished he would look back and gasped in shock when it happened. I gave another little curtsy and waved awkwardly.

He returned to his retreat but turned again just before the end of the hallway to look at me. He paused for a very short moment and smiled before he turned the corner and vanished from my site. I took a deep breath and wondered if I would ever breathe regularly again. My hands shook, and my breath was shallow. I felt certain the emotions were strong enough to penetrate the veil and wondered why Dyre wasn't teasing me. That's when I realized he'd closed himself off pretty much since I'd come here.

That night my dreams were invaded by loud sobbing cries. I took me a while to fully wake before I realized where the sobbing came from, Zefforah. She had opened her veil, trying to connect with me. I'm sure she was alone. No wonder she felt depressed. Where in the world was Dyre?

I almost spoke to her until I heard one of my roommates wrestling with sleep and thought I had better not. But as I rubbed my arms trying to comfort her Zefforah gave me some impressions. Dyre had left her alone, but another impression felt so strong it almost hurt. Kellam. She missed Kellam.

The next morning Marjeàn gathered the staff shortly after his morning meal. His voice seemed more hoarse than usual, and I thought certainly it hurt him to speak. He looked as if he hadn't slept at all and he had hardly touched his food. He told us he needed to leave for a while. He did not know how long he would be gone. It could be a few days or perhaps several weeks. He wished for the house to be maintained as if he would be here because he would return as soon as he could.

Before he left he approached me, he said nothing as he did. I am sure everyone noted the shock on my face. He handed me a small box. I reached out my fingers to touch his as he gave it to me but he dropped them too quickly.

After he left, I opened the box while still in the hall with several of the other servants. It held a cage. In it, the hairiest, most hideous, and incredibly beautiful spider I'd ever seen. One girl saw it and screamed, another nearly fainted. I felt the opposite. I knew I could create a dish to look exactly like it and couldn't wait to lay my hands on some pasta. I could perfect the look of it by the time Marjeàn returned. He had given me a project. The irresistible anticipation tickled me. I dashed to the kitchen thanking him audibly as I ran.

Zefforah kept me from sleep for the next two nights. Her despondent crying crushed my heart. The impressions again told me she missed Dyre and Kellam.

On the third night, I decided to talk to her, but I didn't want to wake my roommates.

I wrapped a blanket around me, and took a walk around the grounds to see if talking to her could somehow make her feel better.

"Do you miss the children?"

She acknowledged she did, and I talked and told her stories of them ending with, "Now I am sure you miss the children."

She brayed softly.

"I know you miss Dyre too. Where is he?"

She huffed and hung her head.

"I know he misses you."

She shook her head.

"That's impossible, Zefforah. You know as well as I do how much Dyre loves you. I'm sure he will show up soon." I stroked my own arms hoping she would feel the comfort of it. I kept my voice calm. "Zefforah, Zefforah." I chanted her name and tried to be soft. It began to work.

She obviously missed Dyre. Why wouldn't he want her with him?

"I haven't seen Dyre for a while, but I know he is well. You know it too. He would never leave you alone without good reason."

My words comforted her. She found a comfortable position and folded her wings into her body.

"Zefforah, I know Dyre doesn't like it when we connect, but I wish you would do it anyway. I miss you."

Suddenly Dyre's voice came through loud and clear, it made both Zefforah and I jump. "She knows better than to connect with you."

I snapped at him, "Where have you been?"

"I had some things I needed to do without her."

"She has been miserable!"

"I am here now, you can leave."

Zefforah was jumping like a puppy when her master returns.

"Shut her out, Zefforah!" Dyre commanded and instantly she blocked me off. I could still see her through Dyre's eyes, but hers were closed to me.

"I'm glad she feels better. Now maybe I can sleep." I barked at him as I walked back into the house. "Zefforah knows she doesn't have to shut me out."

"I have given her strict commands to do exactly that. She will be punished for letting you in tonight."

"No! You can't do that. It's your fault she felt so bad.

She simply wanted some comfort."

"Why do you care?"

"She didn't do anything wrong."

"Go to bed, Eviona," Dyre commanded, and his veil closed.

Promulgate (v) to make known by open declaration

Marjeán returned after being gone for two weeks. On the evening he returned, I made my pasta dish in the shape of a large beautiful spider which I had worked on since his departure. I heard from the serving girls he had been delighted with it. Thrilled at being able to return his gift to me as a sort of gift to him, I wanted to talk to him. Perhaps to ask for more inspiration or simply to be near to him, but he never came down to the heart of the house, and I didn't dare explore past my boundaries.

His routine changed a bit upon his arrival. Each morning after his sunrise meal, he would go out for a ride on his horse. He would be gone most mornings at least until mid-day. He never missed a day of riding, even in poor weather.

Night often found me with Dyre. He would lie awake not speaking to me, but I felt him there. I never saw anything as his eyes were often closed, or stared at the sky, and sometimes the ceiling.

Sometimes, if I knew my roommates were asleep, I would to talk to him. "Why aren't you sleeping?" I whispered.

"I am waiting for you to go to sleep."

"We are both lying here watching each other not sleep?"

He chuckled. "Close your eyes."

I did and waited a moment before saying, "Alright, my eyes are closed, now what?"

He chuckled again and whispered, "Now go to sleep." He placed his veil, and I fell to sleep.

Again the staff had been called to a house meeting. We lined up in the foyer the way we had each time

Marjeàn went away for more than a day.

We knew the routine and the speech, but today seemed a bit different. As we entered and made our lines, he paced the floor, obviously deep in thought as we arranged ourselves. Once we all arrived, he stopped and took a breath as if he were unsure of what to do next. He looked extremely uncomfortable.

"Dear servants, I am in need of your help. I need a companion."

A very odd appeal. We looked at each other in wonder.

"I am used to having social interaction. Stimulating conversations protect the mind from deterioration. Currently, the only ones I am having are with myself. It's causing me to go mad." He glanced over our lines and looked at our shocked faces. "I know this is a very strange request. However, I have no time to go and find a companion to bring here with me so I am looking to you for help." He stopped to inhale deeply. "Are there any among you who have been educated?" He again looked down the line of us, and I couldn't help but think his eyes rested a bit longer on me. We all wondered what to do. Exasperated he said, "If any of you have had any education at all, please take a step forward."

I hesitantly took a step forward with five others. Marjeàn's face showed relief. He bowed his head and said, "Thank you."

He dismissed the others and looked very hard at the six of us standing there. He approached Bren, his personal assistant. "You may go, Bren. I have far too much for you to do otherwise."

Bren left, and Marjeàn stepped to the girl next to me, one of my roommates, a larger girl with a round, ruddy appearance and a mass of curly black hair. Normally she had a smile which stretched across her whole face, but in that moment she looked terrified.

"Do you read my dear?" Marjeån asked her in his rough, calming voice.

"Yes, sir."

"Would you like to read some books and discuss them with me?"

She stood silent, paralyzed. I wished I could help her. She took a long time with her reply and finally answered him with a question of her own. "Do you want me to be honest?"

Marjeån smiled and asked her gently, "Do you remember my rules?"

"Yes."

"Then you already know the answer to that question."

She smiled her huge smile and answered him honestly. "Sir...," she began and then remembered his other request. She started again, "Sir, Marjeån, sir, I don't want to discuss books with you." Her smile grew bigger. She clearly felt relieved.

"Then you shall not be made to do so," Marjeån said returning her smile. "You may go." She nearly ran out of the room.

I stood next in line. As he walked close to me, his hands moved behind his back. He held his left wrist with his right hand.

"Hello, Eviona." He addressed me sweetly, and my heart jumped knowing he still remembered my name. I nodded in reply. "Would you like to read some books and spend some time discussing them with me?"

How I longed to read a book. I missed my hours of study and learning. My urge to spend time with him felt just as great. "I would love to," I answered enthusiastically.

He raised his eyebrows, surprised at such an animated reply. He visibly made a mental note of my answer, asked me to tarry, and went on to ask the three remaining servants the same question.

The next in line stood one of the riders who carried our masters' letters, a very young man maybe still in his teens. He had a youthful glow to his skin. He declined quickly I think more because he didn't want to spend his time talking with a middle-aged man, but he looked at me and nodded after being dismissed as if letting me know he did it for me.

The head maid, Ginnie, declined the offer due to her busy schedule with the house.

That left one lone wrinkled and weathered gardener. He moved slowly and spoke the same way as if thinking about each word before it came out of his mouth. He responded to Marjeàn, "Yes siree, I would be keen on readin' some books. I would like to run through the meadows too, but that won't be happenin'." He smiled and tipped his chin up at me. "She is a might bit prettier than I am, even though I might be more knowledgeable. I think you would probably like talking to her." Then he leaned forward as if to tell Marjeàn a secret. "If I were you, son, I'd favor the girl."

Marjeàn smiled at him, leaned toward the old gardener and whispered, "Do you really think so?"

The wrinkles on the old man's face changed directions as he winked at me and then smiled at Marjeàn. I couldn't help but beam at him. At that, he started to walk out of the room in his slow and steady fashion.

My face suddenly felt quite flushed as Marjeàn and I were left alone in the room. He approached me, pulled a tiny book from his pocket and motioned for me to take it. He dropped his hand instantly after I had it as if he knew of my desire to reach out and touch him. His hands realigned behind his back and stayed there.

The book felt small and thin in my hand. I did not look down to examine it however, because of my intense awareness of the way Marjeàn looked at me. I intentionally never lost eye contact so he wouldn't know of my uneasiness, but I wondered if he could tell anyway.

"Is it possible to have this book read by the day after tomorrow?" He asked in his raspy accent.

"Yes, I am certain of it." I was sure. It felt very small, like it had only a few pages.

"At mid-day I shall meet you in the garden. We will take a walk and discuss what you have read." He stood still and looked at me for an instant. I so wanted to touch his face, his hair, his hands. At the moment I lost all control, he turned and left me alone in the large foyer.

I looked at the book and knew it in an instant. I had begged Minuette to read to me as a child. I caressed the cover and read the title 'To Be One.' The letters had been engrained in my mind in a way I could never explain, although before this moment I had no idea what they said.

I knew I would enjoy reading this book, and I hated Minuette all over again for depriving me of such a treasure.

Retrospection (n) the action of looking back on things past

I intently examined my small book when Minuette came. I had found it in the rubble of the house and every time I raised my courage enough, I would ask her to read it to me. She seemed to find delight in teasing me with it. I wore the letters to soft grey lines caressing my fingers over the pages so often. I wanted so desperately to know what the words on its cover meant, and maybe its story. Was it a story? Maybe a poem. I simply wanted to know the title. I wouldn't ask her to read it to me today, but I would be brave again and ask her to tell me at least the title.

It had rained earlier, and when she came in, she looked cross and wet. Today would not be a good day to ask her for anything. I hid the little book behind my back. She looked at me with contempt as she noticed my concealment. Before even stopping to shake off her coat she grabbed me.

"Show me what you are hiding!"

I pulled out the little book, and she tore it from my hands with a shriek.

"This book! You want to know what this book says?" She screeched at me.

I kept my head down as I nodded. I knew by her tone she wouldn't tell me anything.

"This book says you are a stupid, ugly, horrible little monster!" Then she threw it to the other side of the small room. She took deep breaths as she paced the floor the way she always did when she grew angry, and I knew not to say anything. I stood not daring to utter a word. Hoping she would forget me. Maybe if I stood still enough, I would somehow disappear into the wall. She shook her head at me and balled her fists until they shook as well.

"I must teach you some manners." She barked.

From her bag, she drew a long leather strap. I had never seen it before.

"Turn around!" She yelled at me.

I shook my head and closed my eyes praying she would go away.

"Turn around!" The volume and strength of her words forced me to do as she commanded.

I turned. I had no idea what to prepare for. I heard a crack and then the most excruciating pain I had ever felt cut across my back.

"AAAHHHH!" Zefforah and Dyre yelled with me. Dyre shouted at me, "Demon! What are you doing?"

Minuette's strap hit me again. This time I knew to brace myself for the worst of it, but I still cried out in pain.

Dyre must have guessed at the situation. "Tell her to stop, you idiot!"

I only shook and stayed as silent as I could muster. She whipped me with only a few more stripes; enough to leave my little body in ruins and my spirit broken yet again.

Dyre raged, both at Minuette and me. I had deep cuts in my back. She told me I would be even uglier now. She didn't stay long with me that day. I hated and feared her even worse than before.

Once she unloaded the few supplies she had brought for me she left to return home.

Dyre waited for her seething the whole time. He normally would have shut me out but that day was different.

As soon as he saw her come in, he began to unbutton his shirt and berated her. "If you ever touch that wretched girl again, I swear I will kill you."

Minuette looked surprised but countered defensively, "She needed to learn a lesson!"

Dyre raised his voice above hers. "Maybe I should teach you a lesson!" His hand came up to strike her. Minuette backed away from him in shock.

I whimpered. I didn't want to see this I didn't know why he would allow me. He stopped, "Don't you want me to hit her?"

"No," I cried softly, "I really don't."

Minuette looked hopeful thinking he might have stopped.

"Well, I want to!" He slapped her hard across her face knocking her to the ground. He turned his back on her as she cried out.

He removed his shirt, and I heard her gasp. "What happened to you?"

He turned around to bark at her face, "You did this to me, you vile woman!" I felt his anger pulse through my veins. "Don't touch the girl again!"

For the first time, it felt like we had an emotional connection. Whether he did it because of his wounds or mine didn't matter. He retaliated against my captor and let me watch as he did, I think as a kind of gift.

Amity (n) friendliness or good relations

I escaped to my empty room and devoured the small book. It held a simple fairytale about a tiny elfin princess who had fallen in love with a giant. They loved powerfully and beautifully, yet in no way could they be together. In the end, the giant had been killed by the people and the princess mourned so greatly the gods allowed her to be with him. His giant body turned into a mountain, and she forever stayed with him in the heart of it.

It took me very little time to read. I promised myself I would read it again before returning it to Marjeàn. I loved the charming story and felt gratified to have finally read it.

I had enough time to make something easy as part of Marjeàn's evening meal. I made perfect little white mice as a gesture of spite to the past. When I presented them to the serving girl to put on the tray for Marjeàn, she jumped away with a shriek. I loved it.

After the mid-day meal as we cleaned up the kitchen the door opened and silence rushed through the room. Marjeàn walked in with his eyes searching until he saw me. "Eviona, may I speak with you for a moment?" He gestured for me to join him in the hall.

I wiped off my hands and quickly retreated to the hallway with the shocked eyes of the rest of the servants burning holes in my back.

"Eviona." His tone sounded urgent as if he were concerned about me. "Why are you not reading your book?"

"I am finished with it, Sir." I kept my hands busy wiping them in my apron.

He looked at me tenderly. And his gruff voice pleaded. "Please call me Marjeàn."

I restated myself. "I am finished with it," I paused and felt slightly uncomfortable saying his name. "Marjeȧn."

He smiled and continued with his question. "How can that be? Every meal I've had, my table has held your work. When have you had time to read?"

"The book you gave me is a child's story really. It took very little time to read."

"Good." He nodded and wanted to say something more.

I dropped my apron and flattened it repeatedly. I knew if he stood there in front of me for too much longer I would lose control and reach out to touch him. "Is there anything else?"

"No, but I wish I would have scheduled our visit for today. I feel like I am wasting time I could have spent with you."

I uttered my shock. "Sir?"

He seemed to realize what he said, "I simply miss conversing. I am looking forward to having a real conversation."

"I see," I said a bit disappointed that his urgency to spend time with me was purely for lack of something better to do.

He nodded, "Alright then. I will see you tomorrow afternoon."

"Yes, tomorrow."

He walked away slowly, and I realized that his hands were clenched behind his back again, the left hand holding the right wrist. It seemed the natural thing for his hands to do. Perhaps I could discipline myself to do something similar with mine. Before he turned a corner to slip out of sight, he shifted and looked at me one last time melting me with his gaze.

Anxious for the morrow to come, I barely slept.

Dyre broke the silence of the night, "Eviona, you aren't sleeping again."

"Neither are you."

"Yes, but I have a lot on my mind. What have you to worry about? Whether or not someone will be eating flower or bird-shaped fruit for supper."

"Do you remember that book I used to carry around?"

"The tiny one Minuette tore to shreds? What about it?"

"I finally read it."

"I am truly happy for you."

I had expected him to mock me. "Thank you," I said with surprise.

"Was it as wonderful as you wished?"

"The only thing which could have made it more wonderful is if I could have read it as a child." Then I thought for a moment. "Or you! You could have read it to me through my eyes."

"I should have." It almost felt like an apology.

"Oh well," I whispered.

Dyre sighed. "Now you need to go to sleep." He hummed a slow melody. His voice caressed the notes exquisitely. I'd never heard him sing before.

"You sing beautifully."

He said nothing. He merely resumed his humming. I fell asleep to a voice I once believed would never truly comfort me.

The next afternoon I couldn't stand still. I felt all sorts of anxiety I didn't expect. What if I couldn't make intelligent enough conversation? How could I keep my hands to myself for the whole time I'd be with him? Would he quickly grow bored with me? I walked rapidly through the rows between the bushes of the garden, until I heard him approach.

"Here you are." His hoarse but calm voice put me a bit at ease. He gestured suggesting we walk out in the meadows beyond the gardens. I followed him as he moved and noted again how he placed his hands behind his back. "So, how did you find the book?"

"I couldn't have hoped for it to be any more delightful."

He chuckled slightly, "You sound as if you have wanted to read it your entire life."

"How close to the truth that is." I wrung my hands as we walked doing everything I could to keep them to myself. I separated them to look more natural, but found myself more under control if they held each other. "As a little girl I knew this book and always wanted to read it." I pulled it out of my apron pocket. "I didn't learn how to read until much later."

"Well, I am glad to have given you the opportunity."

I nudged the book toward him to make sure he would know I would give the books back.

He glanced down at my offering. "You may keep this one if you like."

"Thank you," I said, elated. I placed it back into my pocket and patted it with my hand. "I will treasure it. I assure you."

"Would you like to read another one?"

"Wait, you said you would like to discuss the books with me."

"Yes, well, I tested you with this one. I wanted to see if you really could read, or if you simply wanted to take long walks with me."

When I realized his joke, I felt embarrassed. "I don't mind walking, but I truly love to read. Even though I became a teacher for a while, I still have an incredible desire to learn more."

"You were a teacher? You should have been first to step forward when I asked."

"I don't think any of us knew what to think at such an odd request."

"Is it odd for me to need company?"

"No, but it is odd for you to choose a servant be that company."

"Perhaps you could think of me as a fellow servant," he suggested.

I laughed, "I could more easily think of you as a teacher."

He jumped on that thought. "Then I shall be your teacher. What do you want to know?"

"Everything!" I stopped and looked at him as I said it maybe a little too eagerly.

He scrutinized my face. "That one may take a while. Why don't we start with something a bit less complicated, how about animals?" I must have been beaming at him because he turned to face me and laughed. "I thought you might like that. Perhaps you can find some inspiration for your great masterpieces."

"I would love it! Do you have a book with pictures?"

"Here I thought you could read." He teased me. "Let's walk to the house. I have just the book for you."

When we arrived in the library, I found he had already pulled a thick book with many pictures and all sorts of information about a multitude of animals from his shelves, as if he had anticipated our conversation. I sat down and opened its pages. I wanted to consume it right then.

I jumped up and asked, "May I take it to my room?"

"Right now? What happened to my hopes of companionship?"

I smiled humbly and sat down again. "I am sorry, I

forgot."

"That's alright." Marjeàn seemed pleased at my delight with it. "Do you think you could put the book down for a few moments tomorrow afternoon to spend some time with me?"

"Done!" I said, excited at the thought I might be able to read before preparations for the evening meal began.

"Then I will see you tomorrow."

"Thank you." He smiled as I danced out of the room with my new treasure.

That night I wanted to keep reading so I found a candle and read by the light of it. Dyre came into my mind late, after everyone else slept. "What are you doing?"

"Will you look at this?" I pointed to a picture of an exotic creature on the page. "It's amazing! Don't you think?"

"It's only an animal."

"Well, I think it is beautiful. I can't wait to try to make some of these." I said flipping through the pages showing him different pictures.

"Were you thinking about sleeping tonight?"

"No, not until this candle won't give me any more light."

"Stupid girl."

"Getting smarter." I sang back to him.

"Goodnight, stupid girl," he replied with a chuckle.

"Goodnight," I sang again.

He smirked and was gone.

The next day I found Marjeàn waiting for me in the garden.

We walked as we talked about all of the animals that I had learned about. I had to remind myself about my hands often, because as I spoke I animated with my hands as I explained things, and I often found them drawn into his magnetic pull.

He didn't say much. He let me talk on and on about all of the things I had learned. He smiled at me frequently and sometimes when I looked at him I wondered if he really heard the words I spoke or simply watched my mouth move.

When we returned to the house, he led me toward the library. We entered the large room, and he handed me a book from the table.

"I'm not finished with the one I have yet," I admitted.

"I didn't think you would finish it all in one day, but you can use it for inspiration anytime. This one has stories. Read what you can tonight and we shall discuss it tomorrow."

I looked down at the book in my hands.

He said, "Don't worry about the kitchen. I would rather talk to you than have mice as part of my meals."

I concealed a growing smile. "I will gladly start to read it as soon as I can."

"Which reminds me," he said as he turned to begin walking again, "you should read in the library. I am sure the servant's quarters do not have adequate lighting."

Firmament (n) the vault of heaven, sky

Winter came with its flash storms and Marjeȧn only left the house for his morning rides. Sometimes when the snow was too high or the storm too ferocious he would still go, but instead of forcing a poor horse to battle the weather he'd go on foot.

I felt guilty as I spent less and less time with the servants and spent most of my time either reading in the library or talking with Marjeȧn. A room in the upper floor of the house held a large fireplace and on the opposite wall an even larger picture window, during the winter it became my favorite place to meet with Marjeȧn and have our daily discussions.

I thought we must look amusing with our hands so obviously being kept to ourselves. I wondered if he struggled with thoughts of reaching out to me the same way I constantly wanted to touch him.

Every once in a while, he would ask me to do something out of the ordinary. Like the day he asked me to take a nap in place of our afternoon talk, and then meet him after dark in the garden. I did as he asked, but could not rest in the afternoon. I felt certain the other servants were talking about me and yet uncertain of why Marjeȧn would like to talk to me at night. With no way to escape the busyness in my mind, I could not relax.

As the evening approached, I prayed the sun would move faster in the sky. When it finally set, I waited for the darkness of night to settle. The hours felt like days until I thought it might be late enough to go to the garden.

Sitting near a huge bonfire he reclined in a chair with gloved hands behind his head, and a blanket covering his legs. I forced my feet to walk toward him instead of the sprint they begged for. As I came closer, he must have felt my presence behind him.

"Thank you for coming." He said without standing or glancing in my direction.

"I have to confess I am very confused."

Although his position remained constant, his head jerked toward me a bit. "Confused?"

"Why are we meeting in the evening, outside, in the middle of winter?" I came around to face him.

He smiled and pointed to a blanket near him which I wrapped around me over my thick coat. Then he gestured upward. "I simply wanted to enjoy the heavens with you."

I followed the movement of his hand to look upward. I had watched the evening sky through Dyre's eyes but had never regarded it as something to enjoy. My eyes had a different desire and turned to Marjeɑn. He immersed himself in his survey.

"As a child, the night sky held my solace." He stared up as if gazing at an old friend. "I could examine it for hours and escape in the search. Sometimes I could convince my mind to imagine myself right in the heart of it."

I peeked at it again. The night sky and I should be old friends, but before this moment I had never been inclined to notice it. Now, with the stars in his eyes, I found my need for Marjeɑn's attentions reason enough to take notice. I attempted to see it through his perspective.

The moon, though only half full, shone brightly and seemed to cast an iridescent glow on everything, especially the snow. I liked that.

I inspected the brighter lights, and then noticed softer ones, and more even smaller than those. The longer I investigated, the more stars seemed to appear until their magnitude became immense; an eternity of lights creating shapes and pictures.

Some of the stars flickered as if winking at me. I saw a small streak of light and wondered what it could be and where it would go. Slowly, instead of the small dots they had been just moments earlier, the glimmers of the heavens evolved into something incredible.

Marjeȧn brought me back to earth, "Do you like it?"

A bit embarrassed to have my heart beating so madly at the sound of his voice, I nodded. "Um hm."

I fixed my focus on the brilliance of the heavens in Marjeȧn's eyes and listened to his voice sigh. "I love the stars." He tore his eyes from them long enough to smile at me.

I blushed with how deeply I had been gazing into his enchanting eyes and looked up momentarily. "Thank you for sharing this with me. It is truly beautiful."

He smiled wider and whispered, "I agree." He said it as if he were agreeing with me about the stars, but raised his eyebrows at me as if he were saying it about me.

Without my permission, my feet took a step toward him. My fingertips tingled with a familiar anticipation. "I think I should go."

"So soon?" He stood and gestured to a nearby seat. "No, please sit."

At his reaction, I was silently grateful for the cold which gave an excuse to the quivering of my lips. "Honestly, I didn't sleep this afternoon. I'm very tired now, and cold."

"Go ahead." He motioned his chin toward the house to dismiss me.

"Are you coming inside?" I asked. "I'll walk back with you."

"No," He sat and relaxed into his former position of reclining with his hands behind his head. "I am going to stay out here for a while."

I walked quickly back to the house, shut the door between us and leaned against it. "You have to stop." I reprimanded my heart for its intense beating. On the way back to my room I smiled and bit my lip with the memories of his gaze at me and fell asleep utterly giddy.

Early in the spring, before the snow had even fully melted Marjeàn called the staff together.

"I will be leaving for a while. I wish for the house to be maintained as if I were here. Bren, I expect anything out of the ordinary to be reported promptly at my return. Godin, please carry on with your work in the garden. Ginnie ..." He went on with the same instructions he'd given before each time he left.

"Eviona?" He called to me after dismissing us.

My roommates eyed me as they departed, and my heartbeat ran wild as I approached Marjeàn. Each time he left he assigned me new books to read as if he really was my teacher.

As I closed the distance between us, I folded my hands in front of me and leaned in as his hand reached up moving through his hair and then back to the common position behind his back.

"Will you find some time to read while I am away?" He raised his eyebrows chastising me for my lack of doing so during his past departures.

"When you first came you asked us not to be idle. I feel wrong taking time away from my duties when you are not here to converse with."

He laughed, "Education is never idleness." He looked out the window. "I would take you with me if I could."

I pressed my lips together hard and prayed for the butterflies in my stomach to calm.

He seemed to hear the echo of what he had said. "The long rides to and from the house would be far more productive if spent in conversation rather than idleness."

I would have told him I would love to go with him, but never had the chance. Before I knew it he'd rushed away, leaving me with my lips still quivering, my hands clenched together, and my body leaning in the direction I had last seen him, begging for his attention.

Each time he went away I resumed my work in the kitchen with the other servants. Dyre's name seemed a constant buzz in the air. This time, after Marjeàn had been gone for a few days, a cry of an attack on the castle rang through the house. My heart beat too quickly in my chest as I listened to the reports. I stayed silent as the other servants speculated about the news. Never lending my opinions, or letting them know of the obvious lies. My heart fell at the thought of Dyre's destiny and how Sylvaria might change over the next few years.

The next time Dyre's veil dropped as I lay in the darkness of the night I spoke. "I've heard your name a lot lately."

"Really?" He sounded flattered.

"They said Zefforah and her fire-breathing abilities set the castle ablaze."

Loud laughter broke the still of the night. "They think she breathes fire? That's wonderful! We used a catapult."

"So you've started."

"I only want to nudge the king a bit. Let him know I'm as serious as the rumors paint me to be."

"I wish you hadn't done it."

"You know this is what I am supposed to do. Are you surprised?"

"You don't have to do it. Sylvaria has a good king, and you have a good life."

His mood shifted. "You know nothing about my

life." His rough words left me unsettled as his veil closed.

"Don't be foolish." I pleaded as I closed my eyes.

Vie (v) to compete

I hadn't heard of his arrival that morning, but as I headed to gather vegetables, I saw Marjeàn sitting at a small table in the flower garden. I debated about approaching him, but my feet ran before my head could decide on the action. I felt ridiculous when I reached him, panting and eager. "Have you been waiting for me?"

"No." He laughed. "It's nice to have a pretty girl running after me though."

I blushed my embarrassment as I caught my breath and begged my heart to slow its pace.

He laughed heartily as he gestured to the chair opposite him. "Please sit."

"What would you like to talk about?"

Marjeàn's eyes seems to sparkle as he asked, "I understand it is considered a man's game but by any chance do you play cards?"

"Are you a poor loser?" I eyed him as I asked.

He smiled dealt the cards.

Dyre and Horrish played this particular game on long winter days. Dyre could pick two cards and make it look like only one and then discard two just as easily. I always saw it of course, but Horrish never caught onto his cheating. When they had a wager, Dyre always won. Horrish never quit playing the game with him, but he did stop placing bets with Dyre.

As I picked up my cards, I noticed their beauty. The faces resembled flowers and trees. "These are beautiful."

"I purchased them near a garden with each of these flowers, it's a beautiful place."

I took my first turn. "Since you travel so much you must see many beautiful places."

He glanced at me. "There is no place as beautiful as a

sincere smile at my coming home."

I avoided his eyes as my stomach filled with butterflies and tried to make light of his comment. "Now you are simply trying to distract me."

"Is it working?"

I cleared my throat and focused only on the game until I won too easily. I wondered if he had allowed me to win and I called him on it. "Did you throw that game?"

"Why would I do such a thing?"

"Because I am a girl and you have no confidence I could win on my own."

A small smirk crossed his face. "Perhaps I didn't play as well as I normally would have."

"Exactly as I suspected." I raised my eyebrows accusingly.

His smirk transformed into a stunning full teeth smile. "If that is the way you want to play I am prepared to do so."

Although a very close game, he won the next round. He visibly enjoyed my competitive spirit.

"That's one each," I said.

He laughed, "What if we go best of three?"

"Then one more for a winner."

He shuffled the cards and dealt. As I picked up my hand, I couldn't believe my good fortune. I had almost won with the cards I already held. If luck smiled on me, I would win very easily.

"You must have a good hand." His eyes were down when I looked at him, but he had obviously read my face.

"I do," I smiled and took the first turn. "What shall you give me if I win?"

With his head down his eyes shot up at me. Their icy

color shone through his long dark eyelashes. "What would you like?"

I didn't expect a comeback in the form of a question. "I don't know." I laughed in response.

A serious expression grew on his face. His eyes moved to look directly into mine, and his voice declined into a whisper, "If I could I would pick the stars from the heavens to give you."

Chills raced down my arms. I swallowed hard and dropped my eyes. "Oh." My memory of his gaze into the night sky left me speechless.

His eyes released me as he looked back at his cards with a slight smile on his face. We sat motionless for a moment until he stated, "It's your turn."

"Oh, is it?" I quickly took a turn, grateful to have the cards in front of me to focus on.

Only the sounds of our arms moving and the breeze roaming through the grass broke the silence.

A few minutes later Marjeàn asked his own question. "What are you willing to give me if I win?" He didn't look at me. I think to lessen the discomfort he knew I felt.

My heart. I thought the words and felt myself blush. "What do I have?"

"I'm sure you could think of something." The seriousness had vanished from his face and voice, but I still felt the influence of the words he had spoken only moments earlier.

I took my turn and had won again. I looked up to him and smiled as I placed my cards on the table for him to observe.

"I'd better find my ladder." As he smiled at me, I wondered if there had ever been a more beautiful man than the way he looked at that moment.

"What if we play to five?" I offered.

"That sounds like a good plan."

I have no idea how, but Marjeån won the next two hands, the last one by sheer luck. At least that is what I told him. Although I believe he might have cheated.

"May I take the cards for a moment?" I asked as he stood.

He sat back down and placed them on the table. I took the cards and shuffled them awkwardly. It had been a long time since I last played with Kellam, I felt like my hands should remember better than they did. After a few tries, it felt more natural.

"I used to know a card trick. Would you like to see it?"

Marjeån's eyes lit up in amusement. "Yes."

I shuffled one more time, and I played the trick I had watched Dyre perform so many times. Being unpracticed it didn't go as smoothly as I would have liked, but Marjeån watched me with a charming smile.

"Will you meet me again tomorrow afternoon?"

I continued to play with the cards as we walked back to the house, grateful to have them to occupy my hands.

"I'm afraid I am not doing a very good job in the kitchen. Even though tonight's dinner will taste appetizing I'm sure, I have not done anything to help prepare it. I feel like I am letting the other servants down when I spend time with you."

"Do I not have enough staff to allow you time with me?"

"The staff is a good size."

"Then I will change your job title. For as much as I love eating your creations, my time with you is much more valuable."

I smiled and offered him the cards, knowing if he took them from my hands at least our fingers would touch.

He casually offered, "They're yours."

"I couldn't take them. Really." I would have loved to keep them, but my ache for his touch pressed me to plead to give them back.

He stopped walking and stood staring at the cards in my open hand. His eyes moved to mine. His hands shifted from their normal position at his back to resting at his side.

My heartbeat quickened as we both stood motionless. His hand rose toward mine, and he pressed the deck into my palm. "Please keep them."

His hand removed too quickly. My fingers closed around the cards, but I missed the opportunity of touching him by only a moment.

His hands moved again behind his back he bowed from the waist and left me.

Stelliferous (adj) full of stars

The next morning Bren, Marjeån's personal assistant, came to find me. Marjeån had asked to speak with me before he left for his ride. I hurried to his dinette.

He looked up as I walked into the room, "Ah, there you are, Eviona." He dabbed his face with his napkin and looked up at me. "Today will you meet me in my bedroom? I have something I want to show you."

My mind raced. I feared I had misinterpreted what my role in our new situation would be. I froze. I wanted to be close to him, but I wouldn't do that.

"Eviona," his face grew concerned, "You look like you might be getting ill."

I had to tell him the truth, which is what he said in the beginning he wanted. "I will not be a hired woman for you."

He choked on the water he sipped. "Oh, my stars! Is that what you thought I wanted you for?"

I nodded my reply.

"I apologize for the thought to even have come to your mind. I promise I will never ask you to do anything you do not wish to do."

I remained silent, but gratefully so.

"I have something to show you, I had hoped not to move it, but if you wish, I shall bring it out for you to see. We could meet in the library. Would that be better for you?"

Relieved I gave an appreciative nod.

"I will see you later then, in the library."

That afternoon found me too anxious to sit, I waited for Marjeån walking around his library, pulling different books from the shelves and making mental notes of new ones I would like to read.

"Hello, Eviona." He stood at the window across the

room from the door. I wondered how long he had been there watching me.

"Hello." I felt self-conscious. "I enjoy your library."

"I'd allow you to live in it if you would like."

I blushed and looked away to hide.

"Would you like to see what I have to show you?"

I nodded, and he gestured for me to follow.

We walked together down several hallways until we entered a large hall where a large tapestry waited for examination. Its size completely filled the huge wall. I approached it, knowing full well the pictures would be distorted into tiny dots. I simply wanted to touch it. I put my hand out and looked at Marjeàn almost expecting Lady Delsa's voice to come out of his mouth and stop me.

He nodded to me as if he knew I wanted his permission to handle it. His gaze melted my insides and it took all my willpower to refocus on the tapestry. Pleased to know he trusted me I reached my hand forward and caressed it gently letting each of my fingertips have a turn at its beauty. Marjeàn said nothing as I did.

As I backed away, I realized it showed more than a simple picture. It read more like a story. Only the words were stars, planets, and other heavenly beings. Other than its bright background it very much reminded me of the sky on the night Marjeàn had shared it with me that winter. As I looked at it, I could swear I saw stars twinkle at me. I easily fell entranced into it.

"Do you like it then?" Marjeàn's voice suddenly woke me from the vision I had become spellbound by.

"Isn't it the loveliest thing you have ever seen?" I asked.

"No, not the loveliest." His eyes intently gazed at me. "But I do agree it is quite lovely."

"I am amazed someone had the patience to make such an incredible work of art."

"You make wonderful art all of the time. Surely those little masterpieces take much time." He teased me by stressing the word 'masterpieces.'

"That's different. What I do, I learned out of boredom. This, well, this is exceptional."

He looked thoughtfully at me as I turned my attention back to the tapestry. "This is the closest I could come to your payment."

"But I didn't win." I reminded him.

"You won that hand." He smiled at me and walked around me to look at it more closely. "But since I won the five I guess it will be placed back into my room this evening." His eyes sparkled and told me he had no intention of giving it up.

I walked towards it to one more time stroke the texture of it. I caressed its surface with my eyes closed and imagined myself instead caressing Marjeån's face.

"I would like to change things with you even more than I already have. Do you think you would mind?"

I opened my eyes and turned to stare into his. "I don't know. What is it you want to change?"

"I don't want to make you uncomfortable, but over the last few months I have truly come to see you as a companion, I would like for you to take a room upstairs and act as a guest in my house instead of staying in the servant's quarters."

I breathed a small sigh of relief. "Actually, I think it might make me feel a little more comfortable. The other servants, though they are all still very sweet to me, already act as if I am not one of them when you are home."

"I am sorry to have caused you any discomfort." He

looked tenderly at me. "I would very much enjoy having you as my guest."

"I am grateful to you, Marjeàn. I think I would like that arrangement."

"Then let us make the changes. I have a room for you. Go and gather your things, I will have Bren show you there as soon as you are ready. Then I shall come and find you for the evening meal."

I froze in disbelief as he walked from the room. He had clearly planned this far before today.

Bren took me to a large room upstairs. For the first time, I had a room to myself. Other than the one Minuette used to keep me in, but that prison didn't count as a room. This seemed even more beautiful than the one I had shared with Sanura at Aunt Delsa's house.

If I had ever wondered what it would be like to sleep on a cloud, I had the feeling I would find out in that bed. A huge fireplace took up the bulk of one corner. The focal point, however, would have to have been the window. I was drawn to it as it oversaw the beautiful gardens Marjeàn and I often walked in. I had an amazing perspective. I didn't think the gardens could be any more beautiful than when we walked through them, but the view from my room proved me wrong.

I loved seeing the climbing vines dress the garden wall, the lanes filled with beautiful flowers and shrubs which grew in colorful patterns.

Those interesting blue roses lined every edge. I noticed several things from this perspective and wondered how I could have missed them before.

A knock came to the door. I opened it to find a small crew bringing in a large chest. When they left, I opened it to find it full of beautiful clothing. I unpacked the trunk and filled the wardrobe. I loved every dress as if I had picked them out myself.

For someone who had only known me a short amount of time Marjeån seemed to be able to read my mind. I loved his kindness and generosity. I had fallen in love with him, and I believed he was falling in love with me. As I worked, a familiar voice interrupted my thoughts.

"Wow, look at you. How did you accomplish this? Thievery? Deception? Extortion?"

"Dyre," I said, legitimately happy to hear from him. "You haven't been around much lately." I moved around the room to allow him to observe it more closely.

"I've been busy. But you, you have been busy too."

"I'm in heaven," I said as I sat down, put up my arms and fell down backward onto the bed.

He took a minute to process everything I felt. "So, how do you find yourself here then?"

I couldn't resist, "I do believe someone is falling in love with me."

He smirked, "Who could fall in love with a troll like you?"

"Oh Dyre, not even you can ruin my happiness today." I smiled, and I felt his mood change as he smiled with me.

"So, does this love of yours have a name?"

"His name is Marjeån," I said it with all the tenderness I felt.

After a long pause, he asked seriously, "Do you love him?"

I paused, uncomfortable admitting it aloud. "It's still so new."

"What about Jovan? I thought you loved him."

My heart beat quicker at the mention of his name. "I do love Jovan. Is it possible to love two people at once?" I had asked myself the question many times.

Dyre hesitated. I couldn't tell what he thought, but I felt his heavy heartbeat.

"Dyre? Are you angry with me?"

His hand gathered into a fist as his veil closed.

Because of the way he said it I wondered what he thought. Was he trying to protect me? Or was this like before with Jovan? Perhaps he simply didn't like anyone else to be a part of my life. I couldn't put my finger on it.

"I don't care what you think, Dyre," I whispered defiantly. I wished I didn't place so much value on his opinion. I hoped he didn't know I did.

A knock came to the door, and I rushed to answer it. I found Ginnie, the head maid, standing on the other side. "Hello Eviona, it looks like you are now the lady of the house."

I giggled and invited her in. "What if I had never learned to read? It might have been you setting up yourself in this room."

She smiled and shook her head at me. "No, my dear, Marjeàn has had his eye on you from the first day. If not books he would have found another way to spend time with you."

I felt self-conscious at her comment, but asked her what I had been wondering for days, "Ginnie, do the other servants hate me?"

"Not one." Her swift reply helped me feel her sincerity. "There are a few of us who are worried about you though."

"Why?"

"There are things about our master which some of us have been talking about," she whispered.

Marjeàn cleared his throat to announce his presence. Ginnie jumped, visibly startled. "If you need anything Eviona, let me know." She skirted around Marjeàn in the doorway to go, deliberately dropping her eyes.

Marjeán glared at Ginnie as she ran down the hall.

"This room is incredible," I said. "Do you know I can see the whole garden from here?"

His focus shifted from Ginnie to me, and his countenance turned from harsh to gentle. "Which is your favorite flower? I will see to it there are more of them."

"I don't know if there could be any more of them. The blue roses seem to line the whole thing."

"They are the color of your eyes." The intensity of his expression overwhelmed me, and I had to lower my gaze until I could think again. I noticed my dress. "I'm sorry I have been enjoying your gifts and haven't changed my clothes for the evening meal."

"I will be happy to have you come with me in what you are currently wearing."

"Then I'm ready. Shall we?"

Truculent (adj) fierce, cruel, brutally harsh

The next day I enjoyed trying on my new dresses and loved each one of them. I found a great deal of pleasure in feeling elegant again. I wanted to read in the garden before Marjeàn came home from his morning ride.

I found a good bit of shade covering one of the benches there and sat down with my book.

"You look beautiful, Eviona."

I jumped at the sound of his voice and stood to speak with him. "Marjeàn, I thought you would be riding."

"I must go away for a while. I wanted to say goodbye."

I nodded my understanding. "How long will you be gone?"

He smirked as if my disappointment pleased him. "I promise to come back as soon as I can. Would you like me to bring you something?"

I wished I could ask him to touch me. How would one phrase such a request? "I can't think of one more thing you could give me."

"Then I will have to expose you to more of the world so you may tell me what you want."

"You are too generous with me, Sir." He raised his eyebrows at me, and I corrected myself with a shy smile. "Marjeàn."

"Goodbye, Eviona."

"Goodbye." My eyes connected with his, silently pleading for him to touch me. My body moved forward as the hands he usually kept behind his back fell to his sides. Please touch me. I begged the unspoken supplication.

Eternity passed as the distance between us closed.

The crash of tools sounded in the distance. I turned to see Godin the gardener picking himself up from where he must have fallen. Inaudibly his lips formed curses as he picked up the various items he'd dropped. When I turned back to Marjeȧn, his hands were once again clasped behind his back. He bowed slightly and walked away.

As I heard the horse retreating from the house, I stared blankly at the page in front of me. My thoughts lost in the memory of his eyes, his mouth, his shoulders, and chest. I berated myself again and again for not reaching out to him. Even simply to take his hand.

"Eviona." I looked up to Godin and the sun behind him blinded me. My shade had all but disappeared. How long had I been there lost in my thoughts?

"Godin, how are you?"

"Do you have a moment?" His tone seemed pleasant enough, but his face looked very serious.

"What is the matter?"

"Will you walk with me?" He gestured towards the other side of the house.

"Certainly." I stood and walked next to him letting him guide me.

"You are aware our master has a private garden."

"Yes."

"He has been very specific about its contents."

"Yes, I remember."

"There is something in it I wish to show you."

I slowed to a stop. It didn't feel right to invade Marjeȧn's private space. When Godin realized I no longer walked next to him, he paused to look back at me. "Please, Eviona." He motioned toward me his voice pleading. "We all know you are falling in love with him. He seems like a good man, but there are things about him which you should know."

I shifted and looked back toward the direction from which we'd come. As much as I cared for Godin and everyone else in the house, I did not like the implications of doubt toward Marjeàn.

Godin reached out to touch my shoulder. "I simply want you to see something."

I walked slowly, and he helped me with an arm around my shoulders to pull me forward. He led me to the wall of Marjeàn's private garden.

I had been prepared to see an elaborate retreat with fountains and statues. Instead, I found a simple meadow. Although almost empty I could feel the tranquility of the area and understood why Marjeàn enjoyed spending time here. High stone walls surrounded it with a few benches strategically placed in a circular pattern and right in the center stood the largest sculpture made with plants I had ever seen.

My mouth dropped as Godin stated, "He calls it…"

"Zefforah," I whispered her name at the same time Godin said it.

"Do you know what this is?" Godin cried. "This is the beast! Dyre's beast!"

Thoughts and questions reeled through my mind as I spoke his name aloud. "Dyre?" I pressed on my forehead with my fingertips trying to release the ache coming to my head. Marjeàn knew Zefforah. This sculpture showed her soft and beautiful side, not how the masses knew her. A cold chill ran over my skin as I realized Marjeàn must know Dyre as well.

Godin turned toward me, "Master Marjeàn must be working with him. Look at his interesting travels, his odd isolation. It all adds up."

I found myself weak and wandered to the closest bench to sit immersed in my thoughts. Godin followed me continuing his speeches. I had stopped listening. My head swam with information too great to allow any external conversation.

"Thank you, Godin. Don't let me keep you."

He shook his head and opened his mouth to continue.

I put up my hand to stop him. "Please. You have shown me what you wanted me to see. I need to be alone."

He nodded his head and turned to go.

Grateful for the seclusion of the place, I decided to try something I had never tried before. I needed to tear down Dyre's veil. If I could look through his eyes without his knowledge, I might find some kind of clue of what Marjeȧn had to do with all of this.

I closed my eyes concentrating on his veil. Thinking of how I had once learned to build mine, my attempt to pull away his might be similar.

Dyre had a very keen sense of smell. It seemed the easiest of his senses to break through first. I concentrated on breathing in through my nose, trying to match my breath to the rhythm I knew him to have during calm moments of the day. I inhaled. Roses. No. Just beyond this wall, they were close to me, not him. I tried again. What might he smell? I visualized different fragrances, and familiar foods I knew he loved. Nothing. Then I thought of Zefforah. I smiled as I breathed in her scent. I could smell Zefforah. The black of his veil changed to the yellow sheet of smell. I pushed it aside in my mind. The collection of layers between us still blockaded me from pulling any more, but I would work my way through them all.

As I could tell when he breathed in and out through his nose, I concentrated on the sound of his breath. Nothing came. I could barely hear my own breath; I could only feel breathing. Hearing it would be too difficult. I changed my thoughts to listen instead for the sounds Zefforah might create. Could I hear her footfalls? No, but I could hear the faint sound of her wings as she must have been ruffling them. The green layer of sound became more evident as I concentrated on the noises, I pulled it back slowly. I faintly heard Zefforah occasionally moving in the background as well as a scratching sound I couldn't yet identify.

Touch would be more difficult. I placed my hands on my lap with my palms up, hoping to feel if he held something in his hands.

The slight brush of something against my neck kept distracting me. I reached my hand up to sweep it away and felt nothing on my own neck. I realized I might have been feeling the collar of Dyre's shirt. I placed my hand in its former position and moved my head slightly trying to feel the sensation again. There it is. He wore a shirt and a coat as well; I felt the weight of it. My right hand curled as his held something light and smooth. His fingers moved it in quick jerky movements and occasionally his arm shifted to the side and back. He was writing. The fabric of purple seemed to pull back on its own.

Red, the color of taste seemed too easy as I knew the flavor of his mouth as well as I knew my own.

The last piece, the one I wanted the most, the deep blue thickness of sight still barricaded me from him. With great mental effort, I tried to picture the paper he wrote on. I knew how his letters formed on the page, but without knowing what he wrote, it would be impossible to envision.

I pushed against the veil. Nothing. His head moved up, and I felt the softness of Zefforah's nose against his face. I could imagine her. A picture formed in my head and then the picture started to move. The blue of sight gave way, and I finally saw her as if she were right in front of me.

He laughed and pushed her gently to the side before returning his focus to his letter. I kept my eyes closed and matched my breath to his, hoping he wouldn't notice me there. I read through his eyes as he wrote.

Laroke,

Things are going better than I could have anticipated at this point. The last battle seemed almost too simple. The information you have been providing helps us immensely.

Just as we had planned, we are decreasing the number in the king's army. All will be well when the time is right.

I have thought after I am king we should attack Villarosa, our sister kingdom to the North. It should be easily done as they are small. When we take it, I will show my gratitude for the assistance you have shown me throughout the years and place you on the throne there. Your service to me is priceless; I would like to reward you amply for it.

Things are going well with Marjeån and Eviona. She is obviously falling in love and has shown no sign of suspicion at this point. It surprises me but pleases me as well. I know you disapprove of my taking these measures with her. I assure you it is for the best and will work out nicely in the end.

My stomach churned, I tried to take slow breaths still matching his. I wanted to read more, but couldn't seem to move past what I had just read.

Marjeån worked for Dyre. I had been brought here as part of a plan. My heart beat against my chest as if a hammer beat me from the inside. I felt utterly betrayed; sick in my heart, as well as becoming sick to my stomach. I forced myself to continue reading, worried Dyre might feel my presence by the furious beating of my heart.

I have a favor to ask and from what you have told me of your influence over your contact you will easily be able to accomplish it. There is a soldier in the king's army by the name of Jovan. He is young but do not underestimate him. I want him in the front lines of the next few battles. I find him a nuisance in many ways and wish to be rid of him...

I choked with emotion.

Dyre's eyes closed with his surprise and his hands pressed against either side of his head as if holding it together. "Eviona! How did you break through? How much did you see?"

I groaned the words with clenched teeth as tears flowed freely from my eyes. "You are lower than I ever thought possible."

"Eviona wait." I didn't wait. I placed my own veil as I listened to him call my name. "Eviona! Eviona..."

I stood and staggered, unsure of where to go. My lungs snubbed their sustaining function. My eyes, desperate to shut out the pain, refused to open, and the footing beneath me became a chore. A threatening world of uncertainty overtook me, and I collapsed into darkness.

Connate (adj) existing in a person from origin

I awoke in my bed. Ginnie pressed a wet cloth to my face as I agonized over my last few moments of consciousness. My mind raced with memories of my life. Years Dyre and I had experienced together, the last time I saw Jovan, and everything I had thought I felt with Marjeἀn.

I attempted to sit up but realized the strength I needed evaded me.

Ginnie shushed me as she pushed gently on my head with the cold cloth. "You have a slight fever but the master would not allow me to give you any obiberry juice."

"He's here?" I tried to sit up again, but she pushed on my shoulders and forced me to stay in bed.

"He came home the same day he left and found you not an hour later. He must have forgotten something. It's a good thing too, hardly anyone else goes into that garden; it could have been days. He has since gone again."

My words formed slowly. "How long have I been unconscious?"

"Two days. Although you were responsive at times." Her eyes opened widely with concern. "You woke repeatedly crying the name of Dyre. Godin disclosed to me what he had shown you. He didn't mean to upset you."

"This is not his fault."

"Do you feel you can eat? You need the nourishment."

I stared at her blankly, too busy thinking to register what she had asked.

"I will bring something right away."

Over the next few days, she nursed me to health as I

thought constantly of Marjeȧn.

How could he know Dyre? Why had I never heard of him? How much did he know about me and how long had he known it? Did he genuinely care for me, or had it all been an act, part of Dyre's plan? Would Dyre ever tell anyone about us? So many answers I didn't really want to know.

Early one morning I awoke to echoing footsteps in the hall. Marjeȧn? I sat up, and opened my eyes, despite my desire to do the opposite.

My heart sped as a letter came under the door. I listened intently. When the heavy footfalls faded down the hall, I rushed to retrieve the letter.

It had to have been from Marjeȧn. What he would have to say to me? I hoped he would send me away from here, far away from him and Dyre's plans. I picked up the paper. The note had obviously been written in a hurry. Each word slanted at different angles.

My Dear Eviona,
I would like to speak with you when you feel you are strong enough. I know you must wish to ask me some questions. I want you to know my desires are to tell you the truth. I want you to know everything. No matter how difficult the subject may be for either of us to discuss.

Please meet me in my garden. I will wait for you there every afternoon until you feel able to come. Please. Come to me,
Marjeȧn

The words surprised me, but my desire to go to him astonished me more. I did have questions. I wondered if anything we could say to one another could somehow erase the damage of our false relationship. I read the note over and over.

As the morning departed, his ride would end. I couldn't stop myself from going to his garden. I stood hoping my legs remembered how to function. I opened the door of my wardrobe wondering what I should put on. Should I wear my hair up or leave it down? Would it make a difference if I tried to look more beautiful? Should I wait? Put it off? Would going tomorrow make him suffer? Should I eat first? Would it be wise for me to have food in my stomach? What if I became sick?

Before I could think of any answers, I stood dressed and ready at the outside wall of his garden. My time to question had ended. My body had pulled me here without allowing my mind to think.

I entered into the beautiful place, I did not see Marjeån. Grateful for the extra time to allow myself to think, I walked to the sculpture standing calmly in the middle of the space.

"Hello, Zefforah." The sculpture appeared real enough. It might have been a green painted Zefforah. "This is a disaster." I reached out to touch her expecting her to be as soft as the real thing. "I hate Dyre. Jovan's life is in danger. I fear I have lost Marjeån too."

"I'm not lost."

My body froze at the sound of his familiar voice. My heart stopped. I had to concentrate to continue breathing. I didn't turn to face him. I couldn't move. "What does he wish for you to do with me now?" I asked.

"Can you not even look at me?"

I breathed in deeply to gain some courage. Then I slowly turned to face him. I expected to feel nothing for him. After all, I meant nothing to him, a pawn in Dyre's game, but I couldn't have been more wrong.

His incredible beauty, his broad shoulders, his starlight blue eyes, and thick black waves of hair assaulted my senses. I couldn't believe how badly I still ached to touch him.

"Eviona," he walked toward me, "is there any way you would be willing to stay with me, to still spend time with me?"

"How can I trust you?"

"Ever since I met you, every thought in my mind, every action I have taken, every word I have uttered to you has been sincere. I hope you can believe me in that."

"Marjeȧn I …"

His hand rose, I expected it to go through his hair, a gesture I'd watched in anticipation so many times before. Instead, he reached toward my face, I couldn't breathe. He paused momentarily before placing his fingers on my cheek. A sudden jolt of energy coursed through me. Every cell of my body seemed to explode as if alive for the first time. The incomprehensible current surged through me, a ravaging fire flowing through my veins creating a bond with him from the inside. I felt my essence intertwining with his weaving us together. One a perfect fit for the other. Not just my body, but my soul longed to be with his, to struggle against that desire would be vain. The ecstasy of our connection erased the negative thoughts and feelings which only moments earlier had filled my being. I became lost in the fire which burned within me.

Marjeȧn gently pulled his fingers down my cheek until they slid from my jaw and the seal broke. My need to reach out to him intensified a hundred times.

It seemed painful to be separated from him. As if I had jumped into a frozen lake after being engulfed in his warmth. My lungs could only take in fast, shallow breaths. His eyes closed, serenity shone on his face, his chest rose and fell as quickly as my own.

"Am I hallucinating?" I asked him, certain I had imagined the whole thing.

"Eviona," he whispered my name. His eyes opened and looked into mine. His hand reached to take mine. As soon as he touched me, I gasped as the flame reignited and the blissful burn raced through me again. I would do anything in the world to not break that seal of our touch. He moved to put his arms around me, pulling my willing body into his as he whispered my name again.

Being there in the safety of his arms the whole world could have crashed around me and I wouldn't have cared. I felt certain nothing could penetrate the complete serenity I felt in his arms until he spoke the one name I didn't wish to hear. "Dyre and I…"

"Stop!" I begged, and pushed myself away. I stepped away from him further even though I saw how much my rejection had hurt him. His hands reached out to me, the hope he felt clearly discernible on his face. I shook my head and held up my hand signaling for him not to touch me again. I had to lower my eyes. I couldn't even look at him without my thoughts becoming completely muddled.

He stood motionless, but his words were insistent. "I have to tell you."

"There is only one thing I want to know."

When only his silence greeted me, I looked up. He nodded to have me continue.

"What do you know about me?"

His eyes studied me tenderly. "I know you are beautiful, and clever, and..."

"Marjeȧn." I reprimanded him with the word. He knew what I really wanted to hear.

He inhaled deeply. "You have known each other for many years."

He didn't tell me what I actually wanted to know. "Did he tell you anything about *how* we know each other?"

His face cringed as if he knew his words weren't what I wanted to hear. "I know he is mindful of you. He wants you here, to be safe."

I breathed. I only wanted to know Dyre hadn't told him about our connection.

Then he said, "There is more."

I shook my head gently from side to side and put up my hands in protest. "We don't need to talk about him anymore."

"Please. You have to know."

"No," I begged.

He exhaled hard and impatient. "I must tell you one thing." I could see the stress in his eyes. "He gave me a message. It is something he assured me you would want to know."

I forced myself to look at him not knowing what Dyre's message might bring.

"He burnt the letter, and promises not to make the request."

My lungs took in a gulp of quick relief and sobs of gratitude choked from my chest.

As he watched me cry his eyebrows buckled, his mouth pressed together in a thin line. "Do you hate him?"

"More than I ever have before, and I have hated him bitterly."

Marjeàn brushed his fingers gently along my cheek to wipe away my tears. I leaned into his chest and his arms folded protectively around me.

"He may have brought us together, but I don't want

him to come between us."

"Please, never speak of him. If I am to stay with you... you can never speak of him again." I pushed myself deeper into his warmth. "I want to stay."

Conjecture (n) the expression of an opinion without sufficient evidence

Blissful would be the most fitting word to describe my life at that point. Nearly inseparable from that moment on, Marjeàn and I found constant happiness in the simple joy of our touch. As we walked our hands intertwined. He regularly caressed my face, and I often cradled myself into him. We spent as much time as we could together, touching whenever we could. Sometimes we walked or sat in a quiet room to talk. The library saw us often with me reading my books, while he would write letters or conduct other business. I never asked to whom he wrote, or what kind of business he carried out. I knew more than I wanted already.

After his morning meal, he still took his ride with his horse. I despised being deprived of his presence, but his rides were important to him, so I did not object. He never asked me to join him. I would have liked to have gone with him, but my fear of horses never permitted me to ask.

I received a bouquet of blue roses for my room every week they bloomed. They smelled heavenly. Marjeàn often picked them for me as we walked the gardens, cleaning off any thorns then offering them as a gift or placing them in my hair.

One afternoon I brought a pair of swords to the garden with me and lightheartedly handed one to Marjeàn.

He asked too seriously, "What is this for?"

"For some fun," I responded playfully.

"No," a stern look on his face.

"Oh, I see, you don't believe I can," I teased.

"I have no doubt of you." He took my sword as well as the one I had given him and threw them to the ground.

Confused, I stepped away from his evident anger.

He moved to me clutching me closely in his arms and placing his mouth next to my ear to whisper. "Please, never allow the steel of a sword to come between us."

I looked up into his eyes, impassioned and angry.

"Marjeȧn, I only meant..."

"Never." His finger drew a line from my eyebrow to my chin, and his lips moved to kiss my cheek.

He pulled me away from the swords on the ground looking back at them in malice.

During a time when Marjeȧn had been gone for several days, one of his letter carriers approached me.

"I saw you challenge Marjeȧn to a duel a few weeks ago."

"He certainly didn't like the idea." I tried to laugh even though I remembered his fierceness.

He sized me up with his eyes. "Are you any good?"

"Are you willing to find out?" I responded coyly, anxious for the chance to duel again.

He smiled, and we went to find some swords.

"What is your name?" I asked as we exchanged blows.

"Ayrik," he replied. "And to answer your next question, I will tell you I have never met Dyre."

"What was my question?"

"We all suspect Marjeȧn's connections with him. Everyone knows I take his letters away from the house and so almost everyone else has asked me if I have met him."

"You haven't?"

"We do not deliver them personally. We have a contact we deliver them to who takes them from there."

"Are the letters addressed to Dyre?"

"I don't know. I receive a bag from Marjeȧn and pass

it off to my contact without seeing its contents."

I wondered about those letters. Wondered if I should try to take advantage of my new friendship with Ayrik, but I never did. As much as my curiosity kindled, I feared to find out any more truth than I already knew.

Every time Marjeản left me, Ayrik and I would bout. I enjoyed the competition, using my skills, and it helped the time to pass more quickly. He even loaned me some of his clothing so I could move more freely as we fought.

One afternoon after a long and challenging duel he asked me, "Whose side are you on?"

I studied him wondering how to answer.

With my pause, he clarified his question. "Is it possible to love someone as much as you obviously love Marjeản and be enemies with him?"

I smiled a bit playfully and admitted, "Would you think less of me if I told you I love someone in the king's army as well?"

His face held complete surprise. "You love him as much as you love Marjeản?"

"Differently," I nodded. "But certainly as much."

"If you had to, which would you choose to die?"

"You might as well ask me if I would prefer my heart to beat or my lungs to breathe. I couldn't choose."

Ayrik laughed at me. "Do they know about each other?"

"Jovan doesn't know about Marjeản. But Marjeản may know about him, I'm not sure."

"If he did, wouldn't you have been the one to tell him?"

"No, Dyre could have said something."

Ayrik's eyes grew. My hand flew to cover my mouth. I wished I could recall the words from his memory. I had become too comfortable with him and had allowed my tongue to divulge the secret.

Fear grew in his face as he asked, "So he is an ally with Dyre, and you know Dyre too?"

"Please don't tell anyone else," I begged in a whisper.

He studied my scared face. "I won't tell."

Still panicked I pled, "Swear it. You must swear you will never tell." My worried eyes and shaking body begged him.

"I promise, you can trust me. I swear I will never tell anyone."

"Thank you." I breathed.

Ayrik granted me some time to calm down then asked, "How do you know him?"

"I've known Dyre since my childhood. I didn't know until recently, but he asked Marjeȧn to bring me here to keep me safe."

"Dyre must be an interesting friend to have. Since your heart cannot form your loyalties, do your friendships?" The accusation in his eyes screamed his own loyalties.

"I wouldn't exactly call Dyre a friend right now."

Ayrik studied me again. "You still haven't answered my question."

It felt good to have a conversation aloud which I'd had so many times in my mind. "I have always known about Dyre's plans. In my childhood I simply expected him to become king. Logic tells me I should be on his side. Especially now with my feelings toward Marjeȧn, but I can't convince myself to do it. I have an allegiance to Sylvaria which I simply cannot dismiss."

"I understand." My glance shot toward his face. "My brother joined Dyre a few years ago. To coerce my brother Dyre must be very convincing."

"He is."

"My brother and I have had many discussions of Dyre and Sylvaria and no matter what arguments he comes up with my devotion to Sylvaria remains unmoved."

I nodded, grateful to know someone else shared my feelings.

Ayrik continued. "If needed, I would fight for the king even though my brother fights for Dyre."

"Those are my feelings exactly. Am I a fool? To continue my life with Marjeán knowing we are enemies?"

"I don't think you are a fool. I think you are in love. Of course, you are in love with another man too," he teased.

I laughed. "I love my time with Marjeán, but I wonder if our loyalties will separate us in the end." I put my head down and whispered my thought. "I think he feels the same. I suppose that's why he never kisses me."

A roar of laughter rushed from Ayrik. "You cannot be serious. I've seen him kiss you."

I blushed and chuckled self-consciously, "You may have seen him kiss my face. He often kisses my cheeks, my eyes, my forehead, but he has never kissed my lips."

"It may be your allegiance, but I wonder if your old friend has anything to do with it."

I raised my eyebrows and nodded my head. "I certainly haven't dismissed that thought."

Indeed, I had wondered the same thing several times. I always felt Marjeán wanted to kiss me. I definitely wished that he would.

He often traced the outline of my mouth with his finger and then he'd look into my eyes as he broke the contact mentally before he would do it physically as if he'd done something wrong.

I never asked Dyre about it. He and I didn't speak, but at night we usually would drop our veils before we fell asleep. I did it to force my feelings of happiness on him, and to show him he didn't have the control over me he wanted. I wondered if he did it to keep me in check. Like a father waiting on the porch for his daughter to come home from spending time with a boy. I didn't ask. I hadn't spoken to him since the letter. I didn't plan on speaking to him ever again.

Articulate (adj) made clear, distinct, or precise

"Marjeȧn." I grabbed his hand. After several weeks away it felt too wonderful to have him with me again.

He returned my smile, caressed my cheek and kissed my forehead.

"What are we to do today?" I asked as he led me outside. He had something planned.

Each time he went away he returned with something for me. A new dress, some exotic plant or food, a piece of jewelry, I never knew what he might bring, but he showered me constantly with gifts.

"We are going for a ride." He smiled at me.

I pulled away from him and stopped my feet. "No, I don't ride."

He laughed at my reaction and took my hand to keep me walking, "Don't worry, I am not going to have you ride a horse, I am talking about a carriage ride."

He escorted me to the front of the house where a beautiful open carriage awaited us. My eyes grew big, and he laughed at my new enthusiasm as I ran toward it.

"This is beautiful! May we ride right now?" I asked him breathlessly.

"Of course." He finally reached where I stood and opened the door to help me inside.

I bounced on the seats elated with the thought of riding in an elegant open carriage. I had never had the privilege before. Only the wealthy could afford such things. Though Lady Delsa had one, I certainly had never ridden in it. I sat up tall in the seat, and he sat next to me. As we started off, I waved excitedly to the gardeners and staff as we passed.

As we rode, I loved feeling the wind in my face and breathed it in deeply.

Marjeȧn often laughed at me through the ride, he enjoyed watching me.

We rode for most of the afternoon and by the time we came back home I sat contently nestled into his side with his arm around me. "Thank you Marjeàn. I adore your new novelty."

"I'm glad. I love to see you happy." Then a sly look came to his face, and he admitted, "I did have a motive for our ride though."

I looked at him quizzically, "What have you done?"

He smiled and shook his head. "You will simply have to see for yourself."

I felt giddy with expectancy by the time the carriage stopped in front of the house. Marjeàn laughed watching my eager face.

He offered me his hand to help me from the coach and I wound my fingers with his as we strolled to the house. I soon felt as if we were going to my room. We came to the familiar hallway just in time to see several servants come out of my room and shut the door.

Marjeàn smiled and asked if everything had been prepared.

They grinned and nodded knowingly then walked down the hall glancing back at me. I wondered what he could have done.

"Marjeàn?" I eyed him accusingly. "What have you been up to?"

He only smiled and opened the door for me to walk in.

I immediately noticed the addition to the room on the far wall stood a vanity. It had two large mirrors. One on the wall and the other positioned on the top of it like a counter. Both had incredible etchings of flowers and vines framing their surfaces.

The counter top held a beautiful set of ivory combs and brushes. I squealed with delight and ran to it. I sat on the dainty stool and felt like royalty. I primmed in the mirror for a moment and noticed Marjeàn smiling at me from the doorway.

I ran back to him and threw my arms around his neck and embraced him as tight as my arms could muster. "Thank you. They are beautiful."

He laughed and hugged me tightly. "Promise me you will use them often."

"I will, and I will always be thinking of you." I rubbed my nose lightly against his, and he grinned as he released me from his arms. Then he closed the door and escorted me to dinner.

Marjeàn sighed at the end of the evening, "You are anxious to be rid of me tonight."

I nodded, "I cannot wait to use my new gift." When we reached my door, I softly kissed his cheek. "I don't have words enough to tell you how grateful I am for everything today."

His head bowed, and I thought I heard, "I love you." His harsh voice whispered the words especially softly. He'd kept his head and eyes down as he said it. He had never said it before. I wasn't positive I'd heard him correctly.

I placed my hand on his face and lifted it until our eyes met. I wanted to make sure he knew my words exactly. "I love you, Marjeàn."

He smiled slightly, and his chest rose and lowered in slow, deep breaths.

I pulled myself closer to him and moved my hand to the back of his neck drawing his face toward mine. I heard him take a quick breath as his lips opened and advanced. I closed my eyes and just as I could feel his breath on my mouth he lunged backward away from me. I opened my eyes as he exhaled sharply then smiled apologetically.

He quickly caressed my hair and pressed a kiss to my forehead. The connection broke between us as he walked away. His hands clenched into fists at his side. There must have been a very powerful reason for him not to kiss me.

I dressed for bed quickly and sat at my new vanity, purposely opening my veil. I ran my hands along the floral etchings on the mirror and intricate carvings on the brush and comb handles. I slowly took my hair down and reached for one of the brushes. I sat for a long time running it through my hair.

Dyre joined me as I desired and watched as I brushed my hair. By the scowl on his face and the tightness in his chest, I knew he was furious. I worried for Marjeàn for indulging me so much. But I wanted Dyre to see my happiness, to know how well Marjeàn treated me, and to feel how much I truly loved him. I let Dyre watch me enjoy my gift every night he would join me, purely out of spite.

It seemed Marjeàn spent an equal amount of time with me and away from me. Each time he left for a few weeks I would hear word of Dyre's army through Ayrik or the other servants. Dyre seemed to be rising in power and gaining followers as he won more battles. According to the reports Zefforah grew more frightening than ever. Although, I knew those were lies.

After one especially painful goodbye, I slept restlessly for several hours until I opened my eyes to the surprising sight of Jovan. His angry face troubled me.

I stood before him and glanced down to my own hands; one clenched into a fist and the other holding a sword. My thoughts couldn't push my hands to do my bidding. I wanted to release the sword and throw my arms around him. His sword lifted against me and my arms fought back against my will. I then realized the body I occupied belonged to Dyre. I stepped to the side attempting to pull my consciousness away from his. The strain to separate myself from him felt odd and painful. His body pulled against mine, and as we divided into two beings, I felt as if I had physically been ripped apart and fell to the ground.

I twisted to see Dyre and watched him disappear into nothingness as if he had never existed. Jovan appeared unaffected by the happenings and turned to face another approaching foe. Marjeản.

Marjeản rushed at him. I opened my mouth to scream for them to stop but no noise came from my throat. I rose and attempted to stand between them forcing them apart with my outstretched arms. Their swords whipped through me. I couldn't be seen or felt by either of them.

I staggered backward watching in horror as the two men I loved fought like barbarians. Unable to make them stop, desperate for them both to remain unharmed I continued my helpless, silent cries.

As the echo of their swords resounded in my ears, I could not endure the sight. I ran. Crying like a child, hiding like a coward from the thought of what might be.

My eyes opened. My heart pounded wildly in my chest, and I panted as if I had run a hundred miles. I lay motionless in my sweat soaked bed until I could once again control my breath, and feel my heartbeat calm.

It had only been a dream. How much of it could have been real? Had Dyre seen them fight? Had he fought Jovan himself? Could it have been as much of a memory as it had been a dream?

I felt Dyre still sleeping. Nothing. I couldn't see his dreams unless we dreamed them together. He had not seen this dream. I looked to Zefforah. Seven long seconds of a breath in, she still slept as well. This had been my dream. My fears. Not a memory, thankfully.

My thoughts turned to fear every time Marjeȧn left. I worried about his role in the battles. Then I would think about who he would be fighting. I dreamt many nights about Jovan and Marjeȧn facing each other. Not knowing what the other meant to me, and not knowing how my world would fall with either of them gone.

When Marjeȧn returned home, I clung to him and silently begged for him to never leave me again. Never saying the words aloud, but he must have known my thoughts.

Winter fell heavy that year, covering the earth with a thick layer of ice and snow. Marjeȧn's riders did not come or go, only Marjeȧn left for his morning rides or walks. I again quickly learned to love the winter. No word from the outside meant Marjeȧn never left for long. No one could have been happier than I during those deep winter days.

Portent (n) threatening or disquieting significance

I awoke to a sound I feared. The cheery songs of birds outside my window announced the oncoming spring. Their continuous chirps showered me with the sad thoughts of Marjeȧn leaving again for weeks at a time. I opened my window and yelled at the birds, "Go away!" Their wings fluttered, but the song returned to the air too quickly. I slammed the window shut.

I dressed slowly and when I heard his familiar footsteps coming toward my room I ran. I heaved open the door, and threw myself into his arms.

"What did I do to deserve this?" He chuckled.

"Hold me."

"You know it is how I prefer to spend my time." He laughed again but with no reaction from me he pulled my hands from around his neck and pushed me back to scrutinize my face. "Who hurt you? What happened?"

"Nothing. No one."

I wouldn't allow him to study me further. I pressed my body once again to his and wrapped my arms around him holding on as if my very life depended on my grasp.

He held me motionless for a moment before asking, "Did you have a bad dream? Has one of the servants said something to upset you?"

"No." I lied. The servants talk of Dyre and my nightmares both upset me constantly, but those things couldn't have shaken me the way my knowledge of the oncoming spring did.

"Please tell me."

I gave in and spoke. "It's spring. I'm not naïve enough to think you will be staying with me much longer."

He didn't contradict my statement. In fact, his expression told me how right my fears were. He kissed my hand and looped it through his arm. We went through our day as usual.

Every day I woke with new signs of spring and every day my depression darkened. Until one morning as we walked together he announced, "I have a plan. When I arrive home after my ride, I promise you a surprise." He intertwined his fingers with mine. "Come on then, smile for me."

He ducked his head to my level to look into my eyes and smiled at me hopefully. Then he squinted his eyes and pushed his cheeks in different directions making all sorts of faces until I shook my head with a slight smile on my lips.

"There's my smile. I've missed you." His thumb moved across my lips, and he met my eyes. "I'll make my ride short today. The sooner I leave the sooner I can return."

"Then go quickly." My mouth moved against his thumb, and when he left it there, I pretended I would bite it if he didn't go.

He grinned and went to ready himself. Before he left, he pulled Ginnie to the side. Hoping to discover my surprise I searched for her after Marjeȧn had gone. I found her setting up an interesting scene in the library. A large fire crackled in the fireplace. In front of it lay a large blanket set with my tools from the kitchen, several pillows and bowls of different colored silver beets. The multicolored beets made for a very fun medium to create with.

"Ginnie, what is all of this?"

"I simply do what I am told, Eviona. He also told me to find a book called 'To Be One' which he said I could find in your room. Would you mind going to fetch it?"

I did as she asked and waited for Marjeȧn's return anxiously wondering what he could be thinking. I heard his footsteps in the hall before I felt his presence enter. I turned to him with a curious smile on my face.

"You're smiling. Have you discovered what I had planned for you?"

"You wish for me to create something for you out of silver beets."

He grinned, "Then it will be a surprise. You have guessed wrong. I am the one who will create something for you."

"Really?"

He examined the contents of the room, and his expression soured. "Ginnie!" He went to the door and called to her twice before I realized what must be missing.

"Marjeȧn." I held up my little book with a twinkle in my eye.

He growled a bit frustrated that Ginnie would tell me anything but he asked sweetly, "Will you read to me while I work?"

I sat in front of the fire, and he looked at me with annoyance. "You can't watch."

He sat on the blanket with his back toward me. I turned myself and placed my back against his.

I opened my book and read the story to him. He chuckled at the way my voice peeked in pitch to show my delight with his occasional monosyllabic acknowledgments.

"...the end." I closed the book and moved to turn around.

Marjeȧn leaned away from me, "Don't move."

"My legs are going to sleep."

"I need more time. Will you read it again?"

"Can I help?"

"No!" His heavy voice sounded defensive. "Read. Please."

I lay down on my tummy, tucked my foot under Marjeɑn's leg and started to read the story again. This time, when I finished, I put the book down but didn't move.

"Marjeɑn?"

"I'm nearly done." His soft voice showed concentration. I didn't speak or move again until he whispered. "Come see. Very slowly please."

I slid my foot from its place.

He tensed, "Careful."

As I moved, he bent his body slightly away from me as if I shouldn't touch him. I knelt on my knees and moved around him, so I wouldn't bump into him. He had something cupped in his hands; one hand holding his creation, the other covering it.

His eyes blinked slowly, and a small smile graced his lips. "Are you ready?"

I nodded my head, and he moved his top hand away. There in his hand, he had created the most beautiful rose I would ever behold. Reds, pinks, purples, yellows and oranges bloomed as petals over purple and green leaves. He had outdone me in every way. He opened his palm, and it all fell into nothing but a pile of vegetables in his hand.

"Oh no!" I gasped. "Why did you do that?"

"Do you remember its beauty?"

"Of course I do."

"What did you think when you saw it?"

"I thought I've never seen a more beautiful rose."

He nodded in approval. "Hold on to that memory and you can hold that rose forever."

Without words he told me, he would indeed be leaving soon and for longer than simply a few weeks.

I touched his face and kissed his cheek praying to be

wrong. "Thank you for creating it for me."

"Now." He pulled us both to stand. "We have an important task before us. I have never seen the whole house and wish to take a tour."

Cathect (v) to invest emotion or feeling in an idea, object, or another person

We walked through the rooms discussing memories in the ones we knew, the great hall where we had once stood as Marjeàn chose me to be his companion and the sitting room where we overlooked the snowy gardens, the kitchen, and the hallway where we had once collided. Larger than either of us realized, there were many places we hadn't seen.

"Why would one person want or even need such a large house?" I asked.

"I had to find one which would impress a lady enough to spend time with me."

"Yet no lady has ever graced these halls," I reminded him.

"I didn't need a legitimate lady, only the company of a beautiful woman."

"Oh, I see, any one of the servants would do as long as they were beautiful."

He chuckled and pulled me into a large room which had a marble floor and several large windows lining the walls. A fireplace sat on one side with a high hearth.

I clapped my hands together as I ran inside. "Oh Marjeàn, it's a ballroom!" I couldn't stand still. I had to dance. "We should have had a ball!" I turned in circles and drifted from side to side as Marjeàn observed from the doorway. I stopped dancing and scowled at him. "Come here," I commanded.

He walked toward me for a few feet and then veered to the left and sat on the hearth.

"Where are you going?"

"I'm going to watch, you go ahead."

I snickered, "Are you afraid I will step on your toes?"

"I don't dance," he stated firmly.

"Then I shall teach you." I moved to take his hand.

He peeled my fingers away from his. "You dance. I'll watch." His eyes twinkled at me.

I furrowed my brow at him and pretended someone else had come and asked me to dance. "Thank you, sir. I would love to dance." I bowed at my invisible partner and danced.

Marjeån gazed at me. I kept my eyes on him as I turned with my hands holding the air. I could only stand it for a minute or two before returning to him. "Please dance with me."

He shook his head in refusal. "No, but please continue. I'm enjoying this."

"But I want you with me. I can dance alone any time I want. You aren't always here."

"I know." The tone in his voice reminded me of my morning fears.

I took his hand and pulled on it playfully to have him stand. He chuckled at my efforts and continued to sit as I pulled with all of my strength. He smiled mischievously, and he pulled back with one strong tug. I suddenly found myself giggling in his lap.

"I win." He put his arms around me to hold me there.

I fought in vain against him. "You are supposed to be dancing with me." I laughed and struggled.

I stopped laughing when I saw his serious face. "I will miss that laugh."

"No, not yet. The snow hasn't melted. Flash storms could still happen."

"Eviona, I…" he hesitated only a moment. "I love you."

"Marjeån, you know I love you. Please, stay with me."

He closed his eyes and pulled me close to him.

I begged. "We could stay here forever, you and me.

Or we could run away and be lost in the world. Forget the past, forget the future and stay together."

He shook his head and smiled as if waking slowly from a dream. "Dance." He pushed me tenderly off of his lap.

I put my hand out to him. "Dance with me."

"I don't dance," he reminded me.

I kept my hand there, and he eventually took it. He stood up and placed his arms as if he would dance and then he stood perfectly still as I tried to sway with him. It reminded me of trying to move a stone statue. I knew this would be the closest I would be to dancing with him and pushed him with a snicker.

He caught my arm and whispered, "I love that laugh. I love that I caused that laugh."

I pulled away from him. My face serious, reflecting his. I took his hand to walk from the room.

We finished our tour after supper and late into the evening he insisted I put on my coat and join him in the garden. A fire waited for us as well as a blanket.

As we snuggled together, I asked, "What are we doing out here?"

"Enjoying the stars."

With the cloud of the oncoming events hanging over me it felt good to look up into clear skies until I noticed an all too familiar pattern. Seven stars. One in the middle with six in a ring around it. Not a perfect ring, but I knew somewhere within a very short amount of time it would be. An almost exact replica of Dyre's map wounded my eyes.

I dug my face into Marjeȧn's shoulder. I could not hide my emotions. Dyre's mysterious day of reckoning would not wait any longer. Months? Weeks? Days? I didn't know how long it would be, I only knew it would be soon.

He wrapped his arms around me. I sobbed into his shoulder. He didn't ask me why I cried. We both knew. After a while, I looked up into the tear-streaked face of Marjeȧn. Although I hadn't heard him crying, the moist lines could be seen.

"You must know," he whispered, "I never had the intention of…"

I placed my fingers to his lips. "I know." I did know. He never meant to fall in love with me. Dyre hadn't asked him to do that. Once again I had been in Dyre's way. I shivered. "Let's go inside. I'm cold."

We held hands until we reached my door. He hadn't spoken much since our time in the ballroom. Still silent now he brushed his fingers along my cheek, and he traced my lips which left a trail of tingles on my skin and a slight smile on my face. Then they searched my features, tracing my eyebrows and the curve of my cheeks. I closed my eyes and tipped my head back when his hands moved from my neck down my shoulders to my waist, and hips. I opened my eyes to the soft blue of his as if the ice in them were melting.

"I'll see you in the morning," I said, hoping somehow it would be true.

He wrapped his arms around my waist and held me for much longer than usual. He held my hair to his face and breathed in its fragrance. I leaned my head to the side as I felt his lips press against my neck. His eyes were still closed when he pushed away from me. He turned to leave before opening them.

"Goodnight, Marjeȧn," I called quietly after him, unsurprised when he didn't turn around. He ran his hand through his hair and continued to walk down the hall placing his left wrist in his right hand behind his back. He was leaving me. The farther he moved, the more I knew I wouldn't be seeing him again.

I readied myself quickly for bed, and as I brushed my hair, I felt the confirmative feeling of anxiousness from Dyre. His chest rose and sunk in deep restless breaths. I stared into the mirror only to realize my face scowled back at me. I softly put my brush on the table and pressed my palms to the surface. I stood and glared into my eyes with a glower meant for Dyre. As I spoke, my voice sounded exactly as I wished it, strong and resolute. "I'm not letting him go without a fight!"

I felt Dyre's surprise as I turned and threw a shawl around my shoulders and slammed the door behind me. I closed my veil and prayed I would be able to say something which could somehow convince him to stay with me.

I knocked on the heavy door. The strike sounded too low, as if the thick wood had absorbed the reverberation erasing my plea. I tried again pounding harder this time. The door opened before I reached the third knock.

Marjeȧn stood fully dressed with solemn features. My eyes pleaded with his because my head could not find the words. Seconds lasted hours as each set of eyes searched those across from them. When I could no longer bear the distance between us, I threw myself into his arms, which he mercifully wrapped around me.

He quickly pushed me behind him as if protecting me from some oncoming force. His eyes moved toward the hallway which led to the entry of the house. My gaze followed his to Bren who stood with Marjeȧn's coat and hat in hand, obviously allowing our encounter to complete before his approach.

Bren announced with trepidation, "Everything is ready as you requested, Sir."

Marjeȧn's questions shown in his eyes, and I

wondered if he could read the questions in mine. Why would you leave me? Why have you chosen Dyre? Will I ever be with you again? When? How? Where?

"Eviona, come with me."

I froze, unsure if I heard the words correctly.

When his hand cradled my cheek, I placed my hand over his. His eyes urged as he begged, "I want you with me."

"I want to be with you."

A bit of hope gleamed in his eyes. "I know you can fight. Come fight at my side."

"Fight." It took a minute for his meaning to settle in my head. I would have gone if not for one thing. "For Dyre. I can't."

His face grew dark, passionate. I wondered what kind of thoughts could be going through his mind as he stepped away from me and turned his back. "Is it because of Jovan?"

Dyre *had* told him about Jovan. Probably to instill doubt in his mind, it seemed to be working. "No Marjeàn. This has nothing to do with him."

"Doesn't it?"

Then the answer presented itself to me as if an angel had delivered it. I knew the way to possibly keep him with me.

"Marjeàn." His back still faced me, the pain still obvious in his shoulders. "I will give up Jovan right now."

His shoulders lifted, his neck straightened, and he turned to face me with new hope in his eyes.

"I will never speak of him. I swear I will never even think of him, if you will stay with me."

Pain melted on his face. His shoulders returned to the burdened state they had escaped from only moments ago.

"That's not fair." His lips curled into a pained snarl.

"Isn't it?" I whispered. When he didn't respond I asked, "You do love me, don't you?"

"Goodbye, Eviona." His words, though delicate as crystals of sugar tasted the opposite. He approached Bren and readied himself in his coat and hat and did not turn to acknowledge me again before rushing away.

"Marjeȧn?" I knew he heard me, but he did not pause.

Long, cold strides drew him too quickly from me.

I stretched forward willing the magnetic pull to draw him back to me. When it failed, I called to him again. "Marjeȧn!" His retreating footsteps and my cries echoed through the halls. "Marjeȧn!"

Perhaps he could not face me one more time. Perhaps he knew if he saw the tears streaming down my face he would not be able to bring himself to leave me. Perhaps he knew if he were to touch me one more time his desire to stay with me would outweigh his desire to help Dyre. Then again, perhaps he simply did not want me to know of his true feelings and needed me to remember his mission had been simply to occupy my time while Dyre prepared for his war.

Repudiate (v) to cast off or disown

As I dressed the next morning, the sounds of the house seemed much louder than usual. I peeked into the hall and grabbed Ginnie as she rushed by my room.

"Ginnie, what is going on?"

She looked up at the ceiling and raised her hands as if to ask heaven, "Why do I have to tell her?"

"He's gone. I already know."

She nodded her head and looked at me sympathetically.

My whole body felt like the melting ice I had seen in his eyes the day before. "Gone. He's never coming back." The pain struck again in my all too fresh wounds.

Ginnie put her arm around me. "I'm sorry, sweetie. We are supposed clear the house. He rented everything. We have to pack it all to be returned."

I nodded to acknowledge my understanding.

"There are a few things which weren't..." She took a book out of her apron pocket and flipped through the pages. "It looks like everything in your room actually belongs to you, aside from the books." She glanced at the page. "Except a book called 'To Be One,' which is yours."

"I can't take all of these things with me. Will you let the others know they are welcome to come and take whatever they would like?"

"That's very sweet of you. I'll spread the word."

"Where do we go from here?" I asked.

"There have been arrangements made for us. We are all being sent to different houses. He has arranged for carriages from each of our new masters to retrieve us during the next few weeks. The house should be ready for us to leave as soon as we can make it happen."

After she left, I opened my wardrobe of beautiful clothes and found my servant attire stuffed in the bottom. I slipped my hand across the beautiful dresses I would leave behind, my fingers relishing the touch of their soft, refined fabric. I reached for one of my servants dresses. I put it on and found my old bag, packing only my servants attire.

I sat down at the vanity to brush my hair sitting at it one last time. When I found no comfort in it, I stood to walk around the room. My sorrow twisting my heart just as my clenching fists twisted the brush in my hand. Beset with anger and grief I threw it against the mirror. It shattered, and I felt my heart shattering with it.

I fell to my knees, sifting through the pieces of broken glass for the brush. I clutched it to my chest and sobbed, grateful I hadn't broken it too.

Did he ever really love me? I closed my eyes and tried to remember. He'd been wrong. I couldn't remember the beauty of the silver beet rose. I couldn't see anything clearly now. I couldn't remember his smell, or his voice. I couldn't even remember how it felt to touch him. Nothing.

That day I worked alongside the other servants, reminded of where I really came from. Even though my hands stayed busy, my thoughts were plagued constantly by my reality, and what would soon become of the kingdom.

Ayrik came to find me. He panted breathlessly as he excitedly addressed me loud enough for everyone working near me to be heard. "I've done it. I'm now officially a soldier of Sylvaria."

A cheer ran through the servants near us, and word quickly went through the house. Ayrik's news seemed to bring a feeling of victory to the whole household. All except me.

Ayrik put his hand on my shoulder seeing my low

mood. "I'm sorry Eviona. I had hoped to buoy your spirits with the news. I know you must be heartsick right now."

I nodded to him grateful to have an understanding friend.

"I came back specifically to tell you. There is no need of me here. Perhaps I shouldn't have come."

"Thank you Ayrik. I am glad you came, even if only so I could say goodbye. You have been a good friend. Good luck to you."

He swiftly moved toward the door and turned back to me with a smile and shouted. "Good luck to Sylvaria!"

At which the staff agreed with a cheer.

That night I broke into Dyre's mind. The men around him worked, and prepared. I knew he felt me tear down his veil because the rush of emotion I felt from him and the way he looked down and over his shoulder as he always did when my presence bothered him. I frantically searched through his eyes for Marjeàn, but I didn't see him. A large man approached him with a cart. "Where did you want these, Sir?"

"Give me a minute."

I didn't know if he spoke to the man or to me but I wouldn't leave. I had something I wanted to say.

He entered an office like room. Finding himself alone, he closed the door and bolted it. His head resumed its position of looking down, over his shoulder and he tersely inquired, "What do you want?"

"I want to talk to you."

"Now?" His curt answer showed his anger with me for interrupting him. "Talk!"

"I want you to listen to me and consider what I am saying before you reply."

"Fine."

"Dyre." I started to cry when I said his name, cursing

him internally for taking Marjeȧn away from me.

He breathed out roughly, "Don't cry."

I breathed, trying to calm down. "Give him back to me!"

He struggled momentarily. "I can't. My timeline is coming too close."

I allowed my anger to take over. "You arrogant bastard! Do one selfless thing in your life, let Marjeȧn come back to me."

His stomach churned. He wouldn't give in.

"I will block you out forever, give you freedom from me." I couldn't think of anything else. "What do you want? I will do anything!"

"I don't need to hear this!"

"Please!"

"I can't! Aren't you listening? I can't do it!"

"I love him." My pleading moved nothing but me into a deeper emotional state.

"Stop!" I felt his jaw tighten, his frustration at my hysteria revealing itself physically.

"Marjeȧn is only one man. You have a whole army."

He shook his head and rolled his eyes. "Are you finished? I have work to do."

"You aren't even going to think about it?"

"No, Eviona. I'm not. Marjeȧn is here because he wants to be here."

"I know he believes in you. I know that kind of loyalty is rare." I swallowed, "I understand he has chosen you instead of me."

The tears came freely, but I kept my voice steady, "But I couldn't live if he were to die. Please don't let him fight."

"Go away," he replied crossly.

"You won't even consider it?" I gave in and sobbed

as I asked.

"No!" He unbarred the door and walked out he took a deep breath and looked down over his shoulder at me. "Are you still here?" Several of his men scattered.

I closed my veil.

I lay in my bed incredulous at how Dyre wouldn't even listen to my reasoning about Marjeȧn. Not only heartbroken by his withdrawal from me, but scared for his future with Dyre. I ached for him and wondered if he even missed me.

Sleeping came and went in waves. Finally, I rose and stole away to the ballroom. In my mind, I danced with Marjeȧn. I closed my eyes trying to remember the feeling of his touch on my skin. I wondered what would become of him. If he would be involved in the battles his fate held anything but certainty. My emotions overtook me, and I cried imagining his death and realized whether he fought or not he was now absent from my life.

My thoughts wandered to life away from Marjeȧn. Back to happier times and I heard Jovan's sweet hum as I danced around the room. Comfort filled me at the remembrance of one man willing to give up everything for me. I laughed as I relived memories of past dances he and I shared. I could still feel the warmth from his hands the first night he tried to teach me. Tears flowed freely from my eyes as I wondered and worried about Jovan.

Then my visions of Jovan became interrupted, as if a newcomer had asked to cut in. I couldn't put a face to him, but I could hear his beautiful baritone voice singing as he moved with me around the dance floor. Contradicting feelings of love and hate filled me as I lived a dance with Dyre.

I danced the whole of the night with my visions of

Marjeἀn, Jovan, and Dyre. In the morning my carriage arrived first. It felt as if Marjeἀn wanted me to leave quickly. I took my belongings in the bag which now held my combs and brushes and my small book, the only things kept from my time with Marjeἀn.

I hugged Ginnie and thanked her with tears in my eyes.

She wished me well, pushed me toward the carriage and quickly turned back to the house to return to her work. It seemed so cold.

As I rode, I pulled out my little book and caressed the pages almost the same as I had done as a child. I put it up to my nose to try to breathe in the smell of Marjeἀn and his house. It didn't smell right. Disappointed I placed it back into my bag.

Alone with nothing to do for the first time in days, I had time to sit and think. I convinced myself to be strong and by the time the coach pulled up to my new home I had determined not to shed tears for Marjeἀn again.

I quickly learned the rules. I'd been taken to a large household owned by a good family. The house rules were very strict although easy to follow. I found if I simply obeyed the headmistress I would be all right. She made the law. I learned quickly after watching her beat one of the other servants who disobeyed her; an obvious public display to warn other servants of the consequences of disobedience. I stayed in line and worked hard. I had been there only a week when news from the outside came.

Balm (n) anything that heals, soothes, or mitigates pain

"He's coming!" One of the servant girls squealed with delight.

Suddenly all of the women in the household were giddy.

"Who's coming?" I asked one of the other girls in the kitchen.

"The Captain!" She giggled as she spoke.

At the mention of a Captain, my mind immediately turned to Jovan. I fought the hope, certain it couldn't be him. I didn't understand the reaction of this news by the other female servants though. At the end of the day in my quarters, I asked one of my roommates.

"Zelfy, who is the Captain and why are all of the girls in the house so excited to have him come here?"

Zelfy responded, "Oh Eviona, he is one of the king's Captains. Whenever he visits a house, he always chooses a servant girl to have as a companion. He brings a trunk with him full of clothing and a team of ladies to be handmaids. He is so handsome and treats us like royalty. Not only that, but he chooses one for every day he stays!" She let out a squeal of delight, "The master's son is part of his troops. So, the family has invited him. He will be staying with us for seven whole days! Can you believe it?"

"Have you met him before?"

"No, I never have, but I have heard of him. Everyone has heard of him! Where have you been?"

"Do you know his name?

"No."

I hoped. I wished.

One servant girl, in particular, was so excited it oozed from her. Though very young, maybe only fifteen, she talked non-stop most of the time. This made it worse by far. She continually talked about how much she hoped he would pick her. She would tell anyone and everyone how she couldn't wait to see the dresses he packed, or how her hair might be tied up. She went on and on about what kinds of things he might say to her and how she would respond. Her exhilaration overwhelmed the rest of the house, but because of her enthusiasm we all hoped she would be one of the seven.

The morning he arrived chaos ensued as the servants readied themselves. The female quarters were a frenzied mess of primping. Women I had never seen caring about their looks pinched their cheeks and coifed their hair all while eagerly chatting and giggling.

As soon as he arrived, he would choose a companion for the day. The anticipation in the air seemed thick as butter. I lined up with the others in the back of the house as soon as his coach had arrived. My master accompanied him, and as he turned the corner, I caught my breath. So did everyone else in the line, but I did for a different reason. Though indeed handsome, he looked more beautiful to me. My lips whispered his name. "Jovan."

He was alive! I fought the tears of joy streaming down my face wiping them away with my shaking hands and swallowed the lump in my throat.

I felt my heart lighten at the sight of him. Although not the Jovan of my youth, his eyes still held the same light. It seemed he had grown a foot, if not in actual height then in confidence. His broad shoulders looked as if they could carry the weight of the whole world. He held a look of importance and dignity.

He smiled at each girl in line as he walked. He would stop and ask a question every few steps, enjoying making a show of it. Then he came to me and stopped short. The smile he had worn seconds earlier disappeared, and he turned white as a ghost. "Eviona." His shaking voice whispered my name. "Here you are."

My hands reached forward to his. "Jovan, I can't tell you how wonderful it is to see you," I whispered, though my gesture removed any question of our meeting before. I felt the eyes of the others as everything around us fell into silence.

"You will be my companion for the week," he whispered sweetly.

"No." I softly whispered to him, mortified by the thought.

His face fell.

"You know I'd love nothing more, but there are too many hearts which would be broken."

His eyes grew confused.

"Jovan, you have no idea what you do to a household." I chuckled. "You will leave next week, but I will remain here and be hated having deprived them from their time with you."

He squeezed my hands and rubbed his thumbs across my fingers. "I don't care how they feel. I want to be with you."

My heart swelled. "Go and choose someone else for today." I let go of his hands and nodded my head to have him go.

He did not walk away, but stared at me with devastation.

I verbally nudged him to move on. "Pick me at the end of the week."

"What if I am called away?"

"Then come back again."

He scowled, "You're impossible."

I nodded him onward.

He unhappily chose a companion for the day, and his

ladies whisked her away. He glanced back at me in disappointment. When I smiled at him, he shook his head and smiled a little.

The girls standing next to me immediately started asking me questions. How did I know him? Had I been chosen in another household? What was he like? I never could answer any of them as the headmistress quickly put us all back to work.

All through the week as I worked I listened to whispers around me, and occasionally someone would be brave enough to corner me and ask their questions. Which would quickly draw a group around me until the headmistress broke it up.

I couldn't sleep at night. My thoughts of Jovan made sleeping impossible. I wondered how many other girls were being kept awake by thoughts of him. Zelfy tossed and turned in the bed next to mine. "You can't sleep either?"

She answered, "I don't think anyone is sleeping."

"He is wonderful."

"How do you know him?"

"We knew each other a very long time ago. It seems like a different lifetime."

"Why would you turn down the opportunity to be his companion?"

"He asked me for the whole week."

"Ha!" Zelfy laughed, "I'm glad you turned him down, perhaps I will have a chance because of it."

I laughed. "Good luck."

"Goodnight, Eviona."

The days were busy and fun. We would receive reports from the servants who watched the captain and the girls.

One of them became so overcome she would often

trip or almost faint. Captain Jovan took to walking with one arm around her waist and the other holding her arm to protect her. Which I think probably made matters worse.

Another girl had not ever been taught table manners. We heard reports of her mortifying behavior as she ate her food in a most uncivilized manner. Then we heard Captain Jovan took to eating likewise, and the family of the house quickly fell into the fun; the whole of the meal eaten as if in a den of beasts.

It always made me smile when I heard the stories. I wished I would be allowed to watch a little, but the headmistress would have none of it. Especially because it is what we all wished.

There were only two days left, and we girls lined up again early in the morning. Jovan smiled at me as he had each morning. He raised his eyebrows as if to ask if today would be the day I would be his companion. I shook my head and noticed two girls down from me stood the cute, young girl who wanted so desperately to have a chance, she still hadn't been picked. I put up two of my fingers discreetly and nudged my head in her direction. He walked to her and looked back at me for approval. I smiled and nodded.

He asked her sweetly, "Young lady, what is your name?"

"My name is Ariann. If you desire, you may attend me today." She offered him her hand.

He stifled a laugh. He took her hand and kiss it. "What shall you do if I fall in love and want to marry you?"

"I believe I am much too young for you to marry." The young girl said with an obvious air of arrogance, "However, I will allow you to accompany me today."

"Thank you for the privilege," Jovan grinned. He

would have a fun day acting the parts with her.

The rest of us went back to work.

The next morning as I stood in line I could barely contain myself. I bounced with anticipation. He came to stand in front of me.

"Eviona?"

"Yes, Jovan?"

"Will you be my companion today?"

I felt my cheeks would hurt for weeks with the pressure of such a huge smile. "I will."

Ardency (adj) intensely devoted

He nodded to his ladies, and they came and took me to a private room upstairs. They reluctantly held up some men's clothing and told me they had been instructed to dress me in them. I smiled knowing Jovan planned to duel with me.

Then they began to undress me. I shrieked and backed myself into a corner. I begged them to let me dress alone, but they would not give in. It had been a long time since I heard Minuette's voice telling me of my ugliness, but I heard it as they ordered me. Then a knock at the door saved me.

"Are you ready?" Jovan's voice anxiously called.

"Master," one of his ladies opened the door. "She will not allow us to undress her."

Jovan looked in at me. He smiled and told them, "Then you should let her alone so she can hasten and ready herself. I wish to spend as much time today with her as possible."

Astonished at his answer, the ladies froze.

"All right then, out with you." Jovan's voice resonated happiness, and even though he spoke to the ladies, his face beamed at me.

"Thank you," I said in a small voice as he closed the door after his ladies.

"Hurry," he replied from the other side.

I did hurry, and after I dressed, I looked in the mirror, surprised at how much I had seemed to age since I'd last seen Jovan.

"Eviona?" Jovan called again.

"Come in, I am almost ready."

Jovan came into the room, his team of ladies waited just behind him. "Thank you, ladies. You may go."

From the whispers I overheard, he had never been in the room alone with one of the girls before.

He rushed to me twirled me around causing me to squeal with delight.

"Hello, beautiful Eviona."

"Hello, wonderful Jovan."

"I have missed you so much," he said.

"I've missed you too."

"Have you?"

"Of course," I said, offended he didn't believe me.

"You have made me wait this entire week. You deliberately drove me mad."

I chuckled. "You wouldn't believe the hysteria when the household heard you were coming. I couldn't rob my fellow servants their chance of happiness for a day."

"Always the unselfish one. You know you are the purpose of this tradition of mine." He playfully touched my nose as if kissing it quickly with his finger. "I needed to be able to meet the whole workforce of a household, kitchen staff are never seen by guests. If I did this everywhere I stayed, I hoped it would be a way to spend time with you again."

I chuckled. "How is it I am so worthy of a soldier's attentions?"

He smiled and stroked my cheek. Then he took my hand, "Come, we had better converse in a more public location before we are the blather of the whole kingdom."

Outside the door, my master approached us with a sword in each hand. "Are you certain you want to duel with a Captain in the king's army?" he asked me.

"I would feel deprived without it," I responded smiling at Jovan.

We found a field to the side of the house and jumped into our old habits. Very quickly he noted my strength and developed form. He no longer treated me as a novice but had no mercy as we dueled.

We enjoyed our matches, and though his skill still exceeded mine, I occasionally had a good match. He praised me for my effort and form, which made me very happy. At the end, he took some time to show me new ways to stretch and make the most of the skills I'd developed in the last few years.

We went to clean up, change and met again in the garden.

As we walked, he offered me his arm. He smiled as I took it.

"Jovan, it's good to be with you again."

"You may call me Captain Jovan now," he teased.

I laughed at his faux seriousness.

"Do you know I am the youngest man to ever be made a captain?"

I chuckled "I didn't know. How did you manage it?"

"I have increased in rank quickly because of my knowledge and skills."

"I knew they'd be useful. I am so proud of you. You are doing exactly what you always wanted."

"Yes." Even though he had responded positively, sadness resonated in his voice.

"What's the matter?"

"When you are young, you think you know your desires for the future, but as you age you see the past and what could have been."

I tried to arouse a smile and teased him. "Yes, when the lost princess returned to the king and queen your plans took quite a blow."

"Haven't you heard? She was an imposter. Though her outward appearance seemed correct, she lacked the birthmark her parents knew their daughter to have."

"I hadn't heard of a birthmark. What is it?"

"I think only certain people were told, in hopes of

avoiding a deception like that one. I don't know, but my father knew what to look for."

"Well, with the lost princess still out there to be found, I shall wish you luck with your continued search."

He smiled, and when we reached a small patio, Jovan turned to me. "My Lady, may I have this dance?"

I feigned surprise, "Oh, why yes, Captain."

He took me in his arms, and we danced to the music he hummed. He slowly came to a stop and stood with his arms around me, his eyes focused on mine.

"I missed dancing. It feels perfect to dance with you again."

"It does." He offered his arm again. "You even allowed me to lead this time."

I laughed, and we continued our walk.

"Your pride is not something you struggle with now."

He bowed his head. "I have found life to be a good teacher of humility."

"What of your other weaknesses?"

He grinned, "You mean to tell me, after all this time, you never figured out my other great weakness?"

"No." I shook my head in question.

He stopped and turned to me. He touched my face, caressing my cheeks, moving his fingers along my eyebrows and ears. "Try to remember the first thing you mentioned the day we officially met."

Distracted by his touch, I couldn't recall what I'd said.

His grin only increased. "My hands." He held them up in front of me. "They are the way I learn, often the way I communicate, I touch everyone."

My eyes shot open wide with the realization.

"Touching? I love how affectionate you are."

"You do not," he laughed. "You always push my hands away."

"Only because I like it too much."

He shot a glance of disbelief. When I bowed my head to avoid his eyes, he spoke. "My father was right. It does cause trouble. I've done my best not to be too affectionate, especially with the servant girls."

"I'm sure your father is quite proud of you."

"He was," he said softly. "He died last year."

"I'm sorry, Jovan. I know he loved you."

"Yes, he did."

I read many emotions in his eyes. "You've seen so much pain."

"The war."

I knew I couldn't avoid the subject forever. "Of course, Dyre's war," I spoke with too much anger.

"Do you know much of Dyre?"

"Entirely too much." I cleared my throat. "I mean to say, I have heard of him. Everyone's heard of him."

Jovan must have noticed the deception in my voice. I thought about the fact that I hadn't been with Dyre since pleading with him for Marjeàn. I didn't miss him, but speaking his name caused a pain I didn't expect. "I've learned quite a bit over the last few years."

He looked away, distracted. "Dyre's army is gaining in strength. He is shrewd and slippery. It won't be long before he starts winning more. We can never catch him off guard. I believe the king has much to fear."

"Have you seen him? Dyre?" I tried to sound disconnected.

"Yes, standing on the outskirts of the battles in his intimidating black mask. He may be a large man, but I think he's a coward. His beast doesn't join in them either. It circles from above, but never approaches enough to be harmed."

It seemed logical for Dyre to use Zefforah to be the omnipresent eyes of the battlefield. His leadership would be unmatched because of his view through both of their eyes.

Jovan scowled, "Dyre will die. His beast too and anyone connected to them."

Horror raced through me.

Jovan placed his hands on my cheeks. "Don't look like that, don't worry." He wrapped his arms around me as I began to shake. "It will be alright." His soothing voice did not comfort me. His earlier words had set the flames.

I couldn't speak. I didn't want Dyre to win, but I didn't want to die. The thoughts of Jovan and Marjeȧn in the battles ripped me apart as well. Everyone was in danger.

He held me waiting for my shuddering to calm. "What can I do for you?"

"Are you really willing to do something for me?"

"Anything."

"Never go back to the war."

He abruptly let go of me. My words were obviously not the appeal he expected. He ambled around me studying the problem in his mind. Finally, exasperated he exclaimed, "Eviona, you are the reason I am a soldier!"

"I know. It is unfair of me to ask."

He hung his head. "I don't have that option right now."

I looked into the distance to hide the regret in my eyes. "I understand."

His tone changed, and he timidly inquired, "Why can't you love me?"

I didn't want to tell him the truth. Wouldn't it only hurt worse to know I always have?

He turned away from me then took a deep breath and exhaled slowly before starting to speak. "On the day I became a captain I did a great deal of introspection. I had achieved what I had always professed to desire. That night as I lay alone in my bed I could think of nothing but you and how I'd give it all away for you to be there with me." He moved to me, reached his hand under my chin and lifted my face for my eyes to meet his. "I love you. I know you have never felt the same for me. To you, we have simply been friends. But to me, each time you rejected me struck another injury to my heart, even though I knew you did it for my benefit. I've never wanted anything more than you. Even being captain came second to my dreams of being with you." He slowly dropped his hand and turned away.

He'd taken several long strides before I called to him. "Jovan," I rushed to take his hand. "I have loved you since the first time we spoke."

Disbelieving eyes shot to meet mine. "You have?"

"Yes," I beamed.

He pulled me close with one hand, pushing my chin upward with the other. He studied my lips then glanced to my eyes as if to ask permission to kiss me.

I smiled, grateful at having admitted it aloud at last.

His soft, warm lips trembled as they pressed against mine, but his hesitation vanished quickly as our mouths moved together, rising into a passion I did not expect.

His kisses moved to my cheek, and he whispered into my ear. "You love me?"

I nodded with a simper.

"That's all I want."

"We will always be in places which keep us apart," I replied sadly.

"This war will end, and when it does I will find you and renounce my title. But for the moment this is enough." He kissed me again.

We spent the rest of the day enjoying each other as we never had before. I relished having his arm around me, and the way he caressed me, and never feeling like I needed to push him away. He noticeably appreciated it as well. The whole day played out like a dream. The evening rushed upon us too quickly.

"Please don't abandon me yet," he begged.

"I have no choice. We are given strict orders to come back to the servants' quarters after evening meals."

He chuckled, "Yes, I know. Ariann informed me of every intricate rule yesterday. So, during dinner tonight I entreated a special favor from your master. He assured me there would be no punishment for you if I kept you a little bit longer."

"I don't know," I worried aloud. I knew the headmistress' rules well, and her punishments.

"Please, he promised me."

Though hesitant, I wanted to stay with him. I took his arm, and we walked through the house.

"Where are we going?"

He laughed at my question. "Nowhere in particular." He stopped and looked around. A large, dark sitting room to our left called to us with its outlines of chairs and couches. He nudged his head and pulled me into it, "Come with me." As we walked into the room, he stopped me in one of the shadows. "I have something for you." He reached under his collar and pulled out a chain with a small box attached to it. He lifted it over his head and placed it around my neck. "In this box is the key, your key, to my wedding room."

"Jovan?"

"I had it fully constructed before Trew ever completed his. I've enhanced it periodically ever since." He laughed, "It's probably a gaudy mess by now, but it's beautiful to me because I created it for us. This key is yours and yours alone."

I took his hand leading him to a couch and sat down pulling him with me. I moved into him, kissing his lips, manipulating his fingers with mine. We didn't speak, we simply enjoyed being together.

Substantiated (v) to establish by truth

Morning aroused us with the sunlight coming through the windows. We had fallen to sleep in each other's arms. I smiled at Jovan and stroked his face.

"I have to go."

"I know."

We went to the room where his ladies sleepily waited for the dress I wore. They looked visibly disgusted at me, but Jovan ignored their disapproving stares. Everything but my dress had been packed as he needed to leave before the morning meal. I quickly undressed, handed the clothing out the door and listened as the ladies gossiped down the hall. I donned my usual servants' attire, tucking my key box into my dress. I hoped the promise my master had made to Jovan would somehow protect me from the punishments of the headmistress.

Jovan stood waiting as I stepped out.

I asked a bit panicked, "What are you waiting for? You need to leave."

"I had to see you one more time. I don't know when we'll be together again."

I touched his face. "Be safe, Jovan."

He kissed my lips then took my hands and kissed each one in the center of the palm, then placed them together as if in prayer and squeezed them gently.

I nodded, fighting the tears.

He nudged me on, and my footsteps retreated too quickly. I never went to my room that night, and I also would be late to help with morning meals.

Whispers from the servants as I raced past them echoed in my ears. Fear like my childhood grew inside. If I were whipped Dyre would be furious with me, and I knew how she whipped the servant before me which only compounded my fears. When I reached the kitchen, she waited for me. Everyone worked in fearful silence around her.

"You thought being acquainted with our guest you could come in whenever you wanted." Her tone dripped with condescension.

"I spent a few extra hours with a friend," I said it innocently, as if I didn't know there would be a punishment. It didn't change her mind. "Jovan told me he asked for extra time."

"Yes, I have been informed." She moved around the kitchen, a leather strap in her hand. She would expose my back to beat me. "But, you see, I make the rules here in the heart of the house. I am allowed, because rules keep things running the way they should."

My heart pounded. The strap she held looked like Minuette's. I had no idea how to escape. I couldn't let her see my back, but she wouldn't allow me to not expose my skin. I fell to my knees. "Please!"

"Oh child, I have heard begging before. You are new, I really hate to do this but if I allow even one person to break my rules…well, I can't have insubordination on my hands."

When I didn't move but begged more, she ordered Zelfy and one of the other kitchen girls to hold me to the wall. I thrashed, but they held me tight.

Zelfy whispered, "Don't make it worse."

She quickly lost her patience with me, grabbed a knife from a nearby counter and sliced through the back of my dress.

I waited for the screaming, I braced myself for the horror which I knew would surround me in seconds. She pulled my dress open to expose my bare back, and then she gasped.

I was not surprised by the gasp, nor by her panicked

orders to clear the room. As soon as everyone left, she shut me in. I trembled with the finality of the bar going down into the latch; a haunting reminder of my childhood captivity. I shrank to the floor and wrapped myself in a ball. I cried softly until the bar lifted against the door. She returned with my master.

"You must believe me, sir. I never knew. I've never seen it before."

"Are you sure you saw it correctly?"

"Come and look at her yourself."

The master approached me and gave me a weak smile. "My dear, I need to see your back." He spoke to me as if I were a child.

Confused by his request, but still unwilling I shook my head.

"Stand up girl," the headmistress commanded.

"You may not speak to her like that!" His words caused her to cower. He bent down to my level and whispered, "It's alright." He gently looked into my eyes. "I simply need to see the marks on your back."

Though he would run from me when he saw it, I stood and turned around for him to see.

He opened my dress. His hand touched just above the small of my back. He struggled for breath, and I felt him collapse to his knees behind me. "Ready a coach," he whispered. "I shall take her myself."

The headmistress draped a large, heavy coat around me which I buttoned and held tightly closed.

She then escorted me to an awaiting coach and my master offered his hand to help me in.

We rode in silence until he spoke. "Our guest, Captain Jovan, how did you enjoy your time with him?"

I nodded, acknowledging the question but didn't dare speak.

He nodded in return and we rode again in silence.

My thoughts raced. I had no idea where I would be taken or why. Too many scenarios raced through my mind. I couldn't stop them. None of them ended well. My horrible body had started a chain of events I could not wrap my head around. Though I hadn't slept enough, too much terror raced through me for me to close my eyes, even for a moment. My master was taking me somewhere, but where?

Anxiousness grew in his eyes as he looked out the window. Uneasily I glanced out. I'd never been there, but I knew it on sight. The castle. I would be going to the dungeon. The monster locked away forever in a cold cell. To end life the same way I'd begun it.

In my thoughts I relived the dream about Minuette, her scream, her panic. She told me this would happen. I could hear her yelling in my head. I closed my eyes tight to squeeze out the memory, but it simply made her voice louder. *'You ugly, horrible beast! Not simply plain, not even ugly. You are nothing but a gruesome wound on the world. You cannot allow anyone, ever, to see your back. You shall frighten any living creature which does. You'll be locked in a dungeon like the animal you are!'* I hung my head. The events underway proved her right. I clung to the heavy fabric gathering it even more against my chest.

We reached the castle gate, and my master announced to the guard an immediate need for an audience with the King.

We were allowed into the castle wall, and there exited the coach. My master made the guard swear to not let me out of his sight. I assured him I would not run, but he watched me closely nonetheless.

It seemed to have taken forever for my master to send word to the King. I rested on the ground clutching the coat until he came rushing to me. "Oh my, she is on the floor!" He accused the guard.

"I'm tired," I defended him. I couldn't see the use in getting an innocent guard into trouble.

"Come with me, my dear." His civility toward me surprised me. He offered me his hand, but I didn't dare loose the grip on my coat. More guards came to escort us as we walked along the corridors.

The castle held more beauty than any place I had ever seen, even more beautiful than Marjeàn's home. The high ceilings painted with incredible murals. With art in everything from the stained glass windows to the intricately carved moldings around the walls and doors.

We passed an atrium, a world of itself. I wished I could have walked through it. It smelled of summer rain on a meadow. I soaked in everything as we walked. Certain this would be the last I would see of beauty in the world. I wished I could stop for a moment and really appreciate it.

We reached an immense room with two thrones at the end. Fear grew in my heart. It beat as if freshly wound by a key. I stood in the throne room of the King and the Queen. I couldn't force the air into my lungs.

The room swirled in a flurry. Guards, and servants all rushed around, as if some catastrophe had been announced moments before. I recognized the king and queen by the robes they wore. The finest I had ever seen.

I pulled the collar of my coat closer around me. The queen saw me and ordered everyone to leave.

It seemed to only take an instant for the space to be absolutely empty and silent. Only two guards at each door stayed in the room along with my master.

The queen walked toward me. I fell to my knees

knowing myself unworthy of communication other than that of submission. She knelt by my side and the king came and stood over me.

The King shot questions at my master. "How long has she been with you?"

"Not long, she came to work for me only a little while ago."

"Where did she come from?"

"I don't know. I swear to you." Fear choked in his voice.

I couldn't let him be reprimanded for me. I mustered the courage to speak. "Please, don't trouble my master. I shall answer your questions."

As I said the word 'master' the king's eyes raged like wildfire. I hoped I had not caused a problem.

The queen's hand rested gently on my shoulder as she asked, "Do you know your mother?"

"No," I meekly replied. "A woman kept me during my childhood, but she was not my mother."

"Do you know where we may find her?"

Even in the presence of royalty, I couldn't hide what I felt. "In the depths of hell, I imagine."

The queen closed her eyes tightly and stood turning away from me. I regretted telling her of my true feelings for Minuette.

The king offered his hand to help me up. I shook my head and tightened the grip on my coat as I stood.

He spoke to me quietly. "We must look at your back."

I started to quake. With pleading eyes, I begged my master for help.

"It will be alright my dear. No one will hurt you now."

I trembled, terrified.

The queen returned to me. She looked as if this

tortured her as much as it did me. She gently pried my fingers from the thick fabric they held. Silent tears of horror ran down my face as she unbuttoned the coat I so desperately needed. She pushed the thick fabric off my shoulders. It fell behind me. She placed my hands in the kings and asked him to hold me.

My knees quivered, I couldn't breathe. I stared in dread at the king, but his eyes only watched his wife. I wanted to run away and hide, but I couldn't now. I bowed my head and braced myself for the reaction I knew would come.

The queen opened my dress. "You've been whipped," she whimpered touching the marks Minuette's strap caused. Then she reached, as my master had, to touch a place right above the small of my back. "Three triangles connected in the center..."

It didn't look horrific? It held the same sign as Zefforah's?

"It's her. It's really her," the queen sobbed.

The king's arms wrapped around me. "My daughter. Home at last."

Parvenu (n) a person who has recently acquired position or wealth, but has not yet developed conventionally appropriate manners, dress, surroundings, etc.

I woke to again find four ladies surrounding my bed. I really wished not to have to go through this ritual with them each morning.

Before I could object, I had been bathed, dressed and my hair done. They worked swift and silent through the process. I occasionally tried to speak, but they didn't respond. At least they knew how to work quickly.

When they finished, I glimpsed at my dress and shuttered. Made with several colorful fabrics, all of which were lovely had the dress been made entirely of one of them, but together looked quite garish. I would have to ask if I could wear clothing a bit less pretentious.

I had only been at the castle for two days and still felt uncomfortable in the environment. My bedroom with its high ceiling left me feeling very exposed and small. The room could have been a home on its own. One part of it had been arranged like a sitting room. Another part, a private library. Another held a canopied bed draped in velvet, a great marble fireplace, as well as a large vanity and several wardrobes. Even though incredible beauty surrounded me, I felt very alone.

Once dressed, I followed a servant to a large room with a long table set for five. The king, queen and two young princesses Rika and Kira sat patiently in silence.

"I'm sorry, are you waiting for me?"

"Yes Triella," the queen said softly.

I cringed. I didn't like my given name, but I didn't dare tell them.

"We knew we would not be waiting long. You will have time to become accustomed to your new surroundings and schedule."

"Thank you," I said as I sat at the empty place.

I had a few things I wanted to say. However, no words escaped anyone's lips as they ate, surprisingly even the princesses. Over the course of the time I had been here they had spoken almost constantly, but at meals, silence prevailed. Hesitantly I spoke, "I would like to wear something a little less ostentatious in the future." I stated shyly, "Do you think it would be alright?"

Rika and Kira's faces held shock, but the queen smiled cunningly. "Your sisters have been loaning you their dresses. Later today the dressmaker will be here to take your measurements. We will ask him to craft some to fit your taste."

I tried to remedy any injury to my sisters, "I have been a servant for many years and am used to clothing which is much…simpler." By the look on the queen's face, she knew exactly how I felt. "Mother." It sounded wrong coming out of my mouth, but she nodded her head sweetly. "I also am quite uncomfortable with ladies helping me dress. Must I have them?"

"It is customary. You are a princess, you need to learn the traditions," the king insisted.

The queen came to my defense, "You are the princess. You can choose."

"My dear!" The king objected.

The queen smiled tenderly and responded softly, "We want her to feel comfortable in her own home. Don't we?" Her eyebrows rose placing a command at the end of her question.

"Of course," the king unwillingly agreed. "We do want you to be happy here, Triella."

I had one more request, "I have some things at my

master's…" I glanced at the king and changed my words, "at the house where I used to live." The king nodded his head in approval of my word choice. I continued, "Do you think we could retrieve them?"

The queen motioned to one of the servants, and he rushed from the room. My request would be filled without another word from me.

I caught the king's eye and smiled, still uncomfortable with my new role.

He said, "Triella, I have someone I wish to introduce you to today. I think you will have a great deal in common."

Touched with his gesture, I asked, "Oh? Who is this person?"

"Like you, once alone in the world, he has now found a place in the castle and in my heart."

I smiled my approval.

"He has played an invaluable role in our war as well. He is my informant, my right hand, and my friend."

I looked forward to meeting someone who my father thought so highly of.

After our morning meal ended the king asked me to accompany him to the throne room. The queen walked on one side, the king on the other. Standing between the two of them, I had never felt so safe.

As they sat on their thrones, I took a place standing beside the queen. The king made a signal to a guard in the back of the room, who then opened the door. I focused on their faces. I did have the queen's eyes, and perhaps the king's smile. He beamed as footsteps came into the room. After the king's guest knelt on one knee with his forearm covering his eyes as a salute to my father, I looked over to see him.

The king stood and practically ran to him as he called to his name.

"Laroke, Laroke. Please come and meet my daughter."

The air escaped from my lungs and could not be replaced. I felt weak, sick, and angry. As he stood and greeted the king with a firm bow, the face matched the name. Right in front of me stood Dyre's best friend.

The king didn't notice my distress until he brought Laroke to me. He grabbed my elbow as he wrapped his other arm around my waist expecting me to fall over. "Triella, are you ill?"

I leaned on the queen's throne. "No, I feel a bit dizzy is all, probably from standing incorrectly. I'll be alright."

Laroke took my arm. I closed my eyes for fear my spite would anger the king. "Here, allow me to walk with you to your room where you may rest." The king showed obvious delight as he allowed Laroke to take his place holding me up.

I refused his offer, pushing away his arms. "No, I am fine. I simply need to walk outside in the fresh air for a while." I looked at the king's face. I needed to mend this quickly. "Perhaps Laroke would be willing to walk with me in case I feel light-headed again." I hoped it would be token enough.

"Splendid," the king cheered. "Laroke, I will leave Triella in your capable hands."

Laroke bowed again, "I am honored to be of service to you, your Majesty, and to you as well, Princess." He smiled charmingly, a gesture I did not appreciate nor return.

As we walked a sticky silence lingered between us. Once outside I turned and shot the question most prevalent in my mind.

"How did you reach this point?" His face held too

much composure as I berated him with my words. "You come here and slither your way into the king's heart, all while being one of Dyre's men. How can the king trust you? How can Dyre trust you? Does *he* know what you are doing?"

The coy traces of a smile graced his lips. "I see your father has told you of my dual service. Please allow me to explain."

My arms folded across my chest. I chose not to speak and waited for what would certainly be a weak explanation.

He chuckled, which only made me angrier. "I spy on Dyre and bring information to your father. To Dyre I am nothing. I play the role of one of his many, lowly men. I came here to the castle after my father died in my youth. When the king found me without family, he took me under his wing and gave me a home. When Dyre started his battles against the king's armies, I suggested I become one of his followers. Your father agreed with me. I easily found Dyre and became one of his men merely with words, not with actions. I am absolutely loyal to your father."

I despised him even more with his lies, but I had the advantage of knowing who and what Laroke truly was. Information I would keep to myself for now. Nonetheless, my father loved him, trusted him. I took a deep breath debating about what to do.

Laroke misunderstood my sigh as acceptance and his hand reached to touch my face. I stood like stone as his fingers moved down my cheek. "Your father has already told me he wishes for us to become intimately acquainted. I know he sees me as a son. You can solidify that relationship with one affirmation."

"I do not trust you."

His enticing smile disgusted me as did his reply.

"Then I will work for your trust. An employment I shall enjoy until I am successful."

I pushed his hand away from my face. Then I realized what I could learn from Laroke. How could I form the questions in a way he would not suspect anything? I attempted to play the part of a concerned daughter and hide my loathing of the man with me. "Laroke, will you answer some questions?"

"If it will encourage your trust, I will do anything." Charm exuded from him. I felt sick.

"I want you to tell me about Dyre. Does he have family or friends?"

I hoped he would speak of Marjeȧn or Zefforah. His answer shocked me. "He does have a son."

I scowled, unable to fathom what my ears had heard. "What?"

"Other than his beast, there are two people in the world Dyre cannot live without. One is a boy who came to him a few years ago. He ran away from his home. Evidently neglectful parenting forced the boy to seek refuge elsewhere. It seems even the arms of Dyre are more welcoming than those he once knew as parents. He was found by Zeffor—"

He paused and rethought his words. "A friend of Dyre's brought the boy to him. I had never seen Dyre as a caretaker, but the way he loves that boy is unlike anything I thought possible from such a man."

I wondered how Dyre had been able to keep him from me.

Laroke continued "I have thought we could use him as leverage, or bait of some kind if someone could grow close enough to him."

"You must know him."

"If he is not with Dyre, Kellam is with Dyre's beast.

There is no way."

I swallowed the name of Kellam like a mouthful of dirt. My Kellam? I fought the distress threatening to surface in my expression.

My panic went unnoticed by Laroke as he continued to speak. "So, if the boy is not a possibility there is only one person we could use." I prayed to hear Marjeàn's name. Even from the lips of this vile man, the sound would be music to me. Nonetheless, it was not his name Laroke spoke. "Eviona."

"Yes?" I answered in reflex. Immediately realizing my folly, I continued my questioning hoping he wouldn't notice the blood rushing to my face. "What do you know about her?"

"Very little, and until I know more I won't mention her to the king. I have never seen her, nor do I know where to find her. Sometimes I think Dyre loves her, other times I am certain he hates her. But this I do know, he values her life as much as his own. If we can find her, we will have our edge on Dyre."

Certitude (n) freedom from doubt

I awoke with the first light of day feeling my stomach turning. Zefforah happily flew through the air. Joyful, and free. She woke me on purpose. She must have wanted a little fun. She dove toward a lake and let her wings skim the surface of it. She flew in patterns back and forth, up and down. She soared toward the sky and looped her body over and over until I giggled from dizziness like when I was a child. She made a laughing sound and then flew toward a tower surrounded by men, and she anticipated seeing Dyre there. She landed gently and turned to survey the view before going into the darkness. She wanted me to see it, but not for its beauty. She had landed on a tower. Cliffs to her left, the sea to her right and a huge span of land in front of her. Dyre had dreamed of this place often enough for me to recognize it now. This was the place. The time would be soon. His day.

I heard Dyre in the darkness, but she did not approach him she only listened closely enough to press his plans into my head. In a week, seven days, his final battle would take place. She didn't let me see as much as I hoped and ignored my pleas to see Marjeàn. She simply wanted me to know. More than that, she wanted me there. I felt an undeniable urgency to be there.

During our morning meal, I once again broke the sound of the silence with an address to the king. "Father." Speaking to him still filled me with insecurity. "Dyre will attack again soon."

Every person in the room gasped at once.

I pled, "Please, you must allow me to help."

He looked at his other daughters and at his fear struck wife, then anxious eyes came back to me. He dabbed his mouth with his napkin and stood to leave.

I didn't know what to do, but from the doorway, he turned to look at me and nodded for me to follow. I reacted immediately, looking back at my worried mother and sisters.

We didn't speak as we walked. The uncertainty I felt a few moments earlier seemed small in comparison to what I felt listening to my father's rushing footsteps echoing in the long hallways. I ran every few steps to keep up with his pace.

We came to a large room filled with tables of models and maps. It looked like a child's play yard full of tiny toy soldiers. I'd heard about the war room. Each of these tables showed strategies and movements of troops. My father moved to one of the tables and motioned for me to join him. "We believe Dyre is preparing for battle here, it is very close to the castle. We are thinking if we attack first we will have the upper hand."

I looked at the different locations and went to a different table. "No, that is wrong. Dyre's army is set up here." I pointed to it on the table. "This tower is where they are already set up. If you want to go to him rather than have him attack the castle, we need to go here."

My father studied my face. "How do you know this?"

I closed my eyes in panic and pleaded, "Is there any way you would simply trust me? I cannot tell you my source, but I swear my information is reliable."

After several moments spent in silence, I opened my eyes to look at my father. He stood unmoving as his brow furrowed as if in pain. He lunged to the door and opened it to speak to the awaiting guard. "Find Laroke. Bring him to me."

"Right away, Majesty."

Questions visibly reeled through his mind. He paced slow and thoughtful as we waited.

As Laroke joined us, he smiled at me as he talked to

my father. "How may I be of service, Sire?"

My father put his arm around Laroke's shoulder and led him to the table where we had previously talked. "My daughter has told me some information contrary to that which you gave me. Are you certain your facts are correct?"

I caught a glimpse of scrutiny in Laroke's eyes as he glanced toward me and then back toward the king. "I am certain, Sire. My information is undoubtedly accurate."

My father looked at Laroke and then at me, apprehensively.

"Father, have someone study what is currently in those locations and send word back to us. That will tell us what we need to know then we will be able to plan accordingly."

"Very good, Triella."

Laroke's face darkened, but my father in deep thought did not see it. When he noticed me watching him, Laroke stood straighter and avoided eye contact with me.

"I will go," Laroke insisted.

"Send Captain Jovan," I retorted.

"Excellent idea." My father nodded to show his approval.

Laroke's eyes became more and more perplexed and spiteful. "How do you come by your knowledge?"

My father noticed the shadow which had fallen over Laroke. He chuckled, "Are you feeling threatened by my daughter?"

Laroke turned to my father attempting to make light as he had with a laugh, but his words spoke his true feelings. "You're Majesty. I have been with you for several years. Triella, though proven to be your daughter, is still untested in issues of trust."

My father looked at me and spoke tenderly. "Someday you will understand, Laroke. She is my daughter, my flesh, part of my soul. I will do all in my power to establish her as trustworthy. Unless she proves me otherwise, I shall trust her with all my heart."

Warmth rushed through me.

Fear raced over Laroke's face, and my father laughed again. "Don't worry, Laroke. This does not mean I do not trust you. It simply means there might have been a change of plans." My father put his arm around Laroke and the other around me as we walked from the room. "Come! We need to send Captain Jovan on his mission and gather my other captains here."

The next day my father, his captains, and Laroke gathered for a meeting. They filed into the room. And the door closed. I listened only to the beating of my heart until the door open again only moments later.

My father stepped into the hallway. "Aren't you going to join us?"

Elated, I followed him. Critical stares from the men around me forced me to push back my shoulders and lift my chest, presenting myself as I hoped to be perceived instead of how I felt.

My father quickly told the captains of the different intelligence Laroke and I had provided. Until we received word from Jovan, we'd make plans and discuss strategies according to both scenarios.

My father invited Laroke to speak first. Presenting his information and the thoughts he had as to how best plan our defense.

Then came my turn. Laroke stood back from the table to allow me to explain what I understood. I approached and spoke with as much authority as I could muster. "I believe this is where they are currently camped. If our troops can set up along this pass and start the battle here, it will act as a bowl. The cliffs on this side will prevent any retreat in this direction. It will give them nowhere to go unless it is back to the tower."

A very old looking captain challenged me. "Dyre would not set up things like this. There would be nowhere for his troops to retreat. With only the tower for refuge, we could easily capture any men gathered there."

I nodded, "This will be Dyre's last battle."

Laroke questioned me, "You think you know the mind of Dyre now?"

I answered quietly although with no humility, "I cannot say I know Dyre's thoughts, but I understand Dyre believes this will be where he conquers."

The old captain chimed in. "If he truly believes that, this scenario will force his hand. He will either win here or die trying."

A knock at the door in the midst of our discussion brought a letter with news from Jovan. After my father read it, he looked at Laroke and then smiled at me. "It seems my daughter's information is correct." Then he looked at me. "Do you know how long we have?"

I searched my memory for what I had heard.

"Four days," Laroke answered for me.

"*Six* days," I pressed my own answer.

My father did not hesitate. "It is better to be prepared for the earlier date, and wait for them to attack us."

As our plans completed the men moved toward the door. "Father," I spoke softly, wondering if he would permit my request. "I want to fight. I have to be there."

Surprise rose in the room as whispered exchanges brought the eyes of every man toward me.

I made an offering, "I am quite accomplished with the sword."

I found gratitude for the old captain who supported my request. "Your Majesty, the people of Sylvaria already feel the discovery of your true daughter to be a sign of our guaranteed triumph. Think of the confidence it would provide to our troops if she were to lead the battle."

A surprising wave of agreeing nods stirred through the room.

Laroke objected, "The king's place is at the head of the battle."

I moved to my father placing my hand on his. "Your position is Dyre's target. You must not be there."

Several of the captains supported my statement.

My father inhaled slowly and exhaled quickly. "We shall test you, Triella. Laroke, this afternoon, prepare to duel with my daughter."

"Sire?" Laroke objected.

"If she can prove herself, I will grant her desires."

"Thank you, Father." Once again men started to stir. This time I raised my voice. "I have another request. You will not like it."

The room quieted as my father's face grew concerned. "What more do you want?"

"Dyre must live."

The upset of the room fell on me like a stone as voices rose in protest. My father's hands crashed down on the table in front of him quieting the noise. He looked at me and asked the simple question. "Why?"

I couldn't tell them I would die if Dyre did. Unsure of what to say to satisfy them I looked around at the faces surrounding me when I came upon Laroke's and had an idea. "Dyre did not bring this war alone. We need to know who else has been involved, to nullify any future threats." I lifted my eyebrows at Laroke who's eyes shifted downward and then to my father nervously.

The silence in the room only lasted a moment, but it seemed an eternity to me. At last, my father spoke. "Tell the soldiers. I want Dyre alive."

Fray (n) a competition or contest

My mother and sisters sat excitedly chattering at the side of a large open field as my father took long strides around its perimeter.

Grateful for Jovan and the practice I had gone through with him just days earlier, I prepared myself with the stretches he had taught me. He never allowed me to perform any less than my best. We enjoyed our duels, but they were serious work, and Jovan didn't allow me to fall short. Now I wished I'd thanked him more profusely.

Laroke joined us on the field and attempted to talk my father out of the duel. I couldn't hear the spoken words, but obviously Laroke did not want this to happen. My father would not back down. I appreciated his inflexibility on the matter and hoped to make him proud of me as well as earn my place in his ranks.

My mother certainly had not been told what the outcome of the sport would bring. She and my sisters spoke excitedly and cheered me on. I wondered how she would deal with the news of my going to war. She had only found me days earlier and then I would leave her to fight. I understood the pain she would feel.

The intermediary called us both forward. Laroke and I met in the center of the field as my father joined my mother and sisters.

I don't think either Laroke or I heard the instructions. Laroke did not smile, but this time, I did.

The intermediary backed away, and Laroke whispered as we exchanged a few easy blows. "I'll allow you to look good for a while. When I start to become more aggressive, you can quit any time."

"Throw the fight?" I asked amidst our clanking swords.

"I'm not really going to fight you, Princess. I know

you want to please your father, but there is no way you are going to this battle."

"You really think so little of me?"

"You're a woman. Women stay at home. Men go to war."

"Pompous aren't we?"

"I believe others would call it civil."

"What would Dyre say? If he knew he would be fighting against a woman."

"Dyre would laugh at the thought."

"You know him that well?"

He caught himself. "No. Any man would have such a reaction."

"My father did not. My teacher did not."

"It's time to end this." He finally started to really try.

Our swords echoed in the large space and after several minutes of real work the sweat on Laroke's forehead matched my own.

"You're working hard," I commented.

"Merely for show." He countered. But clearly, we performed on equal ground.

After several minutes my father interrupted us. "Come rest a while."

"Father," I called to him. "Can you find a real soldier for me to fight with?"

Fire roared in Laroke's eyes. "We don't need a rest, Sire," he called, and I grinned.

The stench of sweat increased as our wrestle continued. Driven by the oh's and ah's of my family and my sister's occasional screams I enjoyed the work. The minutes progressed, his strength decreased and mine as well. I could not keep up this level of fighting forever. Yet, we went on.

My sword cut down onto his arm, not a large cut but

blood showed on his sleeve.

I mocked, "Would you like to stop and have my father dress your wound?"

He growled and came at me harder than before.

He flew at me with strength rather than skill, a poor decision on his part. I wrapped my sword around his and pulled it from his hands. As it flew to the ground, I placed the tip of my sword against his collar bone. He glared at me as my sisters cheered.

"Looks like I will be going to war," I taunted.

He pushed my sword away and then the sweat from his chin, fire grew in his eyes.

I turned and rose my arms in victory running toward my mother and sisters.

My father met me on the field with a satisfying smile. "You fight well."

"Father, I should tell mother I am going with your troops."

He glanced at her with concern. "No. I did this. You have returned to us once, you will again. I'll help her understand." He then glanced toward Laroke. "I would ask Laroke to look out for you, but it seems I may need to reverse the favor." He laughed and patted me hard on the back before rushing toward Laroke.

Kira danced around me, Rika sang my praises, and my mother beamed. It would be the last time I'd see her smile before I left for the battle.

Dubieties (n) doubts

I couldn't believe the picturesque scene where our battle would be held; bright, lush and alive. I hated to have a battle in such a magnificent place. I pictured it ravaged by war. My heart sank at the thought.

I had been set up in a tent by myself and was grateful for the privacy and small space. The two extra days we spent waiting were excruciating. Tension and apprehension saturated the air. Every extra moment the men waited dipped their nerves further into tatters. My nerves frayed as well, and my mind raced constantly.

I didn't interact much with the troops, too caught up in my own thoughts and fears. I spent most of my time alone preparing myself mentally and physically for the battle I knew Dyre had been preparing for his entire life.

I did check on the preparations of the troops. I watched their skilled planning and felt useless. I didn't know what to do other than check on progress and offer words of encouragement. Although, when they announced the lost princess would be fighting a tangible wave of hope raced through the men. It gave me confidence. Although it felt odd for everyone to still call me the lost princess, like I hadn't been found.

I came to the troops which belonged to Jovan but didn't approach. I watched Jovan from a distance. He talked to them in a voice I knew well, authoritative yet compassionate. His men respected him, even those who were older and had probably been soldiers much longer.

I stayed watching Jovan for quite some time. As his company made their preparations, Jovan found reason to speak to every one of them. I could imagine the words he spoke, encouragement, praise, concern. He left each one of them with some kind of touch, a pat on the back, a hand on a shoulder. It made me smile.

I pulled the chain at my neck and took the box from inside my dress. Holding it in my hand only increased my desire to speak with him. The wish gnawed on my mind, but with so much at stake, such uncertainty about my life, and my future I couldn't find it in me to move toward him. Had it really only been a few days since we had seen each other last? It had to have all been a dream, from a million years ago. The more I watched him, the more I wanted to talk to him. I rushed to my tent and penned a letter instead.

My Dear Jovan,

Is it true we were together only days ago? Much has happened, many things have changed. It seems the only genuine truth I have at the moment is the knowledge of your love for me. I hold it close as the monster of uncertainty claws at the world surrounding the fate of Sylvaria.

Apprehension and uncertainty accompany what is happening currently in the kingdom. Every day some new event challenges the next, every night a new fear for what tomorrow might bring.

My thoughts of you bring me comfort and happiness, but my fear for you is weighty. Both warmth and worry accompany your name in my heart.

I have been moved again. The transition has been interesting for me as my duties are unlike any I have performed previously, and my treatment is decidedly opposite that of how I have been regarded in the past. I am sure I will acclimate sometime. I am not unhappy. On the contrary, I find myself loved and appreciated in ways I have only dreamed. I simply wish I felt more comfortable in my new position.

I have found use for the knowledge you taught me

in our youth. I thank you again for your willingness to teach me. So far I have been more successful than I could have anticipated because of you. I hope to make you proud.

I am troubled by reports of another battle. My thoughts will be with you, as they always are. If you speak my name on the battlefield, I will pray for it to bring you luck.

With all my heart I hope to see you safe again,
Eviona

I summoned a passing soldier, "Do you know a new soldier named Ayrik?"

"Yes, we are in the same company."

"Will you bring him to me?"

"Princess?" Ayrik's voice called outside my tent.

"Come in, Ayrik."

He lifted the flap with a confused expression. "Eviona?"

I ran to him, and we embraced in a gleeful reunion.

"What are you doing here? Are you the princess?"

I nodded grinning, "I guess my loyalty to Sylvaria is in my blood."

We talked, sharing stories of what had happened since we last saw each other.

Then he mentioned, "I requested to be part of Captain Jovan's company. I remembered his name." Then his eyes lit up, "Does he know who you are? Does he know you're here?"

I shook my head, "No. And you mustn't tell him. What if..."

I didn't need to finish. Ayrik understood my apprehensions, and grabbed my hand to squeeze it with comfort.

I gave him the letter. "Will you take this letter to Captain Jovan? Do not mention how you came by it."

He promised me he would deliver it as I requested and we hugged again. "Good luck in this battle, Princess." He lifted the flap to exit and chuckled my title to himself.

I made myself as comfortable as I could with a desire to break through to Dyre. Many subjects reeled through my thoughts, I wanted to make sure Kellam would be safe, I wanted to hear him talk of Marjeàn, I wanted to ask him to surrender, and I wanted to warn him about Laroke.

I concentrated on his veil. I labored harder to break through this time. He had evidently worked to prevent me from doing exactly this.

I started to find my way through. The colors swept from in front of me slowly and at last I could make out the shape of a face. It became clearer and clearer until I saw eyes looking directly at Dyre. They were the eyes of Marjeàn. I gasped, overcome with longing.

His incredible pull on me increased exponentially as Dyre stared at him. I could bear it only for a moment and backed out of my endeavors to talk to Dyre.

I sat alone in my tent after supper questioning, pondering, wishing.

Dyre's voice came into my head as he tried to break through to me. "Eviona?"

I let him in. "I'm here."

"I hope it did not hurt you to see him. You should know you are a constant on his mind."

My heart ached, but I relished his words. "Will you do something for me?"

"I cannot keep him from fighting, Eviona. Not in this battle."

"I understand about Marjeȧn, but please do not allow Kellam."

"Kellam has strict instructions to—" His tone changed as he realized what I knew. "How do you know about Kellam?"

"Laroke."

"Laroke?"

"He confuses me. I don't think he is on your side. I honestly don't know whose side he's on."

"Laroke is my best friend."

"Are you certain? He has been giving the king information about your troops. Although, it's not all correct."

"He's a master of deception. He's just playing the part like he used to when we had Zefforah destroy those villages."

"That was Laroke?"

"Of course. After the fifth town Zefforah stopped coming to my rescue, but Laroke is brilliant when it comes to things like that."

I hated him even more, "He's a traitor, Dyre."

"I don't believe you. Where have you heard these things?"

"Don't you know who I am?"

I felt his confusion at the question.

I asked, "What is your earliest memory of me?"

"I remember the day you were born. I think as soon as you started to breathe we connected. I remember not being able to see clearly through your eyes. Then within a few days, I had an incredible desire to stop the crying. I learned to place my veil to you pretty quickly."

"Ha. I guess we both learned to use the veil because of the other's annoying behavior."

He chuckled.

"Then let me ask you this. What is your first memory of me with Minuette?"

I felt his emotions go cold. He didn't like remembering this part of his life, but he walked me through it anyway.

"I remember when Zefforah brought you to me. Minuette took you before I even saw you. You were probably about two."

"What! Zefforah took me?" For the first time I could remember I felt angry with her.

"All she ever wanted was for us to be together."

"Did Zefforah know I was the princess when she stole me?" I barked at him.

His silence spoke his shock.

"You didn't know?"

"I swear to you, Eviona," He could barely breathe as he spoke. "I did not know. She didn't like the way things were going with Horrish and Minuette and insisted if you were with us..." His words trailed off as the shock of the revelation set in more deeply. "This is all wrong!" He started to panic. I felt him swallow and could feel his heart beating. "This is terrible. You're here! The lost princess is leading the battle! It's all over camp."

"That's right, I am," I said with as much pride as I could muster at the moment.

A deep groan rose from his chest, "No, Eviona! You begged me to send Marjeàn away and then you join the war? Worse than that, you are leading the battle!"

I spoke in only a whisper. "Your war is against me now."

"ARRRRRRR!" He pushed his table over onto its side, its contents crashing to the floor. Then he whispered, "I'm so stupid. I hate this war."

"Surrender. It can stop right now."

His head ached. He pushed on his temples trying to

relieve the pain. "This is the way it started. It must be the way it ends."

"I hoped you would be willing. My men are under orders not to kill you. If you would surrender, I could see to it that you would be—"

"I can't!" Then his feeling changed, his heart quickened, and he whispered hopefully, "Join me."

"What?"

"Eviona, if you would join me we'd both have what we want. You are right there, your father completely at your mercy. No one would even question you."

"No!" I couldn't believe the audacity of his conception.

"I would make sure you were with Marjeȧn."

I caught my breath bitterly, "You're cruel. How dare you!"

"It's your choice, Eviona. I will be King! We could both be happy. You could simply make it much easier."

"No! Tomorrow I will be leading this army against you."

"Eviona!"

I closed my veil with fury pulsing through my veins. I found a dagger and pressed the point of it to my heart. It would serve its purpose. Dyre would be destroyed. Too soon it fell from my hands. I hung my head, disgraced. Knowing my desire to live outweighed my desire to save Sylvaria.

A few hours into my sleepless night, I jerked with surprise when Zefforah's veil opened to me.

"Zefforah," I snarled. "If you would have left me with my parents none of this would be happening!"

I regretted the way I spoke even as I finished the sentence. She bowed with grief, understanding what it all meant. "I know your intentions were good. You can still help fix things. I want you to take Kellam and fly away from here. Leave Dyre."

I had asked her to abandon the person she loved most in the world. She looked to a corner of the room where one figure slept away from the others. It must have been him.

"Zefforah, please listen."

Her anxiety and questioning feelings pressed into me.

"I can't stop the war, and yet I would do almost anything to do it."

She looked at Dyre again, she wanted me to understand.

He must have told her about our conversation.

"I can't join him. I won't. It is impossible for me to break the trust of my father."

We both wanted her to see our sides, she simply wanted our unification. Unable to truly give in to either of us, she felt herself slighting us both.

She settled down on the ground and wrapped her wings around a figure. The slow sound of his breathing haunted me, a ghost from the past. Kellam.

"Please Zefforah, think about what I have said. Save Kellam, Dyre can fight without you, my soldiers have been warned to bring him in alive. Without you, his troops would certainly lose confidence, and Sylvaria could be saved."

Her veil closed. I lay in the dark, alone again.

Sleep unexpectedly came to me and our dreams centered on Dyre's map. I saw the stars, the three triangles touching in the center. The seven stars which looked like the mark on Zefforah's back and the one I had been told was on my own.

Awake, yet again, I moved outside. The stars spoke to me, an exact replica of the map. The day had come. Whatever event Dyre had been waiting for his entire life would happen today. A voice behind me jolted me from my thoughts. "Couldn't sleep?? I turned to face Ayrik.

I shook my head.

"Me neither."

"Do you believe in destiny?" I asked.

"What is destiny more than an end result? If there is such thing as destiny, it must change. With every thought we think, every word we utter, every choice we make our destiny adjusts to fit the consequences of that choice."

I put my head down and chuckled. "You don't believe in destiny."

"I didn't say that."

"What if it is Dyre's destiny to be king?"

"What if his destiny was simply to try, leading all of our lives to this moment in time? What if his end result is nothing more than to have had influence over the people of Sylvaria? He obviously has fulfilled that already."

I contemplated his response.

He put his hand on my shoulder, "In the morning your destiny will be to lead these men into battle. Choose your actions wisely. You may change the course of Dyre's destiny, and all of Sylvaria as well."

Embroil (v) to bring into discord or conflict

In the morning I dressed and practiced with my sword. I wore a soldier's uniform but with my smaller frame I clearly did not have the appearance of one. Perhaps it would benefit me. Dyre's men might feel less inclined to harm a girl, or conceivably more so inclined, knowing the lost princess would be the only girl fighting.

Dyre opened his veil. "Eviona, you can still change your mind."

"No."

"Look at the men around you. How many of them will be dead at the end of the day? You can save them."

"You could surrender before you kill us."

"See you on the field." His veil closed. The time had come.

"They're coming!" I shouted to the camp.

The incredible speed at which every soldier prepared to walk with me proved their excellence. Their strength and constancy granted me all faith in them and their abilities. We walked out to the base of the cliffs and waited in our lines.

I once thought beauty could make one brave. I didn't feel that way as I stood at the front of my men. I had been offered a horse, but declined. I hoped my troops would not see me as a weak and clumsy girl. Even though that is exactly how I felt.

On the other side of the valley at the base of the tower, Dyre's army gathered. At first, I thought the two forces equal in size, but it didn't take long to see we held the advantage in numbers. The animated murmur swept through my men showing they felt the same way. An encouragement.

As the enemy approached, the tone of my troops changed. The fearsome appearance of Dyre's army had an extraordinary effect on our attitude. On their helmets, they wore the heads of ferocious animals. Their shoulders wore the animals blood dipped coats. It felt as if we were to do battle with monsters. The terrifying thought worked its manipulation on our minds.

Zefforah appeared in the sky and circled above our heads. I felt a wave of panic go through my men.

"Are you ready to stop this, Eviona?" Dyre said. My head jerked to the right and left looking for him. "I'm not there. I will be watching from here." I glanced toward the tower and in a top window I saw movement and then myself through his eyes. The mask he wore scratched at my face.

"You could stop it," I muttered back at him.

"Let it begin."

I lifted my sword, pointed it toward the tower window where Dyre stood watching me and shouted the only thing I could think of. It sounded silly in my mind and too simple, but it had the desired effect. "For crown and kingdom! For Sylvaria!"

My men charged into the field and our enemies crashed into our lines. I found myself racing trying to stay with Zefforah. She opened her veil to me which disoriented me at first. I saw the conflict from three perspectives, hers, Dyre's and mine.

The battle raged around me. I moved quicker than most of the swords raised against me. I didn't have to worry too much though. There seemed to be a protective bubble around me.

Most of Dyre's men would turn and move another direction when they saw me. I wondered what he had told them about me. As I saw their reactions, I moved to fight in the places where my men were being hit the worst. I managed each time to scare away the enemy.

They feared me. I felt powerful.

I heard Dyre laughing in my head. Did he laugh at me, or his men?

Zefforah circled overhead. She swooped down close to me. I swished my sword toward her. A reflex. I softly apologized. She flew away, but I saw myself often through her eyes. She watched me closely.

Then I heard my name in the midst of the battle. Jovan. Within only a few feet of me, he fought an obviously well-trained giant of a man. The foe gained ground against Jovan. Panic swept through me.

Dyre cheered on the large man. I growled at him as I looked for a way to help. Then Jovan's sword flew from his hand, and he fell. I ran behind the large foe and in one quick movement turning in a fast circle I sliced his legs, and we both fell to the ground.

"I knew you'd save me, Eviona," Jovan whispered. He stood he offered me his hand. "Thank you, Princess." He lifted me to stand. I moved to him wanting to pull myself into him, but without a second glance he found his sword and rushed away to another fight. I thought he knew it was me until his retreat. I struggled to forgive him for being such a valiant soldier, disappointed he had not noticed me.

Dyre laughed. "No doubt Marjeán would have at least looked you in the face to thank you."

I turned around to glare at the tower window and rising before me stood the man whose legs I had sliced. Evidently I had not cut deep enough. His sword advanced to me, his eyes full of venom. With all of the fear I had experienced in my life nothing came close to the terror I felt at that moment. I ran.

"No, he can't!" Dyre yelled, "Zefforah help her!" Dyre flew down the stairs of the tower. Zefforah was already racing toward the man running after me, mere inches from reaching me. Her tail swished behind me and hit him with a thud. He'd fallen hard. I stopped running.

"Thank you, Zefforah." I panted.

She landed not far from me, and I approached, our eyes locked. Anticipation stung my fingertips. Just before I reached her Dyre yelled. "NO!" It wasn't us he yelled at. The man stood with sword raised behind Zefforah. Zefforah swished her huge tail and knocked him across the field, this time not to rise again.

Zefforah and I walked toward each other anxiously. Dyre called, "Zefforah, Eviona?"

I stopped short a few yards from her. Zefforah darted at me. With no time for me to react she picked me up with her tail as she flew into the sky. At our first touch, my soul breathed in. Light, joy, a surge of power and serenity filled every part of my being. I let it wash over me and relished the peace I found with her. I allowed my sword to slip from my hand. We flew, watched closely through Dyre's eyes.

She and I felt the same, happiness at being together at last.

"This has been too long in coming," I told her. Exhilaration pulled my arms to the side as she shot into the sky. As we raced upward, she grabbed me with her tail and flung me into the air. I flailed and screamed sure I would drop to my death, only to have her catch me and throw me up again. I caught my breath and calmed my heart knowing she was playing with me. She placed me again on her back, and we soared together through the clouds. Then we sailed over the battle and remembered the violence below us.

We flew to the base of the tower, directly in front of Dyre. My heart pounded. Was I to meet him? My tormentor, my mentor, my enemy, my friend.

Zefforah landed gently and pressed me to go to him. She helped me light to the ground only a few yards from a man I feared as well as longed to meet.

We walked toward each other. Jovan's description of him had been perfect. Dyre's large form in his black mask personified intimidation.

After a few steps, I felt a familiar pull and looked at the figures behind Dyre for the source. I called out to see where he was. "Marjeȧn?"

"Don't." Dyre held up his hand to stop me.

"I know he is here."

Out of nowhere came a raging cry, "Aaaaarrrrrrrrrr." Laroke drove his sword toward Dyre. Dyre raised his just in time to stop the blow. I had no sword and turned to find one as Zefforah protected me from the battle.

"What are you doing?" Dyre asked as he avoided the blows from his friend.

"I am winning the crown." Laroke thrust his sword again and again at Dyre who merely batted it away.

"You will have your place with me, just as we have always planned."

"You are a fool if you think I have worked all of this time simply to throw all of the glory to you."

"You *are* a traitor!" Dyre shouted at him.

"You worked for the kingdom your way, I worked for it mine." Laroke returned.

I had found a sword and darted toward them. Dyre cautioned me. "This is my fight, Eviona! Stay away!"

Laroke's head jerked toward me, "Eviona?"

Dyre growled and fought Laroke with his new understanding.

I stood watching, helpless as they struggled. Until I couldn't stand idle any longer. I rushed at Laroke. I pushed him from behind. He fell to the ground. Zefforah grabbed me with her wing and Dyre pushed his arm out to stop our advance.

His hand connected with my arm and her wing and a flash of lightning exploded from the sky crashing into the center of our circle. A wave of emotional electricity raced through our bodies and a blaze of light burst from our circle.

The three of us there alone, separate from space and time. No noise, no distraction, nothing but us. We dared not move. The touch brought us together into an unseen dimension.

Zefforah whinnied, almost a chuckle. Dyre laughed softly, and I too felt delight. Simple. Pure. Happiness.

Time had stopped; the three of us conscious, yet the rest of the world still, silent, in the morose poses of combat. The blood spilling from a wound stopped mid-movement, the sweat from a forehead, motionless, as if painted in midair.

A sharp pinpoint of sound split the silence open, and storms of thoughts crashed into us. We saw the minds of everyone around us, their views, their emotions, what they wanted, what they needed. We knew exactly how to make each person on that battlefield happy.

One man saw his wife and three daughters and a joyful reunion with no more war. His desire to kiss them and tell them he loves them embedded on my mind.

A young man saw his ever unnoticing father. He had come to gain recognition. Pain from a wound he had received flooded his body. He hoped it would move his father. Living or dying did not matter.

Another wondered why he had ever joined this war. He had a simple and happy life before this. He wondered what he would accomplish by being here.

Another, and another, and another.

Laroke's thoughts brought a horrible possibility of the future. Laroke used me and my position for his desires, Dyre was killed, my father slowly poisoned to death, and the entire kingdom of Sylvaria at his mercy.

Dyre growled ferociously. I grabbed his wrist before he could break our connection to take his fury out on his friend. Dyre's anger pulsed through our veins. "He needs to die now!"

I whispered to counter his volume and hopefully have him listen more closely. "First, we need to think of what we are doing. We need to stop this war. We need to be united." I begged.

"Are you going to join me?" Dyre asked hopefully.

Zefforah pushed her head into Dyre pressing him to surrender.

He looked at me.

"I will find some way to work things out with my father. Please surrender."

"I don't *want* this to go on." Dyre pushed his head sharp to the side. Thinking. He looked up into the heavens to find an answer. His whole body vibrated with his struggle. Horrish's words came hot from Dyre's mouth. "This is the way it started it must be the way it ends."

Zefforah pressed him with her head again. We all felt the same way. This is not the way it should have been.

"AAAAHHHHH!" Dyre bowed his head and breathed in deeply contemplating his entire future within only a few seconds.

His heart pounded in his chest as he nodded in agreement. "We will stop this battle, but first Laroke dies."

I nodded, "I'm ready."

"Eviona, let me fight him alone."

"No, we can defeat him together."

"Who's side are you on? Mine?"

I shook my head. "Ours?"

"If your father sees him as his supporter, and then hears you fought against him you will be the one to appear disloyal."

"He has lied to my father for all of these years."

"And to *me*, Eviona! He is a dead man." His tone commanded my submission. I reluctantly nodded my agreement.

Zefforah cried and wrapped her wing around us.

Whole for the first time, none of us wanted the moment to end.

Sanguinary (adj) characterized by bloodshed

Dyre released his hand, and I released mine. Time joined us, Laroke running toward Dyre. Zefforah and I backed away allowing space for the duel.

I hadn't ever witnessed Dyre's use of a sword before. Clearly, he'd been well taught. He grabbed another sword from the ground where a soldier had fallen and whipped them both ferociously toward his traitorous friend.

The wordless battle spoke volumes about their years together. Once brothers now fought as the bitterest of enemies. Dyre moved to higher ground and easily gained advantage over his foe. Until one of my soldiers rushed at Dyre from the back. Dyre saw it happening through my eyes, and Zefforah moved quickly in to assist. She raced to the place she saw the most danger, between Dyre and Laroke and within a mere second I felt steel move through my stomach. Laroke's blade glistened with Zefforah's blood. Dyre doubled over. I fell to the ground where I cried in pain. The salty smell of blood suffocated me as it rushed from my body.

Arms gathered me up. I knew they couldn't be Dyre's. Yet I couldn't open my eyes to see who carried me to the tower and up the stairs.

Zefforah, blood flowing from her, half flew, half struggled, to the vats of obiberry juice close to the tower. She broke them and fell into the juice, trying desperately to heal the wound. Dyre and I combined our screams with hers feeling the fire as she sank deeper into the healing, poisonous pool. Unseen flames raged over my body. I writhed and screamed causing my supporter to struggle with his footing several times.

Dyre roared with the torture. His cries moved through the battle like waves of thunder. Warning his friends and enemies alike to keep their distance.

The excruciating pain couldn't grow any worse. Zefforah struggled toward the water for its cooling relief, but I felt none when she reached it. The pain didn't last much longer. It had been replaced by a wave of release followed by a new unbearable ache. I couldn't feel her. I couldn't see her. I tried to see her veil to open it, to press against it but nothing existed. I had no pain left from the poison, or from the wound, only the agony of her absence as if a part of me had been ripped out from inside.

"No!" Dyre's voice combined with mine in understanding. Zefforah was dead. Our wounds healed, but at what cost?

I surrendered and sank into the void of the empty space within. Dyre wailed pushing his way out of it.

His cries must have become more human because several of my men rushed toward him.

I tried to speak, "Surrender."

He fought instead, continuing his battle, easily beating one after another as adrenaline rushed through his body. More of my men bolted at him. Their swords in constant movement, but he held his ground. He used the surroundings of the field to help him, grabbing items from the fallen to use in his defense, jumping over obstacles and creating them for his opponents.

A door opened, and the arms which held me placed me on the floor. I opened my eyes to see the face of my champion, but shuddered as Laroke lorded over me.

I screamed, and he placed his hand over my mouth.

Dyre's anger against his friend rekindled, but his veil went black. Perhaps he needed to focus, or perhaps he didn't want to see what the traitor had in store for me.

I pushed Laroke's body away from mine only to have his hands grab mine and push them to the floor.

"Stop fighting me! You are hurt. I'm trying to help you."

"Liar! You only want Sylvaria for yourself. You want Dyre and my father dead."

"You are so naïve, my dear." A sickening grin accompanied a sinister chuckle. "You are my secret weapon."

"I'll never help you! I'd rather help Dyre."

"You would detest him if you knew what he was."

"I have always hated Dyre."

"And Marjeàn?" He sneered.

It nearly killed me to think Laroke knew what Marjeàn meant to me. Or that he might know him better than I. "No! You don't know Marjeàn."

With all of my strength, I pushed to one side freeing one of my hands in the attempt. I thrust it forward into his nose hearing a crunch as I pushed.

He stared at me in disbelief as blood dripped from a nostril. One hand released me. I kicked my legs, and rolled again freeing myself.

I jumped up and recoiled to the opposite side of the room, breathing in, finally able to fill my lungs.

He stood and walked around the room slowly pressing his nose to his sleeve to mop the blood. "Do you want to know what your dear Marjeàn is really like?"

I circled the room opposite him, staying as far from him as I could. "You can't know him. Not like I do."

His mocking laugh hurt me to my core. "I know he isn't man enough to even kiss a woman who does little else than throw herself at him."

"You know nothing." I barked at him.

The throaty laugh coming at me clawed at my already wounded soul. "I know how little you know him."

"I know enough. I know his kindness."

"Kindness? Princess, he is not kind. You will see what kindness really is when I save your father from the grief of knowing his precious daughter is a conspirator with Dyre."

"Perhaps I should tell him of *your* life-long friendship with his enemy."

He smiled, "Who will he believe?" Looking at my uncertain face, the laughter started again. "Dyre's Eviona," he snarled.

I had recovered for long enough. A sword rested in the corner of the room I dashed toward it. He saw my intention and drew his own weapon. We began our duel.

We moved in a slow circle knowing with swords we stood on equal ground. This time saw no audience, no one to tell us to stop. This time, one of us would not leave alive.

"Shall I kill you or marry you? Either action would crush Dyre."

"I will not be used in your plans."

He lunged toward me. His sword came down hard and fast yet in too predictable of a blow. I parried easily. We resumed our methodical circle.

"This will be an entertaining marriage. A constant struggle to delight in." He mocked.

"What makes you think I would ever marry you?" I asked as our blades met, high then low, pulling back and pushing forward.

"You will be mine to do with as I please, Princess. And I will rule Sylvaria!" Then he mocked my father as he said, "It is the desire of the king, and I dare not oppose his wishes."

"I won't marry you! You'll have to kill me!" I lunged at him in too much haste, and his sword knocked mine down hard giving him opportunity to rush at me. His blade whipped to my throat, and he pushed my body with his arm and his sword until he crushed me against the wall.

"Killing you will be a pleasure. But I'll make another pleasure of you first. Right here and now to show your lover how easily it is to be done."

I still held a sword in my hand but couldn't manipulate it in any way which would benefit me. He nudged me to drop the sword pressing his blade at my throat until I did.

He murmured in my ear as his sword rested against my collarbone. "You're mine, Princess."

I couldn't move. I cringed as his tongue moved from my jaw to my eyebrow.

The door crashed open. Laroke whipped his head toward the sound. Dyre's figure stood in the doorway. Hope coursed into my body. An overwhelming desire to thank my liberator physically washed over me. Dyre opened his veil.

Laroke forced the sword tighter to my throat, and he turned slightly to keep an eye on Dyre. "I'll kill her!"

Dyre moved forward one slow step, and Laroke's blade tightened. Dyre dropped his sword and put up his hands. His head tilted up and to the side feeling the discomfort of the blade against my throat.

"Don't move," Laroke commanded both of us.

Dyre closed his eyes I could only see black. He wanted me to see something, to feel something, to do something. I tried my best to read his feelings, but my frantic thoughts made it too difficult.

He nodded his head knowing I couldn't do what he wanted. "Eviona." His cool voice shook softly. "Laroke killed Marjeȧn this morning."

"NO!"

I don't know whether my scream or Dyre's sudden rush on Laroke changed things, but I found myself pushing him to the ground.

He scuttled back to his feet but not before Dyre had obtained his sword. The men charged each other continuing a lifelong battle Dyre never realized existed. With only seconds from the first blow to the last Laroke lay bleeding on the floor. Dyre stood silently looking down on him watching the pain in his face. Laroke grabbed his leg, and Dyre kicked him hard in the ribs with the other. Laroke retched and tried to speak. A useless effort which quickly ended as his eyes glazed.

Dyre turned to me. "Eviona, are you alright?"

"Why? How? Please tell me of Marjeàn." I pleaded with Dyre to explain.

He fled from the room moving higher in the tower as the soldiers raged up the stairs.

"Surrender!" I called to him.

"Go!" He ordered.

My grief could not be acted upon. Although I felt the searing pain, my mourning would have to wait. I fled the room and ran down to my soldiers. Hoping somehow Dyre might change his mind I lead them down to the bottom of the tower. We made it outside before my men realized Dyre wasn't on the field and charged up the tower again.

As one man would fall reinforcements from both sides soon took their places. Dyre fought several men at once and lost his footing. As he stumbled, a sword caught the handle of his. It flew from his hand. Several hands tried to grab him. He fought them off, beating them. He would not give up easily. My hands bruised quickly as he crushed his fists into anything which touched him. He dove for his sword. I crumbled with pain as he hit the ground. A hand around his ankle prevented his dive from reaching its goal. He thrashed and fought until overpowered by my men.

It took at least seven or eight of my men to carry Dyre, continually writhing and fighting to a prison carriage. His men quickly surrounded them fighting my soldiers as they tried to shove him inside. Dyre's hands grabbed the door frame, and he kicked a soldier in the face which gave him opportunity. He jumped into the space fighting off the soldiers.

The battle seemed to converge into the area where Dyre fought. Like a tornado pulling men into it and leaving carnage in its path. Men from each side fought and fell. Dyre brawled, willing himself not to be overpowered until a good number of my men started in on him all at once. I felt the beating as they thrust him into the carriage and chained the door closed.

Dyre roared, "I WILL BE YOUR RULER! I WILL BE YOUR KING!" His downfall surged through my veins with the violence of his rage and devastation. His whole life's goal had been to win this battle. His loss stung more than the physical beating.

Men continued to thrash at the carriage. Dyre hammered his fists and body into the carriage walls and screamed obscenities at the men outside.

I staggered toward it as they drove him out of the field. It only had one small window, and as the carriage passed me, Dyre reached out his hand. "Eviona." I watched him until I could no longer see myself.

Expense (v) the price paid

I staggered into the field where the battle continued, but with their leader gone and Zefforah dead many men retreated, and our soldiers easily gathered the rest. Soon the fight ended with nothing left but the evidence of a vile battle.

They took Dyre to a special place in the castle prison. Weighted with chains and prodded along with blades. If he could find the chance, he would try to escape. They had obviously expected it and gave him no opportunity. Once in his cell, he watched through me as I dragged myself through the battlefield.

Several captains set up places for prisoners and others for taking care of the wounded. I heard Jovan's voice. "Bring cots from the tents, bandages, and obiberry juice. We have more work to do!" As he placed himself in charge of the wounded, instinctively I wandered the battleground searching for those who could be taken to him and hopefully saved. Bloody bodies surrounded me. Dead and suffering men from both sides lay scattered on the ground. I moved to one and then the next trying to do whatever I could to help any survivors.

A hand reached out and grabbed my ankle. I crouched down next to him. Dyre gasped, "Kellam."

As fast as I could, I pried off his helmet and put pressure on the wound in his side. I pulled him up into my arms and cried whispering softly to him. "Kellam."

He looked at my face with glossy eyes. "I must be dreaming. You look exactly like..." He stopped and groaned in pain.

"Kellam, it's me."

His eyes closed and he smiled before another cringe came to his face. "Eviona. You came to fight alongside

Father."

I simply nodded unable to tell him the truth and pleaded with him. "Hold on." In panic, I searched for someone with the healing juice. "JUICE! I need some obiberry juice here now!"

His lip twitched with pain, but he tried to smile, "Remember our duels?"

"Can't you do something?" Dyre pressed. "Help him!"

I received juice and tipped it slowly into his mouth as he struggled to swallow. "Kellam. Oh, Kellam." I cried and held him and rocked him as if he were still a child. Guilt filled me as the words Dyre spoke to me this morning rushed back to my mind. 'How many of them will be dead at the end of the day? You can save them.'

Kellam struggled to speak again, and I knew the end of his pain would come shortly. "Did we win?"

"Yes, we won," I spoke the words I knew he wanted to hear.

His eyes closed. "He…didn't want me to fight." He swallowed and his eyebrows buckled, and a moan followed. His face contorted into what I thought must have been an attempt at a smile. His hand grabbed my arm, and he squeezed it tightly. "Tell him…" He tried to breathe in. Three times he tried. His eyes closed and he breathed out slowly.

Dyre whimpered, "Hold on son, hold on. Stay with me."

Kellam fell limp.

Dyre shouted, "Kellam!"

I rocked and wept holding his lifeless body. I couldn't bear the weight of loss. Dyre and I suffered the pain together. We both felt empty and alone without Zefforah, pained at the death of Kellam, and Dyre without his victory, without his dream.

The excruciating ache ate us both beyond what we thought possible. I grieved for Marjeȧn, for Dyre, for my soldiers and his, grieved for their families, and grieved for Sylvaria.

Later as our caravan reached the castle wall, my mother ran to me. Throwing her arms around me, she cried in gratitude for my safe return. After a closer look at my face and clothes she whimpered. "How badly are you hurt?"

"I'll be fine, Mother. I'm home."

My father came rushing out behind her. Cheering as he came. "Victory! Victory!" He picked me up to hug me until I grunted in pain. He released me gently and apologized. Then looking around at the faces of the passing soldiers he questioned. "Where is he? Where's Laroke?" His smile faded as I shook my head gently telling him of his loss.

My mother softly tugged at me, and we continued our walk into the castle. I looked back at my father. Stunned and motionless as he grieved for the loss of a man he never should have loved.

"Come to me, Eviona." Dyre spoke as soon as I woke up. I could sense his urgency to see me. His anticipation when I returned from the battle felt almost unblockable.

"No!"

"I'm waiting for you. Please come to me."

"Why would I?"

"When you are desperate to hear the message Marjeȧn left for you, you will come."

I sighed, knowing he was right. Sooner or later I'd have to face him.

Mordacious (adj) sharp or biting

Anxious for life to go on, I devoted my time to my family. I left my veil open sometimes when I felt too mentally weak to close it, but Dyre didn't say much other than his pleas for me to come to him. He watched me with my family. I think he might have been happy for me to have finally found my true home.

Mornings we gathered for family meetings. Per their request sometimes I told my family a bit about my life. One day as they asked questions about my childhood I decided to answer them honestly. As I spoke, my father's face grew with rage, my sister's with terror, and my mother's with tears. Seeing their distress, I asked questions of them taking the focus from myself. I decided to keep the facts of my life to three areas, my time with Sanura, my life with the children, and my days as a servant, to anyone but Marjeȧn.

My mother had taken upon herself to challenge my education. Several hours of each day were dedicated to studies and tests. The more she tested me, the more pleased she became. When she asked something I knew, I would recite what I'd learned of the subject and watch my mother's face beam at my knowledge. I thought often of my first teachers, Jovan and Elina and hoped they would be proud of me.

Some afternoons and most evenings belonged to my father who introduced me to friends, took me to parties, concerts, small gatherings and large social events. My father, though clearly still mourning the loss of Laroke, spent his time bragging about me and found any occasion to do so.

My sisters took their turn as well, giving me tours of the castle rooms and telling me stories from their childhood. How I wished I had a place in them.

My sisters had always been happy and had never

known cruelty or deception. In some ways I envied them their naivety. They talked of how Mother and Father understood nothing of what it felt like to be young. Their ignorance annoyed me. At least in some areas I felt more qualified to be a queen than the innocent girls who had been trained in my stead. I would bring experience which they couldn't dream of to the throne.

I was very aware of Dyre's presence. Every once in a while he would chuckle or mutter something under his breath. The void Zefforah left seemed a bit more bearable when Dyre and I connected though. I felt more at ease when our veils were open.

One afternoon during one of our tours my sisters took me to the palace atrium. A grand garden room filled with mirrors. Flowers and trees of all kinds burst in colorful assembly appearing to repeat forever through the panes of glass.

I had readied that morning without really seeing what I had dressed in. Now, I had no choice but to notice with my reflection at every side. I wore a simple dress, compared to that of my sisters; adorned with austere patterns. A single braid flowed down my back and wisps of hair dangled around my face. It reminded me of the first time I had ever looked into a mirror. I remembered my surprise at the impossibility of my own beauty. As I stared at myself, I felt a wave of emotion. A longing I hadn't felt in a long time. I heard an audible breath from Dyre, and then he placed his veil.

One day as my mother and I were having our lessons I felt a surprising strike on my face. My hand raced to cover my stinging cheek as I opened my veil and saw my father through Dyre's eyes.

Dyre's hands were raised, chained to the ceiling.

"You do not want to do that, Sire," Dyre warned.

"Are you threatening me?" My father whispered intensely.

My mother, confused by my obvious distress, stopped our lesson. "Are you alright?"

I nodded but asked, "May I take a walk? I need some air."

She dismissed me but pulled my wrist away from my face before I left. "Do not press your hand so firmly into your face. You're leaving finger marks."

I nodded as I escaped to listen to the conversation between Dyre and my father.

"I told you before," Dyre's calm voice obviously upset my father. "I will give any information you wish to know only to your daughter."

"You are not in a position to demand such a thing."

"Then clearly you do not truly want the information you keep asking for."

"I warn you, I will use torture."

I felt Dyre smile. "Ask her if she wishes for me to be tortured. If she does, I will tell you everything, after you do your worst to me."

"I will never ask her to see you."

"Then you will never have your information."

My father's face grew red with rage, and he left the cell. As the door closed, Dyre let out a relieved laughed. Then he spoke low, pleading words. "Please, Eviona. Come to me."

That evening my father and I rode back to the castle after a visit with friends. Anxiousness distinct in his face. "Father, is there something on your mind?"

"Yes, Triella."

I cringed and asked what I had wanted for so long.

"May I beg for you not to address me by my given name?"

"What would you have me call you?"

"Eviona. It's the only name I have known."

The smirk on his face confused me.

"Is it a silly name?"

"No, your mother called you Eviona as a pet name when you were young. It simply means 'mine.' I know she will be grateful to hear it is the name you have gone by and remembered while you were away from us."

I felt grateful to have my name back. "Now, what can I do to help calm your mind?"

"You don't have to. If you are uncertain at all, I would rather torture the man."

"Dyre."

"Yes. He wants to speak with you. He has promised me certain information, but only if he can speak to you."

"He likes to be in control," I thought out loud.

My father nodded his agreement and placed his hand on top of mine. "You do not need to do it. I am already preparing the means by which to force his answers."

"No! No torture. I will go see him."

"I'm not certain I want you to."

At times I would have gladly met him. Now when I needed to, I would struggle to force myself to do it.

My father patted my hand reassuringly. "We have precautions in place already. His hands will be chained to the ceiling and his legs to the floor. He will not be able to hurt you."

"I'm not scared of Dyre, Father."

"You may be brave Triel— Eviona, but do not be foolish."

I opened my veil to Dyre as my father and I continued our journey home in silence. He didn't speak to me, but I could feel his heartbeat, just as he could feel mine.

Sleep, though difficult, finally came somewhere in the dark of the night my dreams conjured wounded men lying around me. Zefforah struggling for breath and screaming as she burned to death in an obiberry pool. I took a sword and approached a man. As I thrust it into him, I looked at his face. Marjeàn. I sat up with a start gasping for breath and crying aloud. I don't know if my startle woke Dyre or if he had been awake before, but he listened to me.

After a long silence, he whispered, "I'm sorry, Eviona. You should have never witnessed such an awful battle."

Even as rare as an apology came from him, I didn't respond. After seeing what I had in my dreams I wanted to curse him, to yell at him, but I didn't. I didn't want to give him the satisfaction of hearing me so vulnerable.

"Eviona?"

"Go to sleep," I commanded.

"I didn't know."

"What are you talking about?"

"I didn't know what the day would bring. I only knew it to be the day the map showed. I still wonder what was supposed to happen."

I remained silent and felt his pain with him.

Not wanting to fall asleep again I asked, "Now we know where I came from. What happened to your parents?"

"I don't know if he was my father, but I do remember being held by a man with strong hands." He looked at his own as he remembered.

"Then my memories run out. I never asked her, but I believe Zefforah may have taken me from him. I wonder what would have been different if I could have kept him with me." His feelings turned angry, and he didn't say anything for a long time.

"Are you thinking of Horrish?"

He clenched his fist, confirming my question.

"Dyre," I whispered.

"That's not my name!" He yelled.

"I don't understand."

"That's the stupid name I made up for myself! Horrish convinced me my name had to be strong, powerful, a name people would fear when they heard; the name of a leader, the name of a king. Dyre was the meanest sounding name I could think of." He scoffed at himself. "Dyre." I could feel his distain. "He was right. People fear the name."

"Guess what my real name is?" I offered trying to change the mood.

"Triella."

I giggled, it sounded juvenile like my sisters, and I stopped myself short. "I guess it is common knowledge."

He laughed. I wasn't sure if he laughed at the name or the way I had giggled, but it did alter his feelings.

"I asked my mother why she had named me Triella. She told me the mark on my back reminded her of the three portions of a soul; one spiritual, one emotional, and one carnal. My name means 'girl of three parts."

"Interesting."

"So, what is your real name?"

I thought it an innocent question, but his feelings returned to their former state of anger, "All those who really knew me are dead."

My heart sank and for a moment we mourned together the loss of Zefforah, Kellam, and Marjeȧn. I fought the tears coming to my eyes, and my voice shook as I asked. "What happened to Marjeȧn?"

"I don't think you really want to know."

"What did he say?" I begged.

"I promised him I would not tell you until we stood face to face."

I debated about breaking the silence of the night with my decision. With nothing but the sound of our combined breaths between us, I whispered, "I'm coming."

His chest tightened, and he closed his eyes smiling slightly. Not a grin, nor a malicious smile, simply a smile of... of relief.

Trachle (n) an exhausting effort

"Eviona." My mother's voice aroused my attention from staring at the piece of food on my fork. "Are you thinking about eating any of that?"

"Yes Mother, I am eating."

"No, my dear, you aren't." She gestured around the empty room. The chairs which had occupied my father and sisters now sat empty and even their place settings had been removed. I wondered how long I had been here without even noticing life happening around me. My mother came and stood beside my chair. "What is the matter, my dear?" Her soft and melodic voice nearly comforted my anxiousness.

"Mother, what was I like as a baby?"

"You were different from your sisters. You lived in another world. You'd smile and coo at nothing, and sometimes cry with no apparent cause."

I chuckled imagining how different from normal babies I must have been.

"Everyone said you were the most beautiful baby, and that certainly hasn't changed." She touched my face. "Eviona. Mine."

My father's tender voice interrupted us, "Eviona." We looked up.

"It's time. He's ready."

My mother looked at me with confusion in her eyes. I nodded to my father. "I can go alone, Father. Stay here with Mother. You will have to tell her."

"Tell me what?" she asked as I left them alone.

I opened my veil to Dyre, he watched, silently waiting for me.

My anticipation grew with each step. The eagerness Dyre felt made me tense. He made fists with his hands; opening and closing them faster and faster as if he could make me walk more quickly by doing so. My heart pounded, and he grew apprehensive.

The prison had two wings. I skirted the one with open cages holding Dyre's men who'd been captured. They called to me as I turned the opposite direction, toward the wing with one lone, closed cell.

I glared down the long hallway toward the door. Dyre lifted his head to see the other side of the same door.

The hallway opened into a small guard's room with a table, fireplace, and bed. The guard greeted me and placed the key in the lock, I stopped him. "Give me the key please, and leave me here alone."

"The king said..."

"Please, Dyre is already in chains, he cannot hurt me. I wish to be alone."

His hand shook as he put the key into my hand. "If the king finds out..."

"I won't tell him. Are you planning to?"

He laughed uneasily, but left me alone.

I put my face in my hands and pushed on my forehead, driving back the fear and incredible emotions. They rushed through Dyre as well. With both of us experiencing so many things it would be impossible to name each feeling.

Making sure I was alone, I bowed my head and pressed my hands to the door between us. "Can we converse like this?" I asked.

"We can," Dyre responded. "But you will not leave with the information you want."

"What about my father's information. What has he asked?"

Dyre laughed, "Only things you already know. He wants to know who helped me. You can give him the names of anyone you can think of. Horrish and

Minuette, and I would love for him to know the truth about Laroke." Anger filled his mouth at the word. He spit into the corner as if trying to rid himself of it. "He was only supposed to become close to a soldier or a guard."

"I will gladly tell my father the truth about him. He loved him like a son, but I hate him."

"Tell him Laroke's father is still alive. It might help him to believe."

"He's alive?"

"Yes, he lives not far from Lady Delsa."

My heart broke for my father's sake, but my own rage toward Laroke could not wait to reveal his secrets.

Silence thickened between us. Neither of us gave in to the wishes of the other. I would not go into his cell, and he would not tell me of Marjeȧn.

At last I whispered, "Did he really love me?"

"Marjeȧn?" His voice caressed the name the way I wanted to caress the man.

I swallowed and entreated again, "Please."

"Come in, Eviona."

I lost all resolve. I needed that question answered more than I needed my heart to beat. I put my arms down, straightened my shoulders and told myself I had prepared myself in every way for this meeting. I had thought of every form his face might have. I had pictured it fierce, handsome, deformed, severe; so many different ways. I stood ready to see him. Whatever his looks, I already knew the man. This, a simple technicality, would change nothing.

I put the key into the lock and opened the door. A force I could not see grabbed me, pulling me as if caught in an undertow. As my body rushed forward, I caught hold of the door frame to hold myself still and looked up to the source of the tide.

"Eviona, now you know." I knew the voice like I knew my own. I hadn't planned to know the face, but I did. My chest constricted, and my breath grew weak. I stepped back and slammed the door. I then pressed myself against it as I whispered his name. "Marjeαn?"

Acquiesce (v) to agree with some reluctance

Grief, frustration, anguish filled me. It seemed every part of me cried out against the truth of this revelation. Tears coursed down my cheeks. I thrashed against the door until pain raced through my limbs. I knew he listened, I knew he felt. He didn't block me. He didn't say anything.

The guard rushed to me pulling my arms from their pounding. He examined me. "He did hurt you. I never should have left."

I shook my head and brushed the tears from my cheeks with a hard swipe of my hand. "The information he gave me hurts." I kicked the door one last time, handed the key to the guard and charged up the stairs. I whispered continually as I stormed away from him. "How could you lie like that? I hate you. How could you?" My body and soul felt weak as if I had been the one tortured.

When the frequency of my chiding diminished, I heard him whisper. "Eviona…"

I screamed and placed my veil slowly and with whispering cries kept repeating. "I hate you, Dyre. I really hate you."

As I closed the door to the dungeon, my father came rushing toward me. He wrapped his arms around me, and I cried helplessly. After a minute he asked. "What did you learn?"

Turning my own anguish into that of my father's I sobbed, "Laroke. Laroke and Dyre were friends from their childhood. He came here as part of a plan. Their intention was simply to have him become close to one of your soldiers or perhaps a guard, you played into their preparations better than they had anticipated."

He grasped my arms tightly and pushed my body

away from him to look into my face. "No, I refuse to believe it."

"We should let Laroke's father know what has happened to him." I whimpered.

"No! He is *my* son. I loved him. He loved me." My father hung his head and pulled me into him.

"Love." I almost cursed the word. We cried through our embrace, each mourning a relationship we once thought of as pure.

My mother's usual calm face had tinged with too much pink and started to turn red. "I still think we should have the gala."

I had never seen my parents arguing before and felt uncomfortable being in the same room with them as they shot short angry sentences in increasingly whispered tones across the table. Having only experienced the volume of anger before, I found the lack of it in my parent's harsh whispers to be far more chilling.

My father gestured to me without really seeing me. "Think about Eviona! She is heartbroken over Laroke." I allowed my father his fantasies of Laroke, it was much easier to explain my own melancholia.

"Mother, Father." I attempted to interject, but my sisters shook their heads at me with wide warning eyes.

"How can you even think about a party?" Father continued.

"I want to celebrate our daughters return to us! It's been weeks since she arrived and after the war, the kingdom is in need of *something*. Anything happy. A celebration is called for right now."

My father's pain for Laroke had not passed, and my own misery about Marjeàn had been too dark. She wanted to help us.

She looked at me in hope. "Eviona, don't you think a gala would help lift your spirits?"

The last time I had been heartbroken my spirits had been lifted by the thought of one man. Jovan. "We should invite the soldiers, of course. At least those of high rank."

Relief glimmered on her face. "Of course."

I met my father's confused stare. "Perhaps?" I offered.

I bowed my head and wondered if a gala really could end my despair. Could seeing Jovan again somehow end the betrayal I felt from Marjeàn? I didn't know the answer to the question, but I did feel somehow lighter as I allowed thoughts of Jovan to flood into my mind.

In the few days leading up to the gala, I focused only on Jovan. My excitement to see him grew with each passing hour until I could barely stand the wait. I wondered how he would take the news of my being the princess. Would he ask me to marry him again right away or would he want to know my family better and gain my father's approval before bringing up the subject?

I found my thoughts occasionally turning traitorously to Marjeàn. I kept my veil to Dyre closed although I wondered what his thoughts were. Every night I wished I could close my eyes and see into his dreams, but I couldn't force myself to sleep, and it seemed the harder I tried the less I rested.

If I did drop my veil, I found myself listening to his breathing wondering if what I felt for Marjeàn could have ever been returned in his feelings, or if I merely played the part of a pawn in his plans. I didn't want to know the answer. If he truly loved me, my heart would be torn with the knowledge that my position would make it impossible for us to be together. If he never did love me, my heart would be broken in the wake of my memories. It would be best not to know either way.

The day of the ball arrived. I chose a pale yellow dress similar to the color of the one I had worn the first time Jovan caught a glimpse of me as a girl. I also had my hair fashioned in a style reminiscent of how Sanura used to do it. I anxiously watched and waited as coaches arrived bringing the guests. I became increasingly pleased as I found myself acquainted with some of them. Most I knew were the captains I'd met in my father's war room, but at least I had some connections in attendance. It helped me to feel more at ease in the crowd.

Then I saw the sight I had looked forward to most. I stood on a balcony overlooking the long drive to the castle as Jovan stepped from a coach. His strong chin and straight shoulders blazed with confidence. I expected nothing less. My heart raced in my chest. Just before my feet could join Jovan turned back to the coach and offered his hand. A petite woman's glove reached from the shadows and a delicate sylph emerged.

My heart continued to beat despite my wish for it to stop. Perhaps she meant nothing. I had almost succeeded at building my courage to approach him despite the presence of the enticement beside him until my sisters approached me.

"Everyone looks so enchanting. Don't you think, Eviona?" Rika said.

"Are you two familiar with that girl there?" I pointed out my subject as she walked arm in arm with Jovan into the castle.

"Oh yes," Kira squealed a little too excited to share in some gossip. "Her name is Lady Zaiah. Captain

Jovan always brings her to the castle, and yet he is totally unfaithful to her."

"What do you mean?"

"When he visits the homes of different families he chooses a servant girl ever day to accompany him."

"I think it's sweet," Rika interjected.

"I think it's devious," Kira countered. "He simply wants every girl he can have, and uses his *kindness* as a rouse for getting what all men want."

"But father likes him. He is smart and very skilled according to father. In fact, if you were to have a contest between him and Laroke, I think Captain Jovan—"

Rika was interrupted by a rude nudge from Kira and a glance at me. They must have thought the talk of Laroke caused the pain on my face.

Rika took my shaking hand in hers. "I'm sorry."

I had to escape. I no longer wanted to see Jovan, and I couldn't stand the thought of pretending to be happy tonight. "I don't feel very well."

Rika touched my shoulder. "You look pale. Do you want something to drink?"

"Maybe you should sit down." Kira took my hand and motioned for me to follow her.

"I need to go to my room."

"We'll help you."

I wanted to be alone. "No, please enjoy the evening for me."

"When you aren't well?"

I made it seem like a favor to me. "I need you to enjoy it for me. You must fill me in on every detail when I'm feeling better."

"Of course," they cheered together.

"We will not let one sparkle of the night go unnoticed."

They allowed me to walk away alone. I escaped the balcony and made my way through the back hallways.

Instead of going in the direction of my room I found myself at the door which led to the dungeon. I walked down the dark stairway and toward Dyre's cell. No guard to distract me left me even more vulnerable. Why had I come? I didn't want to talk to the man being held there.

I tread softly to the door which barred me from him, and sat on the floor with my back against it. I hoped he would not hear me or feel my presence. He shouldn't mean anything to me, he was nothing but a liar. Some strange desire forced me here, to feel his pull. Whether he loved me or not, I ached for him.

He spoke loud enough for me to hear him through the thick door. "Why aren't you at the celebration enjoying time with your precious Jovan?"

His scathing voice hurt as much as the words he spoke. I didn't move. Perhaps, if I sat still long enough, he wouldn't think I stayed.

Then the guard returned and though I motioned for him not to speak he asked, "Princess, shouldn't you be upstairs? Look at you. You are ruining your dress."

I prayed Dyre could not hear him and glanced down at the pale yellow material now streaked with dirt.

The guard continued, "Surely there will be someone at the party who can make you feel comfortable." He twirled the keys in his hands as he spoke. "I know! Captain Jovan is accustomed to spending time with ladies of all stations. I am certain he could make you feel quite comfortable. Shall I go and fetch him?" He turned to leave.

"No," I begged.

Two steps down the hall he stopped and turned around. "Of course, he is with Lady Zaiah. He's never without her. Maybe he's not the best choice."

I had no desire for the guard to continue speaking of how Jovan was breaking my heart, and I prayed Dyre had not heard. I tried to shift his attention. "Will you bring me a small plate from the refreshment table? I think I simply need some strength."

"Of course." He bowed shortly and left me alone in the cold stillness of the dungeon.

"I see. You find the truth about me, and you run to Jovan. Then you find the truth about him, and you run to me." Dyre's thick, dark voice may have been muffled behind the door, but it wrenched my heart. His loathing dripped from every word. "Only faithful when it suits you."

I allowed his words to berate me.

"Why did you come here tonight? Did you think I would comfort you? Did you think I would rejoice in your inconstancy? Did you think I would be grateful for his rejection of you? I am grateful! I am grateful you're alone. I am grateful you are hopeless and hurt. You should be." He hit the door hard, and it shuddered against my back.

I pulled myself slowly from the floor and did my best to brush the dirt from my skirt. The night which had started in a sweet yellow would end in a dull sallow reflecting my heart.

Dulcify (v) to appease

The next morning my parents asked in concern about my health. Because the color of my cheeks still remained several shades too light it was easy to pass myself in need of more rest. For the next few days, I allowed my anger and anxiousness toward Dyre to fester.

One especially bad night I paced my room anxiously. His eyes opened. I hated it. I hated how I longed to hear his voice, hated my ache to be near him. Filled with frustration and wrath, I snapped.

"Why did you tell me you were dead?"

He huffed, "I needed to distract Laroke. It worked well. Your reaction certainly helped."

"Why didn't you tell me who you are? Why didn't you kiss me?"

"Why would I?" He answered coldly.

"Because you loved me?" I sounded pathetic.

"I never loved you. I took you there to be kept ignorant and out of the way."

His words only increased my fury. I wanted to slap him. The pain I'd cause myself would be a small sacrifice. I grabbed a candle for light and raced through the dark halls of the castle. I reached his dungeon, put down my candle, and shook the sleeping guard.

"I need the key."

He opened one eye and squinted with the other. "No precautions have been taken. He'll kill you."

"Then give me your sword, and the key." I enunciated every word to make myself understood.

Both eyes attempted opening but quickly failed to try. "The king will have my head."

I slipped the sword from his scabbard and put the tip of it to his throat. "I will have your head if you don't. You choose."

Both eyes whipped open. His hand touched the blade at his throat. He handed me the key.

I opened the door and dropped the key as I picked up the candle. The guard watched with concern as I pulled the door closed.

There in front of me stood Marjeán. His head bowed. His ice blue eyes locked with mine; red where they should have been white as though he hadn't slept for days. His beard had become thick, and lengthy, along with his hair. He looked broken with his shoulders slouched. His chest raised and lowered in slow breaths.

Wrath coursed through me as I placed the sword and my candle on the floor and ran to him raising my hand to slap his face. He caught it midair and the rush of our connection killed me, especially knowing he never loved me. I sobbed and collapsed.

He caught me pulling me into him and spoke quick and soft. "I lied. I wanted you with me. I would have said anything to make you come. They were lies."

I melted into his arms. The rapture without a veil between us only doubled the fire. Twice the need, twice the ecstasy.

His lips brushed against my forehead, and I smelled my hair as he inhaled.

I grabbed his hand and pressed his palm to my mouth. I closed my lips against it and then pushed it to my cheek and neck. His fingers wound in my hair as my hands moved up his chest.

With my eyes closed, I begged, "Speak to me in his voice."

His low rough voice spoke the words I wanted to hear most. "I love you."

I caught my breath and pulled myself even further into him.

His arms wrapped around me tighter burning me from my innermost parts to every extremity.

He maneuvered my neck with one hand while the other caressed my cheek until our eyes met. The hunger of our mouths pulled us slowly closer. Too slowly.

"Eviona!" My father's panicked voice called from the other side of the door. "Eviona!"

We froze and listened to the key in the lock. Desperation for Marjeȧn and his promised kiss clouded my thoughts. My mind couldn't register how it could be wrong for me to be in his arms.

"Eviona!" My father's voice again.

I could not answer, and my body refused to break connection.

As the door opened, Marjeȧn pushed me away. I looked up, pain expressed in thick scowls on both of our faces. I still couldn't move.

"Eviona!" My father rushed to me placing his body as a shield between me and his enemy.

I looked only at Marjeȧn's eyes. Aching to reach for him again, frenzied at our craving to touch.

"Come." My father moved toward the door forcing my feet in a direction they did not want to go. They dragged like stones digging trenches into the floor.

Marjeȧn tipped his head slightly to the side telling me to go. I closed my eyes and allowed my father's strength to move me out of his gravity. Marjeȧn's footsteps moved toward the back of the cell. I opened my eyes as the guard picked up the sword and candle. Then the door closed between us.

My father cried as he held me in a strong embrace. My arms lay weighted to my sides. Tears fell down my cheeks, but my face remained as the rest of my body, empty.

"The guard came and woke me as soon as he could.

It's a miracle that man didn't hurt you. Why would you go in there?"

I couldn't answer. I couldn't think clearly. What was the question? Why couldn't I be with Marjeȧn?

"Eviona?" My father's voice spoke to me. Meaningless words my deaf ears ignored.

Then I registered his initial question, and more coherent thoughts came to my head. My eyes focused, and I responded, "He has answers no one else can give me."

My father shook his head and with his arm around my shoulder helped me back to my room.

The next morning I found myself in the dungeon, again with no guard. It didn't matter though, I wouldn't be going in. I simply wanted to feel Marjeȧn's pull. Just for a moment. I pressed my body against the door and watched from his eyes as he placed his hand on the other side. I relished the weight of the magnet drawing me through the thick wood.

I expected to hear his voice. Instead, a voice behind me made me jump. "I don't think you should be here."

I turned to see the same guard from last night. "He's very quiet," I commented out of embarrassment for my previous position glued to the door.

"He is." He agreed. "The door is rather thick, but I can hear him sometimes if he talks loud enough to himself and he's made a few requests, but most of the time he's unproblematic. Not quite what I had expected from a criminal of his status."

"What kind of requests?"

"Simple things I suppose; a bucket of water to wash, an extra biscuit and such."

"Do you give them to him?"

"No, Highness," he answered, proud to not allow

Dyre such luxuries.

"I would like any possible requests to be granted." The puzzled look on his face begged an explanation. "I have done my time in a dungeon. Starving. Filthy. Wouldn't you want those things?"

"I didn't know, highness. If you wish, I will grant any reasonable desires."

I nodded and turned from him to press my hand and cheek against the door again. "I need to go."

"Thank you," he whispered, his hand pressed opposite mine.

"I want you to be alright," I whispered lowly hoping the guard wouldn't hear.

The guard cleared his throat. "I appreciate that, Princess."

The sound of Dyre chuckling didn't penetrate the door, but it made me smile as I walked away.

I struggled night and day with my feelings. How could I live like this? Loving Marjeàn meant betrayal to my family and treason to the kingdom. Yet knowing he truly did love me, with as much intensity as I felt for him, too often I found myself entertaining thoughts I shouldn't.

I tried to block him each morning but frequently lost any resolve. I fell back to my old habits of depending on him to close his veil. More often than not the veil between us did not exist.

People filled my days and often I could not speak to him, but it did not prevent him from speaking to me. He made me laugh sometimes, and often sang me to sleep with his glorious voice.

Coaptation (n) the joining or adjustment of parts to one another

"I'd like to introduce you to someone this afternoon," my father told me. He often brought people in to introduce me to. We walked together to a sitting room where I'd spent hours chatting with people my father approved of and hoped I'd become friends with. As we approached a servant came with a message for my father. He read it quickly.

"I must attend to some business. Will you be alright introducing yourself?"

"Of course I will." I kissed his cheek, a gesture he returned before making a swift retreat.

When I opened the door the very shy smile of the sylph, Lady Zaiah greeted me. I took a deep breath and entered closing my veil before Marjeȧn could learn her identity.

"Hello, Lady Zaiah. I'm Princess Triella." I greeted her cordially, and we sat together. We only exchanged the minimum required courtesies. I thought I would explode from the silence. Finally, I asked her about our common subject.

"I understand you generally come here with Captain Jovan."

"Yes."

I asked a question she had to answer with more than one word. "How often do you usually see him?"

"The last time I saw him was at your welcoming gala." She made eye contact with me for the first time.

I asked her a question I really didn't want to hear the answer to, "Do you love him?"

"Of course."

It was not the answer I wanted. "How do you feel about his social practice, with the servant girls?" I wanted her to feel as threatened as I did.

"He's so generous."

Again, her reply was not what I wanted.

She continued, "But he only does it so he can find her."

My heart leapt. "Her?"

"His love. She's a servant somewhere in Sylvaria."

My heart beat madly and yet his devotion to me twisted the guilt in my stomach. "Who are you?" I asked thoroughly confused.

"I'm Lady Zaiah," she answered, obviously concerned for my memory.

"No," I sighed. "Who are you to Captain Jovan?"

"I'm his sister-in-law."

"Sister-in-law?"

"His brother, my husband, died in the war, along with his father."

I finally understood. "I didn't know he had a brother."

"He and my husband were born several years apart. They weren't very close, but Jovan has always been mindful of me, especially now since my husband died. He comes to call as often as he can. Well, he tries. He's busy looking for her now. I do receive letters quite often."

I could barely contain my bliss. Breathing somehow felt easier, and I steered the conversation to subjects I thought she might enjoy.

Though obviously quite shy, Lady Zaiah opened up more and more as I asked the right questions.

When I asked about meeting Jovan she told me how awkward she felt because his physically forward nature. "I'd never been touched so much in my whole life," she exclaimed with giggling wide eyes.

By the end of our time, we laughed together like old

friends. I embraced her as she left and she tittered, "You're affectionate, like Jovan."

After dinner, my father asked me about my time with her.

"I will gladly spend time with Lady Zaiah again. I enjoyed her company immensely."

Rika overhearing exclaimed, "You mean she actually talked to you?"

Kira added, "She never says more than two words to anyone."

My father laughed, "I knew you'd bring her out, Eviona. Well done."

That night as I readied for bed I realized I'd kept my veil closed. Guilt again wrapped its hands around my heart. I almost felt as if I'd spent the day with Jovan, and yet as soon as my veil opened, I'd be with Marjeάn. I hated myself for loving them both. I curled under my covers hoping he'd think I fell asleep and allowed my veil to fall open.

"Your veil has been closed most of the day."

I opened my eyes but didn't speak. What could I say?

"Oh," he whispered. "Did you see him?"

Impossible. "No."

"You spent the afternoon thinking about him then."

"How can you know that?"

"You have this peculiar pang in your chest when he's on your mind. That's why I knew you were lying."

"Did I lie to you?"

"You told me if I stayed you'd never think of him."

"I don't think of him when I'm with you."

"How long had I been gone before your thoughts turned to him?" he scolded. "Could you wait even a whole day?"

"Don't," I begged.

"Good night." He folded his arms under his head attempting a comfortable position to sleep.

I didn't close my veil I wished he couldn't feel the way my heart beat, and yet especially after our conversation I didn't want to leave him alone. I don't know why he didn't close his veil. Neither of us shut our eyes. We let the silence scream in our ears instead.

I needed something to ease my mind. I knew the one place I'd find solace; in the kitchen. The familiar smells and sounds welcomed me. The kitchen staff proved to be friendly, albeit astonished at my presence. I found it therapeutic to shape, mold, and create my tiny art. My family adored them, until my father found out I created them. He demanded I not stoop to levels below me. I continued going to the kitchen, however. I insisted none of my creations be presented to the royal table.

It had been days since we'd spoken but I hoped that would change. I created a pasta spider, and as I did, Marjeȧn broke his silence. "Were you happy when I gave you the spider?"

I paused wondering how the staff would feel about my talking to myself. "Elated." I finally whispered. "I loved that you had challenged me."

"You hardly needed challenging." He smirked. "You only needed a bit of inspiration now and again."

The kitchen maids started to notice my one-sided conversation, but I couldn't defend myself against my ache to hear his voice. "Did you know I made a jelly mold look like a real jellyfish?"

"No, you never made that one for me."

"Jellyfish are beautiful. Everyone told me to move away from them. I couldn't resist getting close enough to really see what they looked like."

"Ah, I do remember the sting, and how angry I was

with you."

I chuckled, and being leery of what the staff must have thought I ended the conversation quickly by addressing the spider as I put him in the oven. "Cook nicely my hairy friend." I instructed the staff when to take out the dish and ordered them to eat it or feed it to anyone other than the royal family. I wandered to the garden to spend a few moments alone with him.

"Are you still angry with me?"

"I'm not angry with you. Although, I shall forever hate him."

"If you could do it over, would you still leave me?"

He swallowed, and his feelings turned dark. "You already know the answer to that question. Don't torture us both by asking it."

"I have so many questions, Dyre."

"Why won't you call me Marjeån?"

"Because of the way you would have answered my question. I have to keep some perspective on who you are."

"I do love you, Eviona."

I shook my head wishing I could push my feelings aside. "If I call you Marjeån, I fear I will have no discipline with myself where you are concerned."

"That is exactly what I want. Come to me. Be with me."

I wanted desperately to be in his arms again. I exhaled hoping the tightness of my chest would loosen and changed the subject. "Why did you have Zefforah sculpted in the garden? Surely you knew what kind of rumors you would be starting."

"I hoped to reveal myself to you there." He scoffed. "I had planned for it to be a happy disclosure."

Our conversation came to an abrupt stop by a knock.

My head jerked quickly wondering where a knock could be coming from, only to realize it must have been the prison door.

"We have a meal for you." The guard laughed loudly as he shoved the tray of my spider pasta through the notch in the door.

Ecstatic at the gift Dyre jumped forward eagerly to consume it. Even though he ate it with his hands and shoved it into his mouth impatiently, I enjoyed experiencing it with him and found myself smiling as I walked back to the castle to eat my own meal.

On the way to the dining hall, I ran into one of the serving girls. She told me everyone had been horrified at my pasta spider so they decided to send it to that villain in the prison. I told her I thought it would be a very wise thing to do, and they should send anything frightful I made straight to him.

"Thank you." Dyre laughed in my head licking his fingers. "I hope all of your creations are looking dreadful these days."

I spoke quietly as I walked away, "I promise they will be."

I arrived at the dining hall and joined my parents and sisters at a meal boring in both looks and taste. I wished I could have been in the cell with Dyre to eat the spider with him.

Mother's voice broke my meditation. "Eviona, I haven't seen you happy for far too long. How wonderful to see a smile on your face. Did something pleasant happen today?"

I hadn't realized my expression and paused for a moment before I answered. "Yes, very pleasant."

"Oh please tell us," My sister Kira begged.

"Yes please," Rika implored.

I looked at their anxiousness. I couldn't be truthful,

they would never understand, but I couldn't lie to them either. I wished somehow I could brush off their remarks, but their faces shone at me with anticipation. I worded it carefully so as not to lie to my family. "I spent some time talking with an old friend today."

They seemed pleased, and my father especially encouraged me to continue to contact my friends in hopes of it buoying my spirits. If they knew who I had talked to their encouragement would never have been so enthusiastic.

Au courant (adj) fully aware

Soon my routine became practiced, but with one addition. Family mornings, days with my mother, sisters, and guests, evenings with my father and my nights spent talking with Dyre, but only in my mind.

The first night as I lit a candle and looked into my mirror I felt him smile. Did he know I specifically wanted to spend time with him? "There are rules you must keep. I want you to agree to them, or I will close my veil."

"Princess, you are already making laws like a queen." Dyre smiled, bowing to the blank space in front of him.

I started my list. "You may not lie to me."

"My sweet Eviona, I have nothing left to hide from you."

My tone escalated, "You may not address me as yours."

"Why?"

My tone softened as I knew my next words would hurt him, "You must be Dyre to me, and only Dyre."

He sat down, noticeably hurt.

I tried to lighten his spirits. "Finally, you must agree to eat every horrible looking thing which is brought to you."

"At last, a rule I will gladly keep."

We spent several hours of each night together. Any spare time I found during the day I spent in the kitchen. I created horrible creatures from all sorts of wonderful foods. I also made it look as if I failed several attempts at other things specifically so my failures would be sent to him.

One especially weak night on my part I admitted, "I would do anything to find a way for us to be together."

"I know."

"You've always been the clever one. Can't you think of a plan?"

"No."

"I could help you escape, and we could run away."

"No, Eviona."

I stood, walking around my room, planning in my head. "What if I were to tell everyone Dyre had died? You could hide away for a few years and come back truly as Marjeȧn!"

"Eviona. No."

"I really think we can do it!"

He shook his head.

I asked him desperately. "Don't you even want to try?"

"I have a plan." He told me tenderly. "You need to start a new life." He paused and smiled sadly. "A life without me."

"No!" I answered irate. "I can't live with you locked in that wretched cell, pretending like you don't exist."

"You must. You must live *for* me. Do the things I wish I could do. Live and be happy."

"Knowing you are there and miserable."

He smiled countering my feelings. "Think of it as reciprocation for your childhood."

I shook my head bitterly.

"No more time in the kitchen either. It's time for you to really be a princess."

"You don't like my creations?"

"It's time for you to create something different; a kingdom."

"Why are you saying this?"

"I will allow you to finally be happy with Jovan."

I stared at my mirror with a glare meant for him.

"You cannot hide the beating of your heart, Eviona.

Even when I mention his name it flutters."

"Don't," I begged.

"I have to tell you something."

"What?" I asked sharply.

"There are a few of your people who I'm sure are still against your father. Others who, like me, craved power. I organized them and gave them hope with my ferocious beast." He scoffed at the idea of Zefforah being terrifying to anyone. "They aren't gone forever, but they currently don't have a leader."

My tone softened, "I will tell my father."

"You should also know your father has been a good king. I couldn't have done better."

I took a deep breath. "Thank you for saying that." I sat down on the ledge of my window and looked out into the night sky knowing how much he missed doing so himself.

"Do you want to hear something good?" He asked.

"Is there anything good to tell me?"

"Kellam."

I felt his pain and asked, "Is he too hard to talk about?"

"I want you to know." He took a deep breath before beginning. "Without you, he refused to stay with his parents. He ran away only a day or two after you left. I've often wondered if his parents even cared. Zefforah found him at the lake where they met. She brought him to me, and I learned about the time she spent with him." He shook his head and laughed a bit, "I was furious with you both."

I smirked, "We knew you would be."

"It didn't take much for me to love him. When he talked about you... I treasured how he talked about you, how much he loved you." He smiled as he spoke, but his heart weighed heavily in his chest. "I felt like I had been given your child, like I raised our son. I love him so much."

I swallowed the lump in my throat, unable to speak.

"You taught him my favorite card games. He made me laugh while we played trying to throw me off." He chuckled, "It worked sometimes. He won more than he should have. I had a bit of an advantage though when he'd pull the tricks on me I used to pull on you. Everything that boy did gave me joy."

"He made me happy too," I agreed.

"I told him everything. He knew everything. Other than Zefforah, he is the only one I ever shared it all with. He looked forward to the crown as much as I did. When I became king and married you, he would be our son."

I nodded, as ache filled our chests.

"We spoke of you often. When you came to live with me, I would tell him all the cute things you did. It was terrible in the beginning when I didn't see you. Every morning he begged for more stories. I must have told him twenty times how you didn't even notice me standing in the middle of the hallway as you looked over your vegetable basket that day. I moved at the very last moment simply so you wouldn't bowl me over. Fortunately, only your basket hit me."

"You said you didn't see me either," I protested.

He shrugged with a snicker, "I lied."

"Your morning rides... you went to see Kellam and Zefforah."

"That's why I couldn't take you with me. I hated time spent away from Zefforah, but she understood my plan, and she loved having Kellam with her. I debated about bringing him to the house as a servant or something, but when I'd mention it, he'd threaten to tell you who I was." He chuckled. "That boy."

"Manipulative," I laughed.

He sighed, "We couldn't wait for the day of the battle. Afterward, we would all be together."

We spent a silent moment reverencing memories.

I interrupted the quiet tribute, "Kellam said you didn't want him to fight."

He barked, "No, I ordered him not to fight! He had strict instructions on where to go and wait for me until after the battle." Anger raced through him, and he balled his hands into angry paws. "Why didn't he listen?" He pounded his fist into the floor next to him.

I grabbed my hand and whimpered with the pain.

"Sorry," he muttered. "I'm tired, Eviona." As he closed his veil, he began to weep.

That night our dreams took us to a familiar place. The stars. We saw them in the sky in the exact locations the map showed. Our perspective changed as we rose into the heavens and looked down. We saw ourselves being joined in marriage with Zefforah and the rest of the kingdom watching from the cliffs and the tower in the place we had seen in our dreams many times before.

We saw ourselves as rulers of Sylvaria. Our people loved us and trusted us. With our incredible ability as the three of us touched we knew their thoughts, saw their needs. We had the ability to discern how best to help our people.

Our kingdom was truly perfect. We saw Zefforah acting as protector. The people loved her. Children ran to play with her. Their parents praised her, grateful for her presence.

We saw industry, harmony, work, service and happiness in Sylvaria and our own happiness. Together, the three of us, as it should have been.

As the dream dimmed and we woke, we both realized

what we had seen. The vision. The dream once seen by an old man. Our hearts pounded in unison.

He rose to his feet and paced back and forth, rocking in pain. I sat up in my bed.

"Did you see it?" He cried.

"Yes, I did."

He hollered and fell to his knees. He hit the stone floor with fists of anger. "I could have been happy! I could have had everything!" He pressed his forehead to the floor. "Ahhhhhhh," he roared.

I couldn't hold back my own tears. We sobbed together. Me in silent misery, him repeating the words, "I'm sorry. I am so sorry."

I had no words to say. Our torture united. We knew what could have been. We also knew there could be no chance of it now.

Anamnasis (n) recollection or remembrance of the past

The next day seemed a blur. The weight of the dream pressed into every moment. At the end of the day, I had to see him.

During my time in the kitchen, I made a plate of mice crackers. After our family supper, I spoke to him as I crept with them toward the dungeon. "I am coming to see you, but you have to promise not to touch me."

"Why would I promise that? I won't. I can't keep that promise."

I stopped walking, my shoulders slouched in disappointment. "Then I can't come."

Both of us froze waiting for the other to give in. Neither did.

I finished my walk to the dungeon and handed the plate to the guard nudging my head toward Dyre's door. When I turned around and started up the stairs, he called out, "Stop." He sat and folded his arms across his chest, "I won't touch you."

I turned around just as the guard went to open the small door to push the food through.

I stopped him. "I'll take those in to the prisoner." I took the plate and motioned for him to open the door.

He froze with a concerned look on his face.

"Is something wrong?"

"You told me to grant his requests," he reminded me.

"Yes, that is correct."

He very hesitantly whispered, "A few days ago he asked for some scissors and a razor. I insisted he return them within an hour but daily asked for the razor so I've allowed him to keep it. Your highness, I do not think it will be safe for you to visit him."

I nodded my head. The guard had no idea how dangerous this visit might be for me. I knocked.

"Dyre..." I felt stupid calling to him through the door. "Give the razor back to the guard."

I motioned for the guard to reach down and open the notch in the base of the door. He took the instrument and closed the notch again.

The guard looked at me curiously, "Would you like me to chain his hands and feet?"

"Perhaps you will allow me to take your sword for protection instead," I offered. He handed me his weapon and allowed me to enter.

Dyre sat at the point of the room farthest from the door, but it didn't lessen my craving to run to him. In fact, the shock of seeing Marjeàn's face again pricked every nerve in my body. His coal black hair hung in loose waves which only seemed to act as a frame and make him even more striking. I attempted to remind myself this man was Dyre, the enemy, but it didn't help.

Keeping my voice down, I whispered, "You look good." I struggled to pull my eyes away from his face, I couldn't.

"I feel more like me." His eyes stayed in constant contact with mine.

I pushed the tray of crackers across the room toward him. They only slid half way. I attempted to push it further with the sword but to no avail. I knew I wouldn't be able to control myself if I walked forward to push them any closer. Instead, I sat and pressed my back against the door.

I couldn't think very clearly. "This is harder than I thought it would be."

He smiled shamelessly.

"Why don't you have some crackers?"

His eyes sparkled. "If I move forward at all, I will break the promise I just made." His eyebrows rose. He knew his words and tone all added to the beckoning I already felt to go to him.

I placed the sword by my side, pulled my legs against my chest and buried my head on my knees. "I shouldn't have come. Did you know the pull would become worse once we touched?"

"I had a similar connection with Zefforah. While ours is more of a physical connection, hers was different...more..."

"Spiritual." I raised my head and finished his sentence.

"Yes," He nodded and smiled, "you felt it as well."

"I did."

"I often thought I might have something similar with you. I didn't want to touch you until I knew you loved..." He stopped himself and looked into my eyes before bowing his head and admitting. "I had a very hard time keeping my hands to myself, even before we touched."

I smiled, reluctantly remembering having to school my own hands. I looked at his face and could feel his need for my contact, just as I ached for his. I lowered my head and asked, "Why didn't you tell me the truth about who you were?"

He leaned his head back against the wall and looked up at the ceiling as he spoke. "You won't believe this, but I've always loved you."

I laughed, "You're right. I don't believe you. You hated me."

"I tried to hate you, but after the first time I saw you..." He didn't finish the sentence. He didn't need to. I felt how hard his heart pounded in his chest and knew he felt mine echoing it.

"Why didn't you ever let me see you?"

"You were supposed to be a monster. I couldn't have

you falling in love with me," he laughed.

"Then why not after you had seen me?"

He thought as he stared at me. "My cruelty for all those years wasn't exactly an ideal beginning. Besides, I wanted you to be able to fall in love with me as any girl might fall in love; not because I am part of you, but because of who I am, alone."

"Trust me, you could have walked up to me in the street, and I would have been yours."

He shook his head, his face cringed. "I couldn't be sure of that. You'd already met Jovan. Your feelings for him, your dreams..." He whispered, "You love him. It hurts knowing you feel that strongly for someone else."

What could I say? We both lowered our eyes.

I felt him looking at me tenderly, pushing his hand through his hair the way he used to when he wanted to touch me. Even from across the cell I felt the magnetic pull it had on me. When I recoiled, he folded his arms across his chest.

"I wanted you to know it was me. I made it so obvious; the book, the stars, everything I knew about you. Did you honestly think you could have this kind of connection with anyone else?"

He was right, I should have seen.

"I tried to tell you the day we touched, but you hated me too much. You didn't want to hear it."

I had no words. I dropped my eyes from his gaze.

His soft voice broke the hush of the room. "That's why I never kissed you."

"What?" I looked up as his eyes closed and he brought a finger to his lips tenderly tracing their outline.

I felt his touch on my own lips and gasped placing my hand on my mouth.

He opened his eyes and smiled at me mischievously.

"I wanted to kiss you."

I looked away from his impassioned eyes melting my defenses. My body trembled as I asked, "So, I don't understand. Why didn't you?"

He sighed, "I'm a liar. I admit that, but kissing you without you knowing it was me you were kissing…" He bowed his head, "That would be lying to myself, I couldn't do it." His eyes locked on me. Even with his head bowed I could see their beauty through his thick dark eyelashes. "I wish you could have known."

His face turned playful as he took his hand and rubbed it again softly against his lips watching my reaction.

"Stop!" Smiling, I whispered the command as I again pressed my fingers on my mouth. I loved the feel of it, but I'd already come too close to giving in to my desires.

He looked at me, and I felt him lose control just as I did. I had to leave.

Frantically he begged, "Please don't go."

"You know I can't stay."

"Please."

"No, Dyre."

He felt frustrated, but he spoke softly, "I don't want to be Dyre anymore. I want to be the man you love. The man I know you ache for. It's all I have left."

I shook my head emphatically.

"One moment. *One* moment to be who I really am, to have you speak *my* name, to hold you close to me, and tell you—"

"Stop it!" I grabbed the sword and stood to leave.

He jumped up, ran to me and grabbed my hand. With his touch, I fell helplessly into the overpowering ecstasy and didn't dare move. The emotions flowing between us communicated without words. I allowed my fingers to mingle with his feeling the explosion of fire rush through me as I manipulated his hand. I needed to gain control of myself and begged, "You promised me once you would never ask me to do anything I didn't want to do."

"Yes, Marjeȧn told you that. He simply wants to be with you, one... more... time." He spoke softly making his words stick in my mind.

I turned to face him, and he reached out to me. I pointed the tip of the sword toward his heart and begged, "Please release my fingers."

He dropped my hand, and we both quivered in pain.

"You would put a blade of steel between us? I could easily fall forward. And we could die here together."

"Step away," I begged, lowing the sword. "It hurts too much to be this close."

He stepped backward relieving some pain.

I knocked on the door. "Let me out please."

"Eviona?" His supplication washed over me.

"What do you want me to do, Dyre?" I asked in desperation.

"I want you to come back, and when you do call me Marjeȧn."

Coalesce (v) to unite

We couldn't sleep. In the middle of the night, I called out to him. "I can't come to see you again."

"I know you will."

"No," I said pointedly.

"Alright." He softly acknowledged, unbelieving.

I groaned and closed my eyes and tried to sleep. He began to hum. The sound of his beautiful voice made it easier to relax, and I found myself finally lost in slumber. I followed Marjeàn through all of my dreams. I dreamed again of the battle, of watching Zefforah die, of Minuette, of meeting my parents, he appeared in each scene and through all of them I could never catch him. He always managed to stay beyond my reach. When I woke, I felt like I had run all night. My body ached and once again I spoke aloud. "I can't come."

"I'll be waiting for you, until you are ready to be with Marjeàn again."

I spent several days avoiding the prison and even our nightly talks.

I asked my father to take me on a tour of the kingdom. I needed to keep myself as far from Marjeàn as possible. My mother did not like the idea of father and I going alone. "I do not trust you two. You find dangerous things to do without me. Eviona fighting in the war, or going to see our worst enemy in the dungeon alone. The girls and I will be there to keep a good eye on you."

My father loved the idea and my first family excursion planned. We spent several days traveling, meeting people, seeing new places and learning more about each other. I found my father had indeed served his people well. There were problems in the kingdom as there are always problems. However, for the most part, his subjects felt him a fine ruler.

Rika and Kira found ways to make every day adventuresome. They had us play games as we traveled and laughed easily. I slowly learned to love their voices in constant banter. I even saw maturity in the way they spoke to the people we came in contact with. My respect for them steadily grew.

Dyre spoke to me as we traveled. I never closed my veil, but I couldn't talk to him with someone continuously at my side.

We visited the town where my good friends Sanura and Trew lived. It was cheerful reunion for all of us and my family enjoyed meeting someone who had been so good to me. Sanura had a beautiful little family with two sons and a daughter named Eviona, for me. I wondered as I held that beautiful baby if my future would hold children. Dyre seemed to read my thoughts and told me I'd be a wonderful mother. Both of our hearts sank as we thought more on the subject and its impossibilities for the two of us.

At one point Sanura and I talked quietly while my father and Trew discussed Sylvaria, and my mother and sisters busied themselves with the children.

She asked, "Have you seen Jovan?"

Dyre and I both stiffened at the question.

"Yes, he is doing very well," I told her. "He is Captain Jovan now."

"Yes, we were at his ceremony. Isn't it wonderful? His life is going exactly as he wished it." I felt Dyre's sorrow at the mention of his name. I couldn't bear the weight of it.

"Tell me about your boys," I chose a topic which would lead to hours of conversation, and relieve Dyre from the subject of Jovan.

As we settled down that evening, my sisters readied

for bed in another room, and my parents spoke quietly to each other while I relaxed near them. Dyre took the opportunity to speak to me.

"I hope you find happiness the way Sanura has."

I rubbed my arm to acknowledge him.

He stroked his hand along his jawbone, and I felt it leave a tingle of warmth in my skin. I thought it was sweet until he moved his fingers to caress his lips and I felt him smiling.

I slapped my own hand, and my father looked up at me concerned.

"A bug." I brushed off my hand and then squeezed it tightly as a reprimand to Dyre.

He laughed, "I couldn't resist."

I wished we could have had this kind of relationship our whole lives. We should have always made each other happy instead of hating each other.

On the last day of our journey, the closer the castle came, the more I knew I would go to see him. I couldn't control my ache to be with him.

We arrived home in the late afternoon. My parents wanted to allow us time to rest properly from our trip by going to bed a bit early. I only thought how it would grant me more time with Marjeàn. I quickly went to the kitchen and cut up some fruit. Then I rushed to the dungeon to see him.

"Weak, weak, weak." I chanted to myself as I approached the door of his cell.

He smiled as his heart raced along with mine.

The guard teased, "Are you here to see me?"

"I've been away so long, I've missed you," I replied.

He smiled sweetly and chuckled. Noticing my plate, he asked, "Does he tell you more if you bring him something?"

I turned my expression down, making it stern and

gestured toward the cell. "It's a bit of encouragement. He will give me what I want today. I'm sure of it."

"Would you like to borrow my sword again?"

For show, I pondered the question for a moment then said, "I'll let you know if I think I'm in danger."

"Right. Good luck, Princess," he said as he unlocked the door.

I stepped in and kept strong eyes on the guard until the door closed. Then I placed my tray on the floor and ran to the anxious arms awaiting mine. "Marjeàn," I whispered.

A huge smile spread across his face, his heart raced as he wrapped his arms around me and breathed in the smell of my hair. He didn't let go for a long time as his hands moved slowly down my back. I had no desire to push him away and fell into the inextinguishable fire of his influence.

He did pull away from me, but only enough to search my face. He brought his fingers to study it; tracing my eyebrow, the curve of my cheek, the length of my jaw. Absorbing every contour of my face and neck as if relearning the way they felt.

I captured his hand, pressing my lips to each of his fingers as I turned it in my hands, gazing into his eyes as I did. I felt his desperation as greatly as I felt mine.

I lifted my face to kiss him. He confused me by pulling away.

His hand found mine and our fingers intertwined as he guided me to a wall. We sat down, and he leaned against it.

I took his hand in mine lifting it to my face to rub the back of it against my cheek. "I love you," I kept my voice low uncertain of how much the guard would hear.

He whispered, "And I love you. You hurt me terribly

the night I left when you questioned whether or not I really loved you. Your distrust of me, Dyre, was so great as to make you doubt me, Marjeān."

"You never answered. It hurt me too."

He nodded in understanding and pulled me forward until my cheek and my hands rested against his chest.

He seemed content. Perhaps because of the freedom I had given him with no need to hold back. I fondled the collar on his shirt as he ran his fingers through my hair. I melted into him, lost in the delicious satisfaction of his touch.

"Did it hurt to speak in your voice?" I asked.

He responded in the voice I wanted to hear. "I had to disguise it, you knew mine too well. It took me months to develop an accent I thought you wouldn't recognize. I tried out all sorts." He laughed as he remembered and spoke in a few of them saying, "I love you, Eviona. I love you. I love you."

"I love them all." I laughed quietly.

He took a deep breath and asked, "Will you do something for me tonight when you leave the prison?"

"What do you want me to do?"

"I miss riding. Would you take a horse and ride for me? So I can feel the sensation of it again."

I sat up my eyes open widely questioning his sanity. "Are you mad?"

"Shhhhh." He nodded toward the door to remind me of our volume. "Please," he begged with a smile he knew I would not refuse.

"Of course, you know it will be me feeling it and not you. It will be a rough ride."

"I don't mind."

I made a face at him to express my doubt. "I will do it for you." I shook my head and whispered, "I must be insane."

He gazed at me with a smile. His hands moved to hold mine.

"This is all I have wanted for so long. To be myself, Marjeẚn, having you know who watched you and loved you from the other side for all of these years."

"I would have liked to have had more than this."

He nodded in agreement, "I would have had you be mine forever." He eyed me tenderly caressing my face, "My wife, my queen, my lover."

A sad smile crossed my lips as I thought of the things he had listed and how none of them would ever come to fruition. I needed to be content in stolen moments like this.

"May I see your back?" I asked.

He paused with a glint of pleasing curiosity in his eye and then stood and took off his shirt.

I rose with him and motioned for him to turn around.

I touched the markings from Minuette's beating and then moved my hand and eyes to the small of his back. I had expected the same mark on his back as I had seen on Zefforah's, but his was different there were only two triangles.

I traced their outline.

"There used to be three," he said.

"Zefforah?"

"I'll bet your mark only has two now as well."

I placed my arms around him, pulled myself into his strong back and together we mourned the loss of the other part of us.

"Come here." He turned and wrapped one arm around my waist and held the other in his then started to twirl in a slow circle.

"Marjeẚn, are you dancing with me?" Pleased and shocked I placed my hand on his shoulder and moved with him. He wore a smile, with his eyes closed as a soft melody sung by his beautiful voice resonated from his lips.

After a few moments, he stopped. "I wish I could really dance with you. I know how much you love it."

"Thank you for trying."

His eyes consumed mine, and his chest rose as he inhaled. The hand he held in his, came to his mouth. He kissed the pads of my fingertips and then pulled them down his chin and neck until he found a place for them to settle on his bare chest. His fingertips lifted my chin until my lips waited impatiently across from his. The smirk on his face showed he felt the way my heart jumped at the realization that he would finally kiss me.

The combination of our emotions rose up to engross us. Agony. Hunger. Weakness. Desire. His hand pushed back across my jawbone, down my shoulder, and continued its way to my waist where it drew my body to be one with his. With his eyes focused on mine I parted my lips and offered them to him. Our eyes closed as he gently touched his lips to mine and brushed them back and forth creating sparks of excitement which raced through our bodies. His mouth pressed onto mine, and a wave of passion surged through us.

Explosions of fire followed his touch and mine. The same fire doubled in depth and area, raced through both bodies at once, bringing intense ecstasy to the long forbidden contact.

Breathless and grinning our lips separated.

He laughed quietly. "If I would have known it felt like that I would have kissed you a long time ago." Then his mouth found mine again, pulling us into the rapture of fire. I caught my breath as his mouth released mine.

He gently grabbed the back of my neck and pulled me forward to kiss my forehead. "Eviona," he said with his lips still on my skin. He put his hands on either side of my face and pulled it away from him to look into my eyes, his expression too serious. "It's time for you to go."

"No!" I wrapped my arms around him as if my entire life depended on my grasp.

He pushed me away and took his shirt from the floor drawing it over his shoulders. His voice rose to call out harshly to the guard. "I think it's time the princess left." He smiled at my distress as I pushed myself again into his body.

The key clicked in the door.

I panicked as seconds slipped away from me and he stepped back.

"Why so soon?" I touched his face forcing him to lock eyes with me.

"Don't forget my ride," he reminded me.

I nodded though still tormented, "I'll be back tomorrow."

The door opened behind me. The eyes of the guard burned into my back as Marjeàn took my hand from his cheek. We stood together for several moments until I found the strength to tear my hands from his. As we separated the pain of our disconnection resonated throughout my whole essence. Violently excruciating. Once on the other side of the door, I turned to see him as it closed. Marjeàn bowed keeping his eyes on me.

"Did he give you the information you've been wanting?" asked the guard.

I sighed heavily and shook my head. "This prisoner has so much more to give me."

Marjeàn chuckled.

The guard bowed, and I fled to the stables.

Certain it would be a disaster; I found a horse with

Marjeàn's help. He then walked me through preparing the animal. Grateful for his calm voice and direction I slowly grew more confident. By the time I made it outside the castle wall, darkness covered the kingdom. The faint moon lit my way as Marjeàn told me the direction to steer. When he felt me become comfortable, he instructed me on how to kick my legs to speed the animal beneath me.

Wind pushed my hair behind me, and it whipped against my face. Marjeàn breathed in through my lungs and cherished the rush. I enjoyed myself much more than I thought I would. I rode for several miles and stopped only when he asked me to. I dismounted the horse and lay down in a meadow. Placing my hands behind my head, I looked up to the sky to stare at the stars with him.

"Thank you for tonight," I said.

"It is I who am grateful." I felt a wave of emotion I didn't understand wash over him as he whispered, "I love you, Eviona. Goodbye."

His veil closed and I felt a rush of urgency. His words held too much finality. I ripped and clawed at the veil between us tearing it down as I heard Marjeàn's voice, "Would it be possible to have a cup of obiberry juice?"

"NO!" I screamed.

The guard grumbled and said he would bring some.

"Eviona, let the veil close. I don't want you here for this." He closed it again, and I continued to rip it away preventing his efforts.

I ran to the horse and tried to climb back on. "Marjeàn! What do you think you're doing?"

"I am taking Zefforah's lead. She died so we could live. I'm doing the same for you."

"No!" I couldn't find where to put my foot, and Marjeán no longer talked me through what I should do. I finally mounted correctly and kicked as hard as I could. My horse bolted forward.

The calm voice I had so recently learned to love whispered, "I am giving you a gift. Take it with gratitude."

"I don't want it! Don't! Please!" I begged.

"I have tortured you for your entire life. Even our happiest times have held their own kind of misery. I don't want you to suffer anymore. I don't want to hurt you anymore."

The horse seemed to know where to go, I hoped his instincts were correct, and we were heading toward the castle. Darkness hid my whereabouts, but I had to go to Marjeán. I needed to stop him.

"I want you to be free of me, Eviona. If I stayed, you would still know where I am, what I feel. You would make choices not for you, but for both of us. I want you to do the things which are best for you, without my pain, without my past, without me."

"You have to help me! I can't rule Sylvaria without you."

"You can. You will."

"Marjeán, don't you love me?"

His gentle and soothing voice caressed the words, "I do love you. I know you can feel how much I love you."

"Then don't drink that!" I panted frantically.

Thankfully the castle came into view. I couldn't go any faster, but I held close to my horse hoping to somehow lighten the load.

"NO!" I screamed as the notch on the door opened, and a cup slid through.

Marjeán thanked the guard who grunted in response.

"Marjeàn, Marjeàn," I called to him. "Please, please don't do this." I passed the outer wall of the castle, jumped off the horse, and fell to the ground. I twisted my ankle, or maybe broke it.

He stumbled. I prayed the cup had spilt.

I forced myself to rise. I still had time to stop him. Pushing through the pain, I half staggered half crawled toward the castle door. He lifted the cup to his lips. I felt the sting of it as he breathed in the fragrance.

"Stop! Dyre!" It had the effect I wanted. He put the cup down for a moment.

"Ouch," he whispered, "that hurts worse than the poison."

"Don't drink it. Please." I pleaded with him as I stumbled again, falling helpless to the ground.

"Tell Jovan he is a lucky man." He lifted the cup, toasting me and drank it all in one swallow.

Fire raged down my mouth and throat. I screamed through the excruciating pain.

"Go." He lay curled in a ball of pain on the floor, his eyes focused on the small empty cup next to him. "Live." He closed his eyes.

"No." I wept. "No, don't leave me alone. Don't leave me." I looked for him everywhere in my mind. Nothing remained, no veil, no breath, no feeling, nothing; only me and the suffering of what was left of my soul.

Sole (adj) being the only one of a kind

I don't know how long I struggled crying on the ground before I heard voices. "Hey, over here!"

I cringed at the thought of having to face anyone, but I opened my eyes and slowly sat up. "I'm here." The words came out breathy and flat, with no heart.

Several guards ran to me. "It's the princess."

One of them brought his torch close, "Are you alright, Highness? We heard screaming."

"I went for a horseback ride and fell off. I think I may have broken my leg."

He ordered, "Go find the king and queen."

Only moments later my father's arms picked me up.

"We need to take her to bed," my mother said.

After I was carried to my room, a doctor shortly appeared to tend my ankle.

My father stood by my bedside stroking my hair as I cried. I hoped my mask of pain sufficiently covered my despair.

My mother, when finished talking to the doctor, quickly cleared the room. "Eviona dear, you look tired," she said sweetly. "Try to rest. The doctor said you will heal much better if you rest well and stay off your leg for a while. Shall I have your ladies come in to undress you?"

"Please send in only one."

"Of course." She kissed my forehead and pulled my father away.

"I'll be here first thing in the morning," My father promised then they closed the door.

A young girl came in, "How may I help you, Princess?"

"Bring me a cup of obiberry juice. My head hurts."

She stammered, "But we were told never to give you

obiberries."

"I know how to use it," I barked.

She curtsied, "Yes, Highness." She rushed from the room.

I turned over on my bed and cried with renewed intensity.

The vanity of my room called to me. Though it didn't look at all like the one Marjeȧn had given me I had placed my ivory combs and brushes on it. I crawled over to them and caressed each one. I looked at myself in the mirror and felt so alone. I had never known true loneliness until that moment knowing I would never again see through any eyes but my own.

I received the delivery of an ornate crystal goblet filled with the golden juice and thought of the incredible contrast it held to the cup from which Marjeȧn last drank. I stared at it knowing if I didn't drink it I would be lost forever in the void of my aloneness.

I slowly took off my dress then struggled back toward the vanity and caught myself from falling by grabbing the edge. I took a small mirror and held it up to my eye as I turned around to examine my back in the large mirror. There under the scars of my whipping was my mark. One lone triangle. I had never seen it before. I only knew what it looked like from seeing their marks; three on Zefforah, two on Marjeȧn, and now one, only one.

I didn't sleep that night. I stared at the juice and debated my fate instead. As the morning light flooded my room, it hurt to realize I still lived. Not even brave enough to drink a cup of juice.

I spent several weeks in bed to recover from what I had done to my ankle, grateful for the excuse to spend the time alone. Although my parents and sisters were attentive and individually spent their turns in compassionate visits, they did not press me to speak.

Any time I spent alone, my mind moved to memories and anguish easily overtook me.

When the doctor announced I should be well enough to be out of bed, I failed miserably as I endeavored to fall back into our routine. I struggled to strengthen my ankle by walking for a while each time I left my room, relying on someone else to be there with me prepared to hold me up.

One night I crawled to the window, pushed back the curtains and stared at the night sky. Tears I could not control came to my eyes as I thought about Marjeàn. I would never look at the stars again without thinking of him. Did a place exist where I wouldn't be reminded of him? I had experienced everything with him. I would never be safe from his memory. I fell to sleep there at my window lost in the stars he loved.

The next morning my mother woke me. She knelt down beside me, put her arms around me, and allowed me to cry in her arms. She must have known more than the pain of my ankle hurt me, but she did not press me to explain. She simply held me.

Later that morning, with the help of one of my ladies, I visited my father's private office. After I knocked on the door, a servant opened it. I looked inside to see my father's surprised face. He sat at his desk and motioned for me to come in. Watching me struggle he stood and met me half way, where my lady then returned to the door to wait for me. My father took my arm, led me to a sofa and sat down with me.

"Eviona," he placed his hand on mine and looked at me tenderly. "I am glad to have you come. It's good for you to be walking again."

"Father," I looked at him seriously. I already knew

the answer but asked for my father's benefit.

"How is your prisoner, Dyre?" It hurt to say the name. I would forever regret not being able to talk about him in pleasant terms.

He took a deep breath. "He is dead, Eviona. Poisoned. The kitchen staff told us you made several dishes specifically for him. You are a smart girl."

Praise came where I would have liked sympathy. I attempted a smile to please him but did not find it in my power to give.

"What was done with his body?" I asked quietly.

"To the burning place where the rest of the bodies from the battles were taken."

"Of course." My heart ached.

"Don't look so sad. I'm pleased with your brilliance and thank you for it. After all, you are the one to which we owe his death. Did you lace all of his meals with poison or just the fruit you took him that night?"

I lowered my eyes. How deeply my father's words cut.

His hand touched my shoulder. "You seem unwell."

"Still in pain," I answered honestly.

"Perhaps you should return to your room."

"Thank you." I stood to leave.

"Eviona," He stopped me, "I don't like how much time you are spending by yourself. You are too alone."

I turned from him to hide the tears running down my cheeks and motioned for assistance to quickly escape his gaze. How could I ever tell him of my utter aloneness?

On the next clear night, I stayed awake until I knew most of the castle slept. I withdrew to a large pond in the castle gardens. I looked into it for the reflection of the stars and watched them twinkle and dance in the night. It was the only way I could think to surround myself with stars. I hoped he would approve of my meager memorial. I whispered the memories I held most dear, reliving the best parts of our times together. I ended by blowing a kiss to the stars. "Sweet dreams, Marjeȧn." Then I hobbled slowly back to my room. I put my little book into the fire and watched the flames slowly devour it.

Before going back to bed, I sat down at my desk to write a formal request to the castle gardeners for blue roses to be planted along the edges of the pond. I hoped it would be granted.

Extant (adj) still existing, not destroyed

Rika complained. "You were much more fun before that stupid accident last fall."

"I'm sorry Rika. What were we doing?"

"The game. Are you playing or not?"

Kira whispered. "I think when she fell off that horse something happened in her head."

I looked out the window of the coach, unaffected by the comment. My dead heart weighed in my chest like a rock tied to a robin's breast. I thought of little else.

"Girls, be nice to your sister," my mother encouraged.

"Try to be civil when we are at the soldier's training grounds," my father reprimanded.

"You know the threat is gone, Father," Rika said. "Eviona brilliantly did away with him."

I couldn't hold it in any longer and exclaimed, "I do not wish to be praised for Dyre's death anymore. It is a horrible thing to have taken a life."

"But he was our enemy." Rika countered.

I glanced at her young face and couldn't believe my confession as the words escaped my lips. "I loved one of our enemies."

Silence gathered thick, and my emotions spilled over. My mother wiped an escaping tear from my cheek, "Why didn't you tell us?"

"Without judgment, without conditions, you took me in and loved me. Would you have trusted me if you knew I loved one of your opposers?"

Without a word spoken each of my family members' eyes awoke with understanding.

I confessed more, "I cannot tell you how hollow I feel without him."

My father squeezed my hand. "I know. *I know*."

I thought of Laroke. My father couldn't truly

understand, but I knew he felt hollow too.

My mother joined my emotion with tears rolling down her face.

My father promptly realized, "That's how you knew about the last battle. It must have been terrible for you to fight against him. Were you with him when he died?"

"He did not die until later, but I did see him on the battlefield. He even came to my rescue that day, fighting against his own."

Kira interjected, "You found out he died, which is why you took the horse out that night. I've always wondered. I know you're scared of horses."

I smiled without response. I would allow them to believe it happened that way.

My mother asked, "Would you like to tell us about him?"

"Tell you about Marjeȧn?" I hadn't ever thought I would tell anyone about him. I wouldn't tell them everything but at her invitation, I couldn't resist. "Yes, I would." I sighed, as a burden lifted. "He was a very interesting master from the beginning…"

We arrived at the training grounds quite late and were shown to our rooms. In the morning I woke slowly, dressed and went to join my family for the morning meal. Afterward, my sisters and I toured the grounds together. Most of the soldiers bowed as they passed us and several of them smiled flirtatiously, which always sent my sisters into fits of giggles. I found myself often looking for one particular face.

When we came upon a sword training arena, my sisters insisted we stop to watch. The instructor quickly noticed our presence and bowed in acknowledgment. Unexpectedly he stopped the duels.

"Men." He gestured to me. "This is the lost princess,

and Dyre's conqueror."

I cringed and waved hesitantly as my sisters pushed me forward.

"I watched her fight in our last battle against Dyre."

Rika grabbed a sword and shoved it into my hand. "Anyone up for a challenge?

At first, no one moved. I handed the sword back to her.

"I'd like a go." A voice not from the company but from a doorway on the other side called out. I recognized it instantly and smiled at Ayrik.

Rika placed the sword back into my hand as Kira pushed me toward him.

He took his sword, and we faced each other. It felt good to be moving again even in a dress. To hold a sword and move the ways I used to. In the end, I won the duel, but I wondered if he had allowed it, I knew he hadn't worked his hardest. I smiled at him in question. I then looked up to see my father's face glowing at me from across the room. I returned the smile back to him.

The soldiers noticed and several turned to see. In an instant the whole company knelt on one knee, saluting my father with one arm crossed over their eyes.

"Are you up for a duel Father?" Kira playfully entreated him.

"What would I do if she bested me? I should never hear the end of it."

"Maybe some time when we are in more intimate company then." She called.

I held up my sword as if to salute him and he nodded to me and walked on with his guards at his side.

Once he left the room Ayrik called out, "Who's next?"

This time, I had more than enough opponents.

Weaker than I wanted to admit I dueled only two

more times before my body felt too tired to go on. With my sisters at my arms, we went back to our rooms to clean up. I laughed easily with them. Laughter had been foreign to me for far too long. I savored the way it brought me back to myself.

That night after dinner I went in search of my old friend. As I wandered toward the quarters of the soldiers, I came across him.

"Princess." Ayrik bowed low as I approached. "I hoped I might be able to talk to you."

"I came looking for you," I laughed. "Shall we take a walk outside?"

"Certainly," he said opening the door for me.

"I'd like to thank you for today. I enjoyed dueling with you again, even if you did throw the match."

"Well, I couldn't have you lose," he snickered. "Besides, you had to wear a dress."

"Next time I'll really make you work." I threatened with a grin.

"Why did you kill Dyre?" His sudden question and flat tone hurt. "I know logistically why you would do it. Only I can't bring myself to believe you could ever be so cruel as to kill anyone in such a terrible way, especially since you were once friends."

"I know the whole kingdom thinks I did. He poisoned himself."

Ayrik eyed me curiously. "Why would he do that?"

"He did it for me. In the end, we became friends again."

"I see. He made it look like you did it simply to reinforce your reputation. Wow, that's a better friendship than I anticipated."

I chuckled and looked up to the sky. Even at dusk, a few bright stars could already be seen.

"Have you seen Marjeȧn?" He asked with a soft tone, he must have seen the moisture rising in my eyes.

"He's dead too," I whispered hoping I could hold back the tears.

"Did your heart stop beating, or did your lungs stop breathing?"

I lost the fight and began to cry, "That's the problem. I'm still here."

He hesitantly put his arm around my shoulder. "What about Captain Jovan? Are you still in love with him?"

"I still love him," I assured.

"It's been a year since the battle, have you seen him yet?"

"Not yet. I needed to allow myself to breathe again. I think I'd like to see him now."

"Good." Ayrik agreed with a nod. "I'd like to see you happy."

"What about your brother?" I asked as we continued our walk.

It felt good to be with an old friend again; to catch up on each other's lives and reconnect with the world outside the palace and my own mind.

My family stayed there for quite a while. I spent time with my sisters watching the soldiers as they marched and trained. They made sure I participated at every given chance. I enjoyed the interactions I stole with Ayrik and my thoughts fixed more and more on Jovan. I found myself anticipating our next meeting with great eagerness.

As we embarked on our journey toward home my mother commented, "You seem happy, Eviona."

"I feel much better."

"Both your father and I noticed the change in your attitude these past few days."

"One of those soldiers is an old friend. I enjoyed

being there."

"Obviously," agreed my mother. "We didn't need to stay this long, but it's been wonderful to see you smile again."

"Thank you for extending our stay."

With a pleased grin on his face my father added, "Eviona, you are back to yourself."

"I am, Father," I agreed. "I want to be married."

"What?" Upset voices hit me from all sides.

"I thought you would all be pleased."

"I thought you were heartbroken over Marjeán," Rika said.

"I was." I paused and admitted, "I am, but there is someone I am sure you all will approve of."

"Someone?" My father asked. "You already know who you want?"

"Yes. Jovan."

My mother's eyes widened. "Captain Jovan?"

Kira looked at me in terror. "We told you about him. Eviona, how could you even think it?"

Rika interjected with a nudge in Kira's side, "That's probably how she knows him. Did he choose to spend time with you when you were a servant?"

I nodded. "He made me feel exceptionally important. Kira, I assure you he is a complete gentleman."

Kira's face showed her disbelief.

My father thought aloud. "He's a fine soldier. He is intelligent and loyal. I know he has opinions very similar to my own. He seems a fine choice, Eviona."

"Will you ask him for me?"

"Why him?" Kira pouted.

I would tell them the whole story, but not yet. For now, I only said what they needed to hear. "There would be too many willing to marry me simply for the position. I don't believe Captain Jovan would take advantage. He proves himself humble with his social habits, and yet serves Sylvaria faithfully. I trust him."

My father seemed pleased. "I will ask him for you. I like the thought of the match."

"Don't ask him too soon," my mother whispered.

"I promise, Mother, if he turns me down I shall not marry at all."

"Don't say that, dear."

I smiled. "But if Jovan says yes, you will gain a son."

She nodded unenthusiastically.

Then I turned to my father. "However, if he does turn me down would you please give him this?" I pulled the chain from the neck of my dress, over my head and placed the key box Jovan had given me in his hand.

"What is it?" He asked.

"He gave it to me on the day he spent with me."

The rest of the ride we spent in silence, my father glancing curiously at the box, my mother obviously planning in her head, Kira glaring in concern, and Rika smiling at me as I felt that familiar pang in my chest thinking about Jovan.

Betide (v) to happen to, or come to pass

A week later I peeked into the throne room as Jovan met my parents. The way he walked and presented himself allowed me to easily see him in the role I wanted him to accept. He approached my parents until he stood only a few paces away. Jovan could tell me exactly how many feet he needed to place between himself and the King. He knelt down as faithful soldiers always do before my father, on one knee with his right arm across his eyes to signify the blind loyalty which soldiers should have for the King.

My father spoke to him in a diplomatic voice. "Captain Jovan."

He looked up, and my father signaled for him to stand.

"I assume you know, my daughter who had once been lost to us has been found."

"Yes, your Majesty. I fought with her against Dyre. I believe I owe her my life."

My father's eyes widened with surprise, but he continued. "While she lived away from us she worked as a servant girl. Your interesting companionship practices allowed her to feel like a queen when you chose her for a day. For that we are grateful."

Jovan looked pleased and bowed his head.

"She too is grateful," my father continued, "and wishes to repay you. She would like you to be her husband."

Surprise shone in Jovan's eyes. "Um, a royal marriage is quite a reward for such a simple kindness."

"I agree with you." My father's face grew with respect toward Jovan with this comment. "My daughter, however, sees you as one who would rule well with her. I believe she is right."

He stood silently for a long time, visibly gathering his thoughts. "I do not wish to seem ungrateful. I am honestly very flattered. I must, however, refuse." He bowed from his waist as if to ask to be dismissed. "Your Majesties."

My father gaped at him, mystified. "I don't understand. You do realize what you are giving up."

Jovan smiled and offered, "With your permission, I will tell you of my reluctance."

My father gestured with his hand upward as an invitation to continue.

"I am desperately in love with a woman. She lives her life as a servant; thus my invention of the plan to ask household servant girls to be my companions. I've only done it so I could spend time with her. I do not know where she is. I have not seen her for some time, but I cannot willingly give up even the slightest chance of spending one more day with her."

"Not even for a royal marriage?" My mother asked, reminding him once again of the consequences of this choice.

"I hope every day to see her again."

I inhaled filling my lungs as they threatened to collapse with joy.

My parents looked at him in awe. They believed at this moment since Jovan had turned him down I would not be married. Nonetheless, my father followed my request. "I understand your position and admire you for your devotion. It seems a very good reason to deny a marriage, royal or not." He then reached into his pocket, approached Jovan and placed the box and chain in his hand. "I hope you find your love."

Jovan's hands began to shake when he realized what the king had given him.

I entered the room and stood silently behind him.

With mere breath Jovan asked, "Sire, where did you find this?"

"My daughter told me you gave it to her," he responded in question.

Jovan quietly inquired, "Where is she?"

I replied, "Here."

He spun quickly, his eyes met mine and he caught his breath with the surprise. He rushed to me, lifting me up and twirling me around. I felt very self-conscious with my parents watching from only a few feet away, but secretly delighted he would lose all sense of propriety at seeing me again. He put me down and wrapped his hands around my face, the chain dangling from his fingers felt cold on my cheek. Then he placed his forehead on mine. "Eviona, I've been looking for you everywhere."

I backed away from him pushing his chest lightly with my hand as if alarmed at his behavior. "You may call me Princess now." I teased him the way he had once teased me.

He took my hand from his chest and kissed it. "I will call you whatever you like."

"Then call me wife."

He smiled and the pang in my chest magnified.

My parents glowed at me in curiosity. I took Jovan's hand and led him to them for my confession, "I am Jovan's servant girl."

They welcomed him with literal open arms. I felt elated and filled. Filled.

My father released him from his embrace and hit him twice on the back as if he were an old friend. "You must stay with us for a few days before you go to put away your old life. I would like to know you better."

Jovan stood straight as if to elevate himself to what

his station would be. "I will enjoy being here." His eyes turned toward me.

"Please come." My father offered my mother his arm and they strolled out of the room.

Jovan likewise offered me his arm, and I gladly wrapped mine around it. We followed my parents as they walked. Every few seconds I couldn't resist looking at Jovan's face. Each time I did, he would glance at me with a tender smile. I felt almost shy and would look away quickly.

When I saw my parents' destination, my footsteps slowed. We reached the mirrored garden room, and they walked in quickly motioning for us to follow. The last time I had been in this place I had felt Marjeàn's desire for me to come to him. The memory of it stung even now as I gazed at the doorway. I didn't realize my feet had stopped moving until I looked up into Jovan's gentle eyes.

"Are you alright? You look… distraught."

Grateful to have his hand holding mine, I quickly glanced toward the garden. My parents had disappeared from immediate sight. I placed my hand on the back of Jovan's neck and pulled his lips to mine. He eagerly gave in to my unspoken request. A new tender memory ensued.

When our kiss slowed our lips rested against each other for several moments before his forehead tilted forward to touch mine. "I love you, Eviona."

"Thank you, Jovan."

His head jerked backward and a scowl crossed his face. "Thank you?"

"I love you too." I laughed and kissed him again to reinforce my feelings.

"That's better," he said sweetly and invited me into the garden with an open palm.

I kept my focus on him as we walked the path until we came to a sitting area where my parents waited for us. By his expression, I knew my father wanted to talk to Jovan.

My parents had positioned themselves together on the only bench. Jovan led me to a single chair and sat opposite of me on another. His countenance changed as he mentally readied himself to talk with my father.

I couldn't have been prepared for my father's first question. "So, Jovan," he started. "How many grandchildren will you be giving me?"

My jaw dropped and I am sure my face showed my mortification. My mother's foot gently kicked my father's leg in my defense.

Jovan laughed heartily from his gut, which visibly pleased my father. Then his face turned to me, and he spoke softly. "We've had very little time for discussions of such things, Sire." His eyes seemed to bore into mine as he continued. "I will give you as many as Eviona decides."

My father, pleased with this response, turned to more pressing thoughts. The discussion shifted to politics and events of the kingdom. I had expected to remain silent but found I had many thoughts and ideas.

For the first time I thought of being queen not as a burden but as a way of making life better for the people of the kingdom. Who better than I, who had held so many stations, would understand my people? I promised myself to do all I could to build the kingdom I had once seen in a dream.

Unbosoming (v) a confession

On his last evening with us, Jovan walked me to my room. He had been quiet all night.

"Is something wrong?" I asked.

"Your sisters mentioned another man to me." I didn't like the pain I saw in his eyes.

"Marjeȧn." I knew it would be hard to answer these questions. I invited him to sit with me.

He settled next to me, his eyebrows pulled down. "You loved Marjeȧn?"

"Yes," I admitted. "I did."

His face showed his sorrow and he struggled with whether or not to inquire further.

"He's dead, Jovan."

"If he wasn't? Would you still be sitting here with me?"

My heart fell at his question. "I can't answer that." My words hurt him. I placed my hand on his. His love for me filled my emptiness, but if he knew the truth would my love be enough for him? As the words I could tell him entered my mind a cold frost swept through my body.

"Jovan, I'm going to tell you things which will be very hard to believe, but you must know them. I have a dark and secret past. I will understand if you feel you cannot marry me once you have heard. You will be the only person I ever tell."

His eyebrows knit together further. "Nothing could change how I feel about you."

"I knew Dyre and his beast."

"Everyone knew them."

"No, Jovan. Listen." I told him of my connection to them. I explained the things we went through together and about the veil we could place between us. He asked several questions, and I knew when he finally started to understand.

He wrapped his arms around me and whispered, "I'm so sorry."

I pushed him gently away. "There's more." I told him about Marjeán, how we met and about the pull between us.

Jovan leaned away from me and listened with a scowl on his face occasionally inhaling deeply as I continued.

I told him how Marjeán left me to fight for Dyre and how I felt when I thought he had died. Then I told him about seeing Dyre for the first time in the dungeon.

"That's why you poisoned him. You must have been furious with him for lying to you."

"I didn't poison him. I know the kingdom thinks I did, but he did it himself, so I would go on with my life. When he died, I loved him. To me he was Marjeán."

Silence.

I touched his cheek, "I'm sorry to hurt you."

He pulled my hand away from his face and placed it in my lap. He sat motionless, quiet, for a long time. I worried about what he might be thinking. His voice whispered soft and wounded, "How can I possibly rival a man, living or dead, who is quite literally a part of you?"

"I love you."

He didn't move. I wondered if he heard me. He placed his face in his hand. "If I had never let you go in the first place..." He stopped speaking.

"I made that choice, just as I'm making the choice now to always be yours."

"But I'm second choice."

"Second? Is that what you think?"

"Isn't it true?"

"You *were* my first, Jovan. The first man I loved and the first to show me what love should be."

"But I will never measure up. It won't matter the extent of my love, you can't feel it like you could his."

"I feel *my* love for you." He finally turned to look at me as I explained, "Even when living in his house I thought of you. Every battle I worried for you. I dreamed about you, and he saw those dreams. He could feel every emotion I felt for you, which only deepened his jealousy."

"Jealous of me?" He didn't believe it.

I nodded slowly allowing the thought to sink in. "He hated you. He felt my love for you. He feared it."

"Feared?"

"I cannot explain the power of the pull between Marjeàn and me. It felt like lightning when we were together. Instant, intense, even frightening. With you, it's more like sunshine, warm and inviting, with effects lasting even when the sun has set."

"So, you no longer love him?"

"He is a part of me. I will always love him. Memories are potent and undeniable," I took his hand and placed it against my cheek. "But I love you, Jovan, and always have. I want you. The man who loves me whether I am scarred or beautiful, a servant or a princess, who calls my name in the midst of a battle when you are certain all is lost, the man who has always been willing to sacrifice everything for me. Marjeàn could not do that. Not until the end. You continually showed you would."

He searched my eyes then closed his. I hoped my words echoed in his mind.

His response didn't come in the form of words. He opened his eyes, studying me, debating my future. Then he leaned forward and his lips parted against mine in a kiss truly unequaled in gentleness and sincerity. When he released me he whispered, "I know you cannot feel my love for you like you could his, so I will show you. Every day. I promise you will know how much I love you."

I cried for joy, embraced in the arms of the man who would rule the kingdom at my side and love me despite my past.

Our wedding day was the happiest of my life, and my happiness increased exponentially every day afterward. Jovan indeed proved his love for me daily and in every way possible. He somehow even convinced my father to allow me to spend time in the kitchen especially during stressful times such as my pregnancies.

I enjoyed being a part of the decision making process and both Jovan and my father found my experiences with the people invaluable in planning for the kingdom. Shortly after the birth of my second child, my father bequeathed the crown to me.

I became the people's queen. I visited with them in their towns and villages. I served with them in their employments and played with their children. I loved them in a way I hadn't expected, but felt grateful for.

I relished the love of my life. I had been blessed to know love from every side; from friendship, to adoration, fiery passion and everything in between.

I had truly found my destiny, not that of a dream, but in the smiles of my children, the hopes of my people, and the heart of the man who held me close yet left me alone when I looked at the stars.

Eudemonia (n) happiness

Suggestions for Book Club Questions

One of the major themes of The Tripartite Soul is destiny versus choice. Do you believe in destiny? Do you believe destiny can change?

Do you think when Dyre, Eviona, and Zefforah realized the part they played, they could have changed things to reflect what was supposed to happen? When do you think each of them had that realization?

Considering the ending, do you believe Eviona fulfilled her destiny?

How do you feel about the lives lost in the story? How might the story have been different if those characters did not die?

Another major theme of the Tripartite Soul is love. Which is your favorite "love" story? (A love story does not necessarily mean romantic love.)

Do you believe in soul mates?

Eviona and Marjeàn represent soul mates and yet, considering their history, could they have been truly happy together?

Would you rather have a relationship like that of Marjeàn and Eviona, or Jovan and Eviona? Why?

Who was your favorite sub-character? Why?

As Eviona's mother pointed out, there are believed to be three parts of a soul; one spiritual, one emotional, and one carnal. Zefforah, Eviona, and Dyre represent those three parts. Do you think they still possess all three parts in and of themselves?

Do you feel the theory of having a tripartite soul is correct?

Made in the USA
Middletown, DE
03 November 2016